Jenny Holmes has been writing fiction for children and adults since her early twenties, having had ies of children's books adapted for both the BBC and ITV.

Jenny was born and brought up in Yorkshire. After living in the Midlands and travelling widely in America, she returned to Yorkshire and brought up her two daughters with a spectacular view of the moors and a sense of belonging to the special, still undiscovered corners of the Yorkshire Dales.

One of three children brought up in Harrogate, Jenny's links with Yorkshire stretch back through many generations via a mother who served in the Land Army during the Second World War and pharmacist and shop-worker aunts, back to a maternal grandfather who worked as a village blacksmith and pub landlord. Her great aunts worked in Edwardian times as seamstresses, milliners and upholsterers. All told stories of life lived with little material wealth but with great spirit and independence, where a sense of community and family loyalty were fierce – sometimes uncomfortable but never to be ignored. Theirs are the voices which echo down the years, and the author's hope is that their strength is brought back to life in many of the characters represented in these pages.

www.transworldbooks.co.uk

THE MILL GIRLS OF ALBION LANE

Jenny Holmes

CORGI BOOKS

TRANSWORLD PUBLISHERS
61–63 Uxbridge Road, London W5 5SA
www.transworldbooks.co.uk

Transworld is part of the Penguin Random House group of companies
whose addresses can be found at global.penguinrandomhouse.com

Penguin
Random House
UK

First published in Great Britain in 2015 by Corgi Books
an imprint of Transworld Publishers

A CIP catalogue record for this book
is available from the British Library.

ISBN
9780552171496

Typeset in 11½/14pt New Baskerville by Kestrel Data, Exeter, Devon.
Printed and bound by CPI Group (UK) Ltd, Croydon, CR0 4YY

Penguin Random House is committed to a sustainable future
for our business, our readers and our planet. This book is
made from Forest Stewardship Council® certified paper.

MIX
Paper from
responsible sources
FSC® C018179

1 3 5 7 9 10 8 6 4 2

For my mother, Barbara Holmes, and her stalwart sisters-in-arms, Sybil, Connie, Joan and Myra. All young Yorkshirewomen in the 1930s.

And with heartfelt thanks to my dear friend, Polly Collins, fount of information, encouragement and wisdom.

CHAPTER ONE

Lily Briggs was dog-tired from working all morning in the noisy, stuffy atmosphere of the weaving shed at Calvert's woollen mill. Her job was to check the bobbins that fed the looms. The blue and white reels ran out first and replacing them kept her constantly on the move, up and down the central aisle between the giant machines with their well-oiled cogs and flying shuttles. She was thankful that the yellow, green and red bobbins lasted longer, giving her occasional relief from feeding the relentless apparatus that clanked and rattled from here to eternity, or at least until the midday buzzer sounded to signal the end of work.

At ten minutes to twelve, during one of those short, unexpected respites, Lily took the chance to ease her aching back and glance out through a grimy window on to the yard overlooking the canal.

She'd spent all her working life at Calvert's Mill so she knew the cobbled approach to the sooty, three-storey building like the back of her hand.

Every morning at half past seven, come rain or shine, she would trudge with 150 other mill workers through the stone arch of the main entrance. Combers, finishers and twisters would turn left for the spinning shed while Lily and her co-workers turned right into the cavernous weaving shed. Above them, on the first and second floors, were smaller rooms devoted to processes like dyeing, mending and flipping, all aimed at getting the high-quality finished cloth out of the factory on to new-fangled, motorized lorries, which then transported it to tailors across the country.

Gazing out of the window, Lily pictured dozens of scavengers and lap joiners in the nearby spinning shed working like ants to fetch and carry, comb and twist and wind. Here in her own roaring, rattling workplace, were more ants – bobbin liggers like her and piecers who reached over the looms to tie up broken threads, together with loom cleaners, weavers and weft men. Upstairs were the more skilled workers – menders and burlers – alongside office staff (considered snooty by the shop-floor girls) and canteen workers (generally jolly and easy going) who slaved all morning at big gas ovens designed to warm up the soup, bacon and eggs and pies ordered each morning by Calvert's employees.

Lily was brought back into the moment – a Saturday morning in late November 1931 – by her friend Annie.

'I wish the buzzer would hurry up and go,' Annie

mouthed at Lily from her position at the nearest loom.

Lily lip-read her words then nodded. 'At least it's Saturday,' she mouthed back, which meant the twelve o'clock finish then home for the rest of the day.

Until then, the whole shed roared on – much too loud for normal conversation – and the smell of hot engine oil filled the room.

'Yes, Saturday – thank goodness!' For Annie the midday buzzer couldn't come soon enough.

'What do you fancy doing tonight?' Sybil asked from her station across the aisle.

'Cinema?' Lily suggested. There was a new picture with Jean Harlow at the Victory that she fancied seeing.

'Or dancing?' This was dance-mad Annie's idea of heaven after the hard graft of the factory week: finish work, nip off home to get dolled up then out again to the Assembly Rooms.

'I don't mind either way,' Lily chipped in, dipping into her pinafore pocket for a spare hairgrip and using it to tame her mass of unruly curls. With five minutes to go before the buzzer sounded, she ran quickly through the afternoon jobs she would have to do at home before she could get out to join her friends for their evening's entertainment: take the mutton stew out of the oven and feed the family a hot dinner, sew her sister Evie's work pinafore ready for Monday, bake scones for tea if there was time then half an hour to get good and ready for the girls' night out.

'Thank you, ladies, that'll do for today,' Fred Lee, the weaving shed overlooker announced on the dot of twelve, though the sound of the buzzer had been swallowed up by the racket of the looms. Instantly the giant cogs ceased turning, levers were pulled and shuttles stopped darting from side to side across the wide looms. Dust from the morning's work began to settle.

'Oh, my poor back,' Sybil complained as she and thirty other women eased backwards from their machines.

'Here, let me give it a rub for you,' Fred offered with a wink.

'You'll do no such thing.' Sybil pulled her pinafore over her head and rolled it neatly. 'You'll keep your hands to yourself, Fred Lee.' They all knew their boss had an eye for the girls and generally picked out the best-looking ones to flirt with at the end of a shift. And there was no doubt about it: Sybil's upswept auburn hair and curvaceous figure put her firmly into Fred's favoured category.

'Or we'll tell your missis on you when we see her,' Annie threatened, safe in the knowledge that her short, bobbed hair and lithe, boyish figure kept her out of the running as far as Fred was concerned.

Lily and Sybil laughed to see the cocky little man's reaction. His shiny round face puckered into a frown

10

and he gave a nervous cough. 'Now, now – no need for that,' he insisted.

'She's only kidding,' Lily told him as the women weavers and liggers queued up to clock off at the antiquated machine by the exit.

Fred Lee coughed again then recovered. 'By the way, Lily, I need a little word.'

Annie, who disliked the overlooker for his puffed-up, oily manner, wanted him to squirm on the end of her hook a while longer. 'Uh-oh, Lily!' she cried. '"A little word". Why don't I like the sound of that?'

A number of the girls smirked at Annie's jibe and Fred's frown reappeared. 'In the main office,' he told Lily sharply, casting a dark look in Annie's direction as she slid her card into the slot in order to clock out.

'This doesn't have to do with Evie, does it?' Lily asked as he led the way down the corridor towards the office. 'I mean, my sister, Evie Briggs. She left school yesterday and she's due to start here first thing Monday.'

'Why should it have anything to do with her?' Fred snapped, still smarting from Annie's cheeky comment.

'Mr Calvert – he hasn't changed his mind about taking her on in the weaving shed?'

'Why – do you think he should?'

'No, Evie's a good little worker, none better. She came away from school with an excellent report. It's just that, with things being the way they are . . .'

'I know – orders are low and getting lower,' Fred agreed. 'They're laying off workers down the road at Kingsley's or else putting them on short time.' He came to the office, turned the brass knob and opened the glass-paned door.

'That's what I'm afraid of.' Expecting the worst, Lily felt her mouth go dry as she entered the room. Did this mean Mr Calvert was about to give Evie her marching orders before she'd even started?

'And you're right – your sister does come into it,' Fred confirmed, stepping in after Lily and closing the door behind him. 'But not in the way you expect.'

Inside the office there was a large mahogany desk with a neat pile of black ledgers labelled 'Order Books' stacked to one side, next to a black Remington typewriter. A wooden Windsor chair stood behind the desk and beyond that a tall set of shallow drawers beside the long window that overlooked the cobbled yard. A small figure stood silhouetted against the light and Lily drew comfort from the fact that Stanley Calvert was nowhere to be seen.

'There's no need to look so worried,' the figure said in a high, quick voice as she stepped towards Lily and the overlooker.

Lily recognized it as the voice of Miss Valentine, who oversaw half a dozen girls working in the burling and mending department on the first floor of the mill. She was an exceptionally tiny woman –

dainty and thin as a sparrow. A lifelong spinster, she was always nicely dressed in a brown outfit flecked with cream. The dress came almost to her ankles and was neatly pinched in at the waist by a belt with an elaborate silver buckle. She wore her greying hair in a bun high on her head and her unfashionable look was completed by round, horn-rimmed glasses. She would be about forty-five to fifty years old, the girls in the weaving shed reckoned.

Self-consciously, Lily smoothed her navy blue serge skirt and patted her wavy hair. 'What's this about Evie?' she ventured.

'Nothing for you to worry about,' the manageress assured her, measuring the exchange of uneasy glances between the pretty, dark-haired bobbin ligger and the overlooker. 'Fred, you haven't been giving Lily the wrong impression, I hope.'

He sauntered towards the window, hands in his trouser pockets, and stared down at the steady stream of departing workers. 'Me? I haven't given her any impression that I'm aware of.'

'Well, in any case, Lily will be anxious to get home to her family for the afternoon so let's come to the point.' Miss Valentine circumnavigated the big, leather-topped desk and came up close so that Lily could see the fine lines across her high forehead. Her glasses magnified her short-sighted, dark brown eyes and added to the birdlike impression she gave off. 'You know that Evie will start as a learner here in the weaving shed at seven shillings per week and that means Maureen Godwin will move up from learner to loom cleaner and Florence White will in turn move on from cleaner to bobbin ligger.'

Lily listened carefully to Miss Valentine's methodical speech, reassuring herself that Evie's position was safe and wondering where all this was leading.

'Florence will take your job,' Miss Valentine explained.

Lily's heartbeat faltered then raced. 'And where does that leave me?'

'Upstairs with me, if you would like,' came the rapid reply while the birdlike stare fixed itself on Lily's puzzled face. 'You understand what I'm saying?'

'You want me to come and work in the mending room?' At first Lily couldn't believe it. Only the best, quickest workers at Calvert's Mill got the offer of a job in the burling and mending department – it was extremely skilled work and was a sitting-down job to boot.

The steady gaze continued. 'You'll start at twenty shillings per week, going up to thirty when you've learned the trade. What do you say?'

'That's . . . I mean, that's . . . Well, it's champion!' Lily was lost for words at the prospect of earning so much money. Just wait until she got home and told her mother.

'It's a step up from the weaving shed.' Fred pointed out the obvious. 'And it's me you have to thank. I'm the one who put your name forward.'

'Yes, thank you – thank you!' She was blushing and trembling like a leaf.

'I expect promptness and a smart appearance at all times,' the manageress went on in a severe tone. 'You will buy your own burling irons and scissors and you will need size-five needles and a thimble, plus a tin box to keep them in.'

Lily nodded. She caught a reflection of herself in the window – eyes wide open in disbelief.

'I take it you want the job?'

'Yes. Oh yes. Thank you, Miss Valentine. Oh, yes please.' Lily could think of nothing better than this move up in the world and she wondered just why she'd been selected. Yes, she'd been punctual and hard working during her six years at Calvert's, but then so had Annie, Sybil and a dozen other girls in the weaving shed. And yes, she kept herself as smart and fresh-looking as she could, taking care to brush the dust from her dark hair each night and to arrive at work the next day in a neat blouse and skirt beneath her grey winter shawl. But it must have been more than this that had led Miss Valentine to single her out.

'As a matter of fact, it wasn't necessary for Fred to recommend you. I keep my wits about me whenever I have reason to walk through the weaving shed and I've paid particular attention to you and the way you work,' the manageress said, as if reading Lily's thoughts. 'I like what I see.'

'Thank you, Miss Valentine,' Lily breathed. Her

face felt flushed and she gave a shy smile.

'Good. Then I'll see you on Monday at seven thirty sharp,' the diminutive manageress concluded, allowing Fred to open the door for her and stepping out into the corridor. Then her dainty leather shoes pitter-pattered along the polished wooden floor and she was gone.

'I hope you won't forget your time with me in the weaving shed,' Fred said to Lily as she gathered her wits and left the office. He came so close that she could smell the Brylcreem in his sandy-coloured, thinning hair and there was no mistaking the leer on his broad, fleshy face.

'I won't,' she vowed, hurrying on. But she knew without having to think about it that Fred Lee was one person she wouldn't mind spending less time with in future.

'More haste, less speed, Lily Briggs!' he crowed after her.

She took no notice. Her feet hardly touched the ground as she grabbed her shawl from its hook by the main door, flew out under the high stone archway and across the greasy November cobbles, out into the foggy afternoon.

Number 5 Albion Lane was the third in a row of sooty, terraced houses built for workers at the half-dozen mills that overlooked the canal. Albion Lane ran uphill to join the main Overcliffe Road where the trams rattled their way out of town. It backed on to Raglan Road, which overlooked a patch of scrubby grassland called the Common – a poor, unfenced grazing area for six shire horses from the local brewery. The neighbourhood was by this time badly run down, with blocked gutters and grass growing between the cobbles. Though women still made an effort to donkey-stone their steps and keep their windows washed, most of the shabby front doors were in need of several licks of paint. These days there just wasn't the money and some-times not the will to keep up appearances as they once did.

This Saturday, the day of Lily's meteoric promo-tion, was too damp and cold for outside play so her little brother Arthur sat at the steamed-up window of number 5, waiting eagerly for her to come home.

'Why isn't she here yet?' he asked Evie who was busy lugging a heavy coal bucket up the cellar steps ready to feed the kitchen-range fire.

Evie reached the cellar head, clanked the bucket down on the floor and groaned at the weight of it. 'Give her a chance. She'll be here soon enough.'

'How long, though?' Arthur cleared a patch in the window pane and watched the moisture trickle down on to the sill where he perched.

Evie shook her head. 'Hold your horses,' she told him. 'And instead of sitting there twiddling your thumbs, why not help me fetch this coal?'

'Can't – too heavy for me,' he replied, pressing his face against the wet, cold glass.

'Excuses,' Evie grumbled, but she let him off as she always did.

Arthur was just turned six and far and away the baby of the family. Lily, Margie, Evie, Arthur – four kids and that was four too many for a broken-winded, out-of-work war veteran to bring up on a wing and a prayer, according to their father. So Rhoda and Walter Briggs had stopped at four children and had scraped along for years on what Rhoda could earn as an unofficial midwife in the neighbourhood and on Public Assistance until first Lily and then Margie grew old enough to earn a wage. Now it was Evie's turn to start contributing to the meagre family pot.

'Where's Mam?' Arthur wanted to know, feeling cramp in his legs but refusing to alter position until Lily came into view carrying his precious bag of Saturday sweets.

'You know where she is.' Evie carried the bucket to the fire and tipped a few coals into the glowing grate. There was a billow of black smoke up the chimney and then a crackle of yellow flames. 'She's up the street with Mrs Lister.'

'What's she doing there?'

'Don't ask me.' Done with the coal, Evie went to the stone sink and turned on the tap to wash her hands.

Actually, she knew what their mother was doing at number 21 because Mr Lister had coming running to their door at six that morning and frightened the living daylights out of them with his loud knock and urgent cry of, 'Can you come, Rhoda? Baby's on its way!' Their mother had got dressed straight away and left the house with hurried instructions for Evie to mind Arthur while Lily and Margie went to work. 'Your father's not feeling too good so best leave him to sleep,' she'd added on her way out. Now Evie didn't fancy giving an answer to Arthur's question that might lead him to pester her about how babies were born so she left it at three short, dismissive words.

'Here comes our Margie!' the spy at the window reported when he spotted his middle sister hurrying up the street. Margie entered the living room with a rush of cold air, bringing with her the smell of factory oil and untreated wool. 'What a morning I've had,' she complained, lifting her shawl from her head and throwing it on to a chair. 'I only had Sam Earby on my back the whole time, telling me this was wrong and that was wrong and if I wasn't careful I'd be put on short time and I don't know what else.' She removed her work apron, threw it down on top of the shawl then went to the sink, took up the block of carbolic and elbowed Evie aside. 'Just you wait,' she warned her. 'You'll soon find out.'

'But I'm not at Kingsley's with you, I'm at Calvert's.'

'Same thing.' Margie lathered her hands and arms then ran them under the water. 'Work's work wherever you are, and it's drudgery from seven thirty to five, five days a week, plus Saturday half days. It's a rotten life, ask anyone around here.'

'At last, here's Lily!' Arthur spotted his favourite

sister at the bottom of the hill and jumped down from his perch. He ran to the door and flung it open, waiting on the top step for her to arrive. 'Where's my chocolate?' he yelled down the street, his face falling at the absence of the usual brown paper bag clutched in her hand.

'Oh, Arthur, I clean forgot!' Reaching the house, Lily scooped him up and carried him indoors, skinny legs dangling. She deposited him on the rug then reached into her skirt pocket. 'Never mind. Here's tuppence and you can run down to Newby's and buy some for yourself. How's that?'

Snatching the proffered coins and grinning, Arthur was out of the house like a shot – no coat or cap in his haste to be gone.

'That's not like you to forget Arthur's sweeties,' Margie commented, peering critically into the small square of mirror fixed to the wall above the sink. 'My hair needs a good cut,' she sighed.

'Is Mother not back?' Lily enquired, looking about her.

'No, but Father's up and getting dressed at last,' Evie reported. 'I expect he'll be down in a minute.'

'Why, what's got into you?' Margie asked as she turned from the mirror. 'Evie, why is Lily grinning like a Cheshire cat?'

'I am here, you know,' Lily protested. She took off her shawl and hung it on the hook at the cellar head. 'Go on, Margie – take a guess at why I'm so pleased with myself.'

20

'Let me see – you've bagged yourself a sweetheart at last?'

'Trust you. No – wrong. Guess again.'

'Mother says you can go into town tonight with Annie and Sybil?'

'Wrong. I haven't asked her yet.'

'I don't know, I give up.'

'The truth is – I've got a leg-up at work!' The words were out and Lily could still hardly believe it. 'I'm to go upstairs and work in the mending room, starting Monday.'

'Never!' Margie declared. She felt a pang of jealousy when she realized that Lily would now go to work in a nice hat and coat and would be looked up to by the girls in the weaving shed. With four years between her and her eldest sister, she knew it would be a long haul before she left the spinning section at Kingsley's and reached the same dizzying heights.

And yet they were similar, she and Lily – both quick learners, both smart and easy on the eye, with their mother's dark hair and colouring, though their styles differed – Lily being less well groomed and fashionable in Margie's opinion, and certainly less interested in finding herself a nice young man. Why this was so was a mystery to Margie, who had no trouble attracting the boys and revelled in their attention. 'Aren't you a sight for sore eyes, Margie Briggs!' they would call after her on the street. Or else they would whistle, get off their bikes and walk alongside to keep her company, and she would smile and lap up their compliments and their teasing, giving as good as she got.

'Does that mean I'll be by myself in the weaving shed?' a nervous Evie asked. It had been a big week for her, turning fourteen and leaving school and then getting ready to start at Calvert's before she had time to draw breath.

'No, you'll have Annie and Sybil to keep an eye on you,' Lily promised. 'I'll make sure they do.' Sadly, this wasn't quite the reception she'd hoped for when she'd rushed home with her news. And now she could hear their father moving around on the bare boards upstairs, shuffling to the top of the stairs and making his slow way down.

'Will you tell him or will you save it until Mother gets back?' Margie shot Lily a quick question.

'Save it,' Lily whispered back. She thought she knew how her father would react – there'd be a blank look accompanied by a grunt or a shrug. His silence would take the shine off everything good and proper.

Walter leaned on the banister, taking one bronchitic step at a time. He heard voices below. 'What are you lot up to, whispering in a corner?' he demanded as he opened the door into the kitchen, dressed in shirtsleeves and without a collar, his braces dangling over his broad leather belt. 'Where's Arthur? What have you done with him?'

'What do you suppose we've done with him –

waved a magic wand and made him vanish?' was Margie's risky reply.

'He went down to Newby's for chocolate.' Evie stepped in with a sensible answer before their father could react.

Walter sniffed then rubbed the back of his hand across his grey moustache. 'Did you tell him to buy me my cigarettes while he's about it?'

'No, but let me go for you.' Evie was halfway out of the door before she remembered she had no money. 'Shall I get Mrs Newby to put it on the slate?'

'No – ask your mother to give you a shilling.'

'But she's at—'

'Just go!' Walter wheezed before coughing then hawking into the sink. 'And fetch the ciggies to me at the Cross.'

Behind his back, Margie pulled a disgusted face, which Lily ignored. 'How are you feeling, Father?' she asked.

Out came the usual complaints. 'My chest's bad and my leg's giving me gyp,' he informed her, pulling his braces over his shoulders. 'Anyhow, I'm off to the pub. Has anyone seen my scarf and cap?'

'Here on the hook.' Lily lifted them down and handed them to him. 'Don't you want to eat your dinner before you go out?'

'Keep it warm in the oven. I'll have it later.'

Then he was on with his patched, worn jacket and gone, following Evie out of the front door, head down against the wind, coughing his way to the Green Cross.

Margie shuddered. 'If he hasn't any money for his Woodbines, who does he think will pay for his beer?' she wondered out loud.

Lily chose not to answer. 'Dinner,' she said firmly. She opened the oven door, took a thick cloth and lifted out a brown earthenware pot, which she put on a board on the deal table. By the time she fetched plates and knives and forks from the cupboard and laid them out, Arthur and Evie would be back from their errands.

'And shall you take to the mending work, do you think?' Margie asked as if she hadn't felt jealous and there'd been no interruptions since Lily had announced her news. Sitting down at the table, she ladled out some thin stew and potatoes for herself.

'I hope so,' Lily answered. 'And I hope Mother will be pleased too.'

'She'll like the extra money,' Margie predicted then went on to the topic that really interested her. 'This afternoon, Lil, will you cut my hair for me?'

'I don't know. I've to sew Evie's work pinafore – I might not have time.'

'Before the pinafore?' Ever-hopeful, Margie pulled out the drawer under the table and rummaged for scissors, handing them to Lily. 'These are nice and sharp. It won't take you long,' she wheedled.

Lily sighed. 'Finish your dinner then bring your chair over to the window where I can see. Sit here next to the sewing machine. How short would you like it?'

'Chop off three inches, up to chin length,' Margie decided as she tugged at a lock of her shoulder-length hair. 'And will you cut me a fringe? That would be smart and up to date.'

Despite long practice on Evie and Arthur, Lily wasn't confident of her hairdressing abilities when it came to creating a fashionable effect. Her hand shook as she took the scissors from Margie. 'I don't know about the fringe.'

'Yes, make it like the film stars wear, smooth and glossy like Louise Brooks.' For some reason Margie was prepared to trust Lily with her new style. 'I think I'll look very nice with it.'

So Lily took the plunge, combing and cutting, feeling locks of Margie's clipped hair tickle her legs as they fell to the floor. When Arthur and Evie returned to the house, she pointed to the food on the table and told them to dip in and help themselves. 'And no sweets until after dinner,' she warned Arthur.

Too late – she saw that he'd gorged on chocolate on his way home from Newby's and his lips were coated with the sticky remains.

'Oh Arthur, you've only gone and ruined your appetite,' she grumbled, putting down her scissors to dole out a decent helping of the stew.

She should have known better. Chocolate or not, his stomach was a bottomless pit and he gobbled up the meat and potatoes and was soon asking for a second helping.

'Leave enough for Father,' Lily warned as she returned to the window to snip carefully at Margie's new fringe.

'And for Mother,' Evie added.

Then there was silence in the living room at 5 Albion Lane except for the snip of scissors, the settling of coals in the grate and the scrape of knives and forks on cracked, willow-pattern plates.

CHAPTER TWO

Dinner was cleared away, the pots washed and Lily had sat down at the sewing machine in the alcove close to the window when Rhoda Briggs got back at last from delivering Myra Lister's latest baby, her sixth in nine years. It was two thirty in the afternoon.

'Another boy,' she told Lily with an exhausted sigh. 'It wasn't easy either – in the end we had to call for Dr Moss and he'll be to pay on top of what they eventually give me.'

Lily looked up from her sewing. 'But baby's all right?'

'I can't say for sure. Myra will be wondering about that herself, probably for the rest of her life. The cord caught around his neck and he was slow to breathe, that was the problem.'

'Poor little mite,' Lily murmured. 'You must be done in.' Putting aside the work on Evie's pinafore, she got up to make a pot of tea. She noticed how old her mother looked – only just past forty yet already worn out, her hands red raw from cold, her face pinched and shadowy under her brown felt hat.

'Where are the others?' Rhoda asked, taking off her coat but absent-mindedly leaving on the hat.

'Up in the attic. Evie's keeping Arthur amused and I suppose Margie's busy dolling herself up for a night out.'

'No she's not, she's here!' Having heard the thud of the front door closing, Margie had rushed down two flights of stairs. Now she twirled on the spot to show off her new hairstyle. 'Lily did it for me. What do you think, Mother?'

'I think it makes you look common,' was the blunt reply.

The insult hit Margie hard. Her eager, pretty face fell then she quickly set her mouth in a firm line of defiance. 'Anyway, I like it,' she said as she flounced back upstairs.

'Sixteen years old and not a scrap of common sense,' Rhoda muttered with a shake of the head. She had no energy to follow her middle daughter up the stairs to remonstrate, and anyway what good would it do? Hair wouldn't regrow overnight and what was done was done.

'Here's your tea, Mother,' Lily said quietly.

Rhoda took it without thanks and sat at the table, staring vacantly at the grain of the pale wood.

'Something happened at work this morning,' Lily began cautiously as she sat down opposite.

'Not another accident?' was the gloomy response.

'No, not an accident.'

'I remember there were always girls getting their hair caught up in the machines when I was there, little boys having fingers torn off, and they never stopped the production, not once that I can remember, however badly they were hurt. That went on a lot before the war.'

'Not any more,' Lily assured her. 'They have proper guards on the machines now and big safety notices everywhere you look. Anyway, this is good news. Fred Lee took me into the main office after work today to see Miss Valentine.'

'Iris Valentine – yes.' The name took Rhoda back to the days when the two young women had worked the looms together. That was before her marriage to Walter, before the war, before everything. 'There was nothing of her in those days, she was light as a feather. What's she like now?'

'Still tiny.'

'Never married?'

'No, Mother, she's not got married.'

'She always was a sensible sort,' Rhoda said. 'Cleverer than me, at any rate. And pray tell, why did "Miss" Valentine need to see you in the office?'

Lily smiled. 'Pray tell' was one of her mother's old-fashioned idiosyncrasies, said with pursed lips and a sceptical look. 'Only to offer me work in the mending room!'

'You don't say.'

'But I do – it's true. I've been offered a better job,

more money and everything.' Smile, please, Lily thought. Just take one look at me and give me a pleasant look, a word of praise – that's all I ask.

'My, my,' Rhoda said, staring down at her work-worn hands.

'Starting Monday,' Lily added.

'Which reminds me, Evie will need that pinafore.'

Lily sighed and got up from the table. 'Don't worry – it's half done. I just have the pocket and hem to finish.'

'And I wish you hadn't cut Margie's hair that way.'

'I know. It's what she wanted, though. I didn't have a say.'

'She's sixteen – you're twenty, going on twenty-one. You should have had a say. Now look at her – anyone would think she's one of those girls you see hanging around outside the Victory Picture House – you know the type I mean.'

'Not our Margie,' Lily assured her. 'She's a good girl. But Mother, just think – I'll be bringing home twenty shillings each week, rising to thirty. How about that?'

'Very good,' Rhoda said, softening and meeting her daughter's gaze at last. 'Well done, Lily. I always knew you had it in you to get on in the world.'

'I told you it would be all about the money,' Margie said. 'I bet she still didn't crack a smile, though.'

She and Lily were getting ready to go out in the attic bedroom they shared with Evie. Arthur slept in an alcove in the kitchen on a pull-down bed.

'But I could tell she was pleased.' After dabbing rouge on to her cheeks, Lily ran a wet comb through her wavy hair, hoping in vain that the dampness would smooth it down. 'That's the main thing.'

Margie finished buttoning up her soft cream blouse, the one that had a row of small bows down the front and clung to her curves. She checked her hair in the mirror one last time. 'How do I look?'

'Like a film star, like Louise Brooks, just the way you wanted.'

'Good – that's me! Now I'm off to meet the girls.' Margie left in high spirits, picking up her green coat, painstakingly sewn by Lily on the Singer machine in the kitchen, and clattering down the stairs, out of the front door without stopping to say goodbye.

Ten minutes later, Lily was dressed in her best crêpe de Chine dress in a shade of lilac that she knew suited her dark complexion. It set off her almost jet-black hair and wide, heavily lashed brown eyes and for once she felt a small glow of satisfaction as she gazed at her reflection in the mirror above Margie's bed, turning this way and that to check different angles. Then she flung on her slim-fitting grey coat and pushed her hair up under a matching velour hat.

Her plan was to knock on Annie's door and from there the two of them would go on to Sybil's house on Overcliffe Road, taking in a trawl around the market before heading on to the Victory or to the dance at the Assembly Rooms on the edge of town – she didn't know which. Before she left the house, she made the mistake of popping her head around the living-room door.

The first person she saw was Arthur perched on the window sill – his lookout or his refuge, depending on the circumstances. The second was her father, much the worse for drink and slumped in his shirtsleeves over the table, his head resting on his arms. Third was her mother angrily stabbing the poker into the dying fire. When Rhoda turned and spotted Lily, she let the poker drop with a clatter on to the hearth then marched across the room and took Arthur by the arm, yanking him down from the sill. 'Take him to Granddad Preston's for the night,' she instructed Lily. 'He needs a good night's sleep and he sure as eggs won't get it here, not when his father wakes up.'

'Mam!' Arthur wriggled and twisted to escape her grip but Rhoda wouldn't let go.

'Stay with him,' she said. 'Take him to Sunday School at Overcliffe if you like. Don't bring him back until tomorrow teatime.'

'Mam!' he said again. His face was white and there were tears in his eyes.

'Do as you're told,' she insisted.

Lily got the picture – the usual thing had happened whereby her father had staggered back from the Green Cross and started picking on Arthur, snarling at him for nothing, thrusting his moustached face up against the boy and prodding him with his finger. From past experience, Lily guessed that Rhoda probably hadn't even tried to stop her husband. She'd just let him wear himself out then fall asleep at the table and knew now it would be better to get Arthur out of his father's way before he roused himself from his drunken stupor. Since Evie had left the house before her sisters in order to stay over with a friend, Lily was the only one left for Rhoda to turn to.

Lily's spirits sank as she saw her evening out vanish in a puff of smoke but she bore it as well as she could. 'Come on, Arthur, cheer up. You like it at Granddad Preston's house. You get a bedroom all to yourself.'

Cowed, he put on his jacket and hat with Lily's help and before long they were out of the house, walking hand in hand up Albion Lane.

'We can ride the tram if you like,' she told him to cheer him up.

Free of the dark, tense atmosphere of the house, Arthur's face brightened and he played a favourite game of avoiding cracks in the pavement. Tread on a crack and an angry bear would be sure to leap out from behind a wall. He ran ahead of Lily, concentrating so hard on the stone flags that he ran full tilt into a gang of young men gathered under the gas lamp at the top of the hill.

'Watch out, littl'un!' Billy Robertshaw cried as Arthur cannoned into him and landed flat on his back. 'You want to watch where you're going.'

Lily ran to pick him up and dust him down and she was busy doing this when Harry Bainbridge spoke up.

'Hello, Lily. Where are you off to all dolled up?'

'Oh, Harry, hello.' Distracted by Arthur's accident, she didn't pay much attention to Harry, who was hanging around street corners with his pals in the lull between attending his regular Saturday-afternoon football match and the start of his evening out. 'Arthur, you've got to look where you're going.'

'My arm hurts,' he whimpered.

'Here, I'll give it a rub.'

'Let's start again, shall we?' Harry teased, quickly taking on his own role and that of Lily by facing first one way then jumping round to face the other, clearing his throat and projecting his words like an actor in the theatre. In fact, with his fair hair and clean-cut good looks, and especially in the uniform he wore as Stanley Calvert's chauffeur, Harry did have something of the matinée idol about him – an impression that Lily had noted before and might have appreciated again now if she hadn't been so busy looking after Arthur. At any rate, Harry was set on claiming her attention. 'I say, "Hello, Lily. Where are you off to all dolled up?" Then you say, "Hello, Harry. Thanks for asking. I'm going out on the town with Annie and Sybil. You boys can join us later if you like."'

Lily blushed. 'Sorry, but as it happens Arthur

and me are off to Overcliffe, to Granddad Preston's house.'

'And you needed to wear your best bib and tucker for that?'

'Don't ask.' She sighed. She would gladly have stopped for a longer chat with Harry, except that a tram was due any minute and she still had to drop by at Annie's house to let her know her night out had been called off at the last minute.

'We saw your Margie dashing off into town not long back,' Ernie Durant commented. Ernie stood between Billy and Harry, who were both tall. The butcher's son only came up to their shoulders and, with his fresh face, freckles and boyish expression looked the youngest of the three, though Ernie was twenty-four and Harry and Billy twenty-two. 'She hopped on the number twelve quick as a shot. Blink and she was gone.'

'Ernie was put out because it looked like she was off to meet someone special,' Harry commented with a meaningful wink.

'Don't listen to him,' Ernie blustered. 'Margie's a free agent. She can do what she likes.' But it was true that he had a soft spot for the middle Briggs girl, even though she was eight years younger than him and, as Harry and Billy kept telling him, well out of his league as regards looks and style.

'No need to fret, Ernie. Margie's out tonight with the usual gang of girls from Kingsley's,' Lily told him. 'Anyway, I'm sorry, boys, but I have to go.'

'Everyone's in a rush tonight,' Harry said, his face shadowed by the peak of his tweed cap, which didn't, however, hide the twinkle in his grey eyes.

'Well, I'll be seeing you, I expect,' she told him, intent on hiding her blushes as she hurried off, this time keeping firm hold of Arthur's hand. 'By the way, good news – I've got myself a new job,' she called over her shoulder.

It was Harry who broke away from the group, jogged after her and caught her up at the junction with Overcliffe Road. 'Will you be moving from Calvert's?' he wanted to know.

'No, I'll be in the mending shop there. More money, Harry – that is good, isn't it?' While she talked she kept an eye out for the tram coming up from town and said a reluctant yes to Arthur's request for him to take a quick look at the brewery horses on the Common. 'Watch the road, though,' she yelled after him as he crossed over the steel tracks.

'That's champion,' Harry replied.

'That's just what I said to Miss Valentine – champion!' Her normally serious face lit up with a bright, infectious smile. It was nice of Harry to pay special attention to her news and the smile was meant to show him that she appreciated it.

'I'm happy for you, Lily. You deserve it.'

She blushed again at the compliment then modestly switched attention away from her own success. 'I expect you're glad you never went after mill work, Harry?'

'Yes, I'm pretty settled where I am at Moor House, thanks.'

'Yes, I know you. There's nothing you like better than to swank around in your posh uniform,' Lily teased. Privately she had to admit Harry was a sight for sore eyes each morning as she glimpsed him leaving his house and cycling down the side alley in his light grey chauffeur's jacket with the shiny silver buttons and the matching cap. Not that she would tell him this because it was generally acknowledged that Harry Bainbridge's head was big enough already. 'Oh no!' she said suddenly.

'What?' For a moment Harry thought Arthur must have got into more trouble.

'The tram's coming and I forgot to call in at Annie's house.'

Sure enough the yellow and black tram rattled along the steel rails towards them and Arthur darted out of the gloom, across the road to join them.

'Can you pass on a message for me?' she asked Harry. 'Tell her I've to take Arthur to Granddad Preston's so not to wait for me.'

'Right-oh,' Harry agreed. 'See you in a while, Lily.' And he went away, cheerfully repeating the message to himself.

The double-decker tram spat out sparks from its overhead cable and clicked along the rails as it approached the stop and ground to a halt. To Lily's surprise, Margie stepped from the platform on to the pavement. She looked flustered, red in the face and close to tears.

'Margie, what's wrong?' Lily wanted to know.

'Nothing. Nothing's wrong,' Margie insisted.

Unconvinced, Lily saw the conductor hovering, his finger raised, ready to press the bell. 'You sure you're all right?'

Margie nodded and sniffed back the tears.

'Are you getting on this tram or not?' the conductor barked at Lily from the platform.

'No, I'll wait for the next one,' she replied, not liking to leave her sister in this state.

So the tram set off without them.

'What happened? Did your pals let you down?' Lily wanted to know. 'Did you fall out with one of them?'

'Yes, that's right,' Margie answered quickly. 'Dorothy Brumfitt – I always knew she was a nasty piece of work. To tell you the truth, I can't stand the sight of her. When I found out she was going along to the Assembly Rooms with the rest of the gang, I changed my mind.'

'So you hopped on the tram back home? That's not like you, Margie, to miss out on a bit of excitement over the likes of Dorothy Brumfitt.'

'Well, that's what happened.' Margie sighed and looked deflated. 'Anyway, where are you and Arthur off to?'

Lily told her the tale but was only halfway through when Margie interrupted. 'There's no point us both giving up our night out, is there? Why don't you let me take Arthur to Overcliffe instead?'

Here was another surprise for Lily – Margie offering to help for a change. 'Are you sure?' she asked.

'Certain.' Grabbing Arthur's hand, Margie stood at the kerb, ostentatiously on the lookout for the next tram.

Where was the harm? Lily thought. As long as her sister got Arthur safely installed at Granddad Preston's, what difference did it make who took him? And she still had time to catch up with Annie and Sybil. 'He's to stay over,' she explained hurriedly. 'Chapel in the morning, dinner with Granddad then home for tea.'

'I see. It's like that, is it?' Margie quickly picked up on the reason behind the visit. 'Father's back from the Green Cross and worse for wear.'

'Yes, you know how it is.' Lily sighed, stepping in before Margie could say too much in front of Arthur. 'Is that all right with you?'

'I'm not sure about chapel.' Margie winked at her little brother, who immediately joined the conspiracy to miss Sunday School and grinned up at her.

'Please yourselves about that,' Lily laughed, glad that Margie had bounced back from the disappointment over her ruined evening.

'So off you go,' Margie insisted.

'Ta-ta then and be a good boy,' Lily told Arthur. 'Tell Granddad hello from me.'

She turned to retrace her steps down Albion Lane,

chuffed that she could meet up with the girls after all and share her good news. The three of them would go to the market and buy a treat of chocolate or boiled sweets to celebrate and now she fancied dancing rather than the pictures. She would forsake Jean Harlow and vote for the Assembly Rooms where she, Annie and Sybil would foxtrot the night away.

CHAPTER THREE

'I should raise the hem of that skirt a couple of inches next time you get a chance,' Sybil advised Lily as the three girls walked from the Cliff Street market towards town. Fog had crept into the town from the high moor above Overcliffe and dimmed the street lamps so that they had to watch their footing on the greasy pavements. 'You've got a nice pair of legs – I'd show them off if I was you.'

Lily disagreed. 'Long skirts are all the rage again, don't you know?'

Just like Sybil and Lily, Annie loved to talk of fashion and considered herself an expert. 'I say the legs have it,' she decided. 'It's a shame to let them go to waste, Lil.'

They laughed as they trod the wet streets, Annie jingling her recently purchased slave bracelets and all three discussing the cost of the silver signet rings they'd seen on one of the market stalls.

'With your new wage coming in you'll soon be able

to save up for one of them,' Sybil told Lily. 'You can even get it engraved.'

'Why would she?' Annie objected. 'Lily's got no sweetheart to give it to.'

'No, not for her sweetheart, silly,' Sybil teased. 'For herself. I say she'd suit a dainty ring on one of her slim fingers.'

'Will you please stop talking about my legs and my fingers?' Lily attempted a serious protest but her wide smile spoiled the effect.

'And what about her hair?' Sybil went on regardless. 'Now that she's gone up in the world, don't you think she would suit a nice Marcel Wave?'

'I am here!' Lily objected. It was funny – people were always talking about her in the third person, as if she were invisible. I need to make more of a mark, she told herself, be more like Annie who you just couldn't miss in her jingle-jangle bangles and flowery dresses.

Annie rolled on, sidestepping a muddy puddle then linking arms with Lily as they approached the grandiose Assembly Rooms built by the town council just before the Great War.

'Lily's hair doesn't need a permanent wave,' she insisted. 'It curls all by itself.'

'Worse luck,' Lily grumbled. 'What wouldn't I give for nice sleek hair like our Margie's?'

They went on, absorbed in the pros and cons of naturally wavy hair until they joined the crowd outside the dance hall with its carved stone entrance depicting romantic women with flowing robes and luxuriant locks.

'My treat,' Lily offered as they joined the back of the queue.

'No, you keep your pennies in your pocket,' Annie argued.

'Yes, just this once we'll pay,' Sybil agreed. 'To celebrate you moving upstairs.'

Lily gave in as they shuffled slowly towards the box office where they had to pay their threepenny entrance fees. 'How are you feeling about Monday, by the way?' Sybil asked. 'Are you having kittens?'

'A bit.' Lily nodded. She stood aside for a large, fair-haired girl who pushed through the queue to join Billy Robertshaw at the front. It was Dorothy Brumfitt – trust her to use her elbows, Lily thought, watching her link arms with a moody-looking Billy and recalling the row Margie had told her about.

'Manners!' Sybil grumbled.

'I don't blame you, Lil,' Annie went on. 'I'd be wetting myself if I knew I had to work under Miss Valentine.'

'She's not as bad as they say,' Lily replied, remembering how fair and straightforward the manageress had appeared in the office earlier that day. 'She probably comes across as strict to make up for her size. She doesn't want people to think they can push her around.'

'Lily, wash that blue chalk off your hand. Lily Briggs, what are you thinking? Don't you see you missed two broken ends?' Sybil did a good job of mimicking Miss Valentine's high, quick voice.

'Oh Lily, love, shan't you miss us when you move up?' Annie sang out when she'd got over her fit of giggles. They reached the box office at last and she slid payment for herself and Lily under the glass screen.

''Cos we'll miss you in the shed,' Sybil promised. 'Especially with sourpuss Florence White taking your place.'

Touched, Lily promised to meet up with her old friends every dinner time. 'If I'm late, save me a place in the canteen. We'll be able to have our chats just the same.'

'And it's not as if we've been able to talk while we work in any case,' Sybil observed. 'Not with the racket in there and Fred Lee watching our every move.'

'Ugh!' Annie and Lily shuddered in unison at the mention of the overlooker's name. They handed their coats and hats over the counter at the cloak-room and waited for Lily to do the same.

'Are we ready?' Sybil asked.

Standing side by side they examined themselves in the mirror on the wall – Lily in the lilac dress she'd sewn and taken great pains over, Annie in turquoise flowered silk with a dropped waist and a sweetheart neckline, Sybil in candy-striped voile with a high collar and full skirt. They smoothed and patted their hair, straightened their dresses and checked their lipstick.

'Ready as we'll ever be,' Annie confirmed, leading the way into the hall.

The sight that met them made their hearts beat faster. The dance hall was long and wide with a polished wooden floor and rows of electric lights with marbled glass shades suspended from a high ceiling. Floor-length, red plush curtains added a touch of glamour and were drawn against the cold dark of the November night. As the three girls entered the already crowded room, which was thick with cigarette smoke, a five-piece band on a raised platform struck up a familiar waltz.

'There's hardly room to move,' Annie complained, but she'd already picked out Robert Drummond standing head and shoulders above the crowd and she quickly made her way down the side of the room to nab him for this dance before anyone else did.

Sybil shook her head. 'That girl's got no shame.'

Lily laughed. 'Maybe we should warn him: "Watch out, Robert – Annie's after you!"'

'It's too late – he's already smitten. He danced with her all night long the last time we were here.'

Sybil and Lily kept on smiling and chatting as Annie reached her target and the tall motor mechanic quickly succumbed to her charms. She said something to him with a pout and a pretty tilt of her head towards the dancing couples. He nodded and stubbed out his cigarette. Next moment, his arm was around Annie's slim waist and they were stepping on to the floor.

Less bold than Annie, Sybil and Lily had to make do with partnering each other for this first dance, which was already well underway. They didn't care – they would still enjoy themselves with Sybil taking the man's part and steering Lily around the room, taking care not to get their toes stepped on by the clod-hopping feet of the butchers' boys, grocers, brewery workers and mill hands who regularly filled the Assembly Rooms on a Saturday night. Though they were done up in brogues, snazzy blazers and neatly pressed trousers, the local lads were no match for Douglas Fairbanks when it came to steering girls through the Viennese waltz.

'Watch out, Ernie!' Sybil cried as Harry's stocky pal backed into them so hard that his partner, Hilda Crabtree, who worked alongside Margie and Dorothy in Kingsley's spinning shed, stumbled against him and had to be clutched to his chest to stop her from falling to the floor.

'You did that on purpose!' Lily protested.

Ernie winked and set Hilda back on her feet. 'Hilda's not complaining,' he pointed out before he whisked her off in another direction. For the moment he seemed to have dropped his long-standing crush on Margie and was discovering that Hilda was a more than satisfactory replacement.

And so it went on from waltz to quickstep to fox-trot, with only an occasional glimpse of a smiling Annie whirling by in Robert's arms, the skirt of her floral dress billowing out, bracelets jingling. Lily and

Sybil danced more sedately until Lily was surprised by a tap on her shoulder and turned to accept an invitation from Harry to dance to a new waltz tune called 'Goodnight, Sweetheart' while Sybil said yes to a man she didn't recognize – older than your normal Assembly Rooms partner, of medium build and dressed in a dark blue suit. He had a streak of grey at his temples, strong features and a confident air.

'Who's that?' Lily asked Harry, who, while he didn't exactly have two left feet, was the type of partner who had to repeat the one-two-three rhythm under his breath in order to keep time.

'No idea. I've only seen him in this neck of the woods once or twice and I've never bothered to ask his name,' he told Lily. 'He looks like a commercial traveller to me.' The answer put him off his stride.

'One-two-three, one-two-three.' Lily counted Harry back in and they were off again, Harry with a gentlemanly hand placed squarely in the small of Lily's back, Lily having to tilt her head to meet his gaze.

'The last time I saw you, you and Arthur were off to your granddad's,' he reminded her when they were firmly settled in.

'I know but there was a last-minute change of plan. Margie offered to do it for me instead.'

'Blow me down – she didn't, did she?' His eyebrows shot up in comic disbelief as he took charge and steered Lily across the floor, his hand firm against her lower back.

'Honestly, she did.' To her surprise, Lily had to struggle to keep her voice calm. Why had her heartbeat suddenly quickened? she wondered.

'Well, it worked out nicely for you, at any rate. It means you could come out and celebrate with your pals.'

Lily was pleased that he'd remembered her good news. She noticed for the second time that evening that Harry, who had dressed up smartly in blazer and grey flannel trousers, was chattier and more attentive than usual, and she felt disappointed when the waltz finished and a new tune began, causing quite a few couples to leave the dance floor.

'What's this music they're playing?' he asked, looking around dubiously at the empty spaces and tugging awkwardly at the knot of the pale blue silk tie he'd chosen especially to impress the girls. He'd seen a picture-house poster of Clark Gable wearing one just like it so judged himself to be at the height of fashion.

Lily held on to him and listened hard. 'Foxtrot, I think. Yes, this is a foxtrot. I could teach you if you like.'

'I think I've reached the limits of my dancing prowess!' Harry laughed, shaking his head as he led her to the side of the room. They were soon joined by Sybil, whose slick commercial traveller had moved on to a new partner, and by Ernie and Hilda, the latter complaining loudly of bruised toes.

'I swear, Ernie, that's the last dance I have with you,' Hilda moaned.

'Never mind – plenty more fish in the sea,' he retorted. And he was off again, trawling down the side of the room, picking a mousy-haired girl in a pale yellow dress who caught his eye.

Still groaning, Hilda kicked off one of her shoes and wriggled her toes. 'Where's your Margie got to?' she asked Lily in passing. 'I'm surprised I haven't seen her tonight. She never turned up outside the market to meet us like she said.'

'Are you sure?'

'Sure I'm sure. We waited for her then Dorothy turned up and said Margie had decided against coming after all. She's not poorly, is she?'

'No.' Lily stayed tight-lipped about the argument between Dorothy and her sister, reckoning that it was up to Margie to mention the topic at a later date if she felt like it.

'It's not like Margie.' Hilda winced as she slid her foot back into her shoe. Then she cast a critical eye over Ernie's new dance partner as they attempted the complicated steps of the foxtrot. 'Yellow's the wrong colour for her. It makes her look washed out,' she concluded.

'Do you fancy this dance?' Lily asked Sybil, partly to get away from moaning-minnie Hilda.

'Not half,' Sybil agreed. And they were back on the floor, smiling at members of the band as they passed the stage, skirts flaring as they twirled.

49

By half past nine, after three hours of non-stop dancing, Lily's face was hot and her feet ached but she'd had a marvellous time.

'You're not leaving already?' Annie called from the arms of her handsome mechanic as they slow-waltzed by. They made a perfect couple – Robert with a lock of his slicked-back hair curling down on to his broad forehead but otherwise dapper; Annie with flushed cheeks, one slim hand raised and resting lightly on his shoulder, the other clasped firmly by her partner, who seemed to have no intention of ever letting go.

Lily pointed to the clock on the wall. 'I have to catch the next tram home, remember.'

'Poor you,' Annie commiserated. Her father was dead and her worn-down mother was way past caring what time she got home.

Sybil too was happily being swept off her feet again by the commercial traveller, so it was Ernie and Harry who offered to ride the tram with Lily.

'Don't bother about me,' she told them, handing over her ticket to collect her coat. 'I'll be fine, thanks.'

'Who says we're bothered about you?' Ernie countered as he loosened his tie, undid his top button then took out a packet of cigarettes. 'It just so happens we're on our way too.'

'What's the matter, Ern – did Hilda warn all the other girls about your two left feet?'

'Say what you like to me, Lily Briggs, it's water off a duck's back.' Undented, Ernie offered his cigarettes to Lily and Harry who both shook their heads. 'As a matter of fact, Harry and me fancied getting back for a pint at the Cross before closing time.'

'The foxtrot was too much for you both, was it?' As they came down the steps of the Assembly Rooms into the fog and heavy drizzle, Lily turned up her coat collar for the cold wait at the nearby tram stop. 'Never mind, I'm sure the girls of Overcliffe Assembly Rooms will get over their disappointment in time.'

The easy conversation between Ernie and Lily flowed on while Harry stayed noticeably quiet until the tram appeared and they stepped on to the platform for the short journey home. The tram was crowded, so Lily stood in the aisle between Ernie and Harry. When the rocking motion on the bend at Chapel Street threw her against Harry, he steadied her with a hand and she gave him a grateful smile. What's come over me? she secretly wondered. Why am I so hot and bothered every time Harry Bainbridge looks at me in a certain way?

'Here's our stop,' Ernie said at last, peering out into the rain-soaked night. Harry pushed ahead along the gangway, making space for Lily and Ernie to follow. The conductor pressed the bell, the tram stopped and the three of them alighted.

'How about fishcake and chips on me?' Harry offered as they stood outside Pennington's at the

51

top of Raglan Road and he felt inside his trouser pockets. 'I reckon I can scrape the pennies together.'

Ernie looked put out. 'I thought we'd agreed on a pint?'

'And anyway I have to get back home,' Lily said quickly, though with a pang of regret. 'Thanks, Harry – maybe next time.'

So Harry and Ernie walked Lily down Raglan Road, through the alley on to Albion Lane where they deposited her at her house then walked on to the Green Cross.

She waited a while, letting their footsteps recede, staring up the three worn stone steps to her front door while she rehearsed what she would say about it being her and not Margie turning the key in the lock.

Let's hope they've both gone to bed and I can leave the explanations until tomorrow morning, she thought. But there was a light on in the living room and she braced herself to face her mother's barrage of questions. 'What's happened? Where's Margie, pray tell?' on and on, with Father slouched in the fireside chair or already dead to the world and snoring in bed.

Lily squared her shoulders. '"Pack up your troubles in your old kit bag and smile, boys, smile,"' she hummed jauntily to herself as she mounted the steps and opened the door.

Nothing, not her mother's world-weary nagging or her father's drunkenness, could spoil this day of all days unless she, Lily Briggs, chose to let it.

CHAPTER FOUR

'Before you ask,' Lily whispered as she opened the door into the living room to find Rhoda sitting alone by the dying fire, 'Margie's at Granddad Preston's with Arthur.'

If Rhoda was surprised, she didn't let it show. 'That's all right then,' she said without lifting her gaze from the embers.

'You don't mind?'

'No. It'll keep Margie out of mischief for a change.'

'Well, I'll say goodnight.' A relieved Lily was about to close the door and creep upstairs to bed when Rhoda stopped her.

'Oh Lily, I only wish Margie had half your common sense,' she said with a sigh.

Recognizing her mother's need to share her burdens – a rare thing with her – Lily came into the room, closing the door to make sure her father wouldn't overhear. 'Why, what's wrong, Mother? Has something happened?'

Rhoda tapped the arm of her chair. 'I don't know.

You tell me – why did your sister give up her Saturday night out?'

For her mother's sake Lily played down the worries lurking at the back of her own mind. 'There was a bit of an argument between Margie and one of her chums, that's all – nothing to worry about.'

'Fighting over a boy now, is she?' Rhoda's voice was sharp and suspicious.

'No, not that I know of.'

'Aye, but it will be.'

Lily faltered and hovered uncertainly by the door. 'What makes you say that?'

'It always is – that's why.' Rhoda gave Lily one of her long, direct stares. 'When two girls fall out over nothing, there's a boy in the picture – mark my words.'

'I don't know about that, Mother.' Lily frowned then offered to help. 'What can I do? Would you like me to talk to Margie when she gets back tomorrow?'

'Yes, if you think you can do any good. Stop fidgeting by the door, Lily, come over here and sit.'

So Lily went and perched on the arm of her mother's chair, thinking through what had just been said. 'I can't be sure that she'll listen to me, though.'

'Well, I'm sure of one thing – nothing *I* try with your sister does any good. She turns right around and does the opposite. If I say don't throw away your hard-earned wages on one big night out, she's on with her dancing shoes and out of the door before you can say Jack Robinson. And she's always hanker-

54

ing after silk stockings and other silly things that she can't afford. I don't know where she gets it from.'

'Not from you, Mother.' Lily smiled sadly. She couldn't ever imagine a time when Rhoda had been young and carefree.

'No, well, I never had the money.'

'I know. It must have been hard.'

'It was. Remember, I married your father when I wasn't much older than Margie is now. I never had two halfpennies of my own to rub together when I was her age and after I married it went downhill from there.'

The wry comment, made without self-pity, summed up Rhoda's early life. The youngest of five children, one of whom – a girl – had died in infancy, Rhoda had lost her mother to scarlet fever at the age of ten and her father, Bert Preston, had stayed on in the rented house in Overcliffe with his young girl and three lads, Robert, William and Richard.

The children were left to drag themselves up while their father went out to work hauling coal from the open-cast mine at Welby to the mills in the valley below, which meant long days for little pay. Rhoda had to pick up where her mother left off, doing the washing, ironing, baking and generally making ends meet. It left little time for schoolwork and by the time Rhoda reached fourteen she found herself employed first as a scavenger at Kingsley's, a job she hated because the machines would whirr and hiss above her as she crawled underneath to gather up fibres of wool, then as a lap joiner in the spinning shed at Calvert's, which wasn't much better.

So it came as a relief when, at seventeen, she ran across Walter Briggs who had recently moved into the area for work and was knocking on doors looking for lodgings. Rhoda's father, strapped for cash as always, squeezed an extra bed into the room he shared with the three boys and charged Walter the princely sum of two shillings and sixpence per week.

Bert Preston might not have raced ahead with the arrangement quite so hastily, Rhoda reflected later, if he'd realized that within the year Walter would have proposed marriage to Rhoda and whisked her off from the crowded house in Overcliffe to live in a basement dwelling close to the canal.

'There was bad feeling between them after that and my father never really got over it,' she would tell her own children. 'I was piggy in the middle. I mean, how was Father meant to cope, with me married and living on Canal Road? That was the thing.'

Down in the damp cellar, conditions were bad, especially when the children came along – Lily in the first year of marriage, then a gap of four years until Margie, then two years between her and Evie, and finally Arthur, a full eight years after that.

Meanwhile the war had started. Two of Rhoda's brothers, Robert and William, were killed early on – Robert at Mons and his brother not long after. Richard, the youngest, survived almost until Armistice Day then died not in the trenches but travelling through Belgium on the back of a supply wagon. It came under attack from the retreating Germans and a shell blew the last surviving Preston boy clean out of the vehicle. He died instantly.

In his house on the hill, Bert grieved for his three sons and turned eventually to his estranged daughter for consolation.

In contrast to the Prestons, Walter had succeeded in avoiding military service on the grounds of having a weak chest. It was at this time that he found their family – comprising Rhoda and Lily, and Margie already on the way – the house on Albion Lane at a rent they could afford. They lived there contentedly until 1915, when the powers that be cornered Walter and shipped him out to France. He was allowed to return home in January 1917 to convalesce from deep shrapnel wounds to his left side, but was then shipped back to the trenches for the rest of the war.

'Never mind that he'd been blown to bits and had bad shell shock,' Rhoda told her eldest daughter when Lily grew old enough to ask questions about the ugly scarring she saw all down one side of her father's body. 'They sent him back without a second thought.'

'As soon as he walked in through the door I saw it would never be the same,' Rhoda reflected from time to time and without obvious emotion. 'Your father's not a bad man – never was and never will be. But I took one look at him when he came back and saw the life had gone out of him for good.'

Despite all this, Walter did try for work in the mills but his experience in the trenches had weakened him in body and spirit and made him bitter. Besides, after the drop-off in government orders for army uniforms, the Yorkshire woollen mills suffered, so he failed to find a steady job and the growing Briggs family had to fall back on Public Assistance while Rhoda brought up the children and made herself useful in the neighbourhood.

For a start, she became expert in herbal remedies – caraway seeds soaked in hot water and sprinkled with sugar for baby colic, liquorice powder for constipation at any age, mustard plasters for bronchitis. More and more of the women in Albion Lane and on Raglan Road turned to her for advice and eventually for help when their babies came. Rhoda was considered reliable and unflappable, unlike her husband who was usually to be found propping up the bar at the Cross.

Now, late on this cold and gloomy Saturday night, Rhoda made the unaccustomed move of sharing her thoughts with Lily. 'The way things are going with Margie, I can't see her keeping the job at Kingsley's much longer, not if she starts falling out with the girls who work alongside her and causing a bad atmosphere in the spinning shed. The overlookers won't stand for that.'

'She only fell out with one,' Lily pointed out as she kicked off her shoes to warm her feet at what was left of the fire. 'And that was Dorothy Brumfitt, who nobody likes. From what I hear, she's a trouble-maker.'

'Watch you don't give yourself chilblains,' Rhoda warned before staring into the fire and saying nothing for a while. 'So if they get rid of anyone, you think it'll be Dorothy?' she asked at last, seeming to take comfort from Lily's view of events. Then she changed tack. 'As for her goings-on with boys and the like, it might help if you told her it's her job to set an example to Evie.'

'Yes, that's a good idea,' Lily agreed. Sitting this close to her mother she noticed again the shadows and lines on her face and the raised veins on the backs of her hands. 'I wish you wouldn't worry and run around after us all the time,' she told her softly.

'And if I don't worry and run around, pray tell who will?' was Rhoda's stubborn response.

'I will,' Lily promised. 'I can do more of the iron-ing of a night, when I get back from work. And you don't need to do all the washing on a Monday. I could do some for you on a Sunday.'

'And what would people think of me hanging my washing out on the Lord's day?' Rhoda shook her head.

Lily gave a little, self-mocking laugh. 'Here I am, offering to help. I thought you'd bite my hand off.'

'No, you know me better than that. I'll carry on until I drop – that's all I know.' Taking a grey car-digan from the back of the chair, Rhoda wrapped it around her thin shoulders. 'If you really want to help . . .' she added as Lily bent to pick up her shoes and head off.

'Yes, Mother, what is it?'

'You can keep a closer eye on Margie from now on, see she stays on the right track.'

'I will,' Lily promised, making her way upstairs at last.

'Good luck, Evie! Good luck, Lily!' At a quarter past seven on Monday morning Arthur stayed at the window to wave his sisters off to work. His piping voice followed them down the steps on to the street and his pale, peaky face was pressed against the glass.

It was scarcely daylight when they set off and the morning was frosty and crisp for once rather than sodden and dank. Evie had on a crimson beret and matching woollen shawl and carried her new work pinafore rolled and tucked under her arm, while Lily had dressed up for her new job in the grey coat and hat she'd worn on Saturday night.

'Cheerio, Arthur. Be a good boy at school today,' Lily called back. As she turned, she noticed Margie scoot out of the house and run down the hill after them, still wrapping her shawl over her head and across her chest.

'Why did you let me sleep in?' she demanded. 'At this rate I'll be late for work.'

'We didn't let you sleep in,' Lily objected. 'We told you the time and pulled the covers off you.'

'Yes, and you refused to get out of bed,' Evie agreed.

'There you go, ganging up on me again.' Margie's walk into work at Kingsley's was five minutes longer than her sisters' route and at this rate she'd be locked out and have to wait in the cold until the mill manager had officially docked her pay and chosen to let her in. Then she'd get a ticking-off and her week would be off to the worst possible start. 'I'd better run,' she decided, narrowly avoiding Harry Bainbridge as he emerged from the passage wheeling his bike.

'Whoa!' he cried, stepping back and leaning his bike against a lamp post. He clutched at his chauffeur's cap with both hands. 'Hang on to your hats, boys, Margie Briggs is late for work!'

Evie and Lily laughed at the way he pretended to be cowed while Margie gave him a disgusted look and hurried on. Then he gave Lily a wink, picked up his bike and cycled on down the hill.

'Ta-ta, Harry!' Evie cried.

He raised a hand to wave without turning round. 'Want a lift?' he yelled at Margie as he overtook her before the turning on to Ghyll Road. 'You can hop on my crossbar if you like.'

'Thanks but no thanks,' she told him crossly. Then she hastily reconsidered the offer. 'Why – are you going my way?'

'I can do if you like,' he replied. 'Come on, you'll get there quicker.'

61

Impulsively Margie changed her mind and in front of dozens of work-bound mill hands, she gathered up her skirt above her knees and perched side saddle on the crossbar of Harry's bike, one arm around his neck, the other hand clutching the handlebars as they careered on down the cobbled street.

Lily and Evie watched from a distance until Harry and his passenger turned on to Ghyll Road.

'Better not tell Mother.' Evie gave Lily an apprehensive glance.

'No, better not.' Here she was – already letting Rhoda down, Lily realized. 'I promised to keep an eye on her and now look – everyone's staring at her.'

'And she didn't give a fig about it,' Evie pointed out. 'Anyway, it means she'll get to work on time.'

'There is that,' Lily acknowledged. She considered the difference a couple of years made to a young girl's life. Three, maybe four years ago, she wouldn't have thought anything of tomboy Margie hopping on to a boy's bike and hitching a ride, or of her aged eight playing a game of cricket on the Common with the older lads like Harry, Billy and Ernie, whacking the ball for six. Not now, though. 'But she's too old to be showing her legs to the world,' she added. 'Anyway, like we said – mum's the word.'

'Yes, mum's the word.'

As Lily and Evie walked on by rows of identical houses to join the flow of workers, they fell silent, each affected by nerves as they turned right on to Ghyll Road and the tall, forbidding walls of Calvert's Mill came into view.

Now Evie clutched her grey pinafore close to her chest and felt her heart race. Instead of being in with the big girls at school and shouldering the responsibility that came with the class monitor's badge, she was now the youngest of the mill girls and on the lowest rung of the ladder.

'Chin up,' Lily told her, guessing her sister's feelings as they approached the main entrance to the mill. 'No one's going to eat you.'

Evie smiled weakly. Her cheeks were flushed from the cold and her fingers were freezing. She knew her hand would tremble when she clocked on for the first time and she wasn't sure whether this would be due to the temperature or to pure fright, though it would probably be both.

'You'll be fine,' Lily assured her. But Evie looked so young in her red beret, with fine strands of fair hair escaping from the thick plait that hung down her back and blowing across her rosy cheeks. As Evie's grey eyes stared up at the sooty archway, Lily's heart went out to her. 'Come on, I'll find Annie and Sybil for you.'

Evie followed in Lily's wake, threading through the jostling crowd, under the arch and past the Enquiries office, past the wooden board advertising vacancies for piecers and lap joiners, past the safety notice reminding workers that it was forbidden to

63

clean, adjust or oil machinery whilst in motion, then down the corridor to the entrance into the weaving shed.

'This is where you clock on.' Lily showed Evie the machine with its large brass dial then spotted Fred Lee approaching them. 'He'll hand you your cards and show you what to do,' she explained.

'Hello, so this is Miss Evie Briggs!' the overlooker exclaimed with an excess of jollity for this hour on a Monday morning. He planted his feet wide apart, folded his arms and appraised Evie from head to foot before giving an approving nod. 'Not exactly a chip off the old block, though, is she?' he commented to Lily.

It was true that Evie looked nothing like her tall, dark-haired sister. She was smaller and altogether more delicate, with a pale complexion and just at this minute she had the wide-eyed look of a wild creature coming face to face with mortal danger.

'She's a good girl and a quick learner,' Lily insisted, putting her palm against the small of Evie's back and giving her a gentle push forward. She was relieved to see Sybil striding towards them with a smile on her face.

'Come on, Evie, come and say hello to some of the girls while Fred goes to pick up your cards from the main office,' Sybil offered with a reassuring wink at Lily. And she took Evie's hand and dragged her past the leering overlooker, down the central aisle between the big looms whose giant, oily wheels were

64

just clanking into action as the seven thirty buzzer sounded.

Evie glanced uncertainly over her shoulder.

'Go!' Lily mouthed, feeling more uncomfortable than ever now that she had to leave Evie to Fred's tender mercies.

'Don't worry, Lil – I'll look after your little sister.' He grinned.

'That's exactly what I'm bothered about,' she muttered under her breath. But she couldn't delay because today of all days she couldn't afford to be late for Miss Valentine. So she turned and ran up the flight of back stairs leading to the mending room, arriving there just in time to see the little manageress enter from the door at the far end of Lily's new workplace.

Between the two women there were six long, narrow tables, each equipped with a stool and a new-fangled electric lamp on a stand – individual stations for the burlers and menders employed by Calvert's to finish and perfect the work carried out in the spinning and weaving sections of the mill. Three women were already sitting on their stools, taking scissors and other small tools out of tin boxes stowed on ledges underneath their tables. Two more hurried to take up their positions under the eagle eye of the supervisor.

Lily's heart beat fast as she failed to catch the eye of any of her fellow workers. She immediately had a sense that they were more stand-offish than the girls downstairs and reluctant to welcome the nervous newcomer, but Lily steeled herself to walk between the tables and meet the manageress who stood waiting for her by the far door. She passed two sturdy-limbed older women wearing dark blue aprons who were busy arranging the tools of their trade, then a woman in her thirties whom she recognized as Ethel Newby, daughter of the elderly Newbys who ran the tobacconist's and sweet shop at the bottom of Albion Lane. Next she walked between two younger women with fashionable bobbed hair, one wearing a patterned blouse, the other a warm-looking brown cardigan and a matching long, straight skirt. The table nearest to Miss Valentine was still vacant and Lily presumed that this would be the station where she would work.

'Good morning, Lily.' The manageress greeted her primly then handed her a pair of pointed scissors, a burling iron, a packet of needles and a long piece of chalk. 'The cost of these will be taken from your first week's wages,' she remarked, leading Lily to the vacant position. She asked the nearest girl, the one in the patterned blouse, to fetch a bolt of cloth and lay it out over the high table, giving time for Lily to perch on her stool and settle her nerves. 'Thank you, Vera, that will be all for now. Lily, Vera will be on hand to answer any questions you may have. She's been with us for ten weeks and is moving on from learner to mender, just as you will if you make good progress in the work.'

Lily glanced at Vera, who gave a brief smile before returning to her station – the first sign of friendliness that Lily had encountered in her new job.

'Now pay attention,' Miss Valentine instructed. 'I want you to take your burling iron and scissors in your left hand and the chalk in your right hand. The cloth is on its reverse side, as you see. Your first job is to mark the flaws with your chalk.'

'But how will I know where there's a flaw?' Lily asked timidly. To her it seemed that the length of grey cloth spread out on the table was perfect.

'You will run your fingertips over the surface.' The manageress spoke precisely and professionally, having been through this process with many new girls before Lily. 'A flaw will be felt as a small knot in the weft and the warp. This is when you take your burler and lift out the knot and loosen it with the small hook on the end then snip both ends of the thread with your scissors, ready to sew them back in so that they can't be seen. Is that clear?'

Lily nodded, eager to begin. 'Yes, Miss Valentine.'

'Don't sew in the ends right away, though. Mark and loosen then snip and move on, rolling up the material as you go. Sewing the ends and picks is more complicated and comes later. You know what I mean by picks?'

Again Lily nodded. 'They're the threads going weft ways, Miss Valentine.'

'Very good. And the threads going warp ways are . . . ?'

'Ends.'

The manageress nodded. 'As I said, Vera will advise you if you feel uncertain.'

'Thank you, Miss Valentine.' In this new situation Lily was thrown back into her schooldays. She felt ten years old again, in school and sitting at an ink-stained desk.

'I'll speak to you again at dinner time,' the manageress told Lily as she walked away, pitter-patter, in her dainty shoes.

Lily swallowed hard and once more picked up a smile from her round-faced, fair-haired neighbour.

'Never mind, her bark is worse than her bite,' Vera whispered as she ran her fingers over the surface of her material, deftly marking a flaw then hooking her burling iron into the knot to loosen it.

'I'll bear that in mind, thanks,' Lily whispered back. Nevertheless, she began work with trembling fingers.

Soon, though, she grew absorbed in her task, appreciating the quietness of the room compared with the noise of the weaving shed and hardly noticing the ticking of the large clock on the wall next to Miss Valentine's small office or the to-ing and fro-ing of Jennie, the matronly looking taker-in whose job it was to lift newly delivered pieces on to her perch, which was a roller fixed to steel rods. The taker-in would pre-check a length of cloth for major flaws and mark them before carrying it to the burlers and menders for further, more detailed checking.

'Take care not to miss the least little thing,' Jennie warned Lily when she brought a fresh bolt to her station. She was a small, round, confident woman with wrinkled, rosy cheeks and an old-fashioned style. 'Miss Valentine has eyes in the back of her head.'

'I'll do my best,' Lily promised, already more at ease. A glance at the clock told her it was just before ten and she paused to wonder how Evie was getting along in the weaving shed below.

'You know what to do with the cloth when you're finished with it?' Jennie enquired. 'You have to call me back and I take it away to the flipping machine to be folded – that's the routine.'

'Ah, but not yet,' Vera reminded them. 'Not before Miss Valentine has come back to teach Lily mending.'

'Quite right,' Jennie confirmed. Then she leaned in towards Lily for a further chat. 'Call me a nosy parker and tell me to mind my own business, but you wouldn't be a Briggs from Albion Lane, by any chance?'

'Yes.' Lily wasn't sure if talking was permitted in the mending room but it seemed rude to ignore Jennie so she continued. 'Rhoda Briggs is my mother. Do you know her?'

'Know her? I should say so. I only went to school in Overcliffe with her, though I haven't seen her in years and her name was Preston back then. We both married and fell out of touch. How is she these days?'

Lily noticed Vera shake her head in warning and

looked up in time to see Miss Valentine leave her office. She heard the click of the manageress's heels on the wooden floor and wondered at Jennie, who didn't seem in the least bit afraid of the ticking-off she was about to receive.

'Tell Rhoda I said hello,' she told Lily, casually moving off.

'We don't pay you to gossip, Jennie Shaw.' Miss Valentine blocked her way and Jennie had to stop short. 'I'd thank you if you left our new girl to get on with her work.'

The stout woman met the beady gaze of the manageress. Lily noticed they were of a similar age but total opposites in every other respect. Where Jennie was easy and relaxed, Miss Valentine was prim and self-contained. Jennie was large and solid, Miss Valentine a little wisp of a thing. In other words, they were chalk and cheese, but if Lily had to bet on who was the stronger personality she would back the manageress every time.

'I was only being friendly and making Lily feel at home,' Jennie protested mildly.

Miss Valentine's eyes narrowed behind her round glasses as she sought a way to put down this minor insurrection. 'Please confine your friendliness to your dinner break,' she reminded Jennie. 'Vera and Ethel both have finished pieces waiting to be taken away for flipping so I'd be grateful if you would carry out your duties. Lily, please move aside while I show you our mending method.'

The reprimand was enough to send Jennie scuttling off to the far side of the room and to make Lily feel very hot under the collar. Still, she paid full attention to Miss Valentine's new instructions.

'Let's start with these two broken ends,' she began. 'You see how I pick up two stitches with a number-five needle, go over the next two then pick up two more?'

Lily concentrated and nodded. 'Yes, Miss Valentine.'

'And so on, for twenty-six stitches. Then thread your needle with the broken end and pull it through. You see – now the end is invisible and you have mended approximately one inch of material.'

Lily admired the dextrous movements of the manageress's small fingers and wondered if she would ever learn to be so clever with her needle.

'A quick mender can mend three yards in one hour,' Miss Valentine told her. 'So you see, Lily, you have no time to stop and chat.'

'Yes, Miss Valentine. I'm sorry, Miss Valentine. It won't happen again.'

The manageress nodded then stepped down from the stool. 'Remember what I showed you and now try it for yourself while I stand by and watch.'

Lily felt her mouth go dry. This was ten times worse than school, she thought, afraid that her fingers would fumble and Miss Valentine would declare her too clumsy to do the fine work required. Before she knew it, she would be back down in the weaving shed, red faced and with her tail between her legs, on the wrong end of Fred Lee's nasty jibes.

'Begin,' Miss Valentine instructed.

So Lily took a deep breath and picked up her needle. Keep calm, she told herself, don't let yourself down. Concentrate, Lily Briggs, and prove you're as good as the next girl at Calvert's Mill.

CHAPTER FIVE

'So how was your first week?' Harry asked Lily and Evie as they left work the following Saturday. He sat behind the wheel of his boss's shiny black Bentley, parked outside the main door, his peaked cap tipped back and his broad smile inviting a detailed account from the weary girls. He smiled warmly at Lily.

'Long.' Evie sighed. The days had been packed with action. From the moment the knocker-up had rattled his lead-tipped pole against the bedroom window of 5 Albion Lane at six thirty each morning until the five o'clock buzzer had sounded at Calvert's she'd been on her feet. The routine was unvaried – get up and dressed in the icy-cold attic bedroom, eat breakfast then trudge down the hill to join the jostling crowd on Ghyll Road, on then almost to the junction with Canal Road and then left under the mill's arched entrance to clock on and run errands for her fellow workers all morning long. Mash the tea and shop for dinners, trying not to forget who took three spoonfuls of sugar and who wanted a pork pie and who had ordered tripe and onions, and Lord help Evie if she got it wrong. Her afternoons had been taken up learning from Maureen Godwin what it took to be a loom cleaner.

'Very long,' Lily echoed. There'd been so much to learn under Miss Valentine's eagle eye, and not a day had gone by so far without her missing a flaw or a broken end, or being reprimanded for working too slowly by Jennie Shaw, standing by with a knowing smile and a fresh bolt of cloth for checking.

It was only at dinner times, when the two sisters got together with Annie and Sybil in the canteen to relax and swap cheerful stories, that the situation had been made more bearable.

'Listen to you two!' Harry teased. 'Anyone would think you had a hard life!'

'Look who's talking, Harry Bainbridge,' Lily retorted. 'Sitting on your backside all day long, driving around like Lord Muck!'

'Sticks and stones,' he replied merrily. 'Oh, you haven't seen Billy by any chance?'

'No – why?' As Evie gave her answer she was forced to step aside by Fred Lee in flat cap and goggles, riding his motorbike out from under the archway, weaving his way through the departing crowd and leaving a whiff of exhaust fumes in his wake.

'He's supposed to be here, working on the manager's garden,' Harry explained. 'I'm meant to pass on a message from Mr Calvert.'

'Oh well, you're in luck. There he is.' Evie pointed

out the figure of Calvert's gardener wheeling a barrow along the path by the side of Derek Wilson's house at the far end of the mill building. Spotting Harry in their boss's car, he left off work and strolled towards them.

'Chatting with the girls as usual, eh, Harry?' Billy began. He was in his shirtsleeves and without a scarf despite the November chill, his corduroy trousers held up by both belt and braces. Lean and wiry, with an outdoor complexion and a naturally cheerful expression, he seemed to bring a breath of fresh air wherever he went.

'Since when did the pot start calling the kettle black?' Harry replied with unshakeable good humour.

'Is this gentleman bothering you, girls?' Billy said with a wink. 'Would you like me to move him on for you?'

'You and whose army, Billy?' Harry laughed.

'No – we want Harry to give us a ride home in his car,' Lily joked. She and Evie knew Billy almost as well as they knew Harry, having grown up together since the Robertshaws had moved into a house at the bottom end of Albion Lane when Lily was six. The two lads were firm friends and it was Harry who had tipped Billy the wink when the gardening job at Moor House fell vacant a year earlier, allowing Billy to move on from a lowly street-cleaning job with the town council. 'We want a taste of luxury after the hard week we've had,' Lily insisted.

'And pigs might fly,' a voice said.

Lily turned to see that Margie had sneaked up on them on her way home from Kingsley's and she greeted her sister with a sympathetic smile. 'You look done in,' she said.

'I am,' Margie admitted, shoulders sagging, her new haircut the worse for wear after a hot, grimy morning in the spinning shed. Then she noticed Billy standing behind the car and she stiffened.

'Well, ta-ta, I must be getting along,' she told Lily and Evie, turning on her heel.

'Wait for us,' Evie called after her.

'Was it something I said?' Billy quipped, leaning against the car and lighting up a cigarette, watching Margie closely as she ignored Evie's appeal and hurried off.

'Anyway, Billy – I've got a message for you from Mr Calvert.' Harry got around to his reason for being there. 'He wants you up at the big house this afternoon, working on the borders.'

'But it's Saturday.' Billy frowned. 'I'm ready to knock off.'

'Ours is not to reason why,' Harry commiserated.

Billy looked and sounded seriously put out. 'Why can't his bloody borders wait until Monday?'

'Because they can't.' Turning on the ignition, Harry listened proudly to the purr of the car's engine. 'Hear that? Sweet as a nut.'

Lily took the hint. 'Better let you go then, Harry.'

'We'll still see you later?' Harry checked with Billy. 'Six o'clock at the Cross?'

'I'll be there,' Billy confirmed, puffing moodily on his cigarette.

'How about you, Lily?' Harry wanted to know. 'What are you girls up to tonight?'

'We're going to the flicks,' she said a touch too quickly, feeling herself blush under Harry's questioning gaze.

Pushing his advantage, he teased her a little more. 'Not teaching me to quickstep to "Goodnight, Sweetheart"?'

'"Goodnight, Sweetheart" is a waltz,' Lily reminded him. 'Anyway, Harry, I'm sorry but not tonight.'

'Ah well, there's always next week.' He grinned. Then he wound up his window and eased away from the kerb, glancing at Lily in his overhead mirror as he left.

'And pigs might fly,' Billy repeated Margie's mocking phrase. 'Harry Bainbridge doing the quickstep – now that I'd like to see!'

A long week, but satisfactory. Lily thought in school report terms as she and Evie walked home together. She was still buoyed up by her recent promotion and willing to learn from her mistakes, and although she only carried in her pocket what was left of her wages after deductions for the scissors and burling iron, et cetera, she knew that at the end of next week she would receive the full twenty shillings, rising as she'd told her mother to thirty when she'd learned her new trade.

She was less confident that Evie had settled into her role in the weaving shed, though there'd been no complaints so far as she knew from the over-looker, and Sybil and Annie had kept their promise of keeping an eye out for her. 'Evie's doing all right,' they had assured Lily at the end of each day. 'We make sure she stays out of harm's way.'

'You're not saying much,' Lily mentioned to her youngest sister as they turned off Ghyll Road on to Albion Lane and called into Newby's for Arthur's sweets. 'What's the matter – cat got your tongue?'

'I'm just tired.' Evie sighed, waiting inside the shop door. 'My fingers are sore, my back aches, sometimes I think I'm going to drop to the floor I'm so hot and bothered.'

Lily was alarmed. 'It's not too much for you? You can manage the work?'

Evie nodded. 'I have to manage it, don't I? What else is there?'

Lily took her change from Alice Newby, an older version of her daughter Ethel with the same polite, smiling manner. She put the sweets in her pocket then walked on with Evie until they came to a stop by the alley connecting them to Raglan Road. Then haltingly she took up the conversation again. 'You're right – there is nothing else.' It seemed harsh, but it was true – there was no other work for girls like them.

Ten or twelve years earlier, soon after the Great War had ended, some school leavers in the area might have dreamed of office work or going into a bank, even of getting their own small grocery shop or working as a milliner, but not in these hard times. 'We have to grin and bear it, hang on to what we've got.'

'I do realize that. Only I didn't know it would be so hard.'

Lily took her hand and squeezed it. 'You'll get used to it and then it'll seem easier.'

Evie's eyes welled up with tears, which she quickly wiped away. 'You won't tell Mother I was upset? She has enough on her plate.'

Lily knew what she meant – despite her efforts to talk her middle sister out of her bad moods, this past week had included more cheek and sullenness from Margie, which had built up on the Wednesday night to an open argument between mother and daughter and Rhoda's deadly serious threat to make Margie pack her bag and leave. Only Lily's calming influence had stopped this from happening. 'I won't say a word,' she promised Evie as they climbed the hill to number 5 where they found Arthur sitting on the top step clutching a tin full of marbles. He looked hunched and miserable until he spotted his sisters then he jumped up and ran to meet them, marbles rattling inside the tin.

'Where's my sweets?' he demanded, dodging in between Lily and Evie, patting Lily's pockets until he felt the paper bag then dipping in his hand to retrieve it.

'You mean, "Lily, please may I have my sweets?"' she teased. She wondered how long he'd been sitting on the cold step. 'Were you waiting for someone to have a game of marbles with?'

'Not really,' Arthur said through teeth stuck together by a half-chewed lump of toffee. 'I don't care – I like playing by myself.'

Evie smiled and ruffled his hair. 'Who's in the house? Is Mother in?'

'No, just Dad and now Margie. Oh, and Uncle George and Tommy.'

'That means they're headed for the Green Cross,' Evie predicted as, just then, their front door opened and their father came out followed by his brother. So far there was no sign of cousin Tommy.

The two Briggs brothers didn't look alike. Whereas Walter's appearance seemed threadbare and stuck in a bygone era, George had managed to keep up with the times. He was clean shaven and upright, always to be seen in a collar and tie, with a waistcoat neatly buttoned under a tweed jacket. The two men were of a similar height, though, and had the same suspicious sideways tilt of the head, as if they thought the world meant to do them harm.

When Walter spied Lily, he gave George a nudge with his elbow then limped towards her. 'You'll lend me a shilling,' he said – not a request but an order.

'Father, I don't have one to spare,' she began. 'Mother needs—'

'I don't care what your mother says she needs. I

need a shilling,' he insisted. 'And I don't want you showing me up in the street neither.'

She shook her head and glanced at her uncle, a sick feeling of humiliation churning in her stomach. This was rotten timing and she saw that she would have to give in.

'Be nice, Lil,' George advised. 'Let the man enjoy a pint of beer down his local.'

So Lily had no option but to take the money from her pocket and hand it over while Evie took Arthur's hand and told him she would walk him up to the Common to see the shire horses.

'Be thankful it's only a bob,' George smirked. 'If you was my girl, I'd take the lot.'

'And I'm glad I'm not your girl,' Lily retorted, aware that Tommy and Margie had appeared on the steps, both in an ugly mood by the look of it.

'What's got into you, Margie Briggs?' Tommy grumbled over his shoulder, taking the three steps in one jump. 'You can't stand a joke these days, can you?'

Margie slammed the door shut.

'Best not to ask 'cos you don't want to know,' Tommy warned Lily. Dressed like his father in his weekend best, with his dark hair slicked back, he was eager to be off, but not without a final upsetting jibe. 'Tell your mother thanks for the dinner. It was a tasty Lancashire hotpot, ta very much.'

'You didn't!' Lily was suddenly furious at the loss of the precious family meal. 'Not all of it?'

'Very tasty,' Tommy repeated. 'Come on, we're wasting good drinking time.' And he overtook the two older men to strut his way down the street.

'Good riddance!' Lily called after them. Then she stormed up the steps to tackle Margie over why she'd let the men eat them out of house and home.

'That'll be two Saturday nights on the trot that you've stayed in,' Lily pointed out to Margie after the two sisters had settled their differences and re-treated to their bedroom. It was then that Margie had announced that she wouldn't bother to go down to the kitchen and wash her hair since she wouldn't be going out that evening. The afternoon was grey and the light was dim. 'Are you sure you're feeling all right?'

'Ha-ha, very funny, I'm sure.' Margie, who was still in her work clothes, had her head stuck in a fashion magazine. She squinted to make out the print, gave up then threw it down in disgust.

'No, I'm not joking,' Lily insisted. 'What's wrong?'

'Why should anything be wrong? I just want to stay in and put my feet up for a change.'

Lily sat down on the bed beside her. 'It's not still this silly row with Dorothy Brumfitt, is it?'

Margie shook her head. 'Dorothy can take a running jump for all I care.'

'So it is her.' Lily sighed, ready to let the subject drop until she remembered her promise to their mother. 'Is there a boy in the case? You don't need to

82

tell me the details if you don't want to, but is there?'

Lily's persistence caused Margie's sullen resistance to crumble. 'What if there is? And what if there's nothing I can do about it and I just have to let Dorothy get on with it? I'm not going to sit there and watch it happen, am I?'

'Sit where?'

'With the other wallflowers at the Assembly Rooms, watching her steal him from under my nose.'

'Steal who?' Lily wanted to know.

'What's it matter who? You've wormed enough out of me already.' Flinging herself down on the bed, Margie lay with her back to Lily.

Lily stood up. What could she do to help Margie snap out of this? she wondered. She quickly decided flattery was her best tactic. 'So this young man, who-ever he is, either he needs a good pair of glasses or he should have his head examined.'

'Why's that?'

'Because you're worth two of Dorothy Brumfitt any day.'

'You're only saying that because you're my sister.' Up came the blanket over Margie's head, making her voice sound muffled.

'I'm saying it because it's true. And the best thing you can do is stop sulking, get dolled up and get yourself down to the dance hall to prove it once and for all.'

'I can't,' Margie said.

'Why not?'

'Because.'

Swift footsteps on the stairs told Lily that Evie was on her way up. 'And that's all it is?' she checked with Margie, whose gloom seemed settled and deep. 'Just a silly fight over a boy?'

'Father's back with Uncle George and Tommy,' Evie warned, bursting into the room with Arthur in tow.

Meanwhile, there was only silence from Margie.

Sensing a confrontation, Evie and Arthur made themselves scarce while Lily went downstairs to find Rhoda back home and doggedly preparing a meal from the leftover hotpot, adding potatoes and onions to what remained of the stew. She kept her back turned as Walter took off his jacket at the cellar head and invited his brother and nephew to sit at the table. The small room seemed full of their beery, sneering presence.

'Where've you been?' Walter asked Rhoda accusingly.

She flinched but managed not to retaliate. 'To Myra Lister's, to help with the new baby. Then over on to Raglan Road to Doris Fuller to treat her bronchitis. I sat with her while her boy William went off for mustard plasters.'

Lily came downstairs in time to hear her father's churlish retort.

'Aye and trust you to put everybody else's family before your own as per usual.' He held on to the back of a chair for balance and his words were slow and slurred. 'You got paid for your trouble, did you?'

'Not yet. They'll pay me as soon as they find the money.'

Walter turned to his brother. 'You see what I have to put up with – a missis who's never here when you need her. You're better off without one, George, that's all I can say.'

Rhoda finished adding the vegetables, put the lid on the heavy pot then tried to lift it from the table into the oven. Lily saw her wince at its weight and rushed to help.

'Let me,' she offered, heartily wishing to see the back of George and Tommy. With them here, her father always seemed twice as bad, if that were possible. 'Haven't you got a home to go to?' she muttered to her cousin. It was a barbed question since Lily knew full well that her cousin, despite his Brylcreemed hair and smart Harris Tweed jacket, still lived with his father in a damp, cramped basement on Canal Road.

'No, Miss Hoity Toity, nor a job to go to, if that's what you're thinking,' Tommy jeered.

'Oh aye,' George remarked, settling himself in the fireside chair and stretching out his legs. 'I forgot – Lily turns her nose up at us ever since she went up into the mending room. But not for long, I reckon, not the way Calvert's Mill is going.'

'What exactly do you mean by that, pray tell?' Rhoda rose at last to Lily's defence, rounding on her brother-in-law and demanding an explanation.

'Oh come on, Rhoda – everyone knows that times have changed for the worse and Stanley Calvert is struggling just like all the other mill owners around here, for all their grand houses, shiny motor cars and people to drive them around.'

Rhoda went to the cutlery drawer and began rattling knives and forks down on to the table. 'But he's not one of the ones who's laying people off so far as I know.'

'Not yet, not "so far as you know",' Tommy mocked, while Lily gave him a look that could kill.

'You think Calvert would tell you his plans, Rhoda?' Walter broke in. 'Not a chance. No, he's got a man studying his order books right this minute, working out how many people he can afford to keep on and how many they must lay off. They do the sums and one fine morning, perhaps this coming Monday, he gets Harry Bainbridge to drive him down to Ghyll Road. He strides into the weaving shed, cock of the walk, and gives two loom tuners and three weft men their cards without even looking them in the eye. Then upstairs to the mending room and he struts in and says, "Last in, first out," and that's Lily being given her marching orders and Calvert doesn't think twice.'

'That's just how it works,' Tommy agreed.

Walter's long speech silenced Rhoda and filled Lily with dread. Neither could deny it – sackings were in the sooty, fog-filled air.

'And you haven't heard the best of it.' Seeing

Margie appear at the foot of the stairs, Tommy seemed to enjoy the women's discomfort. 'Have they, Margie? I take it you haven't given them the full story yet?'

Margie gasped then froze. She seemed to know what was coming but was incapable of uttering a word.

'It was all the talk down at the Green Cross,' Tommy went on, all the while grinning and staring at Margie. 'People came up to me and said, "Whatever was your madcap cousin Margie thinking – acting like that, getting into a scrap with the girl on the gilling machine next to her and putting her job on the line? Doesn't she know that Kingsley is laying people off left, right and centre?"'

Rhoda stood silent at the far side of the room, her face in shadow. It was Lily who made a move to put an end to Tommy's callous crowing.

'Who got laid off?' she demanded. 'Who do you mean?'

Tommy cocked his head to one side. 'Shall I tell them, Margie, or shall you?'

'Me. I will.' Gathering her final shred of dignity, Margie spoke at last – quietly and as if the words cost her everything she had. 'I got the sack, Mother. Sam Earby handed me my cards at dinner time today. So you see, I've no job to go to at Kingsley's on Monday morning.'

CHAPTER SIX

Margie's dismissal from her job was nothing short of a disaster. It sent Walter off into a rant that could be heard out in the street where Arthur played another of his solitary games, scaring the little boy so badly that he took himself off on to the Common, where he stayed until dark. Inside the house there was an atmosphere of dread.

'I won't stand for it!' Walter swore at Margie, standing up from the table and banging it with his fist. 'No one gets bed and board in this house without paying their way.'

Margie swallowed hard, sickened by her father's ridiculous hypocrisy but not bold enough to point it out. 'Don't worry, as soon as I can find a place to live, you won't see me for dust,' she said, her face drained of colour. She didn't expect any mercy from her mother – or from Lily, for that matter – so she ignored their stricken faces, choosing instead to cast a defiant look at Tommy and George.

'Well, that's set the cat among the pigeons,' Tommy

declared, jauntily taking up his cap and heading for the door. 'Come on, Dad, let's leave 'em to it.'

George soon joined his son on the top step. 'Well, Walter, maybe next time you'll stay alert to what's going on around you,' was his parting shot.

Walter leaned heavily on the table, his chest heaving and his breathing coming in short, laboured bursts. 'Sacked from a job and for what?' he raged. 'For brawling and acting the bloody fool.'

'Father,' Lily pleaded as he launched himself towards Margie.

He was so unsteady that he had to clutch the back of a chair, which scraped across the stone floor under his weight. Lily stepped in to help him back on his feet.

'Keep your hands to yourself,' he snarled, pushing her to one side and making a second lunge in Margie's direction.

Margie tried to stand her ground but she was so pale it looked as though she might faint and she couldn't think of any words with which to defend herself against the onslaught.

'You're not staying in my house a day longer, do you hear? I don't care where you go or how you live, just so long as I don't have to look at your nasty face.'

'Mother!' Horrified, Lily appealed to Rhoda, who had scarcely moved since Margie dropped her bombshell.

Rhoda's eyelids flickered and she shook her head.

'Please, Mother, tell Father not to be so hasty. Let

Margie go down to Kingsley's and plead for her job back. You never know, Sam Earby might give her another chance.'

Again Rhoda shook her head.

'You see that? Not even your own mother will stick up for you and I don't blame her!' Walter yelled, his face inches from Margie's. 'We've watched you grow too big for your boots, don't think we haven't.'

'I'll go right this minute,' Margie declared. 'I won't stay where I'm not wanted.'

'Good bloody riddance,' Walter muttered, running out of steam at last and getting caught up in a bout of coughing. He stepped away from Margie and watched her head for the stairs.

'Go where?' Lily demanded, running after her and catching her up on the first-floor landing. She found her dry eyed and determined. 'Think about it, Margie. You've got no money and no job. Where will you go?'

'I'll work something out, don't you worry.'

'But why not just lie low and wait until things have calmed down? You know how Father is when he gets back from the Cross. But he'll sleep it off and by this time tomorrow it'll all have blown over.'

'Stop it!' Margie said with an anguished shake of her head. 'That's not the point and you know it.'

'Then what is the point?'

'The point is me, Lily. Not Father – me!' Margie went on up to the attic, hardly caring whether or not Lily followed. When she got there, she opened the low door into the loft space and dragged out a dusty suitcase with the initials AWP stamped on the lid. 'The point is that *I* won't stay here. I won't, I can't!'

'But this is your home,' Lily wailed, watching Margie open a drawer and throw items of clothing – under-things then her cream blouse and dark skirt; a patterned, long-sleeved dress; her dancing shoes and a silk handkerchief printed with dainty bluebirds, which she'd got from Lily on her sixteenth birthday – into the brown case then slamming down the lid. Everything was moving so fast, like a train without brakes heading for a collision.

'Not any more,' Margie insisted. Looking around the room and seeing nothing else that belonged to her, she picked up the suitcase and held it like a shield in front of her as if to ward off the remnants of Lily's arguments.

'This is where you've lived all your life, you were born here. How can you say it's not your home?'

'It's a poor kind of home where a father steals money from his daughter's purse and a mother looks down on you and calls you common,' Margie said bitterly.

'She didn't mean it,' Lily protested. 'She worries about you, that's all. And when did Father steal your money?'

'Not *my* money,' Margie countered, 'because I have enough sense to hide it from him and keep it safe. It's your money he takes and you're soft enough to let him have it, even though he uses it to get drunk and turn on poor Arthur. You ought not to give it to him, Lily. You really ought not.'

'Hush! There's a lot of things we ought not to do,' Lily replied, almost overwhelmed by her sister's passionate speech.

'Like picking a fight with Dorothy and getting the sack?' a sullen Margie challenged. 'Come on, out with it, Lily, say what you mean.'

'So Tommy wasn't lying – it really was Dorothy who was behind it. What did she say to you that was so bad?'

'It's not what she said so much as what she did.' For a moment Margie faltered and almost let down her defences then she changed her mind. 'In any case, Sam Earby saw that it was six of one and half a dozen of the other so Dorothy Brumfitt got her marching orders as well as me, if you must know.'

Lily shook her head to rid herself of the undignified image of the two girls battling it out on Kingsley's spinning-shed floor. Then she pressed on. 'So what did she *do*?'

'You shan't worm it out of me however hard you try,' Margie retorted. 'What went on between me and Dorothy is my business.'

'All right, have it your own way. But ask yourself – is she really worth walking out of your job and your home over?' A frantic Lily would have done anything to stop Margie leaving but she knew she was running out of reasons to make her stay.

'I don't give tuppence for my rotten job.' Margie

swung the suitcase down to the floor and reached for her green coat hanging on the hook behind the door. 'As for my home – if I'm not wanted here, why should I stay?'

'But you are wanted,' Lily cried, feeling the argument slip beyond her. She made one last desperate appeal. 'I want you to stay. Evie wants you to stay and Arthur does too.'

'It's not enough,' Margie said as she buttoned her coat up to the chin, picked up her case and carried it down the stairs.

CHAPTER SEVEN

At least I walked out with my head held high, Margie told herself uncertainly as she sat on the number 12 tram with the battered suitcase on the rack above her head. She was trembling and fighting back tears as she remembered her father's cruel words and her mother's indifference.

The conductor came and took her fare, gave her a ticket then studied her unhappy face. 'Are you all right, miss?' he asked.

'Yes thanks, I'm tickety-boo,' she replied, chin up but bottom lip trembling. She stared out at the flattened, yellowish grass of the Common and at the escarpment of black rock beyond, noticing rooks circling over bare trees. I'm glad I walked out, she thought defiantly. And I'm glad I didn't tell Lily everything that's been going on lately. What good would it have done to go into details?

'If you call this tickety-boo, I'd hate to see you when you were miserable,' the middle-aged conductor commented as he went down the aisle to take fares from an elderly couple at the front of the tram.

The trouble was that the mysterious 'details' that Margie had kept from Lily wouldn't leave her alone. They kept biting at her heels like a bad-tempered terrier, dragging her back to the first silly argument with Dorothy.

'Hey-up, here she comes, the Queen of Sheba!' Dorothy had mocked as Margie had stepped off the tram in the centre of town exactly a week earlier. She'd been standing under the lamp post where Margie had arranged to meet up with Billy Robertshaw, her blonde hair artificially waved, her eyebrows tweezered, her cupid-lips painted crimson.

'What are you doing here?' Margie had challenged, wanting a clear run at Billy when he showed up, not to be bothering with Dorothy, who should've been down at the Assembly Rooms with Hilda and the rest of the girls, not here at the tram stop, making trouble.

'Oh, look – Her Royal Highness doesn't want me getting in her road, spoiling her night out! Well, this is a free country and I can go where I like. Anyhow, I could ask you the same question – what are *you* doing here?'

'That's none of your business,' Margie had flung back at her. She had her new hairdo, she'd dressed up nicely and though she felt nervous about the meeting with Billy, she wouldn't let Dorothy see this.

'That's as may be, but I know you're here to meet Calvert's gardener and I'm here to tell you you'll have a long wait,' Dorothy crowed, enjoying the sensation of cutting Margie's legs from under her. 'Billy said for me to let you know he couldn't make it after all.'

With a small shake of her head to disguise the shock, Margie started to walk away. Then she turned back. 'That's a big fib,' she challenged.

Dorothy had shrugged. 'Please yourself. He wanted me to pass on the message to save you waiting in the cold. I've done my job, so ta-ta, Margie.'

'Wait. Did he say why he couldn't make it?'

Dorothy had raised what was left of her eyebrows while she considered her answer. 'From what I know about Billy, you must have scared him off. Aye, I reckon that would be it.'

Her smugness had rattled Margie at last. 'Not as much as your ugly mug would scare him,' she'd retorted.

At this Dorothy's temper had snapped and she'd sprung at Margie, would have slapped her cheek if Margie hadn't dodged out of the way. Dorothy had overbalanced and fallen against the lamp post, but Margie hadn't followed up her advantage. Instead, she'd curled her lip and stalked off towards the next stop. 'Billy is all yours,' she'd called over her shoulder, holding back her tears until the next tram had come along.

The worst of it was – she truly hadn't been sure if Billy's message was genuine or if Dorothy had made the whole thing up to spite her. And afterwards she'd been too proud to find out.

Or no, that wasn't actually the worst of it. The really, really bad part Margie had kept to herself and had refused even to think about. Even now, sitting on the tram to Overcliffe, she blocked it from her mind.

'Ada Street!'

The conductor's voice shook her back into the present and she quickly stood up to retrieve her case from the overhead rack, hurrying to the platform at the back of the tram and stepping off into the late-afternoon air. She stood for a moment, gathering her courage as she stared out over the vast, empty moorland beyond Linton Park – again there were rooks sailing on wind currents against dark grey clouds, and a line of elm trees on the near horizon. A man with two thin greyhounds crossed the street and passed between the park gates without looking at her.

Margie turned and set off down Ada Street. When she came to number 10, she rat-tat-tatted on the familiar green door with its lion-head knocker. She heard footsteps in the tiled corridor and waited for Bert Preston to open it – just far enough for him to peer out.

The old man looked at her through the narrow opening, head to one side. 'Where's Arthur?' he asked, as if this could be the only reason for a Saturday-evening visit from Margie.

With a supreme effort she managed to keep her

voice steady. 'He's at home, Granddad. I'm by myself.'

Bert took one look at the suitcase – the one with his initials, AWP – Albert William Preston – which Rhoda had used to cart her meagre belongings down to Canal Road all those years earlier.

'What happened – did your father chuck you out?'

She nodded and shivered. 'Can I come in?'

'Aye, come in,' he said curtly.

He opened the door to let her step inside. He would ask no questions, would offer no opinion or sympathy over what might have taken place on Albion Lane. The simple fact was that Margie was his granddaughter and he would give her a roof over her head, just as he would if it was Lily, Evie or Arthur who had come knocking. 'I'll put the kettle on,' he said. 'You sit yourself down and make yourself at home.'

CHAPTER EIGHT

As Margie took the tram to Overcliffe, Lily stood at the kitchen window fretting and planning how to protect Arthur from the aftershock of their sister's departure. Grateful that she'd heard nothing from their father since he'd taken himself off to his room and glad that Rhoda had been called back to Doris Fuller's house, Lily spotted Arthur's small figure returning from the Common as daylight faded, dragging his feet and looking apprehensive as he came up the steps.

He opened the door and peered in, relieved to find only Lily in the room.

'Where's everyone?' he asked.

'You must be frozen!' she exclaimed without answering. She rushed to take his cap and draw him close to the fire.

'Is Father in bed?'

'Yes.' Lily sat him in the fireside chair then took his cold hands between hers and chafed them. 'And Mother had to go out.'

Gradually Arthur stopped shivering and looked nervously around the room. 'Where's Margie?'

Lily kept her voice steady and she managed to look him in the eye as she answered his latest question. 'Well, you see, Arthur, she's gone away for a day or two.'

'Lucky thing,' Arthur said, brightening suddenly because he knew that days away meant a Sunday School trip to Filey, with donkey rides on the beach and if you were very good, money for an ice cream before piling into the charabanc for the journey home. The idea helped him to put aside the memory of his father's raised voice that had sent him scuttling off to the Common. 'If she's at the seaside, will she bring me back a stick of rock?'

His naivety tugged at Lily's heart strings. She hugged him and wished all the world's problems could be solved by a stick of Blackpool rock. She took him up to the girls' attic bedroom, snuggled him under the woollen blankets and told him to have a nap until she called him down for tea.

She tiptoed back downstairs in time to find Evie and her best friend, Peggy Bainbridge, coming into the house.

'Hush!' Lily warned, afraid that the girls' voices would disturb Walter. 'Peggy, will you do me a favour and run up to Annie's house? Tell her we've had the usual do with Father and I can't come out tonight.'

Harry's younger sister, who was thirteen and still at school, was a quiet, gentle girl dressed in a long grey sweater and black skirt, her thick, dark brown hair loosely tied back by a tartan ribbon. She readily agreed to Lily's request and hurried off.

'What's happened?' Evie wanted to know.

Lily had been relieved that her youngest sister had been spared the sight of their father unleashing his anger on Margie, for Evie was a sensitive soul and would dissolve into tears whenever voices were raised. 'Hush,' she said again, rolling her eyes towards the ceiling and struggling to find words to explain what had gone on.

'Is Father . . . ? Well, has he been down the Cross?' Evie interpreted Lily's signals correctly.

'Yes but, as I said, he's sleeping it off. And Arthur's taking a nap in our room.'

Evie frowned. She guessed there was more to come and that it must be bad. The moment she'd set foot in the house, she'd picked up the Saturday-afternoon, treading-on-eggshells atmosphere and she could see that Lily was struggling to stay calm. 'And what else, Lily? Have Mother and Margie had another row?'

'No, this time it was Father and Margie.'

'Was it very bad?' was Evie's hurried, anxious reaction.

'Yes, I'm afraid it was.' Though Lily could justify keeping Arthur in the dark, she decided it wasn't fair to beat about the bush any longer with Evie. 'I have to tell you something and you're not going to like it,' she began quietly as she drew the curtains, lit the gas mantle and sat her down at the table.

Evie pulled her long plait forward over one shoulder and began to loosen it from its ribbon, a frown creasing her smooth brow.

'Margie's lost her job at Kingsley's,' Lily went on.

Evie's frown deepened. 'But she'll soon find another?' she ventured.

If only it were that easy, Lily thought. 'She'll have to start looking on Monday but with things being the way they are it might take a while,' she cautioned. 'Meanwhile, Mother will have to rely on two wages coming into the house instead of three. We'll have to tighten our belts for a while.'

Evie shook her hair loose then nodded eagerly. 'I've already told Peggy I won't be going out tonight, so that's a start.'

'That seems a shame.' Lily felt sad that Evie couldn't enjoy splashing out a little of her first week's wages on a night out.

'It doesn't bother me. I feel fit to drop.' Evie sighed. 'And now I'm glad I won't be wasting the money.'

Sitting across the table from her, Lily leaned over and squeezed her sister's hand. 'But remember that things are bound to get better, with or without Margie's wage. My money is set to go up just as soon as I've passed muster in the mending department.'

Hearing noises from the room above, the sisters stopped talking while their father coughed and then fell silent.

'How did Mother take the news?' Evie wanted to know when they convinced themselves that Walter had gone back to sleep.

'Badly,' Lily whispered back, scarcely louder than the faint hiss of the gas light. Then she drew a sudden, sharp breath at the memory of Rhoda's silence and frozen expression. 'She didn't stand up for Margie because she feels so let down. She let her pack her bag and leave.'

'What do you mean, "leave"?'

'Leave home.' The two short words fell like pebbles into a deep pool, causing ripples that seemed to be reflected in Evie's sensitive features.

'That can't be right,' she murmured. 'Where did she go?'

'We don't know. But she'll send word as soon as she's found somewhere to stay, with Granddad more likely than not, don't you worry.'

'And will Mother come round? Will she let Margie back into the house?'

'Not for a good while.' Again Lily chose not to sugar-coat the pill. 'Things have been bad between Mother and Margie lately – I don't need to tell you that.'

'But it shouldn't come to this,' Evie protested. The sensation of family ties being stretched to breaking point affected her very badly and made her feel wearier than ever.

Lily sighed then went on. 'My feeling is that Mother is worn out. She hasn't the strength to deal with Margie playing up and causing problems and that's why I promised to help keep Margie on the straight and narrow in the first place.' For the first time since her sister's dramatic exit, Lily was stricken with guilt. Her shoulders slumped and she was glad when Evie came to sit beside her. 'I should've told Margie straight out – it's time to stop complaining and knuckle under because Mother's tired out with your silly goings-on. Only I didn't, and Margie ran headlong into a fight over nothing with Dorothy Brumfitt and quite rightly Sam Earby handed both of them their cards.'

'It's still not your fault,' Evie insisted, gently pushing Lily's hair back from her face. 'Margie's the selfish one, not you.'

'Yes, but I should've made her see how much Mother relies on her money and how hard it is to hang on to a job these days. I didn't do that, Evie, and now I'm sorry.'

'So is Margie, I'm sure.'

'Let's hope you're right.' Lily looked up and managed to smile.

She hoped that Margie would look back on events and tell their mother how sorry she was. She hoped that she would find work quickly. She hoped that Evie would grow stronger and get used to her work in the weaving shed. She hoped that she would succeed under Miss Valentine's supervision. She wished for many things, but as she went to the window and looked out through a chink in the curtains at clouds drifting across the face of a full moon, she didn't wholly believe that any of those wishes would come true.

'What's your Margie doing at Granddad Preston's house?' Annie came knocking on the door of 5 Albion Lane late on Sunday afternoon, exactly twenty-four hours after Margie's sudden departure. Her coat was buttoned up and she wore a blue woollen scarf tied around her head, turban-style. 'Is it to do with the fight between her and Dorothy?'

'Keep your voice down.' Lily stepped out on to the top step and quickly closed the door behind her, afraid that her mother would react badly to the tittle-tattle. 'We don't want the whole world to know.'

'Too late – the cat's out of the bag,' Annie insisted. 'Sybil and me, we were out last night without you and it was the talk of the town, how Margie and Dorothy had a set-to at work. I don't know who started it, but from what I heard, there was yarn everywhere. Dorothy was chucking cones at Margie, who gave as good as she got. It was Bedlam, by all accounts.'

Lily winced. 'Mother will hate that people are gossiping. But you're sure that Margie is with Granddad at Ada Street?'

Annie nodded. 'Flora Johnson went to chapel up there early this morning. She saw Margie standing at the window of number ten, staring out. Flora waved but Margie didn't wave back.'

'Well, it's a relief to know where she is.' For Lily,

having the short conversation with Annie made recent events seem more real – Margie had run away but she was safe and well. After a sleepless night and a miserable day, Lily could begin to relax.

Taking a closer look at her friend's strained expression, Annie linked arms with her and walked her a short way down the street, avoiding puddles and a stray paper bag that flapped against the kerb. 'Anyway, try not to worry too much. Margie will have to let a bit of time go by and then eat humble pie. She'll be back home before you know it.'

'I hope you're right.'

'Of course I am. It seems bad at present but it'll soon blow over – you know what they say: today's newspaper is the wrapping for tomorrow's fish and chips.'

'Do they?' Lily gave a faint smile and thanked Annie.

'What for? I haven't done anything.'

'Yes you have – you've brought us news that Margie is safe and you've done your best to cheer me up.'

'But I haven't though, have I?' Annie's normally cheerful face looked concerned as she turned Lily back towards number 5. 'Listen, Lily, you're catching your death of cold and I have to run. But remember, if there's anything I can do, you only have to ask.'

'Just carry on keeping an eye on Evie for me.'

'It's a promise.' Annie nodded. 'Go inside, Lil, before you catch your death.'

'Righty-ho.'

'And wait a day or two for things to settle down.'

'I will.' With her hand on the door knob, Lily ran through the possible courses of action that were open to her then came to a firm decision. 'When the time's right I'll take the tram up to Overcliffe to see Margie. Maybe on Wednesday, after I've finished my shift.'

'What did Annie want?' Rhoda asked when Lily went back into the house. She stood peeling potatoes at the sink, her face strained, wisps of grey hair falling forward on to her forehead.

Evie stood at the table with Arthur, showing him how to crack eggs into a bowl of flour then add milk and a pinch of salt. Then she handed him a whisk to mix batter for Yorkshire puddings.

'I was right – Margie's gone to stay with Granddad,' Lily told them.

'Oh, thank goodness.' Evie sighed, raising a floury hand to cover her mouth.

Lily waited in vain for a reaction from Rhoda. 'Did you hear me, Mother? Margie's at Granddad's house.'

'Yes, I heard.' Peeling and chopping then transferring the potatoes into a pan of water, Rhoda refused to stop what she was doing.

'Has she come back from the seaside?' a doubtful Arthur asked Evie, who smiled down at him and nodded.

'It gives us all a bit of breathing space,' Lily said.

107

'Lift this pan on to the hob for me,' Rhoda told her, standing back to let Lily perform the task. Her face looked tired, her eyes cold and blank.

'Mother, I'm sure Margie is sorry as can be for losing her job,' said Lily, ever the peacemaker.

'Sorry doesn't bring in a wage packet,' Rhoda said stubbornly.

'But she's learned her lesson.'

Rhoda ran the tap and swilled off her hands. 'Aye, the hard way.'

'And can't you forgive and forget?' The moment the question was out of her mouth, Lily realized it had been the wrong thing to say.

'Forgive?' Rhoda said in a tone of disgust. It was as if a dam had broken and a torrent had been released. 'Do I forgive Margie for making me a laughing stock? Do I forgive her for throwing a perfectly good job down the drain? What do you think?'

Lily shook her head.

'No – you're right, I don't. Do I agree with her running to her granddad's house and telling tales against your father?'

'Mother, I'm sure she hasn't—'

'And I'm sure she has.' With a trembling lip, Rhoda tore off her apron and flung it down on the table. 'And I'm certain of one other thing – we haven't got to the bottom of this. No, don't interrupt me, Lily. Margie hasn't told us the full story. She's hiding something even worse.'

'What?' Lily cried, afraid of the venom in her

mother's voice and alarmed by the hectic red spots that had appeared on her cheeks.

Rhoda had to lean on the table and draw breath. 'Just stop and think about it,' she said in a voice somewhere between a sigh and a groan.

What did her mother mean? For a while Lily couldn't see what could be worse than losing a job and throwing your family further down into poverty. Then it came to her – the memory of Rhoda insisting there was a boy involved in the argument between Margie and Dorothy. Lily's mind spun off in a direction she didn't want to go and she shook her head violently.

'Now do you see what I'm getting at?' Rhoda asked, the mask of indifference suddenly descending over her worn face again as she turned back to the sink.

It was true – Lily recalled how Margie had clasped the suitcase like a shield, defending herself, keeping her secret. The memory of it sent a shudder down her spine. 'But, Mother, you don't know. You can't be certain.' She whispered the protests without believing them.

'I know the signs,' her mother said, cold and hard. 'I've seen it often enough, believe you me.'

CHAPTER NINE

In the event, an overwrought Lily didn't wait until Wednesday to take the tram up to Overcliffe. Instead, she hurried there straight after work on Monday, her mind fixed on everyday affairs such as searching in her purse for the right money to pay the fare and dreading the moment when she must alight from the tram then walk down Ada Street to Granddad Preston's green door. She arrived still in a state of high anxiety and was about to raise her hand and knock when the door was flung open.

'Come in, I was expecting you,' Bert said, his voice thick with phlegm. 'I knew it would be you, not your mother. Margie's upstairs in the spare bedroom.'

'Has she said anything to you?' Lily asked in a low, anxious voice, as they hovered in the narrow hallway. She stood beneath a picture called *The Light of the World*, which had been hanging there for as long as she could remember – a black-and-white engraving of Jesus in his long robe, his crowned head surrounded by a halo and his raised hand holding up a lantern to show the way to benighted souls.

'No, but then again I haven't asked,' Bert replied with a steady look that told Lily that he preferred not to know awkward truths about the goings-on of the modern world. Once a tall, strong man, the years of hauling coal from the mine out at Welby had stooped his shoulders and curved his spine so that now he wasn't much taller than Lily, and it was as if the coal dust had worked its way under his skin into the deep wrinkles around his eyes and mouth.

So Lily climbed the bare stairs, her light footsteps warning Margie that she was on her way, her heart beating fast as she thought of the conversation she must have. She opened the door into the cold back room with its iron bedstead, its bedside table with the clover-patterned ewer and basin, the faded quilt – everything the same as always except for the one vital difference that Lily had come to talk about.

'Go away, Lily.' Margie's hostile greeting came from the window overlooking a small back yard with shared brick privy and ash pit. A clear sky allowed a full moon to shine its silver light into the room.

'There's a fine thing,' Lily teased, taking off her hat and putting it on the bed. She'd decided to aim for a cheerful tone but even to her it rang false. 'I've come all this way straight after work and that's all the greeting I get.'

'I never asked you to come,' Margie said flatly without turning away from the window.

'It's dark in here. Shall I sort that out?' An old-fashioned oil lamp was the only lighting in the room, as if time had stopped for Bert Preston thirty years earlier, before the advent of gas and electricity.

'Please yourself.' There was a long pause before Margie spoke again. 'How did you guess I was here?'

'Annie told me. Her friend Flora Johnson spotted you.'

'And did Mother send you?' Margie's outline against the moonlight made her look small and young, almost childlike, and her question had a yearning quality that she soon repressed. 'No, don't answer that. I already know this was your idea.'

Lily went to the window and stood beside her sister, looking down on the flat stone roof of the outhouse. 'Will you try to find another job?' she asked quietly. 'If you do and Mother sees that you're making the effort, she may come round.'

Margie shook her head. 'I've spent my life trying to please Mother, but the truth is I never will, not with you to measure up against.'

Lily was startled by her sister's rueful remark. 'That's not true, Margie. I'm not the apple of Mother's eye, not by any means.'

'Yes you are. You're a good girl, Lily – you're kind and clever and steady, all the things I'm not.'

'If I am, then it's not as easy as it looks,' Lily argued. 'It takes a lot of effort to be thought of as steady by the likes of Mother, believe me.'

For the first time Margie turned her head to look at Lily.

'You're surprised?' Lily quizzed. 'Don't you know that there's a part of me that would love to hitch up my skirt and ride tandem on Harry's bike like you, or to have my hair cut short if I had the courage? And wouldn't I just love to go dancing whenever I felt like it and not have to slave away five and a half days a week at Calvert's, week in, week out? Wouldn't we all, deep down?'

Another long silence developed as Lily and Margie followed two different trains of thought. Margie was the first to break it and when she did her tone was whimsical. 'What would be your dream, Lily? If I could wave a magic wand, what would you wish for?'

Lily gave a little sigh. 'There's no point even thinking about it.'

'But if I could, what would it be?'

'Promise me you won't laugh?' Lily squared her shoulders and took a deep breath. 'All right then, if you could wave your magic wand I would leave Calvert's and set up in my own dressmaking shop. I would have my sewing machine on a table by the shop window and a little bell on the door that tinkles whenever a customer comes in. There would be shelves with bolts of cloth of all colours – cotton, wool and silk – and I would make a beautiful dress for one and sixpence plus the cost of the material.'

Margie's slender frame shook with suppressed laughter.

'What? You promised!' Lily protested when Margie's giggles broke through. 'Oh, I suppose a shop on Market Row wouldn't do for you, Margie Briggs. You'd be a princess wearing a ball gown and a tiara, or a Hollywood film star.'

'Definitely not a dressmaker,' Margie laughed, and for a few seconds, silhouetted against the moonlight, the sisters were back to their old, warm familiarity. 'I do have a dream, though, and it's to get away from mill work, just the same as you.'

'And then what would you do?' Lily asked gently.

'Why, I'd do all the things I love to do. I'd go to the seaside but not just with a bucket and spade. No, instead I'd get on board a white ship, an ocean liner, and I'd sail away across a blue sea. Or I'd go dancing in a grand ballroom like the Tower Ballroom in Blackpool and the most handsome man in the world would sweep me off my feet and carry me around in a Bentley like the one Harry drives, and he'd take me to meet his family in a house with a big garden and two more cars in the driveway.' With the smile fading from her lips, Margie paused to let Lily imagine the scene. 'There.' She sighed, blowing softly on the window pane, which grew foggy from the heat of her breath. 'Now you know.'

'And it could happen,' Lily said, valiantly standing up for her sister's fading, unreachable vision.

'And pigs . . .'

'. . . Might fly!'

They stood side by side as their brief laughter

turned to wistfulness again and then Lily hugged Margie and held her until Margie eventually drew away.

'There's something else,' Margie murmured.

'What is it?' Though Lily dreaded the reply, she felt she owed it to her sister to meet the problem without flinching. 'You know you can trust me not to let on.'

'Can I?'

'Yes. I only want to help.'

'Very well.' Taking a deep breath and summoning her courage to share the secret that would put paid to her pipe dreams once and for all, Margie took the plunge. 'I'm in the family way,' she sobbed. 'Help me, Lily – I'm six weeks gone. I don't know which way to turn!'

CHAPTER TEN

Margie's confession in the cold back bedroom at Ada Street confirmed Lily's worst fears; the ones that lay deep below the surface and couldn't be shared, that Lily felt had to be kept secret even from Annie and Sybil. But ever since Rhoda had made her dark prophecy, she had been building to this awful moment. For a while the shock of what she'd been told silenced her and she asked herself how Margie could have been so silly and reckless. After all, despite the trials and tribulations of their childhoods, she had been brought up to know better.

'But who's the father?' Lily asked sternly after the news had sunk in. 'Try to stop crying, Margie, and tell me.'

Her sister wept regardless. Her shoulders shook and she bowed her head but said nothing.

'Please say who it is,' Lily begged, though she still felt weak at the knees with shock. 'It's bound to come out sooner or later.'

'Not if I don't want it to.' Margie took a deep

breath and stopped sobbing, roughly wiping away the tears as she raised her head. 'I don't. And that's that.'

Lily recognized Margie's habit of quickly crying away her distress then putting a tight lid on her emotions – a trait she got from Rhoda, Lily realized when she thought about it later. 'And you're not to tell Mother,' she insisted. 'Promise me you won't.'

'All right, I promise,' Lily said, almost choking over the words.

Sworn to secrecy, she tried other avenues with Margie. 'And you're quite sure?' she insisted.

Margie clicked her tongue impatiently. 'Do you think I don't know the facts of life?'

'No, that's not what I'm saying. But have you been to see Dr Moss?'

'And tell him what? That I'm two weeks late and it's all I can do to stop myself from being sick every morning?'

'Oh, Margie, I didn't realize.' Looking back, Lily could see how her sister's bad moods and reluctance to get up for work were warning signs that she shouldn't have overlooked. 'Why didn't you tell me?'

'Because it's to do with me, my business – not yours.'

'How can you say that?' It hurt Lily to think that Margie hadn't trusted her enough to ask her for help. 'We're close, aren't we – you and I? We tell each other everything. Surely you know that I won't judge—'

'Ah, but you do,' Margie interrupted with a penetrating stare that unsettled Lily. 'Deep down you do judge me for getting myself into this mess.'

Lily felt another hot, awkward flush of guilt and her thoughts scattered in the face of Margie's challenge. Then, when she was able to speak again, she blurted out the first thing that came into her mind. 'Let me look for a place for you to stay – somewhere by the seaside perhaps.'

'I'm all right here with Granddad. Why do you want to send me away?' Margie's face darkened. 'Oh, I see what it is – you'll be unhappy for me to stay here and for people to tittle-tattle!'

Lily hesitated a second time – two pauses that later filled her with shame. Back at home and thinking it through, she wished with all her heart that she'd been braver and more loving, telling Margie no, she would stand by her wherever she chose to be, whatever people said. The impulse was there, but an old Chapel morality held her back – the knowledge that Methodist fingers would point and tongues would wag.

'You are, you're ashamed of me,' Margie concluded and her mood shifted into a settled bitterness which she didn't break out of, even after Lily had talked herself out and prepared to leave. 'You're not to say or do anything, you hear?' Margie warned. 'You're not to tell anyone about this – not Sybil or Annie or Evie. And you're not to bother me about it either.'

'What do you mean, "bother" you?'

'I mean you're not to come back to Ada Street until I'm good and ready.'

'Margie, you can't cope with this all by yourself. It's not right – I'm your sister and I want to help.'

But Margie was adamant and hissed out her response as she took up position by the window. 'No. I've thought about it and I've decided that I want to be left to work it out in my own way.'

'Please, Margie . . .'

Margie's back was turned, her thoughts already elsewhere. 'I want you to go now,' she said with steely determination.

Rebuffed, Lily knew there was no point continuing to hit her head against a brick wall so she said a reluctant goodbye and carried the heavy burden of Margie's resentment out of the room and down the stairs, past Jesus with his lantern and Granddad Preston peering out of the kitchen without saying a word.

'Look after her,' Lily said, in tears and practically running from the house.

The old man waited and listened. Five minutes after Lily had left, he heard Margie sobbing in the room above.

Despite the cold, wet weather, Lily decided not to take the tram home. Instead, she would walk along Overcliffe Road in order to clear her head and reorder her thoughts before she reached Albion Lane, ignoring the rattle and spark of the trams as they overtook her laden with passengers hidden behind steamed-up windows. She paid no attention either to the occasional motor car and the steady stream of men on bicycles still coming up the hill from factories in the valley below.

In fact, the hustle and bustle suited her since it allowed her to walk unnoticed along the high foot-path overlooking the dark moor to one side and the glimmering town to the other. So much raw darkness, she thought, and so much wild, empty space beyond the maze of streets and factory chimneys, with the black canal snaking between tall woollen mills, all silent now that the workers had departed. Breathing in, Lily could smell smoke and soot and hear the faint rumble of town life, but she could glance to her left and see nothing but emptiness.

And so she grew calm and walked steadily as the mist turned to heavy rain, until a familiar figure on a bicycle drew in towards the kerb and stopped under a lamp post a few yards ahead of her.

'Hello, Lily. You look like a drowned rat,' Harry observed, standing astride the bike in a pool of yellow light. He wore a dark grey raincoat over his chauffeur's uniform, with the cap pulled well down over his face.

'That's not very nice.' Pleased to see him, Lily defended herself against the cheeky remark. It was typical Harry and probably true, since her coat didn't keep out the rain and she realized for the first time that she was soaked to the skin. 'Anyway, what brings you this way? Are you on your way home from work?'

He nodded. 'Mr Calvert let me off early. Monday is his night to go to a council meeting at the Town Hall, but they called it off at the last minute. It meant he didn't need me to drive the car.'

'Lucky you,' Lily said, unable to suppress a shiver and surprised when Harry unbuttoned his coat, took it off and put it around her shoulders. His unlooked-for courteousness was new and quite a contrast to his old, teasing way with her.

'Here you are, I'm your knight in shining armour,' he joked.

'Is that right? Where are the dragons?'

'Breathing fire down in the valley. Can't you see 'em?'

'No.'

'They're tucked up in bed for the night then. Anyway, this'll keep you dry, that's the main thing.'

'You'll get your uniform wet,' she pointed out. 'But thanks a lot, Harry. I appreciate it. I'll dry the coat off and bring it round to your house later.'

'No, I'll walk with you,' he told her, continuing in the same gallant way. 'I'd like to make sure you get home safe and sound.'

'There's no need,' she argued.

'But I want to,' he countered, swinging his leg over the crossbar and beginning to walk alongside Lily on the side that shielded her from the worst of the wind and rain. A few minutes ago, when she'd passed under a street lamp and he'd seen her from a distance – a lonely figure wrapped in her own thoughts – he'd set his mind on catching her up then stopping to talk. 'What brings you up this way? Let me guess – you called in to see Margie after work?'

Lily nodded briefly, glad that the noise from a passing tram prevented her from having to give a fuller answer.

'There's no need to go into details if you don't feel like it,' Harry went on after the tram had gone by. 'But just to let you know – Evie spilled the beans to Peggy that Margie had run off.'

'She did?' It was impossible to keep anything to yourself if you lived in this rabbit warren of terraced streets, Lily realized. She should have been cross and ready to scold Harry for gossiping, but somehow she didn't mind the frankness with which he opened up the thorny topic of Margie.

'Yes, but try not to worry – families are always squabbling. Mine is, at any rate.'

'Not Peggy surely? She wouldn't say boo to a goose.' Glancing sideways, Lily saw that raindrops had darkened Harry's uniform across the shoulders and down the front. He looked straight ahead and seemed not to notice, chatting easily as usual while she resisted an urge to draw near and slip a hand through the crook of his elbow.

'No, not Peggy. Mind you, in our house it's only ever money we argue about, or rather the fact that there's nothing left in anybody's purse by the end of the week.'

'It's the same for everyone these days, isn't it? We haven't got two pennies to rub together on Albion Lane, not after the bills are paid.'

'But we all do a bit extra and we scrape by, eh?'

'We do,' she agreed. Though they'd lived cheek by jowl since they were small children, Harry kicking a ball up against outhouse walls, Lily chalking hop-scotch squares on the stone-flagged pavements, she realized this was probably the longest talk she'd ever had with him and that she was relieved to have her mind taken off the recent heart-breaking exchange with her sister.

'I'll tell you another thing – I used to be sure that pounds, shillings and pence were the root of all problems but now I look at the likes of the Calverts and I see that it's not true. It turns out that mill owners and their families squabble amongst themselves just as much as the man in the street, and over daft little things too.'

Trying to match his long stride, Lily nodded. 'I suppose the more money you have, the more you have to lose,' she pointed out.

'That's true. Anyway, by all accounts the Calverts don't have as much as they used to have, not by a long chalk.'

'Yes, but they're not on the breadline. They still have you driving them around for a start. And they have Billy to do their garden and someone to cook for them and clean up after them, I'd bet my week's wages.'

'You're right about that.' Looking over his shoulder and waiting for a motorbike and sidecar to pass, Harry got ready to wheel his bike across the road.

Lily hadn't realized that they'd walked so far so quickly. They'd already reached Pennington's at the top of Albion Lane and she would soon have to say goodbye to Harry so she skipped ahead of him over puddles then stopped on the far pavement, ready to hand over his raincoat.

'No, keep it on for a bit,' he insisted, reaching out to readjust it on her shoulders. It brought them close together, looking into each other's eyes. 'Lily, you would tell me if something was worrying you?' he said without lowering his gaze. 'I could be a shoulder to cry on if need be.'

'I know, Harry.' She felt the weight of his hand on her back and sensed an unusual intensity behind his words.

'Because we're good pals,' he reminded her, brushing raindrops from the coat then tilting her chin up with his wet fingertips. 'And I don't like to see you sad.'

In that moment of gentle concern, all the pain of Lily's conversation with Margie came surging up in the shape of tears, which she tried in vain to brush away.

'I mean it, Lily. What's up? Talk to me.'

'Nothing. I can't tell you, Harry. I'm sorry.'

'No, it's me who should be saying sorry – I've upset you and that's the last thing I wanted to do.' Wheeling his bike with one hand and keeping an arm around Lily's shoulder, he walked her on down the hill in silence until they came to her house. 'You'll be all right now?' he checked.

'I'll be fine, thanks.' Lily kept her face turned towards him as she swung his coat from her shoulders but she wasn't expecting the kiss when it came.

Harry pushed back his cap and tilted his head to one side, leaning in and brushing her lips with his before taking the coat and slinging it over one shoulder. Then, as if nothing had happened, he walked on up the alley on to Raglan Road.

CHAPTER ELEVEN

Surrounded by the day's washing and with her head in a spin, Lily held the hot iron poised above Arthur's school shirt and told herself that she must have imagined it, perhaps even dreamed it – the moment when Harry's lips had touched hers. After all, it had lasted just a second and maybe if it had really happened, it had been a mistake – the accidental result of Harry leaning in to rescue his coat from her shoulders. Yes, that would be it, she told herself, preparing to press the iron down on to the shirt. As far as Harry was concerned, she, Lily, was just the girl next door – they'd lived in the same set of back-to-backs since they were small so how could it possibly be otherwise?

And yet, his grey eyes had looked at her in a certain way that she'd never seen before and he'd been gentle and kind and told her that he didn't like to see her sad.

This memory offered Lily another solution to the conundrum of the kiss – Harry Bainbridge had felt sorry for her, sorry in a way that he would feel if he found an injured kitten or a rabbit in a trap. That was all it was – a moment of sympathy that had quickly passed. Lily nodded and thumped the iron down on to the starched cotton fabric. It was time to forget that doorstep moment with Harry and concentrate on the important thing: Margie.

Meanwhile, Evie left off playing on the hearthrug with Arthur and his miniature army of tin soldiers to drag the zinc washing tub down into the cellar then take washed and ironed items of laundry upstairs to the attic bedroom.

'High time to put away those toys, pull down the bed and get into your night things,' Lily told Arthur when she caught him yawning. She took clean pyjamas from the pile and handed them to him.

'I'm not tired,' he complained, contrary to all the evidence. 'I want to wait until Mam gets back.'

'Mam won't be home till late,' Lily told him, having learned from Evie that Rhoda had been called to Grace Smith down on Westgate Street. Another baby was on the way, this time to a newly-wed, who had caused a scandal by being a good six months gone when she married. Of course at that moment Lily's mind had flown to Margie and her new situation and she'd had to resist a strong temptation to share the problem with Evie, which she'd managed to do. Now, almost at the end of her pile of ironing, Lily licked her fingertips and lightly tapped the smooth underside of the heavy iron to check its heat then insisted to Arthur that it was time for bed.

'O-o-h, why can't I wait?' he whined.

'Arthur!' Lily was tired out and her voice was severe. 'Bedtime.'

Luckily Evie came down and rescued the situation by offering to read him a story while Lily left the iron to cool in the hearth and carried the rest of the sweet-smelling laundry upstairs. By the time she'd finished folding and putting things away, Arthur's bed was in place and he was lying with his single thin blanket pulled half over his face, fast asleep.

'You look done in,' Evie told Lily. 'Are you ready to come upstairs?'

'I am,' Lily conceded and together the sisters climbed the stairs for the last time that day and got ready for bed in the room with the faded, rose-patterned wallpaper and sloping ceilings. Evie was the first into bed – a narrow one pushed deep under the eaves – and while Lily was brushing her hair she asked the question that had been on her lips ever since Lily had come home. 'I didn't like to mention it while Arthur was around, but how was Margie?'

Lily put down the brush and turned down the gas light, taking her time to frame a neutral answer as she put on her nightdress then climbed into the double bed she usually shared with Margie. 'She was her normal self.'

'Has she been out looking for work?'

'Not yet,' Lily replied, which was true so far as it went.

'Perhaps tomorrow?'

'Yes.'

'You don't seem certain,' Evie remarked. 'But you know, Lily, Margie has to pull her socks up and try for a job, even if it means going back to square one in the scouring shed or working as a scavenger.'

'I can't see Margie scouring raw wool and preparing the slivers, can you?'

'No, but beggars can't be choosers.'

Lily realized that Evie's prim assessment would have been comical in the mouth of an inexperienced fourteen-year-old if circumstances had been different. 'No, they can't,' she agreed, wearily turning over to face the wall. 'Now go to sleep, Evie, there's a good girl.'

All through that week, Lily carried the heavy burden of Margie's secret and got on with her daily routine, glad in a way that she scarcely had time to think about either Margie on the one hand or Harry on the other, what with getting Arthur ready for school each morning in order to allow her mother an extra hour in bed then making herself neat and tidy for the walk with Evie down to the mill. They always clocked on at half past seven on the dot and were ready to work as the overseers arrived.

'How's little Miss Briggs?' Fred Lee would call out as he patrolled the central aisle and the great machines began to clank and whir. 'Pretty as a picture as usual, eh, Sybil? Annie, don't you agree that Evie Briggs looks good enough to eat?'

Evie would blush and do her best to ignore him, while the older girls took him on.

'Now, now, Fred, don't be getting any ideas about Evie,' Annie warned as she settled down to her loom. 'Or else you'll have my young man to deal with.'

'And who would your young man be?' Fred scoffed, slicking back his hair as he glanced at his reflection in the nearest window.

'It's only Robert Drummond,' Sybil sang out above the cranking engines. 'You know him, Fred. He's the one who mends your BSA motorbike up at Baines's. He's a local boxing champion, by the way.'

'Righty-ho, then I'm on my best behaviour from now on,' Fred vowed. He kidded along with Sybil and Annie until the machines drowned out their voices and Evie began to go up and down the weaving shed taking individual orders for dinner, getting each worker to write their request on a scrap of blue sugar paper.

Upstairs in the mending room, Lily's skill with the burling iron improved each day so that now she would lightly and expertly run her fingertips over the cloth and pick up the smallest fault, which she would mark then work on with her small metal hook, loosening the knot and straightening out and snipping the threads ready for mending.

'Very good, Lily.' Iris Valentine believed in giving

praise where it was due but not before, so she waited until Friday, the end of Lily's second week, to stop by her table and study her way of working. 'I have high hopes that we'll make a mender of you yet.'

Lily smiled and blushed. 'Thank you, Miss Valentine.'

'You hear that, Vera?' As soon as the little manageress had bustled on into her office, Jennie Shaw made a point of walking past Lily's fellow learner with a piece of finished work ready for flipping. 'Lily's hot on your heels. If you don't look out she'll soon be overtaking you.'

Luckily, Lily's young neighbour was used to Jennie's sly digs and she took no notice. She mentioned instead that there was a rumour going around that Mr Calvert himself was due to drop by later that afternoon.

On her way back from the flipping machine, Jennie overheard the remark. 'Let's hope he's not coming in to lay people off,' she grumbled in her careless way. 'A fine Christmas present that would be.'

Working nearby, Ethel Newby shook her head. 'The word is he's bringing Winifred in to show her the office routine. They say she's to be put to work there.'

'Never!' For once Jennie was rendered practically speechless.

'It's true,' Ethel insisted.

'Well, I never did,' a flabbergasted Jennie tried to

make sense of what she'd heard. 'It just goes to show how hard times have got.'

Vera disagreed. 'You wouldn't be saying that if it was a son we were talking about. Sons always had to learn the business, ready to take over, didn't they?'

'Yes and I suppose this is the twentieth century.' Lily acknowledged that in the absence of a son there was no reason why a girl shouldn't be given the same opportunities as a boy.

'It's about time young Winifred was made to earn her keep,' Mary commented. As one of the older workers at Calvert's she remembered Winifred Calvert as a spoiled child with a whining voice, dressed in a navy blue frock with a white sailor's collar and straw boater, who would be left sitting in the car at the main entrance while her father dealt with mill business. This would be on a Saturday morning and often involved one of the junior girls from the weaving shed being sent out to entertain her, which really meant sitting beside her on the shiny back seat and being subjected to Winifred's demands for sweets and toys. The round-faced, pretty girl had grown up to be tall and slender, fashionably dressed and with a mass of glossy, dark curls about which she was openly vain.

'I bet it's caused ructions at home,' Vera observed. 'I can't see Mrs Calvert being in favour of her precious daughter getting her hands dirty.'

'No, and whatever you think about a girl being worth as much as a boy, Lily, I say it's a sign of the times that these days everyone has to muck in,' was Jennie's conclusion, moving on when Iris Valentine caught her eye.

After this, work went on uninterrupted until dinner time, when Lily joined Sybil, Annie and Evie in the steamy, noisy canteen.

'Here, Lily, we've bagged you a place!' Sybil called from a bench close to a window overlooking the unloading area where wagons delivered raw wool. Shouts from the wagon drivers were combined with the clatter of wooden wheels over cobbles and the droning of vast machines in the engine shed at the back of the mill. The smells that came up from the yard included the sour reek of untreated wool, hot oil from the engines and smoke from the chimneys.

'Brrr, shut that window!' Annie complained as she settled down to a dinner of tripe and onions, specially brought by Evie from George Green's shop on Ghyll Road.

As Lily leaned over to close the window, she glimpsed something that made her heart skip a beat – the sight of Stanley Calvert's gleaming car gliding along Canal Road.

'Lily, stop standing there like a goldfish with your mouth open and hurry up and shut that window!' Jumping up to do it herself, Annie soon saw what had caught Lily's attention. 'Oh, look who it isn't!' she cried. 'It's only love's young dream.'

'Who?' Sybil wanted to know.

'I'll give you one guess,' Annie teased while Lily

blushed furiously. 'Who do you think would make Lily turn beetroot red?'

'Harry,' Sybil said without a moment's hesitation, though Lily hadn't breathed a word about Monday night's kiss. She spoke as if a romance between Lily and Harry were the most natural thing in the world.

'Right first time.' Annie stood with Lily to watch the mill owner's car travel the length of the building then disappear through the main entrance. 'I have to admit, the sight of Harry Bainbridge in his uniform is hard to beat.' She sighed.

'Lily's got good taste, bless her,' Sybil agreed while Evie was quietly embarrassed for her sister's sake.

As soon as Lily had dismissed the memory of the accidental doorstep kiss, she found her voice. 'You're doing it again,' she told Sybil and Annie. 'You're talking about me as if I'm not here.'

'Yes, Annie – leave Lily alone,' Sybil said with a wink at Evie. 'Here, Lil, share some of these mushy peas with me. No? Not hungry? What on earth could have ruined your appetite, I wonder.'

'"I'll be loving you – always,"' Annie crooned as she drew Lily back to the bench. '"With a love that's true – always!"'

'Behave!' Lily implored.

'Yes, best behaviour,' Sybil agreed. 'The boss has arrived so now we all have to mind our p's and q's.'

Stanley Calvert's visit lasted through the dinner break and into the afternoon and included a grand tour of the building for Winifred, who floated through the sheds and warehouses in a crimson crêpe de Chine dress edged with cream lace. Over the dress she wore a fox stole and on her feet she had black patent leather shoes with heels that clicked along the stone-flagged floors. The outfit was completed by a cream cloche hat, which fitted snugly to her head and was decorated with red felt flowers.

'She won't last five minutes,' was Jennie Shaw's dour opinion after Calvert and his daughter had flitted through the mending room.

'Aye, she'll soon have the stuffing knocked out of her if she comes to work here,' Mary agreed.

Vera raised her eyebrows at Lily, as if to say, 'I don't fancy Winifred's chances among this lot,' while Lily merely nodded. Privately she felt a bit sorry for Winifred Calvert, who seemed to stick out like a sore thumb, and she wondered if her being introduced to the business of worsted production was one of the bones of contention at home that Harry had mentioned. And yet Winifred had partly invited the hostile reaction as she minced from room to room, looking down her nose and refusing to catch anyone's eye.

The flurry of gossipy interest surrounding Calvert's visit went on well into the afternoon. When the news eventually filtered through that he and his daughter had left the premises, Lily paused to imagine Harry standing to attention as he held open the Bentley door for them. Harry had done well for himself, she realized. At least he'd managed to steer clear of the usual hard, dirty jobs open to men brought up in these narrow back-to-back streets – coal hauliers and draymen, cobblers, street cleaners and dustmen with old-fashioned horses and carts who came every other week to clear out the ash pits.

'Settle down, please.' Iris Valentine had been the one to show Mr Calvert out of the building and she restored calm as she walked through the mending room into her office. She'd reached the door when she remembered something and came back at a brisk pace to speak with Lily.

'There's no need to look so worried,' she re-assured her when she saw her anxious expression. 'This isn't to do with your continuing here in the mending room.'

It was the memory of her father's 'last in, first out' prediction that had alarmed Lily and she gave a sigh of relief as the manageress went on to explain.

'Mr Calvert confirmed to me on his way out that Winifred is to start work in the office first thing on Monday. He wants her to get a real feel for the business so she'll need a clocking-on card and rules of employment the same as everyone else. I'd be obliged to you, Lily, if you would pop down there and ask Mr Wilson to prepare the documents.'

'What then?' Lily wanted to know.

'Then he'll give them to you and you'll take them home with you this evening and call in with them at

Mr Calvert's chauffeur's house. He lives near you, I believe?'

'Yes, Miss Valentine. Harry lives on Raglan Road just down the alley from us.'

'Very good. So you'll hand Winifred's documents over to Harry Bainbridge, who will take them with him when he goes to work at Moor House tomorrow morning. It'll be quicker than sending them by post.'

Understanding the task, Lily left her position and nipped downstairs to see the mill manager in the office where Iris Valentine had interviewed her for her new job. She knocked on the door and was told to come in by Derek Wilson's secretary, Jean Carson, who was busy preparing wage slips at her typewriter. 'Are you looking for Mr Wilson?' she asked, fingers poised over the keys and peering at Lily over the top of her glasses. 'Because if you are, you'll find him in the weaving shed talking to Fred Lee about the wage bill for tomorrow. If he's not there, try looking for him in the spinning shed.'

Nodding, Lily hurried on along the corridor to her old place of work, down the central aisle until she came to the loom where Annie worked. 'Where's Fred?' she mouthed above the immense racket of the looms.

'Office,' Annie told her, glancing up for a moment and pointing Lily in the right direction.

On Lily went, through all the noise and dust, noticing Florence White hard at work at her own old job, replacing the spent bobbins that fed the giant machines. When she came to the office tucked away in the far corner of the barn-like room, she knocked on the door and went straight in.

It took her a few moments to make sense of what she saw inside the office. She'd been expecting to find Derek Wilson discussing wages with the overlooker at Fred's high, sloping desk, but what she came across instead was Fred Lee in shirtsleeves and braces, standing to one side of a toppled chair. He seemed to be backing someone into a corner of the stuffy room, unaware that he was being interrupted. Lily had a glimpse of a dark grey pinafore and of a slim arm trying to push Fred away. Then she saw the girl's long, fair hair.

'Evie!' Lily closed the door to block out some of the noise then rushed to intervene. She laid hold of the overlooker and managed to drag him back, allowing Evie to dodge out of the corner, her hair loose from its plait, eyes startled and with one hand across her chest to hold her pinafore in place.

Fred shrugged free of Lily and straight away began to cover his tracks, his small eyes set hard, his lips curling in a contemptuous smile. 'A right little vixen, isn't she?' he began.

Cold with fury, Lily ignored him. 'Evie, are you all right?'

Evie nodded, trembling as she pulled the pinafore straight then bending down to pick up her hair ribbon from the floor.

'She scratches,' the overlooker declared, showing Lily several red marks on the inside of his bare forearm. 'There I was, explaining about my bad back and asking her to step up on that chair and reach me a ledger down from the top shelf. I held the chair steady for her like the gent I am and then what does she do? She only loses her balance, falls on top of me then turns on me for no reason and shows me her claws.'

'Stop – don't say another word!' Lily cried as she pushed past him. 'Evie, are you sure you're all right? Can you get back to work?'

Still too shocked to speak, Evie nodded again.

'Grand, then tie your hair back like a good girl, take a deep breath and go.' Lily waited for Evie to leave the office before she spoke again. 'It's not on,' she told the overlooker, pushed into outright confrontation by strong disgust. 'Don't think for a minute you can keep this to yourself. It'll get out, people will talk.'

'No, they won't,' he countered as he reached for his jacket, which was hanging on a hook behind the door. 'Not if they want to hold on to their jobs.'

The threat wasn't even veiled and it deepened Lily's fury. 'You can't keep your hands to yourself, can you? It's the truth and we all know it.'

Fred Lee's eyes narrowed further. '"We"? Who's "we"? You, Sybil, Annie?'

'No – everyone. All the women who work here know what you're like, don't you worry.'

The overlooker's contemptuous grin faltered for a moment as he looked ahead at the possible consequences. 'It's high time for you to calm down,' he told her. 'You'll soon see that this is a storm in a teacup, a silly mistake.'

'I saw what I saw,' she insisted.

Feeling himself back in control, Fred's tone grew more measured. 'You were mistaken. Nothing happened except that your sister fell off a chair and I helped her back on her feet. So if I was you, Lily, I'd go home tonight and tell Evie not to be so clumsy in future. Oh, and I'd point out to her that she's only been in the job five minutes yet she's already causing trouble. You can see the sense of what I'm saying, can't you?'

Furious, Lily had to back towards the door to keep herself from slapping the sneaky overlooker. 'I'll do no such thing!'

He shrugged then slid one arm into his jacket. 'That's a pity since jobs aren't ten a penny these days. I don't fancy Evie's chances if she has to start looking for another.'

The reality of the situation hit Lily like a hard punch to the stomach. She pictured the sequence of events if Evie were to take a complaint to Derek Wilson. Fred Lee would deny it and point out there were no witnesses, Mr Wilson would take the line of least resistance and choose to believe Lee over Evie. He would hand Evie her cards. Then there would be the scene at home – a repeat of Margie's confession of a week earlier, with Evie telling their mother that she'd been given the sack, followed by Rhoda's unforgiving reaction and Lily having to step up to the plate as the only remaining breadwinner.

'You see,' Fred Lee said smoothly as he watched the changing expressions on Lily's face, 'this is the way thing work around here, and don't you forget it, Lily Briggs.'

CHAPTER TWELVE

'So, spill the beans, Lily!' Annie was in high spirits as usual when she and Sybil met up with the two Briggs girls on their way to work the next morning. Despite the biting cold in the air as November turned into December, with the prospect of more short, dismal days ahead, she was determined to stay cheerful.

'Yes, come on, Lil, there's no need to be such a dark horse,' Sybil added in the same jolly tone. 'You were spotted calling at Harry's house last night. We want to know every single word that passed between you!'

'Oh, that!' Lily laughed. She was thankful not to be talking about Margie or about yesterday's incident between Evie and Fred Lee. 'I had to hand over Winifred Calvert's clocking-on cards, that's all.'

Reaching the bottom of Albion Lane, the girls turned on to busy Ghyll Road, dodging between cyclists to cross the street.

Sybil didn't let Lily off the hook that easily. 'And what did Harry say when you just happened to knock on his door? Did he turn bright red then ask you in for a cuppa?'

Lily shook her head. 'He was on his way down to the Cross to meet Billy.'

'What, and he didn't ask you to join them?' Annie teased. 'Was he too shy?'

'I was busy anyway,' Lily protested, glad that the entrance to Calvert's Mill was already in view. 'In any case, Harry and I have known each other too long to be anything besides friends. You know how it is.' Since the kiss it had taken days of Lily talking sternly to herself and reining in her own feelings for her to reach this position and she was determined not to let Sybil and Annie think otherwise.

'Yes, and you know what they say – there's none so blind . . . !' Sybil winked at Annie who winked back. Then, as they went under the stone archway, Sybil linked arms with Evie. 'But never mind about Lily and love's young dream, what I want to know is what made you so hot and bothered yesterday, Evie. You acted like a scared rabbit all afternoon – if anyone had said boo you'd have jumped clean out of your skin.'

'It was nothing,' Evie hastily replied, her pale face colouring up at the memory of Fred Lee's hot hands around her waist as he pressed himself up against her, his podgy fingers reminding her of the sausage links hanging from a hook in Durants' shop window. She and Lily had shuddered about it in their bedroom; Evie had whispered of how Fred had made her stand up on the chair then grabbed her from behind, pulling her down and turning her towards him, groping her chest and planting a wet kiss on her neck as she struggled to escape.

In the end, Lily's sole advice had been to keep out of the overlooker's way and avoid being alone with him, but she knew that was easier said than done. In any case, they'd concluded that the least said was the soonest mended.

'It didn't look like nothing,' Sybil said now as she walked into the weaving shed with Evie and Annie and they joined the queue to clock on. 'I bet Fred Lee was getting up to his tricks behind our backs,' she said to Annie.

'More than likely,' Annie agreed. 'Listen, Evie, do you want me to mention it to Robert? I could ask him to take Fred down a peg or two if you like. I'm sure he'd be happy to oblige.'

'No, please – don't say a word!' Evie begged, afraid of unleashing a backlash that would work against her.

'No, better still,' Sybil stepped in with a different idea, 'Fred's sister-in-law lives on my street. Why don't I drop a word in her shell-like ear?'

'Don't say anything,' Evie implored a second time. She clocked on then unrolled her apron and slipped it on over her head. 'I don't want a row over it, please!'

'Best not to make a fuss,' Lily agreed.

'Yes, all right.' Sybil soothed the sisters' worries by promising to stay quiet.

'Our lips are sealed,' Annie vowed.

'But watch out, Fred Lee – we're on to you!' Sybil declared as she took up position at her loom.

In the relative peace and quiet of the mending room, Lily spent the morning wondering firstly if she'd done the right thing by agreeing to let Evie smooth over the Fred Lee episode and secondly why it was that Margie hadn't replied to a short letter she'd sent in Wednesday's post.

'Dear Margie,' she had begun, aiming for a tone that she judged to be level headed and low key. 'I'm glad we had our talk on Monday and I hope this letter finds you well. I see that you have to work things out for yourself but if it turns out that you can do with my help after all, you only have to ask. There's still no need for anybody else to know what we talked about – just you and me, and that's a promise. It would be nice to hear from you soon to let me know how you're getting along. Send a letter back or get word to me some other way. There's no news here in Albion Lane except that we miss you, Arthur especially, and we all send our love. Do your best to keep warm in this nasty cold weather and write to me soon. Your loving sister, Lily.'

Having laboured over each and every word, Lily had reread the letter at least ten times, lost heart then read it again before she'd finally sealed the envelope and sent it. How would Margie react to receiving it? she wondered. Would she still be angry

145

that Lily wouldn't leave her alone, or would the letter soften her? And how was the poor girl coping up there on Ada Street, alone except for Granddad Preston?

On Thursday and again on Friday, Lily had rushed home from work hoping for a reply, but none had come.

'Did we have any post today?' she'd asked Rhoda on both days.

Her mother had gone on as usual, sitting by the fireside darning socks or turning one of Arthur's collars to hide the frayed edge. 'No, why? Are you expecting something?'

'No,' Lily had fibbed unconvincingly on the Thursday.

But on the Friday Lily had hung up her coat and replied differently, partly to take attention off a red-eyed Evie who, upset by more unwanted attention from Fred Lee, had taken herself straight off upstairs. 'Yes,' she'd admitted. 'I hoped for a letter from Margie.'

'Well, there's nothing,' Rhoda had said with grim finality, putting aside the half-finished collar, resting her head against the back of the chair and closing her eyes.

On Saturday morning, Lily sat at her mending table building up her hopes of a letter, working at the flaws in a piece of navy blue worsted, speaking only when spoken to but mainly lost in anxious contemplation of what would happen to Margie in a month or two's time when the baby began to show. Had Margie actually thought that far ahead? she wondered. And how would Granddad Preston react? If he was angry, as might be expected, who then would Margie turn to for support?

Lily's fingers ran over the beautifully smooth surface of the dark material as Ethel called for Jennie to come and take a finished piece for flipping and Miss Valentine sat in her office sealing wage packets and making entries in her ledger.

Would Margie even go on with the pregnancy? Lily asked herself, crushing the urge to pass over the painful dilemma as she might skim over a flaw in the fabric. No, she had to unpick and tie up the unanswered question with information she'd gleaned from their mother's years of delivering babies in the neighbourhood. Everyone, including Lily, knew there were always women who didn't want to go the full nine months – wives worn out by the absence of family planning and too many pregnancies, unmarried mothers like Margie, women from hardpressed families who couldn't afford to feed another mouth.

Sometimes Rhoda would come home and talk about such situations and the lengths to which people would go to get rid of a baby. 'If they ask me to help, I tell them no – there are other people to go to in a case like that,' was the upright, undeviating message from Rhoda Briggs. Once, Lily had overcome her reticence and asked her mother what was her objection to helping. She remembered now the steady way her mother had looked at her and her calm voice as she'd replied. 'Do I mind snuffing out a baby's life? The answer is yes, it's not for me, not under any circumstances. Mind you, I don't judge others and I understand why some might want to, especially in this day and age.'

This conversation came back to Lily now and she wondered if Rhoda's response would be the same if she learned that her own daughter, aged sixteen, was in the family way.

I expect it would, Lily thought. 'You've made your bed and now you must lie in it,' would most likely be the stern, unshakeable opinion.

Deep in thought when the midday buzzer sounded, Lily was only roused by Vera turning off her lamp and putting her tools into the tin box stowed under her table.

'Come on, slow coach,' she told Lily as she hurried away. 'It's time to clock off.'

Lily packed up then followed her fellow workers downstairs where she met up with Evie for the walk up to Albion Lane.

While they were waiting at the kerb on Ghyll Road, Annie caught them up. 'I shan't be coming out tonight, worse luck. Grandma Sykes is poorly and I promised to drop by. She's on her last legs, by the look of things.'

The old woman known locally as Grandma Sykes had until recently kept the baker's shop on Chapel

Street before it was taken over by her daughter, Marjorie, and she was in fact no relation to Annie so Lily took it as a mark of her friend's warm-heartedness that she was willing to give up her precious Saturday night out.

'Give her my love,' Lily told her. 'What's Sybil up to – did she say?'

Stepping out across the street during a gap in the traffic, Annie gave an abbreviated reply. 'Gone straight round to her brother's house for tea. Looks like you're on your own, Lily, love!'

'Never mind.' Lily waved after Annie and turned her thoughts towards the longed-for letter from Margie, picturing it waiting for her on the mantelpiece at home.

It was Evie who reminded her about Arthur's sweets from Newby's and who offered to buy them out of her own wages. 'I can see your mind's on other things,' she said sweetly.

'You're right, it is,' Lily agreed.

'Then let me do it. I'll run up the street with Arthur's treat then pop round to Peggy's house for a good chinwag,' Evie decided, happy at the thought of a whole day and a half free from Fred Lee.

So Lily hurried up Albion Lane alone, only to find Arthur running to meet her in his belted raincoat and school cap. 'Steady on,' she told him as he patted her pockets in the search for sugar treasure. 'Evie's at Newby's now, buying sweeties for you.'

'Here, Arthur, fancy a toffee while you're waiting?'

Taking Lily by surprise, Billy stepped out of the alley where he'd been sheltering from the wind with Harry and Ernie. He let Arthur delve into the crumpled bag that he held out for him. 'Ernie mentioned he hasn't seen much of your Margie this week,' he said as casually as could be.

'Did he, now?' Lily decided to bypass Billy and speak directly to the butcher's son, still standing in the alley with Harry. 'Didn't you hear, Ernie? Margie is staying at Granddad Preston's house.'

A bemused Ernie paused then shrugged and carried on talking to Harry.

'Don't be taken in by that couldn't-care-less act,' Billy advised, looking embarrassed. 'Ernie was hoping she'd be at the Assembly Rooms later.'

By this time Lily had worked out that it was Billy himself who was interested in her sister's whereabouts but she played along. 'Well, I'd tell Ernie not to hold his breath if I was you.'

Billy cleared his throat and changed the subject. 'How's the toffee, Arthur? Is it any good?'

'Umm-mmm.' Arthur's mouth was full so he nodded hard. Then he saw Evie emerging from Newby's and he scurried off.

'Toffee, Lily?' Billy said, offering her the bag.

'No thanks.' She smiled and was on her way again when Harry fell into step beside her on the short walk up the hill.

'The Rovers are playing at home this afternoon,' he mentioned, as if this was the very thing that would capture a girl's attention. 'Bert Stanley is in goal. It should be a good match.'

'Champion, Harry,' Lily replied, one hand on the rail leading up to her front door. This was the first time she and Harry had talked since Monday night and her heart fluttered in her chest as she tried in vain to concentrate on whether or not the letter from Margie would be there.

'It'll be two–nil to us, I reckon,' Harry predicted, seemingly unable to steer the conversation in the right direction. After all, he knew Lily didn't have the faintest interest in who played where for his favourite team. His fair colouring made him blush easily so he ducked his head to concentrate on grinding out the stub of his cigarette on the damp pavement until he'd regained his composure. 'Sorry, you're not a big Rovers supporter, are you? Anyway, forget about the football . . .'

'It wasn't me who brought the subject up,' Lily reminded him, raising her eyebrows. She'd seen him colour up and was amused by his effort to hide it.

'I wanted to ask you something,' he went on.

Suddenly the mood changed. She felt her own face grow flushed as she realized that Harry was giving her a serious look, which claimed all her attention. She gave up thinking about Margie's letter while Harry, noticeably less full of himself than usual, swallowed hard.

'Say no if you want, it won't hurt my feelings,' he said, fixing his gaze on her face again and looking as

151

if the words were about to choke him, 'but I wanted to ask if you'd like to come out to the flicks with me tonight?'

Lily felt a spark of delight light up the cold, grey afternoon. 'Tonight?' she repeated. 'Just you and me?'

'Why not?' he confirmed. 'We could go to the Victory, or we could get a tram all the way into town to the new Odeon if you like. My treat.'

'Race you!' Arthur called to Evie as they approached number 5 and he charged up the steps.

'That's not fair, you didn't say Ready, Get set, Go,' she protested, lagging behind.

Arthur barged through the front door and left it standing open. From inside the house they heard Walter grumbling about letting in the cold air. Evie hurried up the steps and closed the door behind her.

'Forget it – you're probably busy,' Harry said, misinterpreting the long pause. He turned away from Lily back towards the alley. He'd done it – he'd asked her and now it looked as if she was about to turn him down. 'Not to worry – another time perhaps.'

'No,' she said quickly. 'I'm not doing anything tonight.'

He stopped and retraced his steps, tipped back his cap and looked up at her questioningly in the way that made her knees turn to jelly.

'I'd love to come,' she told him, her face ablaze

with a mixture of awkwardness and excitement. 'I'll meet you by the lamp post at the top of the street. What time?'

'Half past five,' he told her, as chuffed as could be. 'Let's hope Rovers win and make it a real day to remember!'

With a wage of twenty shillings in her pocket and an outing to the pictures with Harry planned, Lily was determined to rise above her cousin Tommy's cheap jibes, which began as soon as she entered the house, unbuttoned her coat and took off her hat.

He was sitting at the table with a pal of his, Frank Summerskill. A year or two younger than Tommy and without any family in the immediate neighbourhood, Frank lodged in the same overcrowded terraced house on Canal Road as George and Tommy Briggs. His sharp features and small, glittering eyes set in a fleshy face somehow reminded Lily of a large, pouchy rodent – an impression enhanced by his dense, greyish-brown hair, which was cut short all over and was reminiscent of an animal pelt. His worn clothes – a shapeless brown jacket that was out at the elbows and patched, grey trousers – told Lily that he'd still had no success in his long search for a job. In fact, the out-of-work Frank was lucky to have any roof over his head, even one as unhealthy and cramped as the house overlooking the canal.

'You see that, Frank?' Tommy nudged him with his elbow and gestured towards Lily. 'That's what happens when you rise up in the world – you go to and from work in your Sunday best. And look, she doesn't even get her hands dirty – see.'

'Aye, it's all right for some,' Frank grumbled as he drew the back of his hand across the underside of his nose. Then he gathered catarrh in his throat, took aim and spat in the grate.

Lily's top lip curled in disgust.

'You don't have to look far to see where Margie got her habit of looking down her nose at people from,' Tommy sneered. 'And look where that got her.'

Mention of her sister made Lily squeeze past Frank to search on the mantelpiece for the hoped-for letter but she found only a bill for the latest coal delivery and a note to her mother from Doris Fuller telling Rhoda she was very sorry but could she wait until after Christmas to pay her the money owing for the mustard plasters.

'Anything from Margie?' Evie asked from her position by the sink where she wiped Arthur's sticky hands.

Lily shook her head.

'See!' Tommy jeered, thumbs hitched in his waist-coat pockets. 'Gone without so much as a backward glance, living the high life up at Overcliffe and never thinking about the people she's left behind.'

'Tommy, you don't know what you're talking about so why don't you just shut up?' Lily challenged. 'And what are you hanging about here for anyway?'

He grinned and leaned back on two legs of the

rickety chair. 'I'm waiting for Uncle Walter, aren't I?'

'Why, where is he?'

Before Tommy saw fit to answer, Arthur wormed free of Evie and put Lily in the picture. 'Father's upstairs with Mother. He wants to know why she's not getting up.'

'Mother's still in bed?' Lily didn't wait for more information. Alarmed, she took the stairs two at a time, rushing into her parents' room without the usual knock on the door. She found her father sitting on the side of the bed and her mother, white as a sheet, still in her nightdress and lying under a thin woollen blanket topped by Walter's brown overcoat. 'Whatever's the matter?' Lily wanted to know, her stomach churning.

'Nothing that a day or two in bed won't put right,' Rhoda insisted.

Lily turned to an abject Walter for more information. 'Father?'

'I wanted to send for the doctor but she wouldn't let me,' he explained.

'But what's wrong with her?'

'She's been sick in the washbasin all night and she says she's got a headache. That's all I know, except that it's not like her to take to her bed, is it?' Sitting in his shirtsleeves, unshaven and without a collar, he looked somehow younger and more defenceless than usual. He seemed relieved that Lily had got home from work and looked to her for what they should do next.

'Where does your head hurt, Mother?' Lily sat on the opposite side of the bed and clasped Rhoda's cold hand.

Rhoda passed her other hand lethargically over her forehead. 'Across here. It's nothing. I wish you wouldn't make a fuss.'

'And is your stomach upset as well?'

'Not so much. Let me sleep off this nasty pain in my head then I'll be right as rain.'

'That's just what she said to me.' Walter shook his head. 'But you didn't see her, Lily. She was up half the night and she was being sick even when she had nothing to be sick with. I thought at one time she was going to pass out.'

'You should've called for me,' Lily told him. 'Mother, is there anything that you'd like – a cup of tea or something to settle your stomach?'

Rhoda slowly shook her head and withdrew her hand from Lily's, seeming to have just enough strength for this but with none to spare for more words. Instead, she turned her face away and closed her eyes.

'Now, lass, this isn't like you,' Walter said, clearing his throat as he bent over her. 'Arthur needs you up and about, making his tea for him.'

Lily laid a hand on his shoulder. 'Leave her now – she needs to sleep. Me and Evie can make Arthur his tea.'

Walter quickly backed down. 'Aye, that's right,' he

agreed. 'The girls will look after the littl'un, Rhoda. You have a nice rest.'

Rhoda's eyes flickered open and she gave Walter a weak smile and Lily saw in that brief moment the twenty-odd years of history that her mother and father had shared – the days of courtship on Ada Street, their early married life on Canal Road, the years of toil and conflict on Albion Lane – all rolled together in a lingering look and a smile.

'You'll be back on your feet before you know it,' Walter promised as he stood up and, clasping his hands in front of him, clumsily backed out of the room.

Lily waited a while longer, watched her mother's eyes close and saw her drawn features relax in sleep. Gently she adjusted her covers then kissed her cheek and with a thousand things she wanted to say left unsaid, she closed the door and went downstairs.

CHAPTER THIRTEEN

'I didn't think I'd be able to come out tonight,' Lily told Harry as they walked arm in arm along Canal Road. 'Mother's poorly. I thought I should have to stay in and look after her.'

'Can't Evie do that?' he asked. He'd dressed up in his best blazer and a pair of flannel trousers that he'd bought with his last week's wages and he'd topped them with his long grey raincoat, but now he felt he'd overdone it for what was after all only an evening at the flicks.

'That's just what Evie said, once Father had taken himself off to the Cross. She told me Mother would do very well without me hanging over her and she was old enough to look after Arthur by herself, ta very much!' Lily smiled up at Harry, feeling that she'd better pinch herself to make sure she was actually walking out with, let's face it, the best look-ing young man between here and Overcliffe. On top of this, she was slowly starting to realize that the Monday-night kiss she'd spent so much time turning over in her mind might not have been an accident after all.

'That's right – let Evie do some of the work.' As they walked by the locked gates of Napier's scrap metal yard, Harry patted the gloved hand that rested in the crook of his arm.

Just wait until she told Sybil and Annie about her night out with Harry, Lily thought. It would have to wait until they got together for a natter the following week and of course they would tease and crow over the fact that they'd guessed right about Harry and Lily, roll their eyes and tease again, but she wouldn't care.

'It's grand to see you smiling,' he told her as they walked on towards Brinkley Corporation Baths.

'Yes, I'm glad I came out.'

Harry smiled back and considered slipping his arm around Lily's waist then thought better of it. That should come later, he decided, after the film when they were walking home. Slow and steady with Lily – that would be the best way. 'You'll like this picture,' he promised. 'It's to do with a soldier in the Great War. He gets badly wounded and lets the girl he loves think that he's dead so she can get on with her life without him—'

'Hush!' Lily unhooked her arm to put both hands to her ears. 'Don't tell me the whole story and spoil it for me.'

Harry grinned, grabbed her hand back then steered her towards the wide, brightly lit entrance of

159

the modern picture house where there was a giant poster showing the star of the film, Gracie Fields. 'She's not bad-looking but she's not a patch on you,' he told Lily.

'Flattery will get you nowhere,' she protested to hide the fact that she was flustered. Why did this keep on happening with Harry – the tremulous quickening of her heartbeat over some silly remark or the special way he looked at her? And hadn't she better keep her feet on the ground for now until she was sure of where she stood with him?

He squeezed her hand then kept his fingers curled around hers. 'All right. I expect Gracie can beat you hands down in the singing stakes, unless you've got hidden talents, Lil.'

'No, I can't sing a note,' she confessed as they joined the queue.

Buoyed up by the lights and the glamorous, brightly coloured posters inside the foyer, Lily could hardly wait to get inside the cinema and when they took their seats amongst a crowd of other young people with smiling faces, ready to watch the news-reel that came on before the main picture, she felt as if she'd entered a fairy-tale world. Gone from her mind were the sooty streets and bleak moors and taking their place was a plush warmth and dimmed lights, the hum of expectation drowned now by the notes of the organ positioned just under the giant screen. The organist played a romantic waltz to get people in the mood for the night's entertainment.

As the notes swelled to the ceiling and filled the auditorium, Harry made a bold move and slid his arm along the back of Lily's seat and left it there, his fingers resting on her shoulder. 'This is a bit of all right,' he said with a smile.

She smiled back at him and thought of nothing when the curtain went up and the newsreel played, only of Harry sitting close beside her, his hand lightly touching her shoulder.

Then the film came on, with Gracie Fields – a Lancashire lass who could make you laugh and cry in a second, who sang like a bird, her voice pure and high, soaring higher still. The words brought to mind blue skies and a girl called Sally's smiling face. Sally with a heart of gold, soldiering on alone after the war.

Of course Lily cried when the wounded soldier returned, even though she thought he looked old and staid and not at all her idea of a romantic hero. She was still crying and drying her eyes when the film ended (in an embrace, of course) and the lights went up.

Harry stood and let his hinged seat fold sharply upwards, offering Lily his hand. He turned, and keeping tight hold of her, led the way along the row of seats, up the steps towards the exit.

And then they were through the foyer and out on the cold, dark street. A tram rattled by, followed by a Ford car and two men on bikes.

'Hey up, you two!' Ernie called as he wobbled to a halt outside the entrance to the baths. The grin on his face was the widest Lily had ever seen. 'I was wondering when you'd get round to asking Lily out,' he told Harry. 'In fact, I bet Billy a tanner you'd never pluck up the courage. It looks like I'm out of pocket.'

'Not so fast,' Lily shot back, her eyes twinkling. 'You can tell Billy Robertshaw it was the other way around – it was me who asked Harry to come to the pictures with me.'

'Never!' a flabbergasted Ernie cried.

'No, she's kidding.' Harry put him right straight away while Lily laughed at the look on Ernie's face. 'I'll tell Billy you owe him a tanner next time I see him.'

'Which might be sooner than you think, worse luck.' Ernie gestured behind him at the small, noisy group of people still lingering outside the Victory. 'Billy's back there with your Margie.'

It was Lily's turn to be astonished. 'Margie's been to the pictures with Billy?' she asked. 'You mean, we were sitting there in the cinema without knowing they were there?'

'It looks like it,' Ernie said, checking his cycling clips were firmly in place before getting ready to set off again. Then he put on a tragic face and bemoaned his fate. 'Margie's ruined her chances with me good and proper this time.'

'Never mind, Ernie, there are plenty more fish in the sea,' Harry sympathized. 'There's Hilda Crabtree for a start.'

'Stop right there,' Ernie ordered. 'I'll choose my own girl if you don't mind.'

And so Harry and Ernie joked along while Lily tried to catch sight of Margie outside the cinema. The group was dispersing and eventually Lily spotted her sister in her green coat and matching hat, jauntily crossing the road hand in hand with Billy in his Saturday-night-out tweed jacket and best cap. She ran a few steps towards them and called Margie's name. Margie glanced round and though she heard and saw Lily, she kept on walking.

'Margie, Billy – wait a sec!' Lily cried. She had to let a tram trundle by then run again to catch up with them.

Billy greeted her with an open, cheery grin. 'Well, if it isn't Lily Briggs! Fancy seeing you here.' He looked across the street to spot Harry saying goodbye to Ernie and following Lily across the road. 'It looks like I've won myself a tanner,' he said with a wink.

'I never knew you were coming into town,' Lily said to Margie, who had stopped reluctantly.

She narrowed her eyes as if warning Lily not to overstep the mark by plunging into the all-important but forbidden topic of conversation. Lily was offended that Margie felt it necessary to drop the hint. 'Anyway, how's Granddad?' she asked coolly.

'The same as ever,' Margie said with a frown. 'He goes out every morning, and comes back in at tea-time. He doesn't bother much with me.'

'That's all right then. But Mother's in bed poorly,'

Lily told her, sharing family news while Billy and Harry carried on with the joke about the sixpence. 'She's not been herself lately and I'm worried about her. I'm going to tell Father to call Dr Moss if she's not better by Monday.'

Margie raised her eyebrows. 'You think you can get him to pay for that?'

Lily nodded. 'He's worried too, I can tell. Of course, Mother won't hear of it – you know what she's like. We'll have to go behind her back.'

'You hear that, Margie?' Billy broke in. 'Harry thinks I should take you to see Boris Karloff in *Frankenstein* next week.'

Glad of a change of subject, Margie put on a bright, flirtatious smile. 'Why's that, Harry?'

'Boris will frighten the life out of you,' Harry promised. 'You'll be glued to your seat, hanging on to Billy for dear life.'

Margie tilted her head back and grinned. 'Horror films don't bother me so there'll be no hanging on to anyone.'

As Margie played along, Lily saw that she was using it as a way of keeping her distance. And of course Lily was bursting with questions. Billy must have taken himself off to Ada Street after their conversation earlier, but had Margie been pleased to see him? Might Margie have confessed everything to Billy about the baby? Because in Lily's mind Billy was by far and away the most likely candidate to be the baby's father.

Lily's fertile imagination ran through the possibilities then came to a sudden halt when Billy dragged her back into the conversation. 'You'll go to see *Frankenstein* with Harry, won't you, Lil? We can all four go together – you and Harry, me and Margie.'

It struck her then with the force of a blow to her chest – Billy wasn't a man troubled by the sudden prospect of unwanted fatherhood. He was himself – carefree and joking, handsome and pleasant enough but not someone you took seriously or who had hidden depths. No, Billy was still Billy, never thinking beyond his daily routine of getting himself off to work, doing his gardening job for Stanley Calvert, taking his pay at the end of the week and getting out on a weekend to have a high old time.

So Margie hadn't told Billy anything, Lily decided, and she was glaring at her again, demanding that she kept her secret and of course Lily couldn't do anything else, even though it seemed wrong for Margie to take up with Billy again as if nothing was the matter. After all, how long could it go on before she had to confess and then what would happen? Lily had to stop herself from shuddering when she imagined that moment.

'I don't know about Boris Karloff,' was all she said in reply to Billy's question, casting her eyes down at the pavement to avoid Margie's hard stare.

'Maybe we'll go dancing instead,' Harry suggested as he picked up the tension in the air and began to steer Lily away. He turned to Billy. 'Are you two taking the tram up to Overcliffe, or are you walking home with us?'

'Tram,' Margie said, leaving Billy no option but to carry on to the stop with her. 'Cheerio, Harry. Ta-ta, Lily,' she called over her shoulder. 'Don't do anything I wouldn't do!'

They were off in the opposite direction, leaving Harry to walk Lily home along the increasingly deserted streets.

'We'll only go dancing if you'd like to,' Harry acknowledged gently. 'I hope you don't think I was jumping the gun.'

'No – I mean, yes I would like to.' She sighed, her mind still taken up with Margie.

'You can tell me if you've got something else on,' he insisted, walking without taking her hand and trying to judge her mood. He'd felt happier and more confident when they were in the cinema, when he'd stolen glances at the light reflected from the big screen flickering on to Lily's face and watched her surreptitiously wiping a tear from her eye. 'We're coming up to Christmas – there's always plenty going on.'

They'd reached the corner on to Ghyll Road and could see the entrance to Calvert's ahead of them and the tall, square memorial tower rising into the dark sky. 'No, Harry, I mean it. I'd like us to go out again.'

Lily's straightforward admission was music to Harry's ears and he moved in to slide his arm around her waist. 'It's funny,' he said.

166

'What?' She leaned her head against his shoulder and liked how this time he matched his stride to hers.

'Funny how you can live on the next street to someone for donkey's years and never think twice about how you feel about the other person.'

Lily hoped that Harry's comment was leading in the right direction but she wasn't sure so she fell back on a flippant remark. 'Now don't you go hurting my feelings, taking me for granted already.'

'No, I'm serious.' He'd built himself up to make a long speech and went ahead with it regardless, his face unusually solemn. 'We come and go – day in, day out. We have our pals and everything's jogging along nicely as usual. You've got Sybil and Annie. I've got Ernie and Billy and everyone down at the Cross. Then all of a sudden something clicks.'

'Between us?'

'That's right. I wasn't expecting it but when it happened it hit me like a ton of bricks.'

'Ta very much!' His way of putting things made her smile. 'Donkey's years', 'ton of bricks' – you wouldn't find those phrases in a love poem, but they were Harry Bainbridge to a 'T'.

'It was when you were dancing with me at the Assembly Rooms. I tapped you on the shoulder and you said yes and you didn't mind me having two left feet and we were getting along fine – one-two-three, one-two-three.' They were outside Newby's sweet shop, and Harry suddenly seized Lily in his

167

arms and waltzed her round the corner on to Albion Lane. '"Goodnight, Sweetheart" – that was when it hit me.'

She laughed and let him hold her close and wrap his coat around her like a warm cocoon. She looked up at him and knew that she wanted to kiss him, only Harry wouldn't stop speaking until he'd got everything off his chest. 'What hit you?' she whispered.

'That you weren't just the girl next door, the one everyone relies on, the girl I could have a laugh and a joke with whenever our paths crossed on a Saturday night out. You were much more to me than that.'

'Stop, before all this goes to my head.' She spoke words that she didn't mean. *Don't stop, Harry,* she should have said. *Tell me everything that's in your heart.*

'You're beautiful, Lily,' he whispered, stroking her hair. 'I don't know why, but I must have been going around all these years with my eyes closed.'

'Harry . . .'

'Hush,' he murmured, his breath warm on her cold face, his lips pressing against hers.

CHAPTER FOURTEEN

For most of Sunday Lily was on cloud nine. Her feet didn't touch the ground, her heart beat faster, her head was in a spin . . . She smiled to herself as all the clichés and well-worn words of American love songs she'd heard on the wireless rolled together inside her head and made her float on air.

She sewed and looked out on to Albion Lane, crooning softly to the tune of 'I'll Be Loving You, Always'.

'What are you making?' Arthur pestered from his perch on the window sill. It had rained all morning and was still coming down so hard that the gutters and drains overflowed and water streamed down the pavement outside the house.

'I'm making a blouse for Vera at work.' As Lily's foot pressed the treadle and her fingers steered the soft blue fabric under the rapidly pounding needle, she tried not to let Arthur distract her from thoughts of Harry, but as always she'd underestimated her little brother's clamour for attention.

'When it stops raining, will you come up to the Common with me and play football?'

Lily had come to the tricky bit of gathering a sleeve at the shoulder end then pinning it carefully into the arm hole before she tacked then sewed it in place. 'No, Arthur, it'll be too muddy.'

'We could play marbles in the alley,' he suggested.

'It'll be all nasty and wet.' She adjusted the gathers until she was satisfied they were even then turned the half-finished garment the right side out to check that the sleeve had been set in right. 'Why not look at a book?'

'No, I want to play out,' he whined, craning his neck to see who was coming up the street.

'We can't always have what we want,' Lily counselled. Deciding that she was unhappy with the evenness of the gathers, she unpinned the sleeve, drew out the thread and began again.

'Harry's here!' Arthur announced as he leaped down from the sill and ran to the door.

At the mention of Harry's name Lily started and pricked her finger. She sucked it as Arthur let Harry in, buttoned up against the rain with his cap pulled well down as usual.

'I won't stop,' Harry began, taking care not to step off the doormat for fear of dripping everywhere. 'I happened to be passing and spotted Arthur at the window. I was wondering – shall I take him off your hands for a bit?'

'To do what?' Lily asked, her finger to her mouth.

Harry's unexpected arrival had made her forget her manners, had thrown her out of the happy day-dream about him into that painful and real state of uncertainty about what last night's kiss might mean and where it might lead, although this time she was at least sure that it hadn't been an accident.

Now that he'd followed his impulse to knock on the door, Harry too seemed unsure. 'I don't know – I haven't thought that far ahead. But I could see he was at a loose end.'

'You're right about that. Arthur can't sit still for five minutes. Anyone would think he's got ants in his pants.'

'No, I haven't!' Arthur protested with a pained look.

Harry smiled and came up with an idea. 'It's about this time in the afternoon that the horses down at the brewery are getting fed. Would you like me to take you to see Duke and Prince and the others, Arthur?'

'Aren't they up on the Common?' Lily checked.

'Not in this rain. And anyway there's no goodness in the grass at this time of year. So how about it, Arthur, do you want to come with me?'

Arthur's answer was to run for his school coat and hat and in less than a minute he was buttoned, belted up and standing with an excited grin beside Harry at the door.

'They say the rain will ease up by teatime,' Harry told Lily, kicking himself for not being able to think of something more interesting to say. He didn't know what had got into him lately – weather was as bad as football as a topic of conversation and it felt to him as if the magic of the night before might have melted into the puddles on the pavement outside.

'Fingers crossed,' she murmured, smiling and nodding them on their way. She waved at them through the window then went back to her sewing, rethreading the needle and trying to concentrate but thinking only of how clear and grey Harry's eyes were when he glanced up from under the peak of his cap, and how those eyes were full of questions that she'd wanted to answer but hadn't been able to, not sitting here at the sewing machine, with Arthur hopping from one foot to the other and eager to be off.

At the end of the afternoon, as the rain eased and dusk fell, Rhoda managed to get out of bed. She came slowly and silently downstairs, grasping the banister and appearing in the kitchen as Lily was putting the finishing touches to Vera's blouse. There was no one else in the house – Walter had taken himself off straight after dinner to the Working Men's Club on Market Row for a change and Evie was cosily ensconced with Peggy on Raglan Road. The blouse was a pretty forget-me-not blue and would suit Vera well, Lily decided, glancing up only to be taken aback by her mother's appearance. Though Rhoda had made the effort to get up and dressed into her grey skirt and navy blue blouse, she looked washed out and was stooping forward with one arm crossed over her thin body, the other hand still grasping the banister at the bottom of the stairs.

'Don't start.' Rhoda knew that Lily was about to fuss so she cut her off short.

Lily put down the blouse and hurried to help her into the chair by the fire. 'Are you sure you should be up?' she asked.

'I had to get out of bed some time and this way it'll stop your father nagging me to fetch Dr Moss,' Rhoda replied as she sank down into the chair. She winced as she reached up to tuck stray strands of hair behind her ears. 'Don't go on at me, Lily. Just make me a cup of tea, there's a good girl.'

Rushing to do as Rhoda asked, Lily squashed down her fears and cast around for ordinary, every-day subjects. 'Harry called to take Arthur out for the afternoon,' she told her. 'That was nice of him, wasn't it?'

'Yes, Betty Bainbridge has brought him and Peggy up nicely, considering she's been by herself since their father died of the influenza – when would that be? Let me see, it was ten years back, during the winter of 1921. Is that where Evie is now – at Raglan Road?'

Lily nodded.

'And whose blouse have you been sewing?' Rhoda pointed to the garment, finished except for the buttonholes, hanging over the back of a chair.

'I made it for Vera Wilkinson at work.'

'How much will she pay you for that, pray tell?' Rhoda went on.

'I don't know, Mother. We haven't mentioned money. Maybe she'll give me sixpence out of next week's wage.'

'It's worth a shilling at least,' Rhoda said sharply then she grew distracted and stared into the fire. 'You've been to see Margie,' she stated after a lengthy silence, taking the cup of tea and looking directly into Lily's eyes.

Lily found it impossible to deny. 'I have,' she agreed, noticing that her mother's hand was shaking so hard that the cup rattled in its saucer. 'I saw her on Monday after work.'

'And?'

'And again last night. We ran into one another outside the Victory.'

Rhoda pressed her lips together in a thin line and took a sharp breath to overcome a fresh bout of pain. 'That's not what I meant. I want to know how she behaved when you saw her on Monday. What did she say? And don't fob me off because I'll be able to tell and then you and I will have a row, Lily, I'm warning you.'

Lily frowned and moved Vera's blouse on to the table as she drew the chair across the room. 'The last thing I want is an argument,' she insisted, sitting down close to Rhoda. 'But I made Margie a promise not to tell anyone what we talked about. I'm sorry,

Mother, but I can't break that promise.'

Turning her face away, Rhoda nodded then spoke slowly and deliberately. 'That's all right, I can read between the lines as well as the next person. I'd hoped I was wrong about Margie but it seems I'm not.' As embers shifted and sank in the grate, Rhoda told Lily to put more coal on the fire. 'How many bags did Holroyd deliver this week?'

Her face burning from the glow of the fire, Lily was torn between her sister and her mother and shocked once again by Rhoda's ability to deny her motherly feelings. It felt like a cellar trapdoor slamming shut. 'Three bags,' she answered flatly.

'That'll be nine shillings we owe him,' Rhoda calculated, tapping the arm of her chair with her fingertips. 'And where will we get that with Christmas just around the corner? Pray tell me that.'

When Lily took the new blouse to work on the Monday morning and gave it to Vera, her fellow mender was all smiles and praise.

'It's grand,' Vera told her, agreeing to a dressmaking fee of nine pence, to be paid out of her wages on the coming Saturday. 'Why, I could go into town to Merton and Groves and buy one just like it for ten times the price and no one would know the difference.'

'You picked a nice, fashionable pattern.' Never one to blow her own trumpet, Lily pointed out another reason why the end result was so pleasing.

'But the buttonholes are perfectly neat, and look at the cuffs with the beautiful scalloped edging.' A happy Vera showed off the blouse to Mary and Ethel. Jennie, not wanting to be left out, came to deliver her verdict on Lily's seamstress skills and by the time Iris Valentine pitter-pattered into the mending room, the praise was universal.

'Girls, please!' The manageress clapped her hands and sent them to their work stations, telling Vera to put the blouse back in its brown-paper wrapping. Before long, the atmosphere in the room had changed and heads were bent in quiet concentration. It was only when the buzzer for dinner sounded that the women, backs aching and fingertips tingling from their painstaking work, were free to talk once more.

'I'm saving up for a length of plum-coloured crêpe de Chine I've seen in the remnant shop on Market Row,' Elsie told Lily as the menders traipsed along the crowded corridor to the canteen. Though Elsie was well over forty, with two grown-up children, she still kept up an interest in fashion and was vain about her appearance. 'I asked them to put it aside for me and now I'm wondering if you would make it into a dress – one with long sleeves and a little Peter Pan collar, with pearl buttons all down the front. Would you have time to do that after Christmas, do you think?'

Promising to make time, Lily hurried to join Sybil, Annie and Evie at their favourite bench by the window. The talk there was all about Fred Lee, who was absent from work due to an accident on his motorbike on his way home from the Rovers match on Saturday. The rumour was that he'd broken an arm and given himself a black eye when his bike hit a patch of oil and skidded out of control. As a result he'd spent the rest of the day at the King Edward's Hospital having his arm put in plaster.

'Accident on his motorbike, my foot!' Annie scoffed as she dug into a dinner of pork pie and gravy. 'According to Robert, that bike's been in the workshop for repairs since last Wednesday. By all accounts it needs a new gasket, which they've had to order from Birmingham.'

'Oooh!' Sybil gloated over this latest piece of gossip. 'So who really gave Fred the black eye and why is he covering it up?'

'Why are we wasting time talking about it?' Lily's dislike for the overlooker made her unusually curt but at the same time she gave Evie a reassuring nod.

'Because we are!' Annie insisted. 'And do you want to know what I think really happened?'

'You're going to tell us anyway.' Sybil laughed at their irrepressible friend as she swept back a thick lock of hair and pinned it firmly in place.

Annie leaned across the table and spoke in a conspiratorial whisper. 'I think the worm has turned!'

'Which worm? What are you talking about?'

'Fred's wife, Nora. I think she's got wind of Fred's goings-on behind her back and got someone to teach him a lesson.'

177

'Never!' Sybil gasped. 'That little thing? She wouldn't hurt a fly.'

'I'm saying that's just what I heard.' Giving the impression of keeping something back and enjoying the suspense she'd created, Annie returned to her pork pie and for a while the sound of plates being scraped clean combined with the hum of general conversation and the background churn of giant cogs turning in the engine room in the yard below.

'What are you looking for, Lily?' Sybil had caught her friend going off into a daydream and clearing a patch in the misted window. 'Or rather, I should say, *who* are you looking for?'

'If it's Harry, you won't see him. He's already been and gone,' Annie chirped.

'I know that.' Lily tried but failed to stop herself from blushing. She was on the brink of making a clean breast of it and confessing that she and Harry had been to see Gracie Fields together when all heads turned towards the door as Stanley and Winifred Calvert walked in with the mill manager, Derek Wilson, and the office secretary, Jean Carson.

There was an immediate and uncomfortable hush during which there was plenty of time for the mill girls to take in every detail of Winifred's appearance – a process that they executed with forensic precision.

'Why does she come to work all done up like a dog's dinner?' Jennie would say to Mary as they returned to the burling and mending room after

178

dinner. 'Who does she think she is?'

'I liked her dress,' Vera would tell Ethel. 'Black and white stripes show off a girl's figure a treat.'

'But crêpe de Chine?' Ethel would query. 'I like the feel of it, but it's no good for sitting around in all day.'

There were other comments about Winifred's hair – 'natural or permed?' – her black patent leather shoes – 'too high' – which the girls would whisper to each other later.

At the time, though, these thoughts were kept private as Stanley Calvert ordered his manager to create a space for the four of them and Jean asked the cook to brew a pot of tea. They sat down at the table next to Lily's and Calvert pontificated in a gratingly loud voice, as if volume alone were a measure of his importance.

'A full order book is what we're after,' he told Wilson, a small, slight man with prominent teeth, a clipped moustache and round glasses, who dressed in a pinstriped suit of inferior quality that was too big across the shoulders but fashionably wide in the trouser leg. 'Are you listening to this, Winifred? We have to be there before Kingsley and the rest with a better price and an earlier delivery date, which we stick to come what may. That's the secret to modern worsted production – low prices and keen delivery, whatever it takes.'

Lily wondered that a man in Calvert's position could talk so confidently about full order books in times like these. Then again, perhaps this was what it took to keep production going against the odds – an unthinking self-belief that carried you through even while you had your back against the wall.

Stanley Calvert certainly didn't look like a worried man, rather one who was used to issuing orders and getting his own way, with a well-fed, well-groomed appearance and one of those smooth, plump faces without lines and furrows, though the thinning hair, coarsening skin and thickening waistline suggested an age closer to fifty than forty.

As for his home circumstances, he'd been married for twenty-five years to Eleanor, who was five years his junior but a woman who considered herself to be his superior in every other respect. A patron of the ballet and opera, an avid reader of the novels of Dickens and Thackeray, which she discussed with a circle of educated, artistic friends, Eleanor seldom turned her thoughts to the sordid business of manufacturing cloth and refused point blank to accept that she, like everyone else during these pinched, straitened times, must tighten her purse strings. As a result she bitterly resented her husband's decision to involve their only daughter Winifred in the daily grind of Calvert's Mill and had promptly decamped from Moor House to stay with her sister in Scarborough in the build-up to Christmas.

'Now if we find a way of buying wool in the grey at a cheaper price than the one we get from the suppliers here in Yorkshire, we'll be on to a good thing,'

Stanley Calvert told Derek Wilson. 'You'll make it your business to find out how much it would cost us to ship it in from further afield – from Leicester or from the Lake District, say – and come back to me with half a dozen different prices by the end of the week.'

The manager, who valued the three-bedroomed house that came with his job and a wage that gave him enough money to run a little Ford car, eagerly agreed. 'You're right,' he said. 'Local suppliers are getting greedy and now that we don't rely so much on the canals for transport, I can look into cutting back costs in that direction, too.'

As the men talked business and Jean poured tea and produced a plate of neatly cut ham sandwiches, Winifred grew more obviously bored. Refusing both tea and sandwiches, she pulled a silver and mother-of-pearl compact out of her pocket, powdered her nose and touched up her lipstick. Then she examined her fingernails and drummed them on the table, after which she stared sulkily around the room until she spied Jennie Shaw.

'She may be the boss's daughter, but that doesn't give her the right to push in front of me in the clocking-on queue,' Jennie muttered to Mary, not flinching under Winifred's haughty gaze.

'When was that?' Mary asked.

'This morning. She was two minutes late. By rights she should have half an hour docked off her pay like the rest of us.'

At the table next door, Sybil, Annie, Evie and Lily overheard every word and cringed. It seemed to them that Winifred was going out of her way to get herself disliked. Lily bit her lip, waiting to see what Stanley Calvert's reaction would be. When he shoved Winifred's manicured hand out of the way as he reached for another sandwich, she saw a flicker of apprehension pass across his daughter's face before she composed herself and went back to an inspection of her fingernails. It was as if Winifred had overplayed her hand, realized her mistake and would suffer the consequences later, when the two of them got back to Moor House.

'Am I the only one who feels sorry for Winifred Calvert?' Lily wondered aloud to Annie on the way back to work at half past twelve.

'Yes, love, you are,' was the swift, decisive reply.

'Well, I think she's a fish out of water and doesn't know how to behave.'

'That's you all over,' Annie laughed. 'Feeling sorry for those who don't deserve it.'

And so it went on at work for the rest of that week – Winifred rubbing people up the wrong way, Fred Lee recuperating at home after his mysterious 'accident' and Lily looking longingly out of the mending-room window each morning and teatime for a glimpse of Harry dropping off or waiting to collect the boss's daughter.

On the Tuesday, Wednesday and Thursday Lily

was out of luck and she was beginning to doubt herself. Was it possible, she wondered, that Harry had taken a step back after the thrill of their first dance and their cinema outing and was now avoiding her? Yes, that must be it. In the cold light of day, Harry had regretted his long speech about his feelings for Lily and now wanted to go back to their old situation of being just good pals. The notion lodged itself in her mind and gnawed away at her, adding to her ongoing worries about Margie, Evie and her mother.

'Why so glum?' Sybil asked her on the Thursday as the mill girls filed out under the archway. The weather was bitter, with the sort of damp cold that got into the bones and with a northerly wind that brought swathes of mist down from the moor to mingle with the soot and the smoke of the town.

Lily shivered and turned up her collar, automatically checking up and down Ghyll Road for Calvert's Bentley. 'It's this nasty weather – it makes you want to curl up by the fire and not move an inch until the winter's over and done with.'

'We've a long way to go yet,' Sybil reminded her, drawing her shawl over her head. 'We've got Christmas before that. Then January – that's usually the worst.'

'Cheer up, you two, for goodness' sake,' Annie chided before steering the conversation in another direction. 'What's Father Christmas bringing you this year, Evie – a shiny new overlooker?'

They all laughed and agreed how much nicer it would be if Fred didn't bother coming back to work.

By the time the girls came to the parting of the ways, Lily felt more cheerful. She and Evie said their goodbyes and walked on up Albion Lane arm in arm, discussing whether or not they would need to ask for Peggy's help again the following morning to take Arthur into school.

'Mother swears hand on heart that she's feeling better,' Evie pointed out.

'But she's not seen Dr Moss and she's not put her nose outside the front door since she fell ill. They're saying it'll be cold and wet again tomorrow.' On balance, Lily felt they should ask Peggy to help out after all and sent Evie down the alley to pass on the message while she hurried on home.

It was so foggy that Lily could hardly see two feet in front of her and almost ran slap bang into the person she'd been longing to see all week.

'Harry!' she exclaimed as he put out both hands to steady her.

'Lily!' For a moment he was tongue tied, his thoughts scattered.

'Where have you been?' she asked. 'Have you been avoiding me?'

'Crikey, no!' In fact, Harry had been doing some loitering of his own, trying to run into Lily and fix up a time for their next outing but missing her by a few minutes here and there. Getting control of his jitters, he resumed his old, teasing manner. 'I take it you've been missing me something rotten, Lil?'

'No, I've been far too busy,' she retorted, her heart beating to the new fast rhythm it adopted whenever Harry put his hand on her arm or her shoulder, or around her waist. 'Anyway, why aren't you at work?'

'I knocked off early because I wasn't needed,' he explained. 'Mr Calvert said he would drive to town to collect Winifred for a change. I just popped into your house to see if Arthur fancied coming down to the brewery again but your mother said he had to stay in to learn his five-times table and she gave me that stern look, the way she does.'

'Mother's been poorly,' Lily said by way of excuse.

Slow to release his hold on Lily, Harry was happy to let the conversation meander on. 'He loved those horses. He says he wants to drive a wagon when he grows up, not that there'll be many horses and carts left by that time, I reckon.'

'He's a funny little lad,' Lily murmured as Harry finally let go of her arms. Her heart felt light as she read between the lines. 'Did you really drop by to see Arthur? Is that the truth?'

'Yes. No. Oh, what the heck – I came to see if I can call for you this Saturday,' he announced bluntly and then realized he ought to have made the invitation sound more enticing. 'You can tell me if there's something you fancy doing – the world is our oyster!'

'No, it isn't,' she laughed. 'Our world doesn't go much beyond Overcliffe Common, remember.'

'All right, then – how about that *Frankenstein* picture that Billy mentioned?'

'That didn't sound very cheerful, did it?' Lily was working out a way of telling Harry that she would like it better if just the two of them went out without making it sound too forward.

'Greta Garbo in *Mata Hari* then?' he ventured.

Lily shook her head. 'Doesn't she end up facing a firing squad?'

He laughed at the squeamish face she pulled and resisted the urge to lift her off her feet and swing her round under the gas lamp on the foggy December street. 'You think about what you want to do. I'll be happy with anything, just so long as you agree to consider me as your young man.'

'Oh.' She smiled, surprised and excited all at once. 'You mean . . . ?'

'I do,' he confirmed. 'You're my sweetheart, Lily, and from now on I'd like to be more than the boy next door – for as long as you'll have me.'

CHAPTER FIFTEEN

Lily had been so happy at work just thinking of the words Harry had said that she hadn't been able to stop smiling all day. Of course, Annie was the one to winkle the secret out of her at dinner then broadcast it far and wide.

'Lily's admitted it – she's fallen head over heels in love!' she told Maureen and Florence at the next table. 'With Harry Bainbridge, and about time too!'

'Oh, Lily!' Evie gasped from the bench opposite. Her expression made it plain that, despite weeks of teasing from Sybil and Annie, the idea of Lily and Harry really falling in love had never seriously crossed her mind. Within seconds, however, she had the pair of them walking up the aisle with herself and Peggy as bridesmaids in shell-pink satin dresses with corsages of white carnations.

'Good for you, Lil,' Sybil said, grasping Lily's hand. 'At this rate you'll beat us all to it. You'll be happily married with babies at your feet and we'll still be toiling away at the looms.'

'Steady on – Harry and me have only been out to the pictures together once,' Lily reminded them, her face aflame but not really minding their well-intentioned fun.

'But you've lived on the next street since you were babes in arms,' was Annie's reaction. 'How much more do you need to know about him?'

'Yes,' Sybil agreed. 'Harry may come across as too big for his boots now and then but he really doesn't have a bad bone in his body. He's just right for you.'

Later, as Sybil and Lily strolled home together, Sybil was happy to let Lily talk to her heart's content about her new suitor.

'He's asked me to walk out with him again tomorrow night,' Lily confessed. 'I'm to choose where we go. What do you think – shall it be the Assembly Rooms or the pictures?'

'Let him take you dancing,' was Sybil's advice. 'Wear your best bib and tucker and I'll lend you my silk stockings. Harry will be putty in your hands.'

'I don't know about that.' Lily sighed. Somehow she didn't see herself as a femme fatale. 'Anyway, will you and Annie be there?'

'Not Annie. She's meeting Robert up at Cliff Street market. They're catching a tram and heading off to the new Pavilion in Hadley, his treat.'

'Poor Sybil,' Lily commiserated. 'We're leaving you all on your ownio!'

'Don't you be too sure.' Sybil nudged her arm and

winked. 'How do you know I haven't got my very own beau lined up?'

'Not the commercial traveller?' Lily enquired, remembering the mysterious older man with whom Sybil had danced a few weeks before.

'No, not him. I haven't seen hide nor hair of him since. But speak of the devil – here comes my new Prince Charming now!'

Leaving the crush of homebound mill workers to head on up Albion Lane, it was easy for Sybil and Lily to spot Billy whizzing down the hill on his bike, though at first Lily didn't recognize him muffled up behind a thick scarf, with his cap pulled down. He arrived ringing his bell and squealing to a halt beside them.

'Hello, girls!' he sang out, staying astride his bike and planting his feet firmly on the cobbles. 'Seeing you two bobby dazzlers brightens up my day, I must say.'

'I bet you tell that to all the girls,' Sybil countered, while Lily tried to hide her confusion. Had she got this right? Had Sybil really said that Billy was taking her out tomorrow night?

'Oh, and it helps that we only have four and a half more hours of drudgery tomorrow morning before they set us free from our chains, eh, Lily?'

Lily nodded and out of consideration for Sybil's feelings she swallowed back her questions about Billy and Margie. She waited until Sybil had waved goodbye and disappeared down the alley on to Raglan

189

Road before she tackled the awkward topic. But it was Billy who jumped in before Lily had the chance.

'I've been meaning to ask you something,' he told her, swinging his long leg over the crossbar and propping his bike against the wall. 'Will you pass a message to your Margie? Tell her not to expect me outside the Victory tomorrow after all.'

'Yes, I can see that you'll be busy doing something else,' Lily said with a frown. She was trying to sort out in her own mind who was most in the wrong – Billy for breaking a promise to take Margie out or Margie for not being truthful with him about her present condition.

'Don't be like that,' he protested. 'It wasn't a proper arrangement between me and Margie, not really.'

'But Billy, this is the second time you've stood her up that I know of. How do you think she'll feel?'

He had the good grace to shuffle his feet and try to explain. 'All right, I admit I was feeling bad about letting her down before and that's why I went up to see her on Ada Street – to say I was sorry.'

'And why did you let her down in the first place?' Lily wanted to know, pushing for more information than she normally would. 'She got all dressed up and took the tram to meet you and what did you do? You sent Dorothy to tell her that you weren't coming after all.'

'I know. I took the coward's way out,' he admitted. 'But I paid for it by having Dorothy hot on my trail all the rest of that night and for days afterwards. She was like a dog with a bone.'

'Poor you, Billy.' Lily looked him in the eye as she delivered the sarcastic comment. 'But you'd better get used to girls fighting over you, the way you carry on.'

'I expect I deserved that,' he said quietly. 'But I did tell Margie I was sorry and I did take her to the pictures to make up for it.'

Yes, you took her to the pictures and led her to believe you would treat her better from then on, Lily thought gloomily, but now you've let her down all over again. 'I'm sorry, Billy,' she told him, 'but I won't pass on the message. You'll have to tell Margie yourself.'

Her answer made him turn away sharply. He looked as though he was about to cycle away but then changed his mind and looked straight at Lily. 'You know the trouble with your Margie?' he said angrily. 'She's the sort of girl who doesn't go in for half measures. No, not her – she just throws herself at a fellow.'

'Billy!' Lily interrupted. 'I don't want to listen to this.'

'You might not want to hear it, Lil, because you're different. You're a nice girl, you don't chuck yourself at a bloke the way Margie does.'

'Billy, she's sixteen!'

'I know. You don't need to tell me that. But some-one should have taught her by this time how to behave. You can't have her dolling herself up and coming on strong the way she does, not without something bad happening.'

Lily let out a deflated sigh and gave a single, defeated nod.

'She did it to me again last Saturday, after we took the tram back to Ada Street. We got off at the stop and you know the gates into Linton Park? Well, Margie stopped there and wanted me to take her into the park and it was freezing and pitch black and there wasn't a soul around. So I said no I would take her straight back to her granddad's house, and that's when she did it – she chucked herself right at me.'

'Billy, stop – don't tell me any more.' At that moment Lily could have cried for her sister and her desperate state of mind.

'Anyway, that's why I'm not taking her out again, even though she's written me a letter, all cheerful and saying how much she was looking forward to meeting up again this Saturday.'

'She wrote you a letter?' Lily said faintly. Poor Margie, stranded up at Overcliffe with Granddad Preston and making more of a mess of things with each day that passed.

'It put me into a right stew,' Billy confessed. 'I did feel sorry for her for a day or two and I thought, Why not take the poor girl to the pictures again – what's the harm? But then I decided no, on the whole it's best not to have any more to do with Margie Briggs.

And now I've told you and got it off my chest I don't think there's any more to be said.'

'No, you go out and enjoy yourself with Sybil instead,' Lily said, thinking him callow and resisting the urge to give him a sharp slap on the cheek.

Billy winced then jutted out his chin. 'It's for the best,' he insisted.

'Best for who, Billy?'

'For everyone,' he concluded, leaving Lily standing on the street, picking over the ins and outs of what Billy had said and working out with a sinking heart the bleak future that surely lay ahead for her headstrong, misguided sister.

CHAPTER SIXTEEN

'Arthur has collared me to make Christmas decorations with him when I get home,' Evie told Lily as they clocked off from the morning shift next day. 'I promised I'd buy some gummed paper in Newby's. We'll cut it into strips and make a chain of coloured hoops to string across the front window.'

'That's nice, ' Lily answered absent-mindedly. The busy morning in the mending room had kept her mind off the ever-present Margie problem but now as she and Evie walked home along the icy pavement she had to make up her mind whether or not to deliver Billy's message after all. She shared her dilemma with her youngest sister as they stopped for traffic and stood well back from the hooting, chugging Austins and Jowetts that threaded their way through the crowds.

'Make sure Margie doesn't take it out on you if you do go up to Ada Street,' Evie warned. 'Tell her it's not your fault – it's Billy's.'

'Ah, but it'll be a case of shooting the messenger,'

Lily predicted. 'It usually is with Margie.'

There was more riding on Billy's change of heart than Evie knew, of course. In any event, by the time Evie had slipped into the newsagent's for the brightly coloured gummed paper, Lily had decided to carry on past number 5 to catch a tram to Overcliffe. After all was said and done, it wouldn't do to have Margie turning out on this cold night and catching the tram into town, only to find herself stood up once again by Billy Robertshaw.

She didn't relish the task and was pushed further down in the dumps by having to wait longer than usual for the tram on one of those grey days that scarcely gets light, standing in a bracing wind and trying not to mind the cold. Shivering at the stop for ten minutes, she eventually turned her back against the wind and stared down Albion Lane in time to see her mother struggling up the hill towards her.

Startled, Lily ran to meet her. 'Mother, what are you doing out of the house?' she demanded, almost afraid that the wind would knock her over.

'What's it look like?' Rhoda trudged on up the hill. 'I'm heading for the stop to catch the next tram out to Overcliffe.'

'To see Margie?' The news came to Lily as a bolt out of the blue. 'Are you sure you want to?'

'Yes, and why not?' Rhoda demanded. 'Margie's still my flesh and blood, isn't she?'

'But, Mother, are you sure you're well enough?'

'It's high time me and Margie had a talk,' Rhoda

said with an air of defiance strongly reminiscent of Margie at her most stubborn. 'If I know her, Saturday afternoon will be a good time to catch her in. She'll be washing her hair and primping and preening ready for a night out.'

Lily was still trying to get over the shock of seeing Rhoda make her laborious way up the hill, her face pinched and exhausted, her figure as small and slight as a child's, but she nodded and said that they should go to Granddad Preston's house together. 'I have to pass on a message from Billy to Margie,' she explained.

For a moment Rhoda knitted her brows and clung to her argumentative air. 'Very well then, you can ride on the tram with me but when you get to your granddad's house, you have to let me talk to Margie on my own.'

'If that's what you want.' As a tram hove into view, Lily reluctantly abandoned her planned role as mediator and decided to let her mother and sister argue things out.

With a grind of brakes the tram jolted to a halt and the two women climbed on, Lily paying the fare for both of them and allowing Rhoda a seat near to the window where she sat without speaking, staring out across the moor. Fellow passengers who bothered to give the pair a second glance would have noted a small, upright woman with a heavy grey shawl crossed tightly over her chest, wearing a brown felt hat held in place by a feathered hatpin sitting next to a striking but nervous younger woman in smart grey velour hat and coat, possibly her daughter though the softness of her face and fullness of her lips plus the strands of dark, wavy hair escaping from under the hat of the latter disguised the family resemblance. Look more closely, though, and it was there in the brown eyes and the shared mannerisms – the upward tilt of the chin and the crossing of the hands on the lap, the polite 'excuse me' and 'thank you' as they rose from their seats and made their way down the crowded aisle to alight at their stop beside the entrance to Linton Park.

'Let's get this over and done with, shall we?' Rhoda said through clenched teeth, crossing the road and heading on down Ada Street to her childhood home.

What memories it must hold. Lily thought back to the days when the young Rhoda had lived here with her three brothers – this house on the hill with its back turned to the soot and the smoke of the town, overlooking crags and hills, buffeted by wind and rain. Back then, at the turn of the century, there had been sunny gala days with processions and brass bands, jubilee celebrations and Empire Days with red, white and blue bunting strung across the smartly kept street. She'd seen faded photos of these events – the women standing at trestle tables in long skirts and big-sleeved white blouses, their hair pinned high on their heads, the men in shirt-sleeves and waistcoats, some in bowler hats, leading

197

carthorses bedecked with brasses and ribbons or perched on the seats of monstrous traction engines that puffed and trundled along the cobbled streets.

Those were the days, people said – more prosperous, more hopeful, before the Great War had cast its long shadow and the Depression had set in, when Rhoda's little family had lived happily here on the hill.

Rhoda's stride was slow but purposeful over the short distance from the tram stop to her father's house. There was no hesitation as she climbed the stone steps and lifted the door knocker. Lily's heart raced. She hoped against all the odds that there wouldn't be conflict, that what had to be said between her mother and Margie would take place reasonably and harmony would result.

Bert Preston showed no surprise as he opened the door and let Rhoda and Lily into the house. 'You took your time.' The old man's hoarse comment was directed at Rhoda. He stared hard at her through narrowed eyes, bushy eyebrows knotted, then let the visitors walk ahead of him down the narrow passage, past the unfrequented front living room with its black horsehair sofa and grey marble fireplace and on into the back kitchen. It was much like the kitchen at Albion Lane, with its cooking range and rough deal table but minus the womanly touches of lace curtains and china ornaments and without the precious treadle sewing machine in the corner that Lily set such store by.

Rhoda cast an eye around the sparsely furnished room. 'I've come to see Margie. Is she in?'

'She's upstairs. She'll have heard you arrive.' If Bert had an opinion about this delayed visit, he kept it to himself, merely filling the iron kettle at the tap and setting it on the hob. 'Shall I bring her down?'

'No.' Rhoda spoke in her usual decisive way. 'I'll make my way up.'

'Please yourself.' He shrugged and pulled out a chair for Lily. 'We'll let them lock horns, shall we? Then we'll be here to pick up the pieces afterwards.'

From the back bedroom Margie heard her mother's voice then her steps on the uncarpeted stairs and steeled herself for what was to come. Best get this over and done with, she thought in a curious, un-spoken echo of Rhoda's own words. She turned from the window to face her mother as the knob turned, the door opened and Rhoda came in.

'Mother!' Margie couldn't help herself – the word fell from her lips as she took in the frail yet deter-mined figure who seemed to have shrunk almost to nothing in the few days since she'd last clapped eyes on her.

Rhoda breathed hard after the effort of climbing the stairs but she stood straight and came up close, looking Margie up and down. 'This is a fine mess,' she said, leaving no room for doubt. The stare let Margie know that Rhoda was aware of the state of play and that was all there was to it.

'I told Lily not to say anything!' Margie cried petulantly, turning away. 'She promised me she wouldn't!'

'And she didn't,' Rhoda contradicted. 'I can draw my own conclusions as well as anyone, can't I? And I've seen it all before. How many weeks are you gone?'

'I don't know. Seven or eight.' Her mother's piercing gaze threw Margie off balance and she was filled with dread, but she did her best to affect a carelessness. 'And don't bother to ask me about the father. Lily already tried that and I'm not telling.'

I'm telling on you! The childish phrase popped into Rhoda's head and reminded her of how young Margie still was. *I'm telling Mother on you, just you wait!* The angry little voice echoed down the years. Rhoda shook her head and sighed. 'Yes and I don't want to know, not right now. I only want to find out what you're going to do about it. Are you going to go ahead and have this baby, or not?'

And here was another shock for Margie – the word 'baby'. Not 'it', but 'baby', spoken by her mother whose job it was to help infants into this world. A baby was on its way, growing inside her, making demands on her body, getting ready to be born. With a heavy sigh Margie slumped down on the bed and let her head hang low.

'Well?' Rhoda demanded in a relentless tone, without for a moment taking her eyes off her middle daughter. Where was Margie's blithe confidence now? Where was the devil-may-care spirit that had brought mother and daughter into so many conflicts, ever since Margie was old enough to walk, talk and stamp her tiny feet? 'Don't go crying and bemoaning your lot,' Rhoda warned. 'Tears don't wash with me, Margie, and you know it.'

Pulling herself upright, Margie took a deep breath. 'I suppose I am – going to have the baby, I mean.'

Rhoda gave an imperceptible nod and seemed to brace herself for further discussion. 'And have you told anyone else besides Lily – your granddad, for a start? Because if you haven't, he's the next person you should talk to.'

Margie closed her eyes and gripped the edge of the bed, feeling her head swim. 'I'll tell him when I'm good and ready,' she argued.

'No, it has to be today, before I leave. That's only fair.'

Margie's shoulders slumped again with the weight of what she had to do. 'And if I don't tell him, you will?'

'He's giving you a roof over your head, isn't he? He deserves to know.'

'All right, Mother, don't go on.' An exasperated Margie admitted defeat. 'I'll tell Granddad everything then it'll be his turn to put me out on the street, just like Father.'

Rhoda winced then walked across the room to stare out of the window. 'Don't go blaming your father,' she warned. 'It was you who got yourself into this mess, Margie Briggs, no one else.'

Now Margie's desperation surfaced as anger. She stood up and paced the floor. 'And don't I know it! Yes, it was me and yes, I'm paying the price with no one to help me. It's no more than I expected after Father turned me out!'

'Who says there's no one to help you?' Rhoda asked in a softer tone, her gaze fixed on the yard below. 'Why am I here now, pray tell?'

Margie stopped pacing and came to the window. 'To help me?' she asked in a faltering voice, her eyes wide and brimming with tears.

'That goes without saying,' her mother murmured, for once letting go of all judgement and taking her daughter by the hand. 'As long as I'm spared, Margie, I'll be here when the time comes and that's a promise.'

'She doesn't look well,' Bert commented as he closed the kitchen door on Rhoda.

'Who – Mother?' Lily knew who he meant but she played for time until she was sure that Margie hadn't blown her top the second their mother had entered the bedroom.

'Yes. Has she seen the doctor?'

'No, she says she doesn't need to and anyway she hasn't the money.'

'What's been the matter with her?' Taking four cups from a cupboard over the sink, Bert set them out on the table and waited for the kettle to boil.

'She was poorly last weekend – sickness and a

headache. This is her first time out of the house.'

'She chose a rotten day for it.' Bert glanced out of the window at a heavy rain that had started to fall. 'This lot could turn to snow in a bit.'

'I'll see she gets home all right,' Lily promised, settling down now that she'd had time to ascertain that the voices from upstairs hadn't turned to screaming and shouting, not yet at least. 'How are you, Granddad? How are you and Margie rubbing along?'

Hovering by the kettle, the old man sniffed. 'I stay out of the road mostly. Margie does what she likes.'

'And you don't mind her staying here?'

'No, I like a bit of company every now and then, especially at teatime before I head off to the New Inn for my usual pint.' Listening to the noises from upstairs, Bert lowered his voice. 'I hope your mother goes easy on the poor girl. She can be a bit harsh at times, can Rhoda.' Sensing a hidden knowledge behind her grandfather's words, Lily sat up with a jolt but said nothing.

'What's up – has the cat got your tongue?' Bert's gap-toothed smile had the effect of further silencing Lily. 'You're sitting there wondering if I know the truth behind why Margie hot-footed it up here to stay with me and yet you don't want to say something you shouldn't.'

'Granddad, I—'

'Well, love, I'll put you out of your misery. It's plain as the nose on my face that Margie's scared to go back home because she's in the family way. I'm right, aren't I?'

Lily felt a blaze of embarrassment burn up from deep inside and turn her cheeks bright red, quickly followed by a strong desire to defend Margie. 'Don't blame her, Granddad. Margie was too young to know what she was doing. She might not let on, but she's having a hard time coming to terms with this.'

'I can see that,' the old man mumbled as he reached for a thick cloth to protect his hand as he lifted the steaming kettle from the hob. 'And I'm thinking that Rhoda arriving on the doorstep isn't going to help.'

Lily glanced at the ceiling as she heard Margie's quick, light steps pacing the floorboards. 'I don't know about that – we'll have to wait and see.' She sighed, crossing her fingers as her mother spoke and Margie replied.

'You can stop feeling sorry for yourself,' Rhoda told Margie, sitting beside her on the hard mattress in Bert's spare room. 'You're not the first and you won't be the last that this has happened to.'

Margie's throat constricted as she sniffed back the tears that threatened to engulf her. 'But how can I help how I feel? This . . . well, it alters everything for me, doesn't it?'

Rhoda didn't deny it. 'A baby takes a lot of look- ing after,' she agreed. 'You might not be ready and if not there's plenty of people who would be willing to step in.'

'You mean, give it away to a stranger?' Instinctively Margie shook her head and placed one arm across her stomach. She'd only just acknowledged that this was a real baby she was carrying so she was far from being ready to consider giving it up. In fact, the idea made her almost yelp with painful protest.

'It could be for the best.' Long experience told Rhoda that life as a young girl struggling to bring up a baby alone might be more than Margie could manage. 'Where would you live, for a start? What would you use for money?'

'I know, I know,' Margie bleated, her heart thudding in her chest as she battled with the reality of what was happening.

'In any case, the main thing is to go down and tell your granddad, see if he'll let you stay on here for a bit.'

Margie nodded. 'Give me a minute to pull myself together, will you?'

Sitting beside her tearful daughter, Rhoda's thoughts flew back to those early days when Margie woke at the crack of dawn and rattled the bars of her cot, yelling to be let out. Her baby hair had been gloriously dark and curly, her round face pretty as a picture. And it had been four-year-old Lily who'd kept the baby happy by sewing simple clothes for little wooden dolls and later playing with a bat and ball in the street, until Margie had joined up with a gang of boys and gone off to muck about all summer's day long on the Common and there'd been neither sight nor sound of her until she'd shown up at teatime, her legs muddy and grazed, her face ruddy and the smell of fresh air clinging to her hair.

'It's funny,' Rhoda recalled, 'I was by myself when you were born because your father was away at the war. It wasn't so very different after all.'

'But you knew Father was coming back,' Margie reminded her, intrigued in spite of her own weighty preoccupations.

'No, I never knew for certain. So many men didn't come home,' Rhoda said quietly. 'My brothers went away to the trenches and I never saw them again, not one of them. In that case, women were left to deal with things by themselves and by and large we got on all right.' There was a silence as each pondered their own thoughts. 'It was an odd time, though. Enlisted men lived life as if every day was their last. They got engaged in a big rush before they went off to France, and some girls didn't even wait for a ring on their finger. No one thought the worse of them for that.'

The notion that this was a familiar situation to Rhoda and that it was not so shocking after all sank in and Margie risked a faint, brave smile.

'We'll manage between us, you'll see,' Rhoda insisted. 'Lily will always be ready to offer a hand and so will Evie. But you mustn't expect your father to come round to the idea straight away. It'll take a bit more time for him to get used to it.' There was another pause and a loud sigh. 'I'm partly to blame, I know. I shouldn't have left you to yourself so much. I should've kept a closer eye, only I hoped I'd brought you up right and you'd turn out sensible like your sisters. And you might have done if this hadn't happened.'

'Mother . . .' Margie began a sentence but couldn't finish it, stung by the comparison with Lily and Evie.

'You never were like them, though.' Sighing again, Rhoda stood up from the bed. 'Now if you had half of Lily's common sense and she had a little more of your get up and go—'

'Mother!' Margie said a second time. 'You'd know that Lily has plenty of get up and go as you call it if you could see her at work or tripping the light fantastic down the Assembly Rooms with Sybil and Annie. It's just that at home you put too much on her shoulders.'

'Yes, I do – I take her for granted,' Rhoda acknowledged, pulling her shawl tight across her chest and heading for the door. 'Are you ready to face the music, Margie? Shall we go down and see what your granddad has to say?'

'Well,' Bert said when Margie had blurted out her news. Nothing else – just one terse word and a nod of his head in confirmation of what he'd already guessed.

Margie's heart was in her mouth. Why it was so

much harder and more painful to risk losing her grandfather's good opinion than it had been with Lily or her mother she couldn't work out. She only knew that the undemonstrative old man's disappointment in her would cut her to the quick.

'She says she'll go ahead and have the baby,' Rhoda told Lily and Bert.

'Aye, poor lass, that's what I expected to hear.' Bert stood with his back to the kitchen window, his work-worn face lit by a glow from the fire.

'You're not cross with me, Granddad?' Margie struggled against a fresh bout of crying, picking up and clinging to the two words of sympathy in his short, non-committal sentence.

'Of course he's not cross.' Relieved at the turn of events, Lily jumped in. 'No one's angry with you, Margie. Just the opposite – we all want to do our best to help.'

'Let me speak for myself,' Bert chided, thrusting his clenched fists deep in his trouser pockets. 'It's not you I'm down on, Margie. It's the devil who took advantage of you – that's who I'd like to get my hands on.'

'Aye and she's not saying anything on that score.' Rhoda settled herself on a chair at the table, inviting Margie and Lily to do the same. 'I think, Lily, you have an idea of your own about that, though.'

Alarmed, Lily threw Margie a quick glance, which was returned by a glare of defiance. 'What makes you say that?' she asked her mother.

'Because you do,' Rhoda insisted. 'And if Margie's too pig headed to tell us, you'd better do it for her.'

'Honestly, Margie hasn't said a word to me. I'd only be guessing if I gave you a name, and that wouldn't be fair, would it?'

'A guess would do for a start,' her granddad countered, coming to sit at the table. 'If it turns out you're wrong, Margie can set us straight.'

'I'm not going to say anything!' Margie herself assured them. They could do and say what they liked, she wasn't about to give them the name of the father. She didn't see clearly the reason why not, but the fact was, with everything else in her life unravelling and out of control, this was the one thing she could keep back and decide what to do about at a later date.

Bert, though, wouldn't let it drop. Yes, he was secretly disappointed in his granddaughter, and yes, he foresaw big problems ahead for her, but for now he fixed his attention on the one thing that Margie wasn't prepared to share with them. 'The way I see it, the father, whoever he is, needs a good hiding for getting you into trouble. Who is it, Margie? Is it one of the lads in your neck of the woods?'

Like a child brought up before the headmaster in school and facing six of the best, Margie pursed her lips and stared at her hands, which she held tightly clasped and resting on the table, allowing Lily, Rhoda and Bert to run through a few names in their own minds – Ernie Durant, Billy Robertshaw, the dreaded Frank Summerskill, or perhaps someone at Kingsley's, such as the overseer, Sam Earby, or one of the workers under him in the spinning shed.

After a long, tense silence, Rhoda turned to her eldest daughter. 'So, who do you say it is, Lily?'

Lily wriggled on the hook of her mother and grandfather's piercing stares but she stayed loyal to Margie. 'It's not my place,' she insisted. 'Margie will tell us when she's good and ready. In the meantime, I say we all rally round and help her get ready for this baby to be born.'

Margie drew a sharp breath and gave Lily a grateful glance. 'Anyway, Granddad, I don't want you getting into trouble on my account. I'll fight my own battles if I have to, thank you very much.'

Touched by her bravado, the old man coughed to clear his throat then stood up and busied himself by picking up the coal bucket and throwing more lumps on the fire. 'Well, the first thing we have to get straight, Margie Briggs, is that you stay put here in Ada Street. There's no need to think of shifting back to Albion Lane, not while your father carries on the way he is. Anyway, your mother's not well – she needs her rest, not to be worrying over you.'

Rhoda didn't argue with this, Lily and Margie noticed. In fact, she nodded and seemed happy to let her father make plans for Margie.

'Lily, you can do some shopping for Margie every now and then,' Bert decided. 'I'll give you the money. She'll need good food to build her up – meat and potatoes, plenty of eggs, milk, that sort of thing.'

'I'm not poorly, I can go to Cliff Street and do my own shopping,' Margie protested.

'But later on Lily can do it,' he insisted with a meaningful look at Rhoda.

'And you're not hiding me away either,' Margie was adamant. Her grandfather sighed and drew her mother out into the front room to talk in more detail about the money and other necessities for Margie's upkeep. 'By the way, it isn't Billy,' Margie confided in her sister. 'I know that's what you were thinking but you're wrong.'

'All right, I'll cross him off the list,' Lily conceded. 'I've always had a soft spot for Billy so I'm glad that he's out of the picture, even if it leaves the mystery unsolved.' Mention of his name brought to mind the message she had to pass on. 'By the way, he's not going to be there tonight – he asked me to tell you.'

If Margie was upset, she didn't let it show. Instead, she took it on the chin. 'That Billy, you never can believe a word he says!'

'It's probably for the best, if what you say is true – about him not being involved.'

'The thing is, I've been doing my best to make him think he was,' Margie confessed with an air of having nothing left to lose.

Lily's eyebrows shot up. 'Could he have been?' she demanded. 'I mean, could Billy have . . . ?'

'Like I said, I was doing my best to turn it into a possibility.'

'Oh, Margie!' Lily thought back to her embarrassing talk with Billy about Margie's behaviour outside Linton Park gates. 'That was wrong of you. You were jumping straight out of the frying pan into the fire if that was your plan.'

Pressing her lips together, Margie nodded. 'But I thought if he liked me, we could maybe make a go of it, Billy and me.'

'Not by tricking him. Anyway, he'd have worked it out for himself eventually.'

'Not if I waited and told him the baby had come a few weeks early. That happens, you know.'

'Margie,' Lily groaned.

'Don't "Margie" me like that, Lily. You don't know what you'd try if you were in my position. And if Dorothy Brumfitt hadn't jumped in and stolen Billy from under my nose, it could have worked out just fine.'

'Well, she did and it didn't.' Lily set the seal on that situation. She knew they only had a few minutes left before their mother and grandfather would return. 'You still have time to tell me who the real father is,' she whispered.

'No, but what I will say, between you and me and these four walls, is that none of this was really my doing.' Still at the table, sitting opposite each other, Margie waited nervously for Lily's reaction.

'So someone took advantage of you?' Lily gasped. 'When? Where was this?'

Margie shook her head as if trying to rid herself

of the memory of what had happened. 'You won't squeeze a lot more out of me, but I want you to know this much – this person, the man responsible – he'd invited me into town to the City Varieties and afterwards he took me to the pub next door and he bought me a sherry or two – enough to make me giddy. And after that, that's when it happened.'

'Where?' Lily repeated as Margie drew to a faltering conclusion.

Margie shuddered, and when she spoke again her voice was hesitant and her eyes brimming with tears. 'It doesn't matter where. All I'm saying is, it came out of the blue. I wasn't ready for him and it was all over almost before I knew it was happening.' Her face pale and stricken at the memory and her hands trembling on the plain pine table, Margie had reached the end of her confession, leaving no time for Lily to say anything before Bert and Rhoda came back into the room. Rhoda was obviously ready to depart.

'We've decided that I'll be the one to tell your father and Evie,' she announced to Margie who tried in vain to dry her tears. 'It'll be best to keep Arthur in the dark for now, though.'

'But, Lily, we'd be happy for you to drop by with the young'un whenever you feel like it,' Bert added. 'My door's always open – you know that.'

Nodding, Lily reached out, took Margie's hands and held them tight. 'Tomorrow afternoon,' she promised. 'I'll bring Arthur up to see you. I'll bake a cake in the morning and we'll bring it with us. Victoria sponge – you always like a slice of that.'

Margie smiled through her tears.

'We'll love you and leave you,' Rhoda said, turning for the door. 'Goodbye, Father. Goodbye, Margie. Come along, Lily, we've got a tram to catch.'

CHAPTER SEVENTEEN

It was a thoughtful Lily who got ready to go out dancing with Harry that night. She hardly concentrated on what to wear, taking a dress that was three years old from the hook on the back of the bedroom door – a navy blue one in heavy crêpe de Chine that was shorter and straighter than the styles that were currently in fashion and rather young for her now, Lily thought as she glanced in the small mirror over Margie's bed. 'It needs a new lace trim around the neck and cuffs to bring it up to date,' she said to herself, putting on Sybil's silk stockings and her own black leather shoes then treading carefully over the floorboards so as not to disturb her mother who had taken to her bed as soon as she returned home after the expedition to Ada Street. Lily took her coat and hat from the bed and was halfway down the stairs when Evie flew up to meet her.

'Harry's here!' she cried in a hoarse, excited whisper.

Lily paused, took a deep breath, then carried on

along the landing and down into the kitchen where Harry stood on the fireside rug chatting to Arthur and smiling broadly. 'What's it to be?' he asked her when she came into the room, which was already decorated with the chains of coloured paper made earlier in the day. 'The flicks or dancing?'

'Let's head off to the Assembly Rooms,' she said, feeling shy in front of their audience even though it was only Arthur and Evie. 'Arthur, you've to go to bed when Evie tells you. And tomorrow, if you're a good boy, I'll help you to write your letter to Father Christmas in the morning then in the afternoon I'll take you to Granddad Preston's house to see Margie.'

Arthur couldn't have been happier with the plan and with Evie explaining to him that tomorrow would come all the sooner if he went to sleep nice and early, Lily and Harry closed the front door on the contented scene.

Outside, Lily was surprised to find that her grandfather's prediction about the rain turning to snow had come true. She frowned at the thought of what the covering of white on the pavements would do to her best shoes and quickly accepted Harry's arm as he led her down the steps.

'Uh-oh, you'll ruin those shoes if you're not careful. Why don't I give you a piggyback ride?' he suggested with a pantomime wink.

'Some other time,' she responded with a playful shove that sent him slipping and sliding across the pavement, almost taking her with him.

'Anyway, it won't be more than an inch or two of snow,' he promised her, 'not enough to spoil our evening.'

Still, it meant that the trams were delayed and they stood arm in arm at the stop waiting with three or four other couples for a full fifteen minutes before one came into sight. Then, just before it did appear, who should join the queue but Sybil and Billy, both in high spirits and ready to tease Lily and Harry for stepping out together a second time.

'Brrr, it's freezing!' Sybil sang out from the back of the queue. 'Harry, why not put your arm around Lily and keep her warm? Or better still, be a gentleman and let her borrow your coat. A little bird tells me that's what you do.'

'Sybil Dacre, that's the last time I let you into my secrets!' Lily cried with a self-conscious grimace at Harry who put an arm around her shoulder and pulled her close. A glance at Billy had told her that he was feeling uncomfortable and rightly so, given that he'd unceremoniously ditched Margie by carrier pigeon, as it were.

Inside the crowded tram, Lily and Sybil found seats opposite Maureen and Flora while Harry and Billy hovered on the open platform at the back. Flora spent the short journey asking Lily searching questions about Margie's stay on Ada Street, which Lily fended off until Maureen jumped in with a question for her about the finer points involved in making a machine-sewn buttonhole, with Sybil putting in her halfpennyworth and so the talk went on until they'd travelled the mile and a half along Cliff Street to the Assembly Rooms where most of the younger passengers disembarked.

Harry, who had hopped off promptly, waited for Lily and offered her his hand. 'See, the snow's easing off,' he commented, looking up at a starlit sky.

'Harry Bainbridge, promise me one thing,' she said with a laugh.

'Anything, your majesty,' he vowed. 'What is it?'

'If you really are to be my sweetheart, and I hope you are, you've got to promise me that you'll never mention the weather – never, ever again!'

'Done!' Harry laughed. 'Or who's playing centre forward for the Rovers. But on one condition.'

'And what's that, Harry?' she asked, tilting her head and looking sideways at him as if butter wouldn't melt. She held tight to his arm as they crossed the snowy street.

'That you promise I can stick to the waltz and you'll never try to teach me to do the foxtrot or the quickstep.'

'Done!' she agreed.

Then they skipped up the steps of the Assembly Rooms into the light and warmth of the entrance, where strains of band music drifted through from the dance hall.

'I like this tune,' Lily murmured into Harry's ear.

They'd danced non-stop for an hour or more and

the band had struck up after an interval with their version of 'Dancing in the Dark', a slow waltz whose melancholy words drifted into her head as Harry took her hand and led her back on to the dance floor.

The song lyrics spoke of a couple dancing at night until the tune ended, of waltzing and wondering why time hurried by until all too soon they were dancing together no more.

She shook her head clear of the sad lyrics and enjoyed the sensation of being whirled around in Harry's strong arms, her eyes half closed and her head spinning.

'I'm not holding you too tight, am I?' he whispered, his head bent and his cheek resting against the top of her head.

'No, I like it,' she replied. The feel of his hand in the small of her back drawing their warm bodies close together, his sinewy strength beneath the dark blue blazer.

'That's all right then,' he said. And he drew her closer still.

But the tune ended too soon and the band livened things up with a quickstep, which left Harry floundering and apologizing to Lily as usual for having two left feet.

'Never mind, I'll stick to my side of the bargain and let you sit this one out,' she said and grinned, waving at Sybil who was having a high old time teaching Billy the basic steps and rhythms off to one side of the floor, giggling at his mistakes and insisting that he take his lead from her.

'Poor bugger,' Harry commiserated as they walked through the grand entrance hall for a breath of fresh air. 'I'm glad you don't press gang me like that, Lil. I always thought Sybil had a bit of the sergeant major about her.'

'Anyway, Billy deserves to be made to feel hot under the collar.'

'Why, what's he done now?'

'He's only stood Margie up and taken up with Sybil instead.'

Harry considered the information. 'Margie's a bit young for Billy, don't you think? There's something not quite right there.'

'Why, has he said something to you?' she asked quickly, fearing that Billy might have blabbed to Harry about the episode outside the park gates.

But Harry shook his head. 'I'm just saying – she's a bit young. How's she doing up at your granddad's by the way?'

'Tickety-boo,' Lily said unconvincingly then steered the talk away from Margie. 'I was chatting with Maureen on the tram and she asked me to make her bridesmaid's dress for her sister's wedding. That's on top of promising to sew a summer dress for Elsie at work as soon as we get Christmas over and done with. At this rate, I don't know how I shall find the time.'

'You will,' Harry assured her. 'That's one of the

220

things I like about you, Lily Briggs – you always find time for other people.'

'Do I?' she wondered.

'For young Arthur for a start. That little lad really loves you and I don't blame him.' It was a bold statement and Harry held his breath as his words settled.

'Well yes, I'd do anything for Arthur,' Lily agreed, giving way to a shiver and awkwardly side-stepping the second half of Harry's sentence.

Harry put his arm around her shoulder. 'Did you hear me? I said I don't blame him for loving his big sister the way he does. What little lad could help clinging on to every soft word and loving look from you, Lil?'

'You don't know the half of it,' she warned. 'Have you seen Arthur when I try to get him to go to bed early? He's not so keen on me then.'

The word 'bed' sprang out at Harry and he instantly tried to shake off the tempting but unworthy image that flashed into his mind. He was a bad lad, he told himself, thinking of Lily in that way, but the idea of him and Lily in bed together wasn't easily got rid of. 'Are you ready to go back inside?' he asked.

She shook her head. 'Why don't I fetch my coat and we can take our time walking home?'

'You don't want to dance any more?'

'No, I'd rather walk.' Was this a step too far? she wondered. Would Harry think her forward for suggesting a long, romantic stroll in the dark?

His answer came in a ready smile and an eagerness

to take her cloakroom ticket from her to retrieve her coat and hat. Before long they were walking hand in hand along an almost deserted Overcliffe Road.

They talked about this and that and matched each other stride for stride. They slid and skidded on the snowy pavements, laughed and steadied each other, stopped to kiss by a lamp post, the cold of their lips sending more icy shivers down Lily's spine. They didn't notice trams trundling by and though the dark moor to their left seemed empty and endless, they were happy in their own little world. Eventually they came to the lighted shop window of Pennington's and Harry walked Lily down Raglan Road through the alleyway on to Albion Lane.

When they emerged, they found Walter Briggs standing on the top step of number 5, staring up the hill towards the Common so that at first he didn't notice Harry and Lily. He was so still and pre-occupied that he seemed made of stone.

'Father's back early,' Lily murmured, moving out of Harry's reach and quickening her pace. Walter must have heard her because he turned to look, his face in shadow, only illuminated by the small glow from the cigarette hanging from his lips.

Harry held back and watched Lily reach the steps to her house.

'Doctor's here,' Walter told her in a weary voice drained of expression. 'Your mother's had a bad turn. Best come in and hear what he has to say.'

CHAPTER EIGHTEEN

Dr James Moss was a tall, deep-voiced man with a florid complexion, built on such a large scale that he seemed out of place in the kitchen of the tiny terraced house – likely to walk into things and wondering quite where to put his big, soft hands which he consequently thrust deep into his jacket pockets. Jutting out his full underlip, he stared for a long time at the black Gladstone bag that he'd placed on the table.

'You might want to take the little lad upstairs while I have a word with your dad and sister,' he told Evie, who hurried off with Arthur.

Lily swallowed hard and tried to contain a rising panic while Walter shook his head and backed into the corner by the sink, pulling out another cigarette and putting it to his lips without lighting it.

'I've found the reason for Rhoda not being herself lately,' Dr Moss began slowly, constrained by the size of the room as well as by the grave news he had to deliver. 'I'm afraid it must have been building up for quite a while. I expect you've seen that for yourselves, haven't you?'

'She's not been well,' Lily acknowledged. 'But Mother said she didn't want to make a fuss – you know what she's like.'

'Until tonight, when she took a turn for the worse,' the doctor continued. 'Walter, I gather that she sent Evie down to the Green Cross to ask you to come home?'

Walter nodded. 'I got here fast as I could, Doctor, and it was just in time. Then I sent Evie to call on you.'

'She was trying to get out of bed when your father arrived, but she fainted away,' Moss explained to Lily.

'How is Mother now?' Lily wanted to know. 'Has she come round?'

Dr Moss nodded then suggested that she and Walter sit down at the table. 'You'll need to steady yourselves,' he warned.

A sense of dread descended on Lily as she followed the doctor's advice, noticing only dimly that her father had chosen to stay in the shadows in the corner of the room. She looked up at Dr Moss's florid face and tried to concentrate on what he said next.

'I gave Rhoda something to help her revive and then she agreed to let me examine her. I found she has a tumour pressing against her stomach – quite a large one, I'm afraid – big enough to stop her from eating normally, at least. That's why she's grown so thin and tired.'

'Can you take the tumour away?' Lily whispered.

'I'm not sure. Your mother would need to go to the hospital to find out about that.'

'But they could try?'

'Yes, but if Rhoda has had this tumour for a while, then small parts may have broken away and got lodged somewhere else – in the lungs, for instance. Then the situation would be very bad, I'm afraid.'

The implications behind the doctor's cautious, carefully considered words sent Lily into a downward spiral of fear for her mother. 'Why didn't she say something?' she cried. *Why didn't I pay more attention?* was the unspoken question that quickly followed.

'I expect she soldiered on, hoping that it would go away,' Dr Moss said. 'But now she knows it won't.' He turned to Walter and addressed him simply. 'You understand about the tumour, don't you? You're prepared for what might happen?'

'I know Rhoda hasn't been herself,' he murmured abjectly. 'We have to get her to the hospital, let them sort her out.'

A frown formed between the doctor's brows as he realized he could take things no further for the time being. He picked up his bag and prepared to leave the family to it. 'Your mother's comfortable for the moment,' he told Lily. 'Let her rest as much as possible, give her some warm milk with sugar or honey to keep up her strength and I'll get in touch

225

with the hospital on Monday to see if we can find a bed for her.'

After this, he saw himself out and left Lily alone with Walter.

'I did the right thing, calling for the doctor?' Walter asked after a long silence when all that was heard in the dimly lit kitchen was the familiar settling of the last coals in the grate.

'Yes, Father,' Lily answered in a dazed voice. She wasn't sure how much of Dr Moss's news he had taken in and she didn't have the heart to elaborate, not now.

'This is a right to-do.' He sighed, removing the un-lit cigarette and sliding it into his waistcoat pocket.

'Yes. I wish we'd sent for the doctor before now.'

'Ah, but she wouldn't have it.'

'Shall I go up and see her, or shall you?' Lily wondered.

'You do it,' Walter said, one hand to his temples, the other resting for support on the edge of the sink. 'Make her go to the hospital, will you, Lil? Tell her not to mind about the money.'

'I'll try.'

'They can do wonders there, tell her – I shouldn't be surprised if they don't get her back on her feet in no time.'

'Yes, Father, I'll tell her.' Lily sighed, her head spinning as she stood up and slowly climbed the stairs.

*

'Don't worry, I knew it was coming.' Rhoda sat in bed, propped up by a rolled-up blanket and a thin pillow. Her pallor was deathly white, her manner resigned.

'I wish you'd told me sooner,' Lily said, feeling a tight band around her chest as she tried not to cry.

'You've enough on your plate.' Rhoda's hands rested on the fawn knitted bed cover, palms down, one on top of the other. Her hair was pushed clear of her face. 'To tell you the truth, Lily, I was hoping I'd see Margie through the nine months but now it doesn't seem likely, not after what Dr Moss told me.'

Lily found herself clutching at straws. 'You might if you let them give you an operation? That's what Father would like.'

'No, I don't think so.'

For a moment exasperation at Rhoda's blunt stubbornness flared in Lily. 'What do you mean, you don't think so?'

'Where would we find the money for me to go into hospital for a start? And anyway what would be the point? No, I'm quite happy for Dr Moss to carry on looking after me here at home.'

'Mother!' Feeling the force of Rhoda's steely resistance on this matter of life and death, Lily let her head drop forward.

'Don't cry, Lil.'

'I'm not.' Lily was aware that the staccato exchange hid a depth of underlying emotion that she couldn't even begin to fathom. With a great effort she took her lead from Rhoda, fought back the tears and looked up at her mother's wan face.

'It'll be up to you to look after Margie when the time comes,' Rhoda told her steadily. 'And in the meantime there's Evie and Arthur to think of, not to mention your father.'

'He'll want you to go into the King Edward's,' Lily warned her again.

'Yes, but you and I can see that's cloud-cuckoo-land.' Rhoda's lifelong pragmatism didn't fail her now. 'We both know that it's not going to get any better, whatever the doctors try.'

There was nothing that Lily could say to this so she sat and stared sadly at her mother, wondering how best to pass on the news to Margie, Evie and Arthur.

'Don't look at me like that,' Rhoda objected, wearily turning her head away. 'Send your father up to me, there's a good girl. Then go upstairs and talk to Evie for me.'

Lily's heart was heavy as she stood up to carry out her tasks. She paused, one hand on the door knob, then offered the only mite of reassurance she could scrape up from the very bottom of her heart. 'Don't worry, Mother, we'll manage.'

Rhoda nodded. 'I know you will, Lily.' She sighed. 'That's what it's all about when it comes down to it. I've brought you up not to let anyone down and now's your chance to show everyone that I didn't do too bad a job.'

*

When Walter took Lily's place at Rhoda's bedside he thought at first that his wife had fallen asleep. He felt as helpless as a bird with a broken wing, prey to all the nightmarish visions that years of mind-numbing drinking at the Green Cross had kept at bay.

Now, though, he came face to face with those terrors that had first come over him in the front line trenches. He smelled again the stench of mud and rotting flesh, heard the whistle and thud of shells, the ack-ack of gunfire. He could see his pals going over the top into a hail of bullets, sliding back down into the mire with half their faces missing, limbs blown off or with gaping wounds in their chests. He remembered them now – Joe Taylor and Dick Waterhouse, Brian Lawson and William Todd – in all the gory detail of their dying, their hands clutching at him while their last breaths escaped in long sighs and groans.

It might have been him, Walter Briggs, rotting there with the rest, and once it almost was when a shell had exploded nearby and a piece of shrapnel had torn into him, the rest of it showering him with mud, blood and much worse until he'd lost consciousness. He'd woken up in the field hospital, thinking of Rhoda and Lily and the new baby that was scarcely walking when he'd last set eyes on her.

'Walter?'

His wife's faint voice brought him back to the present.

229

'You know it's no good thinking about the hospital?' She reached out her hand and he took it, his own shaking uncontrollably.

'But it's worth a try,' he objected.

'No, Walter, it's not.'

He held her hand between his as if he were a condemned man, face to face with what in the end no one could avoid. And as his eyes met hers, he brought charges against himself: the endless counts of neglect and petty cruelty of his married years, his manifold failures as a husband and father. 'Don't leave me,' he pleaded with his sick wife. 'Not yet.'

'I have to, Walter,' she whispered back, fixing him with her steady gaze, though her courage almost failed her. 'I'm ready to go. Honestly, I am.'

Sunday brought Harry knocking on the door of number 5 with the offer of a trip over to Ada Street in the car he'd borrowed from Wilf Fullerton down at the brewery.

'It's Harry,' Evie told Lily, who was inserting a layer of jam into the middle of a sponge cake, the scent filling the room.

Arthur perched on the window sill showing none of his usual lively enthusiasm for the arrival of a visitor. Instead, he concentrated on his game of cat's cradle, looping and twisting a knotted piece of string around his fingers to make the outline of a see-saw, a mattress then a cradle.

'Now then, Arthur,' Harry said as he stepped inside. 'What's that you're up to?'

'Nothing.' Arthur pulled the string loose from his fingers and chucked it down on the sill. 'Mam's poorly. I have to keep quiet.'

'Then it's a good job I've brought the car to give you and your sisters a spin out for a change. I thought we might drop in on Margie at Ada Street.' Glancing apprehensively at Lily as he picked up the grim atmosphere, Harry tried to judge how bad Dr Moss's verdict on Rhoda had been. He thought now that the notion of a jaunt out to Overcliffe might not be one of his brighter ideas.

'I'll stay here,' Evie said straight away, selflessly giving Lily the chance she needed to say yes to Harry. 'I don't mind staying in. There's a pile of ironing to do before work tomorrow. I can get on with that.' And it would give her time to settle her thoughts and get used to the nature of their mother's illness. Lily had gently told her Dr Moss's diagnosis in their attic bedroom while Arthur slept and Walter sat by Rhoda's bed in the room below. Evie had absorbed the shock without crying, somehow rising to the occasion and steeling herself to be a help to Lily rather than a hindrance. 'You go,' she insisted now, while Harry hovered on the doormat and Arthur kicked his heels against the wooden panelling beneath the window.

'Shall we?' Lily left Arthur to decide, her face flushed partly from the heat of the oven and partly

231

because Harry was giving her the look that seemed to see deep inside her. She glanced down at her floury apron and the old wooden clogs belonging to Rhoda which she wore around the house and thought how far away she was from looking her best.

'It's a Jowett Seven,' Harry told him. 'Look out of the window – see where it's parked?'

The shiny maroon car stationed directly outside number 5 persuaded Arthur to leave off kicking the wall and he jumped up to try to unhitch his coat from the high hook on the back of the door. Grinning, Harry helped him while Lily took off her apron and changed her shoes, packing the cake up carefully for the journey.

Within five minutes they were out of the house and sitting on the grey leather seats of Wilf's car, the engine choking, turning then spluttering into life on a cold, clear morning with the remains of yesterday's light snowfall already dirty underfoot.

'How's your mother?' Harry asked Lily as he approached the junction with Cliff Street.

Sitting next to him in the passenger seat she rolled her eyes backwards towards Arthur, who was gazing eagerly out of the window at the great stretch of the Common rolling out on to the moors and the distant white horizon. 'She has to stay in bed for a bit,' was all she said.

'How do you like the car, Arthur?' Harry asked by way of diversion, his heart going out to Lily. She might not know it but she looked lovely sitting there next to him, her face still rosy from the oven, hair uncombed, holding her breath as she looked straight ahead, as if letting it out would be bound to end in a sigh and tears.

'It's grand,' Arthur chirped, leaning forward and pointing to the instrument dial. 'What's that clock thing for?'

'That tells you the speed we're going in miles per hour. And you see that little chrome box perched at the front of the bonnet? That's a temperature gauge to show how hot the engine gets.'

Arthur's small features lit up as he learned about the car. Lily meanwhile sat back and took in the open views. 'This is nice of you, Harry,' she said. 'There must be a lot of other things you could find to do on a Sunday leading up to Christmas.'

'Yes and all of them include me doing jobs for Mother,' he countered with a wink. 'She wants me to wallpaper Peggy's attic bedroom and then get out the cobbler's last and put new soles on three pairs of shoes – that's just for starters.'

'Ah, so this is an escape.' Lily managed a smile. 'Heaven knows it's ten times better to be driving out with Arthur and me than mending shoes!'

'A hundred times better, if you ask me.' Harry noticed a smudge of white flour on Lily's cheek and he breathed in the sweet smell of baking still lingering on her skin. 'But listen, I can sit outside in the car and wait for you when we get there.'

'Why would you want to do that?'

'I was thinking you'd rather have Margie all to yourself, that's all.'

'No, come in and have a word with Granddad,' she insisted as they came to Linton Park and met a tram coming towards them. Harry pulled into the kerb to give it plenty of room.

'There's a man sitting in that tram wearing a black patch over his eye.' Arthur pointed out the curiosity, straight away imagining pirates. Suddenly the tram was a galleon sailing the white ocean and he was the ship's cabin boy being made to walk the plank.

'Harry,' Lily said in a voice not much above a whisper and knowing that on the one hand it was a big decision to break her vow of silence yet on the other hand the burden of knowledge might be eased by sharing it with the one person in the world she'd begun to trust above all others. 'If I tell you something, can I rely on you not to pass it on?'

Harry gave her a quick glance and a nod then turned his attention back to the road.

'Then I have to warn you – Margie's in the family way. I thought you should know.'

He waited for the tram then eased the car on to Ada Street. 'I realized something was up,' he murmured.

'You've been so good to us, Harry – I wanted to let you in on it before it . . . Well, before the whole world gets to know, as they will sooner or later. Don't let on that I told you, though.'

He concentrated on his driving and it was a while

234

before he spoke. 'This is a right going-on, eh? Who's the father – do we know?'

Lily shook her head. 'She won't say. It'll come out eventually, I dare say.'

'There's Granddad!' Arthur called out from the back seat, home from the land of Long John Silver. He leaned far out the window. 'Look – he's sweeping snow off his front steps. Hello, Granddad! It's us! We're in a Jowett Seven. I've just seen a man with a patch over his eye!'

'She's not taking it too badly, considering,' Harry mentioned to Lily after he'd dropped Arthur back at home and she'd snatched the chance to drive back up to Chapel Street with him to drop off Wilf's car. It was coming up to dinner time and she'd left Evie to dish up lamb chops with sprouts and potatoes for their father and hungry brother. Rhoda was in bed, accepting a warm drink but refusing food.

'Who's not taking what too badly?' she asked in response to his tentative remark.

'Margie. She seemed to be keeping her chin up at least.'

It was true – the visit to Ada Street had gone off without incident. Granddad Preston had sat at the kitchen table and presided over his brown teapot with the usual inscrutable air, passing the time of day with Harry by chatting about the finer points of the internal combustion engine. Arthur had leaped at Margie, almost knocking her over and

235

planting a big kiss on her cheek. Margie herself had seemed pleased to see everyone, including Harry to whom she'd offered the seat closest to the fire, together with home-baked ginger snaps from Granddad's best biscuit barrel, the one made of oak with a silver rim and knob, which harked back to the early days of his marriage to Rhoda's mother. 'Made by my own fair hands!' Margie had told him with a touch of her old brightness.

'She puts on a good show,' Lily told Harry as they pulled up outside Wilf's house. She felt unsettled by the events of the morning – the way things had seemed so normal and calm as they'd sat in the kitchen at Ada Street while underneath were the dark undercurrents of Margie's pregnancy and Rhoda's illness ready to drag them down.

Stepping out of the car and hurrying round to open her door, Harry offered Lily his hand. 'Hang on while I hand these keys back then we'll walk across the Common together.'

Harry linked arms with Lily upon his return and walked her past the wide steps and imposing entrance of the Wesleyan chapel at the top of the street. The plain, solid building with its leaded, arched windows towered over the soot-blackened terraced houses to either side.

'So what's up?' he asked. 'Don't you think Margie's going along all right?'

'It's not so much Margie I'm worried about right now.' Lily sighed, leaning in towards Harry as they crossed the street and stepped out on to a narrow footpath that crossed the Common. The sky was blue for once and the air unusually clear, with the chimneys of the small mill town of Hadley visible in the distance.

'It's your mother?' Harry guessed. He felt proud to be walking with Lily so he puffed out his chest and threw back his shoulders. What, he wondered, would Ernie or Billy think if they could see him now, striding out and offering his arm to the best-looking girl in town?

'I couldn't tell you earlier,' Lily confided. 'Not with Arthur waggling his big ears, listening in to every word. But it's bad news, Harry.'

'You don't say,' he murmured, the right words failing him as they so often did. He unhooked his arm and put it around her shoulder as they carried on past a cast-iron bench, until they came to a halt on the crest of the hill.

Feeling the full force of a biting wind, Lily nestled closer. 'She has a tumour pressing against her stomach and Dr Moss says it's been there a while. Mother thinks it's too late for an operation.'

'But is it?' he asked. 'Couldn't they try?'

'She says not.'

'And you believe her?'

Lily nodded. 'She's had more to do with medical matters than the rest of us. She ought to know what she's talking about.'

There was a gap in the conversation before Harry

took the bull by the horns. 'Did the doc say how long she's got?'

'No. But Margie's baby is due some time in July and Mother's certain she won't live to see it.' Recounting the facts brought home to Lily the reality of what was happening and she felt tears well up. 'I didn't have the heart to tell Margie – best for her not to have to worry about Mother for the time being.'

'It's a bad job,' Harry murmured, turning to face Lily and drawing her closer. 'Here comes another trouble marching left-right, left-right straight towards you.'

'It feels more like a steamroller,' she admitted. 'It's funny, though – the news about Mother makes Margie's problem take a back seat, at least for a while.'

Harry watched the brimming tears overflow and felt his heart melt. 'I'm a useless so-and-so,' he muttered. 'I never know what to say.'

Lily looked up at him through a blur of tears. 'You're not useless, Harry. I'm glad you're here.'

'I am,' he insisted, his arms around her, his lips almost touching hers. 'And I'm not going anywhere.'

CHAPTER NINETEEN

Still, when the next morning arrived and she was about to set off for work, it seemed to Lily that, despite Harry's tender support, with her mother ill and her sister out of work and expecting a baby out of wedlock, her precious family was falling apart at the seams.

'Where's my school cap?' Arthur wailed, reluctant to fasten his satchel and be dropped off at Peggy's house.

'On the stool by the sink,' Evie told him, hovering by the door. 'Hurry up and put it on. Lily and me are going to be late clocking on if we don't watch out.'

'I want to say goodbye to Mam,' he whined, scooting off upstairs before Evie could stop him.

'Be quick about it,' Lily called after him. 'Father, be sure to stay in until Dr Moss arrives.'

Walter sat at the kitchen table, arms clasped and head hanging, staring into the unlit grate.

'Did you hear me, Father? Dr Moss will be here

later with news about a bed in the hospital for Mother. Even if she says she doesn't want it, she might change her mind after she's talked to the doctor again. Oh and have a shave, smarten yourself up.'

'Lily, we have to go!' Evie insisted as Arthur clattered back downstairs.

'Right, we're off.' Walter hadn't stirred but Lily had no more time to spare, herding Evie and Arthur out on to the front doorstep and closing the door smartly behind her.

They joined a steady flow of glum, Monday-morning workers trudging down Albion Lane for the start of another week's drudgery at combing and spinning machines – slaves, every one of them, to the Holden Comb, the Lister Comb, the Noble Comb and goodness knows what other kind of infernal invention. Or else they were tied to the relentless Cap Spinner and the Ring Spinner, great cast-iron machines that spun as many as sixty-four bobbins of yarn at any one time, on and on through the working day.

'Good morning, Lily love,' cried Sybil from the opposite side of the street, just before Lily turned off down the alleyway with Arthur.

Lily waved briefly back. 'You go on with Sybil,' she urged Evie. 'I'll drop Arthur off and catch you up.' Halfway down the alley she stooped to tie Arthur's shoelace.

'Hey up, you're in the road!' Billy called out as he wobbled towards them on his bike.

'You're not even meant to ride down here,' Lily grumbled back. 'The sign says "Cycling Prohibited".'

Billy winked and edged past. 'Harry's already left for work, in case you were wondering.'

'Thanks, Billy, but I wasn't.' Blushing, Lily hurried on with Arthur, depositing him with Peggy then setting off at a run to catch up with Evie and Sybil. When they reached Calvert's main entrance, several girls from the weaving shed stood together, moaning about the fact that Fred Lee's motorbike and side-car had been spotted in the yard by the engine shed.

'Then he's back, worse luck,' Florence commented to Maureen, while an out-of-breath Annie rushed to join them.

'Talk of the devil,' Annie warned, pointing down the corridor to where the overlooker had stationed himself next to the clocking-on machine, his hair well oiled, tweed waistcoat stretched taut across his belly.

Meanwhile, Lily said a hasty goodbye to Evie and climbed the stairs to the mending room.

Positioning herself on the far side of Sybil, Evie avoided Fred's eye and waited to clock on.

'Come on now, ladies and gents, no time to hang about,' the overlooker cajoled. If he was aware of the rumours of domestic discord that surrounded his absence, he gave no sign, standing with his legs wide apart and arms folded, ready to get every ounce of work possible out of his weft men and weavers, his bobbin liggers, loom cleaners and learners. 'Get a move on, Sybil. And who's that hiding behind you? Oh, if it isn't little Miss Troublemaker. Don't worry, Evie Briggs, I don't bite – not as a general rule.'

Blushing fiercely, Evie slid her card into the slot. Try as she might, she couldn't get rid of the memory of Fred Lee's clammy fingers pawing her or the fear of what might have happened next if Lily hadn't interrupted him. Why does it have to bother me so much? she wondered. Why can't I brush it off with a laugh and a joke the way Sybil or Annie would?

'Take no notice,' Sybil whispered as she steered Evie safely past the overlooker. 'Keep your head down and do your job. He'll soon lose interest.'

'Hello, Fred – how's the missis?' Fresh from clocking on, Annie treated him to her usual cheeky stare. 'I bet she's glad to see the back of you.'

Her manner angered Fred and made him flinch. 'What do you mean?'

'I only meant she'll be glad to have you back at work and out from under her feet. Why, what did you think I meant – that she'd turned you out of the house for good?'

His eyes narrowed and he shook his head. 'Take care not to go too far, Annie Pearson, I'm warning you.'

'Ooh, and don't you be so touchy, Fred Lee!' Annie cooed, pulling her apron over her head and taking up position at her jacquard loom. 'Come along, Evie love, stand in for Florence and fetch me some fresh bobbins – I'm almost out of red and blue.'

*

Back at home that evening, Lily learned from her father that Dr Moss had persuaded her mother to go to the hospital after all and that the deed had already been done.

'She wasn't happy,' Walter reported.

'But she agreed to it for your sake?' Lily surmised.

'Aye, but she insisted on doing it her own way. She refused the stretcher and said she would walk out of the house on her own two feet. She wouldn't have ambulance men carrying her.'

'Did she take a lot of persuading?' Lily wanted to know.

Her father nodded gloomily. 'She gave way in the end, though. I've never known her do as she's told before. I don't know – it looks somehow as if the fight's gone out of her.'

Lily neither confirmed nor denied her father's observation. 'I'll take the bus into town and pop into the hospital at visiting time,' she decided, searching in the cupboard for pearl barley to add to carrots, onions and the remains of yesterday's lamb chops to put in the pot for a hearty Scotch broth that would satisfy the ever-ravenous Arthur.

And so began the new routine at number 5, with Lily and Evie taking care of all the cooking and the washing and the ironing, in between visits to see Rhoda in hospital and the usual nine and a half hours a day at the mill.

Neighbours on Albion Lane stepped in to lend a hand whenever they could, but still the main burden fell on Lily and as the days went by without firm news from the hospital, she began to feel worn down and hopeless.

It was Friday morning and Lily was already at work, looking out of the window as usual for a glimpse of Harry delivering Winifred in his boss's Bentley to lift her spirits. Sure enough, the car arrived and Harry hopped out to hold open Winifred's door. Winifred stepped out, very fine in a chocolate-coloured coat with her fox-fur stole and a bright orange hat. She smiled at Harry and thanked him. From her first-floor vantage point, Lily took it all in – Winifred's smile, which Harry returned, then her touch on his shoulder – the very lightest, fingertip touch, as if she were brushing dust from his epaulette, except that she rested her fingers there a moment too long and his gaze met hers. They both smiled, she leaned in and said something, he replied, then Winifred nodded and stepped under the archway, disappearing from view.

What had they talked about? Lily wanted to know. What was the meaning behind those exchanged smiles? Smitten by a sharp and unexpected stab of jealousy, she paused, burling iron in hand, until Miss Valentine passed by.

'Daydreaming, Lily?' she asked. 'That's not like you.'

'I'm sorry, Miss Valentine.' Turning her back to

the window, she steadied her trembling fingers and tried to concentrate.

'I know I'm being silly,' she reasoned later in the canteen as she shared her troubles with Annie and Sybil during their dinner break.

'Daft as a brush,' Sybil agreed. Lily had broken into the talk they were having about a winter coat that Annie was making for one of her cousins. She'd been having trouble making the lining sit right and was eager to hear Sybil and Lily's opinions on the matter. She looked around the crowded, noisy room, leaned across the table and lowered her voice to a whisper. 'If you want to know, I feel sorry for anyone who has to cart Winifred Calvert around from pillar to post. It can't be easy, putting up with her dishing out orders from the back seat.'

'Sybil's got a point,' Annie agreed. 'Anyhow, Harry's only got eyes for you, Lily. He's not interested in Miss Snooty.'

'Sshh!' Sybil warned. The subject of their conversation had just come into the canteen to fetch a tray of tea and sandwiches from Betty, the mill's cook.

The entrance of the boss's daughter brought down the level of noise as others besides Lily, Annie and Sybil were suddenly on best behaviour.

Winifred, though, seemed oblivious to the effect she'd created, swanning down the aisle between the rows of tables with her nose in the air, leaving no doubt that she considered herself a rose amongst thorns. 'I didn't ask for meat paste,' she told Betty in a loud voice as she curled back the edge of one of the sandwiches. 'Today is Friday. My order is for tinned salmon and cucumber.'

'I'm very sorry, Miss Calvert,' a red-faced Betty stammered, taking back the plate and slicing fresh bread.

Annie raised her eyebrows and tipped the end of her nose with her forefinger. 'Ooh, tinned salmon and cucumber!' she mocked behind Winifred's back.

Sybil spluttered into her raised mug of tea while Lily frowned.

'Come along, I haven't got all day,' Winifred chided.

Poor Betty was all fingers and thumbs as she corrected the order but at last the salmon sandwiches were made and handed over to Winifred, who took the tray and exited the way she'd come without a sideways glance.

'Never mind, Betty, let's hope they choke her,' Annie called out after she'd gone.

'See,' Sybil pointed out to Lily. 'Surely that sets your mind at rest.'

A frown still creased Lily's brow. 'What do you mean?'

'I mean, what man in his right mind could warm to that stuck-up trollop? No, Lily – Harry's got eyes for no one but you.'

Sybil's reassurance helped carry Lily through the last weekend before Christmas into the start of the next working week.

She spent the time quietly at home with Arthur and Evie doing everyday things that would keep the little boy's mind off his mother's being in hospital – a jigsaw at the kitchen table, rehearsing his spellings for a test on Monday and, best of all, icing the Christmas cake and decorating it with holly leaves made from sugar-coated angelica, together with the miniature reindeer and sleigh that Rhoda kept all year round in a cardboard box behind the clock on the mantelpiece.

Otherwise, there was the organizing of visits to King Edward's Hospital – Evie on Saturday afternoon, Walter in the evening then Lily on Sunday morning – and only an hour on Saturday for Harry to drop in on Lily for a cup of tea and a chat.

He was there on the Saturday when carol singers came down the street and was ready at the door with Arthur to hand over a couple of coppers for their spirited rendition of 'Good King Wenceslas' and 'While Shepherds Watched'. Arthur grinned as he heard the clink of his pennies land in the collecting tin and the carollers wished them all a Merry Christmas.

Harry closed the door and glanced at his watch. 'I'd best be on my way,' he told Lily. 'Mother's finally roped me in to mending those shoes.'

'Ta for coming, Harry.' Busy drying tea things and with her mind flying ahead to the next job, Lily was slow to turn from the sink but when she did she saw him cap in hand, still hovering awkwardly by the door and so she started to pay more attention. 'What's the matter?' she asked.

'Nowt,' he said, a fraction too quick with his reply.

'Mam says not to say "nowt",' Arthur cut in. 'She says it's "nothing".'

'Your mother's right,' Harry said, his face reddening as he fiddled with the rim of his cap. 'Nothing's the matter. But I was wondering, Lily, do you fancy doing something later tonight?'

'Oh, Harry, I can't!' Lily hadn't thought that far ahead, but when she did she realized that Evie was going straight from the hospital to visit Margie, and that she would have to stay in to keep an eye on Arthur. Walter, of course, would be down at the Green Cross.

Harry's face fell a mile. 'I was thinking maybe just a walk up to the Overcliffe Road to see if we can join up with the carol singers? Surely you can get away for half an hour?'

'I really can't.' Lily put down the tea towel and joined him at the door.

'Don't worry, that's fine by me,' he blustered. 'I can join Billy and the rest of the gang, find out what they're up to.'

'I'm sorry, Harry,' she said, looking into his eyes and laying her hand lightly on his arm. He nodded and departed hurriedly without returning the touch, leaving her dejected and uneasy. She felt a sharp pang as she pictured Billy, Ernie and the rest scooping Harry up and railroading him into dancing and having fun without her at the Assembly Rooms. On the last Saturday before Christmas she knew that balloons and streamers would decorate the hall and a tempting bunch of mistletoe would hang just inside the entrance.

But Harry came back to the house for tea on Sunday and told her how the shoe repairs had taken him longer than expected so he'd decided to stay in after all. I needn't have worried, Lily thought. 'Why not give Arthur a hand with his jigsaw while I finish the lining on this coat?' she suggested, smiling as Harry sat at the table and spouted silly music-hall jokes for the benefit of a giggling Arthur.

A short while later Walter arrived back from the hospital, a triumphant smile lighting up his face. 'They're sending your mother home!' he announced, flinging his cap down on the table, loosening his scarf and demanding a mug of good strong tea with two sugars and plenty of milk. 'Tomorrow morning,' he added. 'We'll be back to normal, eh, Lily? Just you wait and see.'

CHAPTER TWENTY

'Merry Christmas, Fred!' Annie chirruped at the overlooker as she entered the weaving shed arm in arm with Evie on Monday morning. '"And a merry Christmas to you too, Annie!"' she answered for him, so that the sour look on his face darkened to a deep scowl. '"And to you, Sybil, and to you, Evie, and to you too, Florence and Maureen, and to all my wonderful, hard-working girls. It's Christmas – let's give you all a five-shillings bonus, why don't we?"'

'I'm warning you, Annie,' Fred snarled over the other girls' amused tittering, then he retaliated by choosing an easy target, following Evie to the rack of pirns that she was about to load on to a low metal trolley for distribution around the shed. 'Leave off from that and come with me,' he ordered roughly.

Evie swallowed hard and pressed her lips together. She put back the big reel of prepared weft yarn and got ready to follow the overlooker.

'Now, Fred, where are you taking her?' Annie

demanded in the same teasing tone but when Sybil gave her a warning look, she stopped.

'This way,' Fred told Evie, marching ahead of her between the tall looms, criticizing as he went. 'Maureen, this loom needs cleaning properly, not half-doing. Florence, why aren't those bobbins ready? George, those shafts need oiling – the noise is giving me a headache.'

Meekly, but with a sense of dread, Evie followed her bad-tempered boss out of the weaving shed, down the corridor, under the main entrance and out into the back yard where Harry had just finished dropping off Winifred.

'Which daft bugger parked this bike right where I can't get past?' Harry wanted to know. In order to turn around he'd been forced to reverse Calvert's precious car through a narrow gap between Fred's machine and the entrance to the engine room. One small scratch on the gleaming paintwork and he was done for, he knew. That would be it – no job and no prospect of finding another, not with times as they were. 'Was it you, Fred? I might've known.'

'Call yourself a chauffeur,' Fred retorted with a typical sneer. 'You could reverse a coach and horses through there.'

'I take it you're not going to move it,' Harry grumbled, spotting Evie in the background and toning down his language. He got back into the car and began to edge forward, using his wing mirror to judge the distance between himself and the offending motorbike. But he braked and stopped when he caught sight of what the overlooker was up to.

'I need these bobbins moving,' Fred told Evie as he pointed to a trolley laden with wooden spools of yellow yarn. 'The testing boys need to get at those bales stacked against the wall. They're taking them down to the Conditioning House.'

One look at the loaded trolley told Evie that it was too heavy for her to shift, but she went behind it and did her best while Lee, who seemed to have over-looked the fact that Harry was still there, stood by with his arms folded.

'I'd lend a hand, only my back's still bad after my accident,' he said with evident enjoyment, moving in so close that she could feel his breath on her neck.

Even with all her weight put into the effort of moving the trolley, Evie found she could only shift it a few inches. She paused and glanced down the empty corridor that they'd just walked along as if help might be at hand.

'Here, let me show you how it's done,' Lee muttered, standing behind her and placing both arms around her waist, leaning her forward into the trolley so that the length of his body pressed against her.

Evie gasped and jabbed backwards with her elbows, catching him in the stomach. But he held on, lifting her off her feet then swinging her sideways against the soot-covered wall.

It was then that Harry acted. He leaped out of the car and charged at the overlooker, grabbing the back of his collar and wresting him away from Evie, finally flinging him down on to the cobbles and planting one foot on his chest. 'Go, get out of here,' he told Evie. 'Make yourself scarce!' She obeyed, sobbing as she ran back to the weaving shed.

'You'll regret this, Harry Bainbridge!' Fred swore as he squirmed under Harry's foot.

'I doubt that,' Harry replied grimly. 'I saw what I saw – your nasty hands all over the poor girl. That's more than your job's worth if Mr Calvert gets to hear of it.'

With a struggle his adversary rolled clear and hauled himself to his feet. He snorted and lowered his head like a bull about to charge but when Harry crouched and put up his fists, he thought better of it. Instead, he cleared his throat and tugged at the hem of his waistcoat.

'You hear me, Lee? I saw you.' Each short word brought Harry closer to the sweating overlooker until he was towering over him. 'I saw it with my own eyes. And if anything like this ever happens again with Evie Briggs, I'll be on to you like a shot.'

Outstared and overpowered, Fred Lee backed off, colliding with his bike and sending it skidding backwards against the wall. There was the scrape of metal and the crack of glass as the headlamp shattered. He tripped and swore, righted himself and strode away, leaving Harry staring after him.

From the first-floor window, Lily and Miss Valentine looked on. They'd been in discussion about the unusual number of flaws in a particular bolt of brown worsted and they'd witnessed the whole thing – the sound of the car engine coming into the yard that signalled the arrival of Winifred, the sight of Harry carefully reversing the car, followed by the altercation with Fred.

'Thank goodness Harry was there and that's an end to it.' Lily sighed, willing her heart to stop thumping at her ribs.

But her manageress shook her head. 'Let's hope so,' she said quietly before ordering Lily back to work.

Then, later that morning, just before the buzzer sounded for the dinner break, Iris Valentine took Lily to one side to issue a warning that sent shivers down the young woman's spine. She took up from where she'd left off. 'Let's hope that was the end of the matter,' she remarked in her high voice. 'But take it from me – I know for a fact that, after what happened today, Fred Lee is not likely to let it rest.'

Lily felt a fresh alarm shoot through her body. 'Why, what will he do?'

'Who can tell?' came the reply. 'All I know is that Fred is spiteful by nature – always has been. So you and Evie must be on your guard.'

Lily struggled to quell her fears and keep her voice even. 'Thank you, Miss Valentine, we will.'

The manageress gave a characteristic, birdlike

nod then issued her final word on the subject: 'Picture the worst that Fred Lee can do and expect it to happen. Then at least he won't catch you off guard.'

CHAPTER TWENTY-ONE

'They say the cancer started not in my stomach but in something they call the pancreas,' Rhoda confided in Lily once she was safely back in her own bed on Albion Lane. In the end, the hospital had done little more than confirm Dr Moss's suspicion that the cancer had spread and then prescribe something to alleviate the pain. After this they'd given in to her insistence that she be sent home and Walter had greeted her with unthinking relief and a nice cup of tea before sloping off to the Green Cross to celebrate. 'Not many people have heard of the pancreas or what it does for you,' she continued. 'Anyway, they decided there was nothing they could do to help me, which I could have told them without all their fancy tests. But don't let on to your father – I haven't got round to telling him about Margie yet and that on top of this latest news won't go down well.'

'What about the others?' Lily resisted the urge to cry out about the unfairness of it all and gently plumped up her mother's pillow then pulled up the blanket to keep her warm.

'You can tell Margie – she should know the truth. But not Evie and definitely not Arthur.'

'And what will you have now to keep up your strength?' Lily wanted to know, turning to the practical to hide the turmoil within. 'Would you like some tasty Bovril in hot water? I can send Evie down to Newby's to fetch some.'

Letting her head sink back on the pillow, Rhoda refused the pick-me-up. 'It'll take more than a cup of Bovril to set me back on my feet,' she said with grim humour. 'Do you know, I couldn't walk back into my own house? They had to carry me out of the ambulance and up these stairs. That means I'm going downhill fast, doesn't it?'

'All the more reason to eat and drink something,' Lily argued, trying to ignore the gnawing, hollow feeling in her stomach and her rapidly beating heart. 'Let me make you a nice sandwich. Or how about another cup of tea?'

'Lily,' Rhoda protested with a slight shake of her head, 'don't go on, there's a good girl. Just turn off the light and leave me in peace.'

'Are you comfy? Will you sleep?' Loath to leave, Lily turned down the gas, waited for the pop that meant the flame had been extinguished and the slow dimming of the fragile mantel then stood in the doorway, staring at the tiny figure on the bed.

'Yes, sleep is one thing that comes easily now,'

Rhoda confirmed wearily. 'Goodnight, Lily. I'll see you in the morning.'

The next day, Christmas Eve, a fight at the Cross was all the talk at Calvert's.

In the mending room, Lily was stashing the small Christmas presents she'd brought in for Annie and Sybil on the ledge under her table. Her mind was on her mother's worsening illness and she didn't notice the strange looks that the likes of Jennie and Mary were giving her. How would Christmas go with Rhoda ill in bed? she wondered. Would her mother try to get up for the occasion and make things as pleasant as possible for Arthur? Would her father come out of the foul temper he'd come home in last night?

It was the arrival of Jennie with her first bolt of cloth for the day that interrupted Lily's musings. 'How's your knight in shining armour this morning?' she asked.

'Come again?' Lily said without paying much attention. She was arranging her hook, scissors and needles on her table, thinking ahead now to dinner time when she and her friends would exchange presents.

'Harry – how's his poor face?' Noticing and perhaps sympathizing with the cloud of confusion that had descended over Lily's face, Jennie drew Mary into the conversation. 'How about that, Mary? It seems Lily hasn't heard about Harry sticking up for her and her sister in the pub last night. And him being so gallant and all.'

Mary took up the story with gusto. 'Apparently Harry had a go at your Tommy for no reason at all and it was only Frank Summerskill who stopped him from laying Tommy out flat. As it was, there were glasses flying everywhere and bottles breaking until Chalky White threatened to call in the bobbies to break it up.'

'If you ask me, the boot was on the other foot,' Jennie chipped back in. 'Tommy's the one who started the argument, I'd bet my week's wages on it. As for Frank Summerskill!' There was no need to go on – her sour-lemon expression said it all.

Lily felt her heart sink. She turned away and stared out of the window on to the yard below, where Winifred Calvert happened to be stepping out of the Bentley while Harry, with his back turned, held open the door.

Jennie followed her gaze and spotted Harry. 'Wait until he turns round and you get a good look at his face!' she warned. 'Black and blue all over, it is. And he got that from sticking up for you and Margie. Ask anyone who was at the Green Cross last night – they'll tell you all about it.'

Winifred was out of the car, a splash of vivid colour against the dark grey background of the mill walls in her orange hat and fox-fur stole. She stopped briefly to say something to Harry then walked on towards the entrance. Harry closed the door and walked around to the driver's side, glancing up and catching sight of Lily and Jennie staring down at him. Immediately he ducked his head and his face was hidden under the peak of his cap.

'There, did you see it?' Jennie cried. 'All cut and bruised from the fight with your cousin Tommy, poor thing! And in front of your father, too.'

'Jennie!' Mary nodded towards the office where Iris Valentine was hanging up her coat and hat.

The taker-in realized she only had time for a parting shot before the manageress emerged into the mending room and she had to scurry back to her station. 'If you ask me, Tommy Briggs needs skinning alive for spreading nasty rumours and upsetting your dad. And coming up to Christmas, too. Ask anyone you like – it's not on!'

'Jennie!' Mary warned again, too late.

The manageress left her office and tip-tapped down the aisle with a good-morning here and a courteous nod of her head there until she met Jennie halfway back to her big canvas skip containing the bolts of unchecked blue, brown and grey worsted cloth. She frowned and tapped her old-fashioned gold wristwatch. 'The time is twenty minutes to eight,' she pointed out. 'That's ten minutes after the buzzer sounded.'

'I know, Miss Valentine.' Jennie held her gaze steady but inwardly she quaked at what might follow.

'It's also the second time this week that I've caught you gossiping when you should be working.'

'Yes, Miss Valentine. I'm sorry, Miss Valentine.'

'Which means I intend to go down to the main office later this morning to tell Jean to dock an hour's pay from your wages this week. I'm sorry, Jennie. I know it's Christmas, but this really isn't good enough.'

Red in the face with silent resentment but having to accept the verdict, Jennie's head dropped and she stood to one side to let the manageress pass by.

At dinner time, with the morning's gossip about the pub brawl all but forgotten by everyone except Lily, it was Winifred who caught the eye as she breezed up to the food counter. There was no denying that Calvert's daughter had style, with her glossy hair tamed into a newly cut bob and her slim waist nipped in by a belt the same shade of emerald green as her closely fitted dress. Sybil especially liked Winifred's tan leather shoes with a thin heel and a T-strap, which was fastened by the neatest little silver button. 'Goodness knows what she paid for them,' she said, pointing out the shoes to Lily and Annie.

'More than we could ever afford.' Annie sighed. 'Unless we saved up for a few weeks and gave up going out at the weekend.'

'Wouldn't it be nice, though, to own a pair of shoes like that?' Lily too appreciated the boss's daughter's taste. She'd been firm with herself and managed to overcome the queasy bout of jealousy she'd experienced over Winifred's close daily contact with Harry and now she was set on being generous. 'Jean says she's settled into office work better than expected. She's good with figures, by all accounts.'

'Here we go again.' Annie shook her head. 'Next thing we know, Lily will be best friends with Winifred Calvert. There'll be no stopping her now that she's moved up in the world!'

'Oh, Lily, don't desert us,' Sybil wailed as Winifred turned and carried her tray through the canteen.

As luck would have it, Winifred caught Lily's eye as she passed and she stopped to talk to her and her friends. 'I was wondering – does anyone know what happened to Harry Bainbridge's face?' she asked in a voice that was mellower and more mature than they would have expected of a nineteen-year-old girl. That, together with her coiffed hair and careful use of lipstick, rouge and mascara, made her seem older than her years. 'You girls live in his neck of the woods, don't you? I was wondering how he bruised his face.'

'Why not ask Harry yourself?' Annie asked without any attempt at generosity. She was no Lily and certainly didn't feel obliged to be nice to their high-and-mighty interrogator.

Winifred frowned. 'I did. I asked him on the way into work this morning, but he brushed it off. He wouldn't tell me how he got hurt.'

Sybil could see that Winifred's enquiry after Harry was making Lily nervous. 'Let's just say he walked into something, shall we?'

'I thought perhaps someone had it in for him,' Winifred said steadily, her tray resting on the table. 'He has cuts to the back of his neck as well as his face, which makes me think that he was set upon by more than one man.'

Lily winced at the notion of Harry being cornered by Tommy and Frank in the Green Cross then became indignant on his behalf. Just wait until I find out the whole sorry story, she thought. Then I can decide what I can do about it.

'Well, if you won't tell me and if Harry refuses to give the game away, I don't suppose there's much we can do,' Winifred decided. 'It doesn't seem fair to let whoever was responsible get away with it, that's all.'

With this she picked up her tray and walked on, leaving Sybil, Annie and Lily lost for words.

'What did *she* want?' someone piped up.

'Did I hear the name Harry Bainbridge mentioned?' called another.

And before long the room was buzzing with new tittle-tattle that linked Winifred Calvert with her father's chauffeur.

'Take no notice,' Sybil advised Lily, searching in her apron pocket for the small Christmas presents she'd brought in for her two best friends. She'd wrapped the identical gifts in white paper printed with small holly leaves and bound by green satin ribbon. 'Made with my own fair hands!' she declared.

'Shall we open them now or wait until tomorrow

morning?' Annie asked as she and Lily brought out their own festively wrapped presents.

'Now!' Sybil replied eagerly and she began untying ribbon to reveal a small red leather purse from Lily and a grey autograph book from Annie. She opened the book and read the inscription written on the first creamy page. 'Annie is my name, single is my station. Happy is the lucky man who makes the alteration!'

'Hah! Does Robert know about this?' Lily laughed, until Sybil dug into her pocket to find a pencil and began to write her own ditty.

'Let's have a gander,' Annie urged after Sybil had finished scribbling. 'Listen to this, everyone. "Good girls love their brothers, But Lily so good has grown, She loves Peggy's brother, Better than her own!"'

'Oh no!' Lily cried, wishing to goodness that her face didn't colour up so easily. To hide her embarrassment she grabbed the book and wrote her own offering. 'Jack and Jill went up the hill To fetch a pail of water. Jill came down with half a crown But not for fetching water!'

'Lily, I'm surprised at you!' Annie guffawed when she read the risqué offering, which brought half a dozen others crowding around the table to make their own contributions.

Meanwhile, Annie and Lily decided to leave their present-opening until Christmas morning. When the buzzer to return to work sounded, they walked out of the canteen together and paused at the top of the stairs before going their separate ways.

'When will you next see Harry?' Annie asked in a low voice as other girls rushed by.

'I'm not sure,' Lily confessed. 'I might try to pop out for half an hour later tonight if they can do without me at home.'

'Yes, try,' Annie urged with a squeeze of Lily's arm. 'Let him know you care.'

'About what?'

'About the fight in the pub, and so on. And ta for the present.' Annie smiled warmly and held up the small parcel given to her by Lily.

'It's not much,' Lily warned. 'But it's the thought that counts.'

'Likewise,' Annie said about her own gift to Lily. 'And Happy Christmas, love.'

'Yes, Happy Christmas.' Lily couldn't disguise the tinge of sadness and apprehension in her reply.

'Let's hope for a better year to come, full of fun for us girls,' Annie called before she ran downstairs to the weaving shed.

The kitchen in Albion Lane was festooned with the multicoloured paper chains made by Evie and Arthur and the mantelpiece was decked with holly that Walter had fetched from the woodland at the far edge of the Common. A leg of pork and a ready-plucked turkey had been bought by Evie from Durant's out of her week's wages, together with vegetables from Cliff Street market, which Walter had fetched on his way back from holly gathering. The Christmas pudding, made by Lily, was trussed up in muslin and placed inside its basin, ready for slow simmering next morning. The cake was iced and decorated. Best of all, Arthur was studying the pile of presents with his name on them, which had been carefully placed under the small tree stationed at the window in full view of the street and decked out with silver tinsel and glass baubles.

'I know what this is!' he exclaimed from time to time, lifting a present from Granddad Preston and shaking it inside its box. 'It's tiddlywinks!' A second shake brought another, different cry. 'No, Granddad's bought me snakes and ladders!'

'Talking of Granddad,' Evie whispered, out of hearing of both Arthur and their father, 'have he and Margie been invited for dinner tomorrow?'

'Granddad has, but not Margie,' Lily replied with a troubled frown. 'Father still swears he won't let her over the doorstep.'

Halfway up the creaking attic stairs with a pile of ironing, Evie bit her lip. 'Do you think he knows . . . ?'

'About the baby?' Lily finished her sentence. 'I'm not sure. Mother hasn't told him yet but maybe he found out down at the pub and that's what caused the fight. Anyway, you're not to mention Margie to him – Mother says.'

'Lily, is that you?' Rhoda's querulous voice came from behind the closed bedroom door where she'd been lying in bed, cut off from all the preparations going on below.

'Coming, Mother!' Lily called back, rushing to see what was wanted, silently running through the rest of the tasks she must do before she could possibly think of popping round to Raglan Road.

'Can I come in?' Lily asked Harry when she finally escaped from Albion Lane. It was cold and dark on the doorstep yet he'd taken his time to answer her knock, though she was sure she'd seen the curtain twitch at the downstairs window and she'd heard noises from inside the house.

'Lily,' Harry said, trying to sound surprised and pleased but failing on both counts. 'Sorry, I didn't hear you knocking.'

A gust of wind got under her skirt and threatened to lift the hat from her head so both hands were kept busy – one trying to anchor the hem of her skirt, the other clutching her hat. 'Don't keep me standing here,' she pleaded.

'Sorry,' he said again, still blocking the hallway. 'Mother and Peggy have gone out carol singing. I'm in by myself.'

The wind gusted again. 'Invite me in, Harry, please!'

He backed off down the corridor, his face still in shadow.

Lily followed slowly. 'Brrr, I'll catch my death. It's all right, Harry, I heard about the fight—' Despite being prepared, as soon as the slanting light from the living room fell across Harry's face, she gasped and stopped dead.

His face was like that of a boxer after a heavy defeat – there was a long cut above his left eyebrow and one on his right cheek. Both eyes were swollen and a bruise was developing along his lower jaw.

Embarrassed, Harry averted his gaze. This was why he hadn't wanted to answer the door in the first place, knowing what a sight he looked.

'Doesn't it need stitching?' Lily wondered, resisting the urge to stroke his face in case it hurt. Her stomach churned and she shuddered at the damage done to Harry's handsome face.

He shook his head. 'I didn't want you to see me like this, though. Are you sure you want to stay?'

'Why wouldn't I? Was it Tommy? Did he really do this to you?'

'Who told you that?' Ushering Lily into the front room instead of the back kitchen, a defensive Harry stood awkwardly in the doorway. He'd been planning to lie low over Christmas, hoping to avoid Lily until the swelling went down and things had begun to heal but now she'd seen him at his worst and he was afraid she would be put off. 'It was nothing,' he tried to reassure her. 'Just an argument that got a bit out of hand.'

'Says you.' She sighed, standing on the fireside mat and clutching the wrapped box of cufflinks that she'd bought at the market. They were silver and mother-of-pearl, with his initials, HB, inset in silver in the centre. But once she'd got over the shock of his altered appearance, she was determined to find out more. 'What was the argument over, Harry?'

'Nothing. Nothing for you to worry about.'

'If I didn't know you better, Harry Bainbridge, I'd say you were telling me to mind my own business.'

'No, it's not that . . .'

'But this *is* my business,' she insisted, trying to ignore the cuts and bruises and to carry on a conversation as per usual. 'What did Tommy say that riled you so badly? It wasn't about Margie, by any chance?'

Harry sighed and sat on the arm of the old-fashioned leather sofa that his mother had picked up for a song at Manby's auction house on Canal Road. He patted the seat, inviting Lily to come and join him, which she did. 'Tommy was dead set on having a go at your dad,' he explained. 'Walter didn't take it well. In fact, he lashed out with his fists.'

'And you couldn't stand by and let it happen?'

'It wasn't just me. When Billy and Ernie saw I was outnumbered by Tommy and Frank, they lent a hand. Then the boot was on the other foot.'

'But it *was* to do with Margie?'

'You're a right little Sherlock Holmes, aren't you?' Harry grinned and tried to lighten the mood. He remembered too late that every movement of his face muscles hurt like hell. 'Ouch!'

'Oh, Harry!' She sighed. 'It's one thing standing up for Evie against Fred Lee at work, but there's no need to go around fighting all the Briggs family battles willy-nilly.' Looking up at him from her place on the sofa and with the light in the hallway behind him, she could only make out the gleam of his eyes and the outline of his closely cropped fair hair. He was in shirtsleeves and pullover, his collarless white shirt open at the neck. 'By the way, Winifred was asking after you,' she remembered. 'She wanted to know how you'd hurt your face.'

'When was that?' he asked more sharply.

'Dinner time, in the canteen. She made a point of coming across and asking me, Sybil and Annie if we knew anything about it.'

'You didn't say too much, though?'

'Not a dicky bird. We only knew what we'd heard at work, and that was all gossip. You know what the girls at Calvert's are like. Anyway, why are you bothered about Winifred asking questions?'

'I don't want my boss thinking I go around scrapping and brawling in the gutter, that's all,' Harry replied. 'I've got my job to think about.'

'Ah, we all have to do that,' she agreed, realizing that this was a natural worry for Harry to have. 'Ta anyway for sticking up for Father – I don't want to sound ungrateful, you know that. But does this mean he's found out the truth about Margie?'

With one short nod Harry confirmed Lily's fears. 'Don't worry, he'll be upset for a bit but he'll get used to the idea sooner or later.'

'Well, I for one am not going to let it spoil our

Christmas,' Lily decided, pulling herself together and remembering the small gift she'd brought for Harry. 'This is for you,' she said, offering it to him and leaving her fingers resting on the palm of his hand. Instead of taking the present, he cupped his hands around hers and pulled her to her feet. 'Do I look a sight?' he asked, looking her in the eyes for the first time that evening. Damn it, what if he did? He ought to trust Lily and believe that her feelings for him were more than skin deep.

'Like Frankenstein's monster,' she teased, releasing one hand to gently push his hair back from his forehead. 'Don't you want to open your present?'

'Wait a sec,' he murmured, putting it on the arm of the sofa then leaving the room and taking the stairs two at a time, returning very soon with his own gift for Lily – a silver heart locket on a chain, still in its white tissue paper. 'I didn't have a chance to wrap it,' he explained.

With trembling fingers Lily took the shining, prettily engraved necklace from the paper and held it up. 'Oh Harry, it's lovely,' she whispered.

'Open it up,' he urged.

Lily slid her fingernail between the two halves of the heart and opened the locket. Inside she found a tiny head-and-shoulders photograph of Harry in his chauffeur's uniform. Unsure of her suddenly tearful expression, Harry hastily said she could change the picture if she liked.

She shook her head, closed the locket and held

the delicate chain up to her neck. 'No, it's just right. Fasten it for me, will you?'

He came behind her, took the necklace and felt the warmth and softness of the nape of her neck. It was too tempting – he had to lean forward and kiss the spot before he fastened the tiny clasp. She turned then hesitated.

'Can I kiss you back?' she whispered. 'Will it hurt?'

He nodded.

'Yes, it'll hurt? Or yes, I can kiss you back?'

'Both,' he murmured, drawing her to him and kissing her. 'Happy Christmas, Lily.'

She smiled and returned his kiss. 'Happy Christmas to you too, Harry,' she whispered in that perfect moment, when the whole world was shut out and her worries melted away like snow.

CHAPTER TWENTY-TWO

Christmas Day came and went at 5 Albion Lane in a flurry of present-opening, party games and over-indulgence.

'I guessed right – it's snakes and ladders!' a delighted Arthur declared as he tore off the paper to reveal the box sent by his grandfather. 'And a jigsaw from Margie. Look, Mam, it's a picture of horses pulling a cart. Margie knows horses are my favourites, doesn't she? That's why she's sent me this!'

Rhoda was up and dressed and ensconced in the one easy chair by the fire, a shawl around her shoulders and her hair tidied back from her face. 'That's grand, son,' she remarked each time he displayed one of his presents. Or, 'Who sent you this one, pray tell?' and 'What's this when it's at home?' when it was something she didn't recognize – a card game or an annual that she'd not heard of before. Her own present to her only son was practical as ever – a set of four linen handkerchiefs with his initials sewn on by hand.

'Thanks, Mam,' he said with evident disappointment. Unless you could play with it or eat it, Arthur wasn't interested.

He cast the hankies aside but soon perked up again when he came to the selection box of Rowntree's chocolates from Evie, chattering ten to the dozen as the girls set about carving the turkey and dishing up vegetables while Walter sat at the table quietly supping bottles of beer brought in from the Cross and kept cold in the cellar overnight.

'Who'll play happy families with me?' Arthur wanted to know. 'Mam, will you?'

'Not now, love,' Rhoda told him. 'Help set the table, there's a good lad.'

Present-opening followed by turkey and roast potatoes with all the trimmings was the unvaried Christmas routine in the Briggs household, then Christmas pud with the usual search for the lucky sixpence, followed by a lull when Walter nodded off and Arthur, perching on the window ledge, played quietly with a new toy – this year a bright red yo-yo from Harry.

'I'm heading back upstairs,' Rhoda told Lily once she'd given over her chair to Walter and made sure that the washing-up was underway. It was three o'clock in the afternoon and she was running out of energy, her face unnaturally flushed by the heat from the fire and from the pain and effort of sitting upright.

It was Evie who broke off from scouring pots to help Rhoda upstairs to bed, taking off the apron that protected her pretty white blouse and best skirt and lending her frail mother a much-needed hand.

'Where's Margie?' Arthur hovered by Lily at the sink and asked the question that had been bothering him all day. 'Why couldn't she come?'

'She's with Granddad,' Lily explained, suddenly pulled back to the here and now, away from the warm memory of being held in Harry's arms the night before in his cold, dark front room. Bert had sent a message that he wouldn't be with them for Christmas Day unless Margie was invited too. 'They're having their Christmas together up on Ada Street.'

Arthur gave a puzzled frown, glancing at his dozing father and somehow making a connection between Walter and the fact that Margie was missing, perhaps remembering the last row before she'd disappeared to live with their grandfather. Nothing had been said directly to Arthur, leaving him to make his own small-boy's sense of the situation and it ended up with him not being far off the mark. 'I wish she was here with us.' He sighed, suddenly losing interest in his present.

'His little face was so sad it would have broken your hearts,' Lily told Annie and Sybil when they came round on New Year's Eve, once they'd spent a long time oohing and aahing over the silver heart locket from Harry, which Lily had worn non-stop since Christmas Eve.

'How about Margie? How is she getting along,

275

really and truly?' Sybil sat at the kitchen table, pinking shears in hand, hovering over a piece of ice-blue satin supplied by Maureen Godwin for the bridesmaid's dress that Lily had promised to make. A hard-pressed Lily had begged Sybil and Annie to lend a hand whenever they could find the time and today was the best opportunity for the three young women to get together and start work on the intricate pattern.

'I dropped in on her and Granddad on Boxing Day,' Lily answered without looking up from the paper pattern, which she'd laid out alongside the fabric – smallish pieces for the bodice and sleeves, larger ones for the skirt. 'She's keeping her chin up, considering.'

'And what does your granddad think?' Standing by with pins at the ready, Annie didn't beat about the bush. 'Does he say Margie's gone and chucked her life down the drain all in one go, that she's a scarlet woman and all?'

Lily shook her head. 'Granddad never says much so you can't tell what he's thinking.'

'No, but he's at least given Margie a roof over her head,' Sybil reminded them. Of the three women she was the one who spoke with most consideration and calmness – a trait she'd inherited from her own mother who had been an overseer in Calvert's spinning shed before the war. 'Are any of those pieces cut on the bias?' she asked Lily, ready to refold the cloth.

'Yes please – the ones for the skirt. It's gored so as to hang perfectly, fitted on the hips and swinging out at the hem.'

'And have you seen Harry lately?' Forthright Annie carried on probing. 'How's his poor face?'

'Healing up nicely, thanks.' Lily had squeezed in a quick Boxing Day visit to Raglan Road on her return from Ada Street. This time Harry hadn't been slow to invite her into the front room where they'd snuggled close on the leather settee while his mother and Peggy made tea and scones in the kitchen, only breaking apart when the door handle turned and Betty had brought in the loaded tea tray.

'Don't worry, he'll soon get back his film-star looks and you won't need to be ashamed to be seen on his arm,' Sybil chuckled as she folded and flattened the satin.

'I'd never be ashamed of Harry,' Lily protested before breaking into a self-conscious smile.

'Here, Annie, lay this sleeve piece on to the material and pin it on good and straight. Then, Sybil, you can start cutting whenever you like.'

'Yes, Miss Briggs. No, Miss Briggs. Three bags full, Miss Briggs!' Sybil and Annie chorused.

'I'm only saying – we need to get a move on if Maureen's to wear this dress at her sister's wedding in a month's time. Then there's that summer dress for Elsie, and your cousin wants us to make a woollen two-piece for her job at the Yorkshire Bank, doesn't she, Annie?'

Annie nodded and handed Sybil the pins. 'At this rate we'll have a list as long as our arms to keep us busy and before we know it there'll be no need to keep on toiling away at Calvert's, at the mill with slaves – you'll see.'

'Well, a girl can but dream!' Sybil laughed at Annie's snatched piece of remembered poetry – John Milton's blind old Samson Agonistes put to work on the treadmill – which they'd all learned by heart at school.

'No.' Lily seized upon Annie's idea and carried on in a more serious tone. 'What if Annie's right? Don't you think we could do it, the three of us together?'

Methodically Sybil began cutting around the paper pattern, bodice pieces first. 'Do what, Lil?'

'Set up shop,' she explained. 'All we need to do is to keep the orders coming in.'

'Which we could do right away by passing the word around,' Annie argued. 'We could even put an advertisement in the *Yorkshire Post* – "Have your dresses made up by experienced seamstresses. Prices on application" – that sort of thing.'

Sybil stayed quiet as she continued to cut, taking care to follow the lines exactly because there was very little material to spare and one slip could ruin the whole thing.

'Wouldn't that be grand?' Lily mused, drifting off on her favourite fantasy cloud. She placed a reel of pale blue cotton thread on to the treadle machine.

First she looped the end of the thread around hooks and small metal cogs until finally she could insert it through the eye of the vertical needle, which she then lowered out of sight through a tiny hole in a metal plate until it connected with the thread wound around the spool hidden underneath. Another slow turn of the large wheel that drove the machine brought both threads back to the surface ready to begin. 'Have you finished cutting out those bodice pieces yet?' she asked.

'Yes, but hold your horses – I need to tack them together before you get to work with the machine.' A perfectionist as always, Sybil refused to be rushed. 'Anyway, say we placed our advert and we got a rush of orders,' she surmised, 'when would we find the time to make them up?'

'That's exactly the point,' Annie said excitedly. 'We wouldn't if we were still at Calvert's. We'd have to give up working there and launch out by our-selves!'

'Whereabouts?' Sybil wanted to know, making large, even running stitches as she talked.

'There's that little empty shop by Sykes' bakery on Chapel Street,' Lily said, quick as a flash. 'It used to be Henshaw's Haberdashers.'

'I know the one.' In Annie's mind she already had the shop window frame and door painted bright green with a sign above that read 'Pearson, Dacre and Briggs – Professional Dressmakers' in fine gold lettering. Or better still, 'Chapel Street Dressmakers' and underneath, in smaller writing, 'High Quality – Low Cost. Why Not Give us a Try!'

'Ah, but that's opposite the rag and bone yard,' Sybil objected. 'There'd be filthy horses and carts trundling in and out all day long.'

'No, Bradley's yard is further along towards the tram terminus.' Lily held to the notion that Henshaw's would be the right choice. 'I'm talking about the top of Chapel Street, as you come to the first set of railings overlooking Linton Park.'

Pausing for a moment from their pinning, pinking and tacking, the three women exchanged excited glances before cold reality crept in.

'Then again, we'd be taking a big risk to start paying rent on a shop without being certain we could keep the orders coming in,' Sybil pointed out.

'Things being as they are,' Lily acknowledged, remembering the unpaid coal bill resting on the mantelpiece. 'Not many people have the money to splash out on having dresses made, even if it is only one and sixpence once in a blue moon.'

'Trust you two to put a dampener on things.' Annie's grumble was only half serious. Even her happy-go-lucky mood had taken a small dip as she thought through the practicalities of giving up her regular wage packet and having to fly by the seat of her pants.

'Here.' Sybil passed the tacked pieces to Lily who sat down at the machine and began to treadle. A rhythmic whir and the rapid pounding of the needle through smooth fabric filled the quiet kitchen.

'So if we're not leaving the mill and setting up as dressmakers off our own bat, what New Year's resolutions shall we make instead?' Annie wondered in an effort to lift the mood again.

'Go ahead – you tell us yours first,' Sybil urged as she began to tidy away scraps of satin into a brown paper bag.

'That's easy!' Annie declared with a wicked grin. 'Mine is to get Robert's ring on the third finger of my left hand!'

'Poor Robert!' Lily laughed at her friend's ambition. 'He doesn't stand a chance.'

'What do you mean, poor Robert? Don't you know Robert Drummond will be the luckiest man between here and Manchester if he manages to snap me up!'

'Yes but does *he* know who'll be wearing the trousers if he ties the knot with you?' Sybil pretended to agree with Lily, just so they could enjoy Annie's reaction. 'There'll be no more dropping in at the Cross or the King's Head on his way home from work once he's hitched to you, Annie Pearson, and no more making the girls swoon down at the Assembly Rooms.'

'What do you mean? Who says we're going to give up dancing just because we've got spliced? That's not my plan. No, we'll still be first on the floor, Robert and me – one-two-three, one-two-three!' Annie held out her arms and whirled with an imaginary partner in the small gap between the table and the sink. 'That ring will be sparkling and catching the light and you'll all be looking at me and thinking, If only I could find one like Robert Drummond in my Christmas stocking!'

Sybil and Lily laughed out loud at their high-spirited friend. 'Not me,' Sybil vowed. 'I won't be jealous of you, Annie, or of anyone who gets themselves tied down to one man, however handsome.'

'Oh, so what about you and Billy?' Lily challenged as she finished the seam she was sewing and snipped the two threads. 'Are you trying to tell us that he's not the marrying type?'

At the sound of the gardener's name, Sybil raised a disdainful eyebrow. 'Who cares about Billy Robertshaw?' she asked. 'Not me, for a start.'

'Oh, listen to her!' Annie teased. 'The last I heard, you and Billy were going strong.'

'Not any more,' Sybil insisted. 'Not since I found out just before Christmas that he was walking out with someone else behind my back.'

'Never!' Annie cried. 'Billy wouldn't dare.'

'Shame on him!' was Lily's response. 'Are you sure?'

'Certain.'

'Who was that someone?' Annie demanded.

'Who cares? Not me – I didn't bother to find out.' Sybil flicked her hair back from her face and gave a little sniff. 'I heard some girls from the weaving shed gossiping behind my back, just enough to know there was a rumour about Billy being seen outside

Merton and Groves with a mystery woman. So I went straight round to his house after work, knocked on his door and asked if it was true. He didn't say a dicky bird but his face turned red as a beetroot and that was good enough for me.'

'You mean, you didn't give him a chance to give a proper explanation?' Lily gasped.

Twisting the neck of the paper bag as if wringing Billy's neck, Sybil gave her no-nonsense reply. 'No. That was it – you two know I'm not the sort to hang around waiting to be laughed at behind my back. I left him standing there bright red to the roots of his hair. And it was after that that I decided to give up men for good!'

Again Lily and Annie laughed. 'Until the next time,' Lily said.

'There'll be no next time.' Sybil stowed the bag of scrap material in the sewing-machine drawer. 'That's my New Year's resolution for you: to make sure I stay single and happy – the end!'

'What about you, Lily?' Annie asked when they'd recovered from their fit of giggles. 'Be honest – wouldn't you like to make 1932 the year when Harry gets down on one knee?'

'I haven't thought about it,' Lily said as she ducked her head and smiled.

'No, not everyone goes about things the same way as you, Annie,' Sybil reminded her.

'Like a bull in a china shop, you mean?' Annie's smile was broad and her good humour undented.

'Yes. Lily's different.'

'How – different?'

'She doesn't charge at things, for a start. She takes everything more slowly.'

'And, let me remind you, "she" is right here, listening to every word you say,' Lily cut in. Not that she minded the game Annie was playing – it conjured up the picture of her and Harry walking down the aisle together, her in a long white dress and veil, Harry smart as could be in a dark blue pinstriped suit, and for a few moments she was happy to dream.

Annie spotted the smile playing on Lily's lips. 'See the look on her face!' she crowed. 'I'm right, aren't I? Lily may not go in crash, bang, wallop the way I do, but it comes to the same thing in the end – her resolution is to have a ring on her finger before the year's out.'

'No,' Lily objected as the dressmaking session came to an end and she placed the wooden hood over the sewing machine. She had to be sensible about her ambitions and look at the realities. 'Do you really want to know what I'm thinking when I look ahead?'

'Yes,' the others assured her. 'Come on, Lily, out with it.'

Lily took a deep breath before she spoke and pulled herself back down to earth. 'Well then,' she said, pained by the need to plant both feet firmly back on the ground, 'my New Year's resolution, which I honestly and truly hope I can keep, is to carry on looking after Arthur, watch out for Evie at work and most of all, help Margie through this pregnancy as best I can.'

CHAPTER TWENTY-THREE

Not that there wasn't fun to be had in amongst the tasks that Lily had set for herself. That same night, for instance, she and Harry had arranged to go to the Assembly Rooms together, where they met up with Billy, Ernie, Robert, Annie, Sybil and the rest of the gang.

'Nice to see everyone's here,' was Annie's comment as they entered the hall together. The place was still festooned with Christmas decorations – paper chains and lanterns, balloons and shrivelled bunches of mistletoe – and the centre of the room was packed to the gunnels with brightly dressed girls while the men lined the edges, pint mugs and cigarettes in hand, watching and picking out prospective partners for the evening.

'Including Tommy,' Sybil warned Lily under her breath. 'There he is propping up the bar with Frank as usual.'

Lily put a finger to her lips – a warning for Sybil not to draw Harry's attention to the fact. Better by far if Harry didn't realize that Tommy and Frank were here.

'Righty-ho,' Sybil murmured, taking Ernie in a waltz hold to dance on the spot.

'The long and the short!' Harry smiled at the ill-matched pair while on the stage at the far end of the hall, the band – complete with pianist, string section and saxophonist – seemed eager to introduce a jazz flavour into a brand-new Cole Porter tune.

The words were to do with the beat of a tom-tom and jungle shadows falling, the crooner's light voice soaring above the noise of the crowd.

'Listen – I haven't heard this before!' Annie seized Robert's hand and drew him on to the dance floor.

'Poor Robert!' Sybil and Lily mouthed at one another, to the mystification of Harry, Ernie and Billy.

The singer went on, convincing his true love in the song that she was the only one who mattered, night or day.

'Dance?' Harry asked Lily, confidently holding out a hand then steering her between couples to a quiet spot close to the stage.

'Slow waltz,' she whispered in his ear as he took her in hold. She counted him in then gave him the signal to start.

He smiled down at her and she noticed that he was no longer self-conscious now that the cuts on his face had healed over, the swelling had gone down and the bruises were beginning to fade.

They danced and the music soared to the climax of the chorus.

Moved beyond words by the lyrics of the song and by Lily's sweet, trusting gaze, Harry's smile faltered. He felt he wanted to sweep her up in his arms and away from the Assembly Rooms, away from these cold and sooty streets, these forbidding mill walls, to a sunny, warm place with blue skies and green fields, trees in fresh new leaf and a wind rustling through silvery grass.

'What's the matter?' she whispered, thinking perhaps that he was finding it hard to follow the music or that his body was still stiff and aching from the fight. If only she had a magic wand she would put everything right and smooth away the frown from his brow.

'Nothing's the matter,' he murmured. 'Everything's tickety-boo.'

The words of the song wound themselves around Lily's heart and stayed there long after the band had finished and broken up for the interval.

'I'm off up to the bar,' Robert announced as Harry led Lily off the dance floor. 'What'll it be, Harry?'

Ordering a pint of bitter, Harry reluctantly let go of Lily's hand and watched her nod and smile at Annie before both girls squeezed their way towards the cloakroom.

'Watch out!' Annie complained when Hilda Crab-tree, just ahead of them, tripped and fell against a bystander's elbow. The warning came too late – beer slopped out of his glass, just missing Annie. It caught Lily instead and when Annie looked round she saw Lily's dismayed face so she quickly rounded on the offending beer drinker – none other than the fly-by-night commercial traveller who had once romanced Sybil around the dance floor. 'Couldn't you watch what you were doing?'

'Keep your hair on – I didn't do it on purpose. Anyway, your friend there should watch where she's going,' the salesman muttered ungraciously. Being older and wearing a pale grey suit instead of the regulation blue pinstripe, he already stood out from the crowd and now that he spoke it was easy to tell from his accent that he wasn't local. Casting a belatedly approving eye over Lily, he decided to soften his tone. 'I'm Kenneth, by the way, Kenneth Hetton,' he said with an ingratiating smile. 'I'm sorry you got splashed.'

'Never mind, no harm done,' Lily said, rapidly brushing her fingers over the wet stain on the bodice of her best lilac dress.

'Need a hand with that?' Hetton offered with a sly wink. It prompted Annie to step smartly on his toe with the heel of her shoe then apologize profusely and insincerely, after which she hurried behind Lily en route for the cloakroom.

'Have you got a hankie?' Lily asked Annie as she surveyed the damage to her dress in the mirror above the row of sinks. 'I need to dab some water on this to stop it from staining.'

'Here's one,' Hilda Crabtree offered, delving into her bag as she emerged from a cubicle. She handed Lily a lace-edged handkerchief.

'Ta.' Lily ran the hankie under the tap and started to dab at the dark stain on her chest.

'This was that clumsy Kenneth Hetton not minding what he was doing,' Annie huffed.

'Is that right? From what I hear, a lot of the girls go hot under the collar for Kenneth,' Hilda smirked. 'Not that I'd touch him with a barge pole, if you must know.'

'Yes and I'm sure Sybil would have a few choice things to say about the way he danced with her and whispered sweet nothings then moved on without a by-your-leave,' Lily agreed. Satisfied that she'd done all she could to rectify the damage, she felt ready to get back to Harry and their next dance.

Sensing a scandal, Annie jumped back into the conversation with both feet. 'What do you know about Hetton that we don't, Hilda?' she demanded, barring the door to prevent Hilda from leaving.

Hilda gave a tut of disapproval then dished out the gossip anyway. 'He's only a married man, that's all.'

'No!' Annie and Lily gasped, wide eyed.

'Yes. He's got a wife and two kids living in Liverpool. They say he moves around a lot for his job selling typewriter ribbons and carbon paper and such like. As a matter of fact, it gets worse. Rumour has it he's like a sailor with a wife in every port.'

'Never!' Lily's mouth fell open.

Pleased that she had created the desired effect, Hilda wanted to be on her way, but she paused at the door with a final, barbed warning. 'Honestly, I wouldn't want my worst enemy getting involved with Kenneth Hetton, which is why I'm letting you two in on his nasty little secret . . .'

'Now hold your horses,' Annie began as Lily put a restraining hand on her arm.

'Out of the goodness of my heart, I'm telling you to steer well clear.' Hilda winked, pushing open the door at last and letting it swing back in the faces of a dumbfounded Lily and Annie.

While Lily and the gang danced the night away, Margie sat alone in her bedroom on Ada Street. She was in a state of indecision, knowing full well that the New Year would soon be seen in everywhere in the land by the linking of hands and the singing of 'Auld Lang Syne', yet she was still umming and ahing over whether or not to pay her mother a visit on Albion Lane. The idea had come to her out of the blue early that morning and had taken a hold over her as the day rolled on.

'Are you not going out?' her granddad had asked as he wrapped his scarf around his neck and put on his cap in readiness for the short walk to the New Inn for his evening pint.

'No, Granddad, I can't face it,' an apathetic Margie had replied.

'Can't face what, love?'

'People staring and whispering behind my back – you know.'

'You have to learn to live with what other folks say,' had been his advice. The old man secretly wished that Margie would show a bit more backbone, not hide away on Ada Street day in, day out. But he couldn't make her stand up to her detractors, any more than he could force her to name the baby's father. 'Anyway, who cares when all's said and done?'

'Me. I do, Granddad.' She found she cared more than she'd expected about the bad opinions of Dorothy, Hilda and the other Kingsley's girls and, truth be told, her old self-confidence had oozed away over the last few weeks to the point where she hardly recognized herself.

For instance, these days she didn't take much care over her appearance, scarcely washing her hair that she was once so vain about, allowing it to grow dull and lank. Neither did she bother with changing her clothes, sticking to a dowdy navy-blue dress and always avoiding looking in the small shaving mirror above the sink in the kitchen at Ada Street.

'Please yourself,' the old man had said gruffly as he made his exit. He'd tried for days to chivvy his granddaughter out of her low mood without success. What more could he do?

So should she go and see Rhoda or not? Margie gazed at the clock as it ticked on from seven to eight. Who would be in if she did? Arthur, of course, but probably not Lily or Evie, unless one of them had stayed in to look after their brother and so take the burden off their mother. Definitely not her father, who was bound to be at the Cross or at the working men's club where there was always a bit of music and a raffle on New Year's Eve.

That decided it – if Margie could be sure that she could sneak into the house while her father was out, she thought she would risk a visit. So she put on her hat and coat then walked the short distance to the tram stop where she was soon chilled to the bone.

'Is that Margie Briggs?' a woman's voice asked uncertainly from inside the shelter. 'It is. Well, I never did!'

As Margie's eyes grew accustomed to the shadowy interior of the shelter, she made out the warmly wrapped figure of Billy's married sister, Ethel Thornton, and said hello.

'I hardly recognized you,' Ethel remarked as Margie joined her, chatting on easily as if unaware of any rumours about Margie that might be circulating in the neighbourhood. 'Long time, no see, eh? Billy told me you'd lost your job at Kingsley's, worse luck. I told him I blamed Sam Earby. He's got no heart, that man. Doesn't he know most of us can't afford to be out of work, especially not coming up to Christmas?'

Margie nodded and shook her head without saying much. She liked Ethel, who was a couple of years older than Billy, with a strong family resemblance thanks to her tall, slim figure and blue eyes. Ethel had been training to be a nurse until she'd met and married Jimmy Thornton, a warehouse manager at Kingsley's, and now she gave the impression of being happily settled.

'You poor thing, you're shivering,' Ethel noticed as a tram approached. She stood back to let Margie get on before her then sat down next to her, chattering on about joining Jimmy in time for midnight. 'And how's your mother?' she asked Margie as the tram approached the top of Raglan Road. 'I hear she's not so well.'

'That's right, she's not.' Margie felt awkward entering into conversation after her weeks of self-imposed isolation but she was grateful to Ethel for taking an interest in her and her family. 'She can't get out of the house much so that's where I'm headed – to pay a visit and see how she is.'

'Well, tell her I was asking after her,' Ethel said as she made room for Margie to stand up and squeeze by. 'And tell her Happy New Year from me, won't you?'

'I will,' Margie agreed, swaying in the aisle as the tram ground to a halt. The conductor steadied her and gave her plenty of time to alight before pressing the bell that signalled to the driver that he could safely move on.

Down on the pavement, Margie drew a deep breath of cold air. Ethel mentioning Rhoda's illness

294

had had the effect of increasing her anxiety and she wasted no time crossing the street and hurrying on down Albion Lane. But when she reached the door of number 5 and heard noises from inside, she hesitated, bending down and putting her ear to the letter box to see if she could make out who was there.

'Lucky you,' Evie was telling Peggy. 'A job as a shop girl at the Army and Navy Stores means you can steer clear of mill work.'

The two girls sat cross-legged on the rug in front of the fire, speaking in low voices while Arthur slept soundly on his pull-down bed in a corner of the room. Evie's fair hair was loose from its plait and spread across her shoulders while Peggy's was still neatly bound by a red ribbon at the nape of her neck.

Peggy nodded. 'It's a stroke of luck that Mother knows the manageress there. They want me to start straight after my birthday at the end of the month. Harry says he'll be able to drive me over there every now and then, or else I can always catch the tram.'

Evie sighed enviously. 'There'll be no noisy, dirty machines for you when you start work, Peggy Bainbridge, just lovely, shiny glass counters and shelves piled high with scarves and gloves and hats, and people coming in and asking for things they need and you smiling and saying, "Is there anything else you need, sir?" and, "Can I help you, madam?" You'll be handing out change and listening to the shop bell ringing all day long.'

'But I hope Miss Arthington takes a liking to me and decides to keep me on,' Peggy cautioned. 'I'm only there on a week's trial, for her to make up her mind.'

'She'll like you!' Evie promised, for what was there not to like about shy, conscientious, pretty Peggy?

Margie let the flap of the letter box click shut and moments later, having heard the noise, Evie eased open the front door to find her middle sister standing uncertainly on the step.

'Margie!' It was the last person Evie had been expecting and her face registered a mixture of surprise and pleasure.

'Sshh!' Margie had been looking for a hug from her sister, but none came. 'Who've you got in there with you?'

'Only Peggy. Arthur's fast asleep. Margie, what are you doing here?'

'I've come to see Mother. Is she still up?'

Evie shook her head as she stood to one side and let Margie into the kitchen, standing with her at the bottom of the stairs. 'No, Mother doesn't get out of bed for more than a couple of hours each day, not since Christmas. She's probably already asleep.'

'So it looks as if I've had a wasted journey,' Margie mumbled, self-conscious under Peggy and Evie's concerted gaze and unable to stop herself from wondering what they were thinking. She wished now that she'd spruced herself up by at least combing her hair and putting on some lipstick.

But as she prepared to back out of the house and retrace her steps to Ada Street, they heard a voice from upstairs.

'Evie, is that Margie's voice I can hear?' Rhoda asked through her open bedroom door, sounding alert and something like her old self. 'If it is, tell her to come up.'

So Evie nodded and made way for her sister who went quickly upstairs and into her mother's bedroom.

Rhoda lay on the bed, bolstered into a sitting position by pillows and rolled blankets. Her thin face was bloodless, her worn hands resting on the outside of the fawn coverlet while a shawl kept her shoulders warm and her hair was combed back off her forehead.

The sight brought Margie up short. She hovered in the doorway, registering once again the ways in which the illness had altered her mother – dark circles under her sunken eyes, lips pressed together and thinned by constant pain, the knot of her drawn brows. Margie's throat constricted and a look of alarm flashed across her features.

'Don't just stand there – come in and sit down,' Rhoda instructed in the old way; it was strange that her voice remained the same while her body faltered and faded away.

Margie took a deep breath and did as she was told, perching on the edge of the bed. 'I came to say Happy New Year,' she murmured, aware that

297

she could have chosen a more suitable opening gambit.

'Yes – 1932,' Rhoda reflected. 'Ring out the old, bring in the new, eh? I wasn't expecting to see you tonight of all nights, Margie. Why aren't you out enjoying yourself, pray tell?'

'I'm sorry, Mother, it's late. I shouldn't have come.'

'You're not hiding yourself away, are you?' Treating Margie to a penetrating stare, Rhoda reached out to take her hand and hold it tight. 'That's not like you to stay in, not on New Year's Eve.'

'The way things are, what else can I do? Anyway, who wants a killjoy like me spoiling their fun?'

'Lily, for a start,' Rhoda interrupted. 'She'd have looked out for you – you can count on that.'

Margie hung her head and stayed silent for a while, valiantly trying to overcome the onrush of self-pity she felt. 'Anyway, what about you, Mother? How have you been feeling? That's really what I came to find out.'

'There are days when I've felt better,' Rhoda admitted, still looking closely at Margie and making up her mind to take what might be her last chance to have a heart-to-heart with the daughter she felt she'd failed the most.

'What does Dr Moss say?' Margie asked. 'Is there some medicine he can give you that would help?'

'No, love, there's not. Dr Moss does his best but his best's not good enough, not with a tumour like mine.'

With her hand still enclosed inside her mother's, Margie's lips quivered and tears came to her eyes.

'There's a lot for me to think about, lying here,' Rhoda confessed. 'There's Arthur for a start. Yes, Lily and Evie can organize things so he gets to school and has his meals and so on – they can look after him very nicely so far as that goes. But . . .'

'But what, Mother?'

'But I've come round to thinking that this house is not where a little lad should be stopping, with me being so poorly and not able to do anything for him. I've decided it's better for you and your granddad to have him up on Ada Street.' It cost Rhoda dear to come out with the idea that had been preying on her mind over Christmas but she continued regardless. 'He should be away from here, up near the moors where there's plenty of fresh air. And you, Margie, you have the time to look after him and take him to school. It'll do you both good.'

Margie looked at her mother with fresh alarm. 'Are you sure about this? Have you mentioned it to Lily?'

'Not yet, but I will.' Now that Rhoda had got this part off her chest, she felt she could go on. 'And you, love – I want to be sure that you're looking after yourself properly and not moping around thinking that what's happened to you means it's the end of the world. It's not, you know.'

Nodding miserably, Margie felt the first tears trickle down her cheeks.

'You might think so now but you'll change your mind once the baby's born,' Rhoda promised. 'One look at him will be all it takes, you mark my words.'

'"He" might be a "she",' Margie pointed out.

'Yes. Which would you rather – a little boy or a little girl? Or twins – one of each, eh?'

'Mother, don't!'

'Why not? It happens, you know.'

'It'll take me all my time to look after one, never mind two,' Margie protested with a self-deprecating shrug. 'Two sets of nappies to wash, two mouths to feed – how does anyone manage that?'

'Ah, but they do,' Rhoda said with a smile. 'I've seen plenty of women cope very nicely with twins in my time. Anyway, you'll know what to do when the time comes, what with Lily standing by to lend you a hand, even if I'm not able to.'

As Rhoda said this, Margie felt a jolt of fear run through her body and she stood up and began to pace the floor.

'Hush, you'll wake Arthur up,' Rhoda remonstrated. She was growing tired and she wanted to make the most of what precious time she had with Margie. 'We've not always seen eye to eye, you and me,' she went on, beckoning her to sit back down. 'Perhaps I've not played my part the way I should have.'

'No, Mother. What's happened to me isn't your fault.'

'That's what it feels like.' Rhoda sighed. 'Right from the start I was too busy delivering other people's babies to spend enough time with my own – I realize that now. It's funny when you think about it, isn't it? Then when you were up on your feet and toddling, I handed you over to Lily to look after and she was a good little mother to you, and that was a blessing. Then Evie came along and last but not least there was Arthur, and I went on letting you get away with a lot, Margie, because there never seemed to be time for me to explain what you should and shouldn't do and I left you to find out for yourself. Now that comes back to haunt me – the fact that I never made time to talk to you about the important things—'

'Mother!' Unable to bear the sorrow and regret on Rhoda's face, Margie leaned in to comfort her with a hug then sat back and placed her hand over her stomach. 'This has nothing to do with me not knowing the difference between right and wrong. I knew that as well as Lily or anyone else. And when he . . . When it happened, I did say no because I knew it wasn't what I wanted. I said it loud and clear.'

'But he took no notice?' Rhoda asked, her gaze penetrating Margie's weakened defences. Miserably Margie nodded and looked down at her hands.

'This man – who is he?' her mother asked gently. 'Tell me all about it, love. The man's name – everything.'

'You don't know him, Mother.'

'But tell me in any case.'

Moved by the soft tone, Margie looked up into her

mother's eyes. And it was then that her resistance finally melted away and she haltingly shared with Rhoda every last detail of what had passed on the terrifying night that had changed her life for ever.

CHAPTER TWENTY-FOUR

'Lest auld acquaintance, eh?' Annie nudged Evie and Sybil as they stood in line to clock on at half past seven on the following Monday. She nodded towards Fred Lee standing beside the clocking-on machine, flat cap, motorcycle gauntlets and goggles under one arm, the wide bottoms of his Windsor-check trousers tucked firmly into the tops of his socks, timing the arrival of each and every worker in the weaving shed.

'Yes, some things never change.' Sybil sighed.

'Worse luck, eh, Evie?' As they approached the machine, Annie put herself in between Evie and the overlooker, whose fleshy face seemed to have grown waxier and his waistline thicker over Christmas and New Year. 'Now then, Fred. Somebody ate too much Christmas pudding, didn't they?'

'Yes and somebody had better mind her p's and q's if she wants to stay on the right side of me,' Lee retorted huffily.

Annie nudged Evie towards the machine and taunted Fred for his feeble put-down. 'Come on, you can do better than that,' she said cheerily.

'Yes, if I could be bothered,' he snapped back. 'Evie Briggs, how long does it take you to get your card stamped and put in the right slot? Come along, Miss Slowcoach, get a move on!'

Blushing, Evie hurried to clock on and get started on her first task of the day. Soon hundreds of bobbins turned, shuttles flew and the workplace was going full tilt all around her.

Half an hour later, as Evie crawled out from under the metal warp beam of Flora's loom carrying the last handfuls of gathered dust and broken threads, she found a pair of sturdy legs encased in wide checked trousers blocking her way. Her heart sank as she glanced up and saw the overlooker frowning down at her.

Lee gestured with his thumb for Evie to stand up and follow him out of the weaving shed, which she did, still clutching the debris from under Flora's loom. Once in the corridor and with the door closed behind them, the overlooker turned to her and bestowed on her the typical lewd scrutiny that made her tremble from head to toe.

'You're not so full of yourself now that your loud-mouthed friends aren't here to stick up for you, are you?' he leered as Evie stuffed the rescued threads and wool dust into her apron pocket. Her hair was coated with the stuff, her hands smeared with black engine oil and her heart was pounding as she wondered what Lee was up to now.

'Wait here,' he barked, leaving her standing in the empty corridor while he walked its length before disappearing into Derek Wilson's office.

Evie waited. Out of the window she saw a green van deliver what looked like brass engine parts, then Harry drove Calvert's Bentley into the yard, stopping to let the boss's daughter step out. Winifred herself soon appeared at the far end of the corridor in her brown coat and bright orange hat and, with a quick glance in Evie's direction, she disappeared into Wilson's office. Ten minutes went by while Evie's heart raced and her head whirled. What had she done wrong? she wondered. Had she not worked fast enough to clean Flora's loom and get it back into production? Was that what Lee was complaining to the mill manager about and if so, what would be her punishment?

At last Fred emerged from the office, jerking his thumb once again for Evie to join him. Without speaking he tilted his head in a gesture that meant she should step past him.

Evie winced as she sidled through the doorway, feeling the heat from Lee's body and breathing in the sour-sweat, stale-tobacco smell emanating from him. In front of her was a large, leather-topped desk. Derek Wilson sat behind it and Winifred stood at a metal filing cabinet to one side. Even though it was growing daylight outside, the black window blind was lowered and an electric lamp on the manager's desk was switched on. The cast-iron radiator against one wall seemed not to give off any heat.

'This is the girl you mean?' Derek Wilson said to the overseer. He peered over the rim of his glasses at Evie, pen poised over a sheet of paper torn from a spiral notepad.

'Evie Briggs,' Fred confirmed, coming into the room and closing the door, the glass panel of which was also covered by a thick blind.

Carefully the mill manager placed his Parker pen diagonally on the paper then rested his elbows on the desk and made a tented shape with his bony fingers. 'Mr Lee says you're a slacker,' he told Evie without preliminaries. 'He tells me, try as he might, he can't get a decent day's work out of you.'

Evie shook her head but in that moment she was too taken aback to defend herself.

'What have you got to say for yourself?' Wilson demanded, taking up the paper and causing the fountain pen to roll towards the front edge of his desk. Winifred darted to save it from falling on to the floor then stepped back out of Evie's line of vision while the manager ploughed steadily on. 'Well, here's Mr Lee's list of complaints about your work, and considering you only started here at Calvert's a few weeks back, it's blinking long.'

'I'm sorry if my work hasn't been satisfactory, Mr Wilson,' Evie managed at last. 'I've been doing my best.'

'Hmm. It says here you can't get here on time in the morning.'

'But that's not true. I've clocked on before half past seven every single day—'

'And that you often take more than an hour to fetch dinner orders from the local shops – a job that should take no more than thirty minutes.'

'That's because Mr Lee often asks me to fetch his newspaper and his cigarettes.' Realizing that her job depended on her defending herself, Evie spoke out clearly now. 'I have to go out of my way to pick them up from Newby's because he buys them there on tick. I call in roughly every other day – you can ask Mr Newby.'

Derek Wilson twitched his nose then drew his hand along his short moustache. 'Be that as it may, there's another complaint here that you don't bring the right things for the girls to eat.'

Again Evie shook her head and launched into an earnest defence of her actions. 'No, that's not right either, Mr Wilson. There was one time when Jennie Shaw changed her mind. She swore blind she'd asked for chops but I'd written down tripe and I know I was right.'

The manager let Evie finish then glanced across at Fred Lee. 'So the worm turns, eh, Fred?' he said with a wink.

'Yes, but she's a sly one. You can't believe a word she says,' the overlooker replied in a conspiratorial tone. 'You know what these girls are like.'

'I know she doesn't look like you can get a good day's work out of her,' Wilson agreed as he looked Evie up and down. 'You're sure you don't want to keep her?' he asked Fred Lee.

'Quite sure.' There was no doubt in Fred's mind that he was winning the argument so he stood complacently by the door, hands behind his back. Getting rid of Evie Briggs would put other girls such as Sybil Dacre and Annie Pearson on notice that they had to toe the line if they wished to hang on to their jobs. This rearguard action meant he would have them where he wanted them – back under his thumb.

It was then that Winifred spoke up. 'Mr Wilson, would you like me to check Evie's clocking-on card?' she enquired, catching the manager's eye with a confident smile.

Irritated by the interruption, he cleared his throat then twisted off the top of his pen to write himself a note. He didn't look Evie in the eye as he delivered the *coup de grâce*. 'No, that won't be necessary, Miss Calvert. I've heard all I need to hear.'

With a small shrug of regret in Evie's direction, Winifred accepted the overrule while Evie stood with hands clasped, listening to Wilson's thin, clipped voice.

'You understand what's happening?' the manager asked, worried by her pale face and stunned silence, anxious to get her off the premises before she fell down in a heap and had to be rushed off to the sick bay. 'You've been given the sack – there's no longer a job for you here at Calvert's Mill.'

'Yes, Mr Wilson. Thank you,' Evie whispered nonsensically, her head spinning as she turned and, without even returning to the weaving shed to retrieve her shawl, walked for the last time out of his office, under the main archway and slowly along Ghyll Road.

There was no use hiding the latest bad news from their mother, Lily decided, even though Evie had tried.

'I had to pretend I was poorly,' she'd explained over their tea of scrambled eggs on toast. 'I told her that was why I came home early.'

Now Lily was carefully packing Arthur's shirts, plimsolls and a spare pair of grey flannel shorts, ready to take him up to Ada Street, as arranged by Rhoda during Margie's surprise visit on New Year's Eve. She'd asked him to choose his favourite toys and a teddy bear to take with him and he was presently upstairs showing Rhoda what he'd decided on.

'No, there's no getting away from it – we have to tell her and Father the truth.' Lily sighed. 'We'll wait till I get back from Granddad's. And don't worry – I'll make it clear it wasn't your fault.'

'No, I'll tell them myself.' Evie decided to shoulder the responsibility. 'I'll speak to Mother and Father while you're out, just as soon as he comes back from the Cross.'

'Good girl.' Lily nodded her approval.

'Anyway, who knows? Perhaps it was partly my fault.' Tormented by thoughts of how she could have avoided the sack, Evie settled on her own short-comings as the cause – her shyness and unworldliness, her inability to stick up for herself faced by the likes of Fred Lee.

For a moment Lily looked up from her task. 'No, you mustn't think that. Fred is a nasty piece of work, that's the beginning and the end of it. But he'll get his come-uppance sooner or later, don't you worry. In the meantime, we'll think of something else for you to do to bring in a few shillings each week. There's a chance of helping out at Newby's for a start.'

'In the shop?' Evie asked with a glimmer of hope in her eyes.

Lily nodded. 'Alice Newby isn't so well these days, according to Ethel. Harold isn't as young as he was either.'

'But it wouldn't pay much, would it?' Evie realized. 'And we don't even know if they want someone.'

'No, it's just a thought.' Hearing Arthur clatter back downstairs with his armful of toys, Lily went back to packing his things into a hessian shopping bag while Evie cut and wrapped some Christmas cake in greaseproof paper for him to take with him.

He bounded into the kitchen, his face alive with the adventure of going to stay with Margie and Granddad Preston for a while.

Lily put on her coat and picked up the bag from

310

the table. 'Have you said your goodbyes?' she asked, hardly able to contain the sadness clawing at her heart.

'Bye, Mam!' Arthur yelled from the bottom of the stairs as he threw his school mackintosh around his shoulders and fastened the top button without sliding his arms into the sleeves, wearing it like a cape. 'We're off now!'

'Bye, love,' came the faint reply.

Then he and Lily were out of the house and running up the hill to catch the next tram while Rhoda lay in bed listening to their footsteps fade on the stone-flagged pavement of Albion Lane.

The curtains were open and the gas lamp outside cast its harsh light on to the bed where Rhoda lay. Her eyes were open and she stared at the ceiling as she tried to overcome the pain of her parting from Arthur. She'd been drifting in and out of sleep since he left, but still the hurt was fresh.

He would be better off at Ada Street, she told herself, and looking after him would give Margie something useful to do. Besides, Arthur always loved being at his granddad's house. But letting go of him was harder than anything Rhoda had ever had to do – far worse than coping by herself when Walter had been called up into the army to serve on the Western Front, and worse even than the dawning realization that she was just as alone after her shell-shocked husband had returned from the war, damaged and without direction, reliving through recurring nightmares his time in the trenches.

It was Arthur's shining face that stuck in her mind now, unmarked by life, with a light in his hazel eyes undimmed by experience, and his voice shouting 'Bye, Mam!' up the stairs before the front door slammed shut after him. He was happy, bless him. He was happy and after she was gone, Lily, Margie and Evie would step in and look after him.

Evie. Rhoda's thoughts shifted seamlessly in the gas-lit silence to what her youngest daughter had just told her.

'I've lost my job,' Evie had confessed to her mother and father not long after Walter had come in from the pub and made his way upstairs to see how his wife was. 'First thing this morning – they laid me off.'

Walter had stamped about, demanding to know the whys and wherefores, had blamed Evie at first then Fred Lee, then the state the world found itself in. 'But you should've kept your head down,' he'd told Evie in the end. 'No one else got the sack besides you, did they? So you must've done something to make them think twice about keeping you on.'

'I'm sorry, Father,' she'd said as she held back the tears. 'I'll go out tomorrow first thing and try for a job at Kingsley's, see if they'll take me on there.'

'Try not to be too hard on her,' Rhoda had said. 'I'm sure she did her best.'

Walter's anger had died down as quickly as it had

flared and he'd soon grumbled his way downstairs and had stayed in the kitchen just long enough to eat his supper before Rhoda had heard the front door open and close and footsteps going down the hill towards the irresistible comforts of the Green Cross.

On her silent sickbed Rhoda's thoughts moved on to Margie. She hoped that her middle daughter would soon reach the point where she would look forward to the future with her baby and not back to the time when her attacker had forced himself on to her. For this reason alone, after long and tortuous thought, endlessly going over the ins and outs of the question, she'd decided to keep the father's name to herself.

What good would it do to go to the police, who might not even believe Margie? They would say there were no witnesses, that Margie should have known better than to go out drinking with a man she didn't know, that it would be her word against his, and so forth. And what was the point of naming names to Walter, who would no doubt lash out and land himself in trouble? No, Rhoda wouldn't follow that course of action either.

She must have dropped off again, coming to as a motorbike came up Albion Lane and passed the house, then horses pulling a heavy cart – probably from the brewery at this time of night – then silence for a while before men's voices drifted up from the pavement. Rhoda recognized the sound of her husband saying goodnight to his pals and again the noises of the door opening and closing.

What time was it? she wondered and she turned her head to peer at her bedside clock. Ten past eight. Surely Lily should be back from Overcliffe by now?

The deed was done. Arthur was safely dropped off without comment or question at number 10 Ada Street. A stone hot-water bottle was warming his bed and a mug of hot milk and a ginger biscuit had been waiting for him when he arrived.

'Look after him,' Lily told Margie, who was alone in the house.

'I'll do my best,' Margie promised, taking Arthur's pyjamas out of his bag and setting them to air by the fire.

Nothing was said about the reason behind his stay. Instead, the sisters chatted for a while, Lily telling Margie about Evie's bad luck on the work front and the two of them tut-tutting over the fact that men like Fred Lee were allowed to rule the roost.

'You look well at any rate,' Lily said as she kissed Arthur goodnight and prepared to leave.

'Come again?' Margie's hand flew to her hair, which she patted and smoothed self-consciously.

'I said you look well. You have colour in your cheeks.'

'That'd be from sitting too close to the fire, I expect.'

'But you're getting plenty of sleep?'

'Yes and eating for two, before you ask. So everything's tickety-boo with me, don't you worry.'

'But I do worry,' Lily concluded as she walked down the hallway and opened the front door. 'And we all have a lot on our plates just now, you must admit.'

'That's right, we do.' Margie sighed then nodded. 'Well, at least Arthur will be fine with Granddad and me.'

'Thank you, Margie – that is a weight off my mind.'

'Ta-ta, then.'

Lily went down the steps then turned back. 'You're sure you can manage?' she asked.

Margie gave a little laugh and threw back her head. 'Get along with you!' she chided. 'And stop clucking around me like a mother hen.'

'Somebody has to,' was Lily's retort. Then she laughed too and went off into the freezing, sooty fog that had descended over the moor soon after night had fallen.

Rather than wait for a tram and preferring to be alone with her thoughts, Lily set off to walk, finding that there was hardly anyone around at this time of night – only a man walking his dog in the park then a thin, stooped woman emerging from the gloom who trudged by without speaking. Maybe the tram would have been a better bet after all, Lily thought, stiffening at the sound of an approaching car, which braked and pulled in alongside her, its

315

headlights barely penetrating the fog. Glancing into the pitch black of moorland to her left then to her right down one of the many cobbled streets, she got ready to rebuff any approach from a passing stranger.

The car stopped a few yards ahead of her and when the driver's door opened, Harry stepped out. 'Look who it isn't. What are you doing out on a night like this?' he wanted to know.

'"Hello, Lily!"' she prompted. '"Fancy running into you." "I know, Harry. I wasn't expecting to see you either. What a lovely surprise!"'

'Yes, that's all very well. But seriously, Lily, you can hardly see your nose in front of your face.'

'It's worse than I expected,' she admitted. 'Mother wanted me to bring Arthur over to Granddad's, that's all.'

Harry took her arm with a gallant display of gentlemanly consideration then guided her towards the car. 'Get in. I'll drive you home.'

Lily hesitated beside the passenger door. 'Are you sure?'

'Yes, hop in. Who's to know?'

So Lily settled herself into the leather seat and watched Harry flick the indicator switch then move off. 'Well, this is a nice treat.' She sighed, leaning back and taking it all in.

'I happened to be late finishing work,' he explained. 'Mr Calvert didn't get out of the Council meeting until after eight then I had to drive him

316

home to Moor House, which took longer than usual, what with this fog and he said to me, "Harry, forget your bike tonight and use the car instead," which was decent of him, considering. It caused a few black looks from Mrs Calvert, who doesn't like handing over the Bentley for my own private use, but he's the boss when all's said and done and he gave me the go-ahead, so here I am!'

'Whoa, Harry!' Lily laughed as he gave her chapter and verse. 'I'm just glad it worked out the way it did.'

'Yes, it's my lucky night, running into you,' he agreed, risking a sideways glance, which lasted long enough for him to veer out into the middle of the road and for Lily to cry out and grab the steering wheel with her gloved hand. The movement was too strong and brought them swerving back towards the kerb and a nearby lamp post. Harry braked and the engine cut out as he jerked to a halt.

He whistled and tilted his cap back. 'Phew, that was a close shave. Are you all right – no harm done?'

'No, I'm champion, thanks.' Waiting for him to restart the engine, Lily grew acutely aware of him sitting next to her inside what felt like a shiny cocoon of leather, glass and metal. She stared at the stitching on his black leather gloves, resisting the temptation to throw caution to the winds and kiss him passionately on the mouth.

Harry, for his part, didn't hesitate. He leaned over and planted his lips firmly on hers, drawing her towards him until the gear stick and handbrake got in the way of an even closer embrace.

'Drat,' he laughed, pulling back to check that Lily hadn't minded his advances.

She smiled then sank back against her seat, eyes closed.

'I've been thinking . . .' he said.

'What, Harry?'

'Nothing. Never mind.' He frowned and got ready to turn the ignition key.

'No – what?' Slowly she opened her eyes and turned her head.

There wouldn't be a better chance, Harry thought. The two of them were alone together in a car in the dead of night, surrounded by a swirling mist that made it feel as though there was no one else in the world besides him and Lily, who was gazing at him with half-closed eyes, lips parted as if ready to drink in whatever he had to tell her. Oh, how he loved this girl!

'What?' she said again.

'I've been wondering how to say this, going over it in my mind until I don't know if I'm coming or going.'

Lily shook herself out of her daze, for a moment falling into her habit of fearing something bad. Could it be that Harry was building up to telling her that it was all over between them? No, surely not. He'd kissed her and told her it was his lucky night and she ought to believe in him and in herself, not straight away go thinking the worst. 'Spit it out,' she implored. 'What is it you want to say?'

He tapped the steering wheel and took a deep breath. 'Righty-ho.' But this was another false start followed by silence.

'Harry!'

Blimey, this was harder than he'd reckoned and he'd known it wouldn't be a piece of cake. He blew air through his lips, tapped the wheel again and tried to grab hold of the words that were whirling through his brain. 'I know we've not been walking out together that long,' he began.

'That's true,' Lily agreed. She felt she had to speak up, to hear her own voice or else she would have to pinch herself to prove she was really sitting here with Harry, in this little world, still with his kiss on her lips.

'But it's been long enough,' he stammered.

'For what?'

'For me to know that you're the one.' He was on the brink of saying the three precious little words that songsters wrote about and film stars whispered on the silver screen – he just needed a little extra push.

Lily shook her head in wonderment.

Why was she shaking her head like that? Was she saying she didn't feel the same? Did she want him to stop now before it was too late? Why didn't he understand?

Lily stared at him, longing for him to carry on.

319

'Here goes. You're my sweetheart, Lily, and I love you. There!'

Her mouth fell open and a tingle ran through her whole body. The declaration had come out of the blue and she struggled to find words that would express how she felt.

Harry too was carried along on an unexpected surge of emotion, like a dam being breached and water pouring through. In too deep and being swept along, words tumbling out, things that couldn't be held back. 'I do, I love you. I'm head over heels. I never thought I would feel this way about anyone and I suppose that's it – love comes along and bowls you over when you're least expecting it. That's what's happened to me, at any rate. I think about you all the time, Lil. I can't get you out of my head, however hard I try. And anyway, I don't want to. I like thinking about you every minute of the day – the way you look, the sound of your voice, the things you do. It's like a magic spell that I don't want to break.'

Still Lily stared, still she shook her head and she thought her heart would burst with joy.

He paused then came out with the other vital words he'd pictured himself saying. 'I want you to be my wife, if you'll have me. Will you marry me, Lily?'

CHAPTER TWENTY-FIVE

'I can't, Harry,' was her reply. The answer sprang out of her mouth and could never be taken back. 'I can't marry you – not now.'

His face took on a stricken look as the words quickly sank in, then he turned the key in the ignition to cover up the explosion of hurt feelings that struck at his heart. The engine whined and spluttered then finally coughed into life. He stared straight ahead as the car set off from the kerb and crawled on through the fog.

'I'm sorry,' she gasped, lost in an agony of her own. 'I wasn't expecting it. I wasn't ready.'

'Forget it,' he mumbled, gripping the wheel. What kind of a bloody fool does this make me? he wondered. He'd been ninety-nine per cent sure that Lily loved him back but it turned out he'd been mistaken all along, a blithering idiot.

'No, you don't understand,' she protested.

'It's plain enough,' he argued. 'No means no, however you hedge around it with excuses.'

'I didn't say no. I said not now.'

'Same thing,' he muttered as he turned off the main road into Albion Lane. 'I'm a right chump, aren't I?'

'No, you're not.' Everything she wanted to say stuck in her throat – not now because Mother is poorly, Margie is expecting, Evie has lost her job. It's a bad time, can't you see? I should have said yes, she thought. Why didn't I go where my heart led me and say yes, I will? I love you too, Harry. Of course I will! Misery and confusion overwhelmed her and trapped the explanations inside her head.

'So let's say this never happened,' he said, his face sullen and shut against her as he pulled up outside her house. He waited for her to open her door then spoke again. 'And we won't mention it to anyone else, if that's all right with you.'

'Harry, I'm sorry,' she began, her voice still failing her, her hand trembling on the door handle.

'No, no, forget it,' he insisted. Why didn't she just get out of the car and walk away, end his misery?

He was angry, pushing her away, not giving her a chance to explain. 'Mother will be expecting me – I'd better go.' Still the right words escaped her and out came the wrong ones, sending her careering off down the track she least wanted to go.

Harry gave a slight nod, nothing else.

Lost in a storm of conflicting emotions, Lily was defeated by his sullen silence. She opened the car door and stepped out on to the cobbles. 'Ta for the lift,' she said, helplessly adrift.

'Any time,' he replied through gritted teeth, hands still gripping the wheel, gaze fixed straight ahead.

She was still reaching for the right thing to say when Harry pressed the accelerator pedal and the engine raced.

Quickly Lily clicked the door shut and stepped back. He left her standing in the middle of the street, cloaked by foggy silence, her heart burdened by a weight that almost made her sink on to the cold ground.

Harry knew it was too late in the evening to consider dropping in at the pub. Besides, it was Monday and there'd be no one there. Instead, he drove aimlessly around the back streets and eventually found himself on Canal Road, idling past the empty mills, public baths and picture house at ten miles per hour and trying to make sense of what had just happened.

For a man used to easing through life with a joke and a ready smile, he found Lily's rejection unfathomable. After all, people didn't say no to easy-going, popular Harry Bainbridge. His pals laughed with him and slapped him on the back, drew him into the middle of their group, bought him a drink and shared football stories, admired his boss's car. They winked at him and told him he could have the pick of the crop as far as girls were concerned, if only he would remember to polish his shoes before he went out, get a decent short, back and sides and steer his partner around the dance floor without revealing that he had two left feet.

He'd been out with plenty of girls, of course. Most recently, in early November, he'd hitched up with Vera Wilkinson, Lily's fellow worker in the mending department. They'd been to the pictures a couple of times but it had soon fizzled out, and before that he'd spent a few evenings in the Cross with Annie's friend Flora Johnson, but she'd proved too much of a handful, so he'd backed off from her and returned to his footloose, fancy-free ways.

So when he'd asked Lily to dance that night at the Assembly Rooms and the band had played 'Goodnight, Sweetheart' and she'd counted him into the waltz, he'd expected it to be pleasant enough but not something that would knock him for six the way it did. He'd got one arm around her waist and she was looking up at him and smiling and for some reason he'd suddenly felt drunk, dizzy, intoxicated. They'd woven in between other couples and he'd breathed her in – her in her lilac dress, with the deepest brown eyes and warm, full-lipped smile that he'd known all his life but taken no notice of until that moment, her hair and skin giving off a scent of fresh flowers from the soap she must use. Later that night, once they'd parted ways, all Harry could think of was the soft feel of Lily's lilac dress, the warmth of her skin beneath and the smile that lit up her lips and eyes.

After that he'd jumped right in and not looked back. For him it was Lily-this and Lily-that every time he opened his trap until Billy had laughed at him one night at the Cross. 'Whoa!' he'd said, as if Harry was a runaway horse. 'You'll scare the life out of the girl if you carry on like that.' So Harry had tried his best not to come on too strong, only giving Lily a small wave if he'd spotted her and her pals on their way to work and not hanging around at the end of her street on the off-chance of running into her the way he wanted to. Nice and easy did it – and slowly he'd felt a growing confidence that he wasn't the only one who felt the way he did.

And now this. Bringing the flow of warm memories to an abrupt halt, he pulled over to the kerb outside Napier's, grasped the wheel and let his head drop forward, thinking it through to the bitter end.

After a while, he let out a long, loud sigh, pulled himself together and sat bolt upright. Well, you won't catch me doing that again in a hurry, he resolved, staring up at the dim yellow halo of light cast by the street lamp outside the scrap yard. Lily Briggs has missed her chance with me and that's that.

They called it a broken heart, as if love was the glue that held the various working parts together and when love fled, the pieces shattered into tiny fragments, leaving you desperately searching on hands and knees for what scraps you could salvage.

In bed that night, with Evie sound asleep under the eaves of their attic bedroom, Lily scrabbled to save herself.

Harry's proposal had thrown her completely. He called me his sweetheart, she remembered, then waited in agony for the fresh wave of regret to pass. When he spoke his face had been clear and honest and more handsome than ever, his eyes bright with expectation. The words had poured out of him, shiny and new though they'd been spoken a thousand times before, up and down the land and through the centuries, and a million other lovers had sworn their love and sealed it with a kiss.

But not her, not Lily Briggs.

Harry thought about her all the time. He couldn't get her out of his head. She cast a magic spell. That's what he'd said. And part of her had soared and sung like a bird in a bright blue sky, but another part was earth-bound, tied down and clogged by heavy responsibility, reminding her she was the good girl of the family, the eldest daughter who looked after others and put them first. The songbird had flown up and up until it was a dark speck, smaller and smaller and finally vanishing, leaving only the solid, dutiful part of her on the ground below.

Yes, Harry, she should have said. *Yes, I love you, yes, I'll marry you!* And she would have been the happiest girl in the world after that. Obstacles would have fallen away. Her mother would have been informed and would have given them her blessing, her father's rant against it would have soon faded to a grumble and he would have taken longer but in the end, what was there to be said against Harry Bainbridge, the lad earning a decent wage as a chauffeur and who lived on the next street? Before she knew it, she, Annie and Sybil would have been sewing a white satin dress for a summer wedding.

That's all very well in a fairy tale, Lily reflected as she lay in the icy silence on her flock mattress, tears rolling down her cheeks on to her pillow. But look again at the facts, consider how much her mother relied on her to take over where she left off once and for all. Lily knew her mother would never be strong again, not well enough to cook and mend, clean and bake, chivvy and knock Arthur into shape each morning ready for school. And think about Father – he'd never allow the wedding to go ahead, not the way things were. He wouldn't let Lily's wage go out of the house, for a start, not now it was the only money coming in.

The more she thought about the family failing to make ends meet, the more misery descended over Lily like a cold shroud. Love didn't put bread on the table, she realized – it didn't fill empty stomachs. And even when – in fact, not 'when' but 'if' – *if* Miss Valentine eventually gave the go-ahead and Lily reached her full burler and mender's wage of thirty shillings, that amount by itself wouldn't pay the coalman, together with the milkman, the green-grocer and the butcher and she would still have to earn extra money by bits of dressmaking here and there, which would use up every spare minute of her day, with nowhere for her and Harry to fit in unless . . . unless she threw it all to one side and ran round this minute to Raglan Road to knock on his door in the middle of the night and tell him she did love him after all. Yes, she could do that, but then what? Then they got married and set up home together, her and Harry, leaving Margie, her new baby, Evie and Arthur to cope on their own without a penny coming in.

See! she told herself. You were right to keep your feet on the ground, Lily Briggs – it's plain as the nose on your face that you can't marry Harry Bainbridge.

But she lay awake all night, as though on her hands and knees in the dark, searching in vain for the lost fragments of her broken heart.

When Lily went to work at Calvert's as usual next morning, Evie took herself off to Kingsley's mill around the corner. Ignoring the curious glances of workers like Hilda Crabtree who were clocking on, she scanned the 'situations vacant' noticeboard at the grimy entrance: they needed rovers, combers and twisters in the spinning shed – none of which she was qualified to do, she realized. A piecer was needed in the weaving shed to join together threads that were broken whilst the machines were in motion – another job that required experience so that was no good either. But right at the bottom of the list she noticed that Kingsley's needed a scavenger, an unskilled job for a school-leaver, which was right up her street. So she screwed up her courage and went with the flow of the jostling crowd down a corridor until she came to a door marked Manager's Office, where she drew a deep breath and knocked. There was no answer.

'There's nobody in there, I can tell you that,' a passing worker informed Evie. 'Mr Crossley doesn't get in until gone eight o'clock. Anyway, what do you want him for?'

'I came to ask about the scavenger's job,' Evie explained.

The stout woman in a threadbare brown apron looked her up and down and seemed to take pity. 'Try Sam Earby's office at the end of the corridor,' she suggested.

Evie moved on along the corridor. Her rat-a-tat-tat on the overlooker's door was followed by a shout for her to come in and she was faced by Earby's sour, harassed expression.

'What are you after?' the overlooker barked, scarcely bothering to look up from a pile of paperwork.

'Do you need a scavenger?' she asked timidly.

'Situation's taken,' came the rapid-fire response. A tick in a column, a scribbled signature, paper on the spike, move on.

'Thank you,' Evie said as she made a crestfallen retreat.

She made her way on to the next mill on Canal Road – a giant structure with a colonnade of stone pillars along the front and an intricate Italianate tower – to scan the noticeboard with the same result, and on again throughout the morning, knocking on doors only to be disappointed and heading back home, passing Calvert's as the workers stopped for dinner.

'Yoo-hoo, Evie!' Sybil cried, raising the first-floor canteen window and leaning out. She'd spotted the dejected figure of Lily's youngest sister down in the street and, sympathizing with her situation, had immediately invented an errand for her. 'Have you got time to pop into the remnant shop? If you do, can you pick up the couple of yards of brown velour they've set by for me? There's a threepenny bit in it for you.'

'Yes, and I need two reels of black buttonhole thread from Cliff Street,' Annie added as she elbowed Sybil to one side. 'Only if you've got time, mind you.'

Soon Evie had a whole list of errands to run – a message about coal delivery to hand on from Ethel Newby to her mother at the sweet shop, a request for Reckitt's blue dip from Jennie Shaw, and finally a mission to Market Row, to Jean Carson's house, to fetch the reading glasses that she'd absent-mindedly left on the mantelpiece that morning.

Evie took them on willingly, repeating them to herself under her breath as she made her way first to the remnant shop then on to Cliff Street market for the thread.

*

'Ta for that.' Lily winked at Sybil, who had set the ball rolling, but she was soon distracted by the familiar sight of Stanley Calvert's Bentley turning in under the main archway. Her stomach churned as she saw Harry at the wheel, his face hidden by the peak of his cap.

'What's Calvert want?' Jennie saw it too and pulled a face. 'Who's going to be handed their cards today, I wonder?'

They waited on tenterhooks for a decree from on high, but in fact it was Harry who soon marched into the busy, steam-filled room with its clashing cutlery and smell of hot dinner, looking to neither right nor left and bending forward to speak only to Winifred who sat with Jean at a table near the counter. He was out again in a flash, determined not to let his gaze wander, then down into the yard below to sit in the car with his boss while Winifred collected her coat and hat from the office.

'Hmm,' Annie noted with a frown and a worried glance at Lily.

'Not now,' Sybil advised, giving Annie a nudge. Lily looked hot and bothered as it was.

The week ground relentlessly on and it wasn't until Friday that Lily felt able to share her situation with Sybil and Annie. 'It's all over between Harry and me,' she told them as they clocked off and set off on the walk home. For four whole days she'd felt weary and hopeless, as if the bottom of her world had fallen out, but trying not to let it show.

Only now that they'd all watched Harry collect Winifred, who they'd heard had gone to visit family in Scarborough – her smiling at him and hopping into the front passenger seat beside him – and Sybil and Annie had been witnesses to him ignoring Lily for the third or fourth time in as many days had it proved too hard for her to conceal the reason.

Sybil's eyes widened and she gasped. 'Don't tell me! I bet Winifred Calvert has been setting her cap in his direction and Harry's been daft enough to let himself get sucked in.'

'No, it's not that.' Lily sighed. If only you knew, she thought. I promised Harry I wouldn't say anything, but it's me. I'm the one who's to blame.

Annie couldn't believe Lily's news either. Lily and Harry were made for each other – anybody could see that. 'What then?' she asked.

'If you ask me, it's not Winifred that Lily needs to worry about,' Florence cut in before Lily could answer. The bobbin ligger had been walking slightly ahead of the three friends and she turned to them with the expression of a nosy-parker unable to hold back a juicy piece of gossip.

'We're not asking you,' Annie informed her.

But Florence chugged ahead like a train without brakes. 'If I were her, I'd be looking closer to home.'

Sybil strode ahead and blocked her way at the corner of Ghyll Road and Albion Lane. 'What do you mean by that?' she demanded.

'Yes, Florence. If you insist on putting in your

halfpennyworth, best come straight out with it,' Annie agreed.

Lily could see colour rising to Florence's cheeks and recognized second thoughts flitting across her face. 'Never mind, take no notice,' she told the others, fearing the worst.

'No, Lil. Florence had better come clean,' Annie insisted fiercely. She disliked Florence's sourpuss ways and was determined to stick up for Lily, backing Florence against a blackened stone wall. 'What do you mean, Lily should look closer to home?'

Pressed for an explanation, Florence quickly flew from defence to attack, letting her vicious streak emerge. 'All right, I'm only saying what Hilda told me when I bumped into her outside the pictures on Tuesday night. And Hilda had it from Dorothy, who had it from Billy, which is practically the horse's mouth, if you must know.'

'For goodness' sake, Florence, spit it out,' Sybil implored.

Shaking her head and overwhelmed by the clatter, rumble and chug of workers departing on foot, by bike and in buses, Lily backed away to the edge of the kerb.

'Oh all right, all right,' Florence snapped. 'Lily has bigger fish to fry than Winifred's silly bit of flirting with Harry, which no one takes any notice of if they've got any sense. No, Lily has to sort her troubles out with her own sister – that's my opinion.'

'With Evie?' a nonplussed Annie asked, while Lily

prayed for the traffic noise to fill her head so she couldn't hear what Florence came out with next.

'No, not Evie, silly. With Margie.'

'Why – what's Margie done now?' Annie demanded.

'It's not what she's done lately, it's what she did earlier – with Harry,' Florence said pointedly, rolling her eyes upwards. 'That's what lies at the bottom of Lily's difficulty, I'll bet.'

Margie and Harry. Margie in the family way. Margie not telling anyone who the father was, and if you put two and two together and this latest bombshell was true, who could blame her?

Annie and Sybil looked at one another aghast.

Margie and Harry! Lily shook her head in disbelief. She stepped back from the pavement on to the road. Her head spun, a horn hooted, brakes screeched, and her friends' hands rushed to grab her as her knees gave way and she fell to the ground.

CHAPTER TWENTY-SIX

'Good job I slammed on my brakes, otherwise Lily'd be a goner,' Ernie told Sybil and Annie later when they took him into Nixon's corner café opposite Newby's for a mug of hot, strong tea, for it was Ernie at the wheel of his delivery van who had so nearly knocked Lily down.

Lily had recovered quickly and reassured her friends she was fine, then shaken herself free and dashed off, lost in the crowd. Sybil and Annie had been left to deal with Ernie, who'd gone pale after the near miss.

Lily still wasn't thinking as she ran up Albion Lane on to Overcliffe Road and on to the first tram that would take her to Ada Street. But once installed in the back seat of the tramcar she found space to gather her thoughts. Harry couldn't be Margie's baby's father – it was unthinkable. Right at the start, when Lily had considered the different possibilities, it was Billy's name and at a stretch Ernie's that had floated into her head – not Harry's. Never Harry's.

Then later, when he'd tried to draw her out about it and understand how things stood, he'd listened steadily and attentively and not acted like a man with something to hide. 'It's a bad job,' he'd said with a sympathetic shake of his head. He'd even had a fight with Tommy in the Cross, sticking up for Margie instead of brushing the whole thing off as many would.

But what if Harry had been defending the family name not for Lily's sake but for Margie's? That might make more sense. Tommy had taunted Walter and dragged Margie's name into the mud and Harry, the baby's father, hadn't been able to stomach the insults.

As the tram rocked and swayed around slow bends, buffeted by the wind that always blew down from the moors, Lily was beside herself. One moment she told herself no, not Harry, and she despised herself for even believing it for one second. Then she swayed the other way, pressed against the cold window, with the darkness of the moors stretching for ever, feeling betrayed. Margie and Harry. Harry and Margie. Margie riding side-saddle on Harry's crossbar, her skirt lifted above her knees, slim legs dangling.

At last she stood up and fought her way to the platform between men in caps and jackets that smelled of wet tweed, down on to the greasy pavement and over the broad cobbled road ribbed with shiny steel rails to Ada Street. Before she knew it, her hand was on the knocker of number 10 and Margie was answering the door.

'Lily!' One hand on the door jamb, a shocked Margie blocked her sister's way.

'Let me in,' Lily begged, stumbling over the threshold and pushing her way down the corridor. 'Where's Arthur?'

'Out with Granddad. They went to buy fish and chips.'

'I need to sit down.' Otherwise her legs would buckle again and she would faint in earnest this time.

'Here.' Margie overtook her and rushed into the kitchen, fetching a stool for Lily and sitting her down. 'What's wrong? You look as if you've seen a ghost.'

Collapsing on to the stool, Lily leaned forward and lowered her head into her hands. 'Who's the baby's father, Margie?' she asked in a voice so low that she could scarcely be heard. Each word was torn out of her, but without an answer she was in agony. 'Is it Harry? Tell me – is it?'

Margie looked down at her in disbelief. For an instant she wanted to laugh then a second later she burst into tears, kneeling beside her sister and heaving loud sobs from deep in her chest.

'Oh, for Heaven's sake, Florence was right – it is!' Lily wailed.

'No.' Controlling herself, Margie grasped Lily's hands and made her look at her. 'Harry's not the one who did this to me. Do you hear me, Lil? It's nothing to do with him.'

Slowly the words made sense and Lily nodded.

In a while her head would stop spinning – it must, otherwise she would be flung apart into a thousand pieces.

'What has Florence White been saying?' Margie demanded, her cheeks wet with tears. 'Who put that idea into her head?'

And so, haltingly, Lily told her everything she'd heard and Margie's temper flared, thinking about cruel girls spreading rumours, and then it cooled as she realized what a state it had left Lily in. 'You mustn't believe a word they say,' she insisted, making Lily stand up from the stool and come to an easy chair by the fire. 'Sit down there. I'll put the kettle on. You and Harry didn't fall out over it?' she checked as she made the tea.

Lily watched her through the tears that kept on falling – tears of relief now that Margie had set her straight. 'No. If you must know, we're not even walking out any more. But I just wanted to be sure he . . . he'd played no part.'

Thank Heavens for that, she thought. Though there was no future for her and Harry, she couldn't have lived with the knowledge that he'd taken advantage of her sister. That was how she phrased it in her own mind – 'played no part', 'taken advantage of' – to smooth over the brutality of the event, even to herself.

Meanwhile, Margie stirred the tea leaves in the steaming brown pot and watched them whirl. This is what happened when a false rumour took hold, she realized. People got the wrong end of the stick, innocent names were bandied about and people were hurt. She was the only one who could put a stop to it. 'Very well, Lily, I'll let you in on what I told Mother,' she decided as she poured the tea. 'It's to go no further, mind you. This is between us three – me, you and her.'

Building up her courage, Margie set two cups in saucers and set teaspoons with a light tinkle on to each one. In the background the front door opened then clicked shut but neither she nor Margie took any notice.

'Promise not to fly off the handle,' Margie pleaded as she struggled to make her confession for the second time.

'I won't,' Lily agreed, distracted by the knowledge that their mother had kept Margie's secret close to her chest and not taken action against the culprit.

'It's no one you know. I hardly even knew him myself.'

'So it was a stranger who did this to you? That's even worse than I thought.'

'Not a total stranger.' At last Margie brought herself to the point of naming the man. 'It was Kenneth Hetton.'

'The travelling salesman?' Coming out of the blue, the truth took Lily's breath away. 'I do know him – Hilda told me all about him. He's a thoroughly bad sort. Margie, we have to report him to the police!'

'No, Lil, I can't do that. I've thought about it a

hundred times – of course I have – but I just can't.'

'Whyever not?'

'Because I'd have to walk into the station and up to the sergeant's desk and tell him all the awful things Hetton did to me. Then I'd have to stand up in court and say it all over again in front of a judge and jury. I haven't got it in me to do that, I really haven't.'

'Yes, I see.' Slowly Lily nodded and she felt a surge of hot anger rise against her sister's cruel attacker. 'I have some more bad news for you, Margie,' she went on. 'The man is married. He has a wife and family.'

Margie groaned and covered her face with both hands. 'I can't bear it, Lily. I feel so ashamed of myself!'

'No, it's Hetton who should be hanging his head. Honestly, I could kill him for what he's done to you.'

'And where is he now?' Gathering herself together, Margie fixed her gaze on her sister. 'I can't get it out of my head – am I likely to meet him on the street? It keeps me awake at night. What will I do if I accidentally bump into him?'

'I don't know the answer to that. What I am certain of is that the last I saw of him, he was hanging around his old haunt – the Assembly Rooms, I mean. I was there with Harry and the usual crowd. Honestly, Margie, if only I'd realized . . .'

'No. Hetton has no idea about the baby and that's the way I want to keep it,' Margie insisted. The cat was well and truly out of the bag and in a way she was relieved. She reached out and grasped her sister's hand. 'It's a secret, Lily, between you, Mother and me. That's it – there's no more to be said!'

Days went by and Lily's head was still reeling from the week's events and revelations. She kept telling herself that life without Harry must go on and that she would carry on doing her best to help Margie. Work kept her steady, methodically picking out loose threads and neatly sewing them back in so that they couldn't be seen by the naked eye. However, on the Saturday, just after twelve o'clock, when Lily prepared to rush home to make sure that her mother had spent a comfortable morning, she couldn't avoid bumping slap-bang into Billy and Harry outside the main entrance. Billy was knocking off from his gardening work and Harry was in uniform waiting for Winifred.

'Hey up, Lil!' Billy cried when he spotted her, irrepressible as always. 'Where are you dashing off to in such a hurry?'

Harry saw her and reddened but said nothing.

She veered off the pavement on to the road and around the Bentley, aiming to get past quickly.

'Sorry, Billy, I can't stop to have a natter. I'm in a rush.'

'"The runaway train goes down the track,"' he sang raucously then imitated the sound of a whistle blowing. '"And she blew, blew, blew . . ."'

Harry stepped between them, his back turned

to Lily, saying something to Billy that she couldn't catch.

Then Winifred swanned out from under the arched entrance, hat in hand, with her fox stole slung casually around her neck, her coat hanging open over a green blouse and black skirt. She glanced at Billy as she waited for Harry to open the car door, then turned her gaze with a curt nod to Lily who couldn't help but feel like the ugly duckling in her blue serge skirt, white blouse and grey coat and hat.

Within a few seconds they'd dispersed – Harry and Winifred in one direction, Billy setting off on his bike after them, Lily crossing Ghyll Road in the opposite direction with a head full of regrets and her heart sore with jealousy and loss.

She arrived home to a quiet house since Evie had succeeded in picking up a few hours' work at the sweet shop. Her father was out as usual and Rhoda was asleep in her fireside chair.

So Lily took up a piece of sewing – a puff-sleeved, cornflower-blue dress for Elsie's young daughter. Lily's fellow-mender had requested red smocking across the front of the dress – a time-consuming job that had to be done by hand but which Lily welcomed as a way of settling down and soothing her troubled thoughts. She soon got lost in the task and when she heard footsteps running up the steps and heard the key turn in the lock, she looked up at the clock to see that it was already half past three and almost dark.

That was it – there would be no more peace, Lily realized, expecting her father back from the pub, but instead Evie came flying in.

'Have you heard the latest?' she cried breathlessly, loose strands of hair escaping from her plait, one hand clutching her fawn cardigan across her chest. She looked from Lily to a waking Rhoda and back again. 'There's been an accident!'

'Where? What are you talking about?' Rhoda got out of her chair and tottered towards Evie. Lily intervened, putting a hand under her mother's elbow to keep her upright.

'Up at Moor House,' Evie told them. 'Peggy came rushing into Newby's and she was in a terrible state.'

'What's Peggy got to do with Moor House?' Lily wanted to know. The news was clearly very bad.

It was Rhoda who asked the question that dragged the truth into the open. 'Calm down, Evie, and tell us what's going on. Did one of the Calverts get hurt?'

Evie closed her eyes and frantically shook her head. 'No, it was Billy. Harry was up there when it happened. He cycled down and told Peggy and Mrs Bainbridge all about it.'

'Billy,' Lily echoed, with Harry's name lurking somewhere in the shadows. The picture was blurred and she was still trying to piece it together.

'Billy Robertshaw – Harry found him in the garden store at Moor House. They fetched an ambulance and took him to the hospital. Harry says it's very bad. He thinks Billy might die.'

343

CHAPTER TWENTY-SEVEN

The usual Saturday-afternoon activities – going to the pub after the Rovers match, visiting Cliff Street market, preparing for a night out – were cast aside. Up and down Raglan Road and Albion Lane people gathered to discuss the catastrophe that had befallen Billy.

'How is he?' Sybil asked Maureen Godwin. 'Do they know if he's come round yet?'

'Last I heard, he was still spark out and hanging on by a thread,' the little loom cleaner reported, a dark blue beret pulled well down over her fair curls. 'My brother, Bob – he's a porter at the King Edward's – he got it from the horse's mouth.'

'Oh, but Billy's a strong lad. What do you bet he pulls through?' Sybil insisted. She'd left the house so quickly when she'd heard the news that she was still in her slippers and cardigan.

But Maureen shook her head. 'It doesn't matter how strong you are, not if a car comes along and flattens you.'

'Never!' Vera's horrified reaction immediately slid into strong denial. 'That can't be right. Didn't Harry find Billy in the garden store?'

Maureen nodded. 'Yes, but they're saying that someone dragged him in there after the accident happened.'

'And they just left him there?' Sybil enquired, aware that they'd been joined by Ernie, Annie and Frank, coming from different directions like iron filings drawn to a magnet.

'That's what it looks like.' Maureen was proud to be the fount of all knowledge for once. 'Bob says there was broken glass and a pool of blood on the driveway outside the main house and they found one of Billy's boots in the flower bed.'

'Spare us the details,' Ernie warned, while Frank leaned on a lamp post with his arms folded, seemingly indifferent to the shock and horror of those around him. 'We only want to hear what they're doing to put him right at the hospital. Did your brother say anything about that?'

Maureen shook her head; she had reached the limits of her expertise.

'The first thing the coppers did was go to the garage and take a good shufti at Calvert's car,' Frank chipped in. 'It turns out the front bumper was bent to billio and a headlight was smashed so the second thing they did was go looking for Harry.'

'How do you know all this?' Ernie demanded,

ready to challenge anyone who had a word to say against his pal.

'I saw them going up Raglan Road ten minutes ago,' Frank sneered. 'I might not have come top of the class but even I can put two and two together. Calvert's car knocks down Billy Robertshaw and the coppers hammer at his chauffeur's door. It stands to reason – they probably already arrested Harry and slung him in Armley for all I know.'

Annie, who had joined the party late, looked with concern at Sybil. 'Does Lily know?' she muttered.

'Does Lily know what?' Evie enquired, drawn to the shop door by the gathering crowd and over-hearing Annie's last remark.

'That the coppers have fingered Harry,' Frank said with juicy delight.

That was more than enough for Ernie. He turned on his heel and strode off up Albion Lane, know-ing for a fact that if he'd stayed a second longer he would have socked Frank in the jaw and knocked him clean off his feet.

That afternoon, at four o'clock, with Lily still keep-ing Rhoda company inside the house and oblivious to the nasty rumours about Harry that had begun to circulate, she was surprised by a loud knock on the door. When she hurried to open it, she found Granddad Preston, Arthur and Margie standing on the step.

'We need to have a quiet word,' Bert began,

dipping into his pocket to produce a sixpence.

'Here, Arthur, this is your pocket money.'

No sooner said than a grinning Arthur was off down Albion Lane with Lily's voice trailing after him. 'Evie's there behind the counter. Buy your sweets then stop a while to keep her company.'

Bert gave Lily a nod of approval as he and Margie stepped over the threshold. 'Where's your mother?'

'She's just this minute gone upstairs for a sleep.' Anxiety rising, Lily made room at the kitchen table. 'What is it, Granddad?'

'Yes, I'm waiting to know why you've dragged me down here,' Margie butted in. 'What happens if Father comes home?'

'You can leave Walter to me,' Bert insisted then without preliminaries he went full steam ahead. 'If you must know, I've tracked down Kenneth Hetton.'

'Granddad, you never did!' Shock drained the colour from Margie's cheeks and she clutched Lily's hand for support.

'I did, and don't interrupt. If you want to know how I knew, I was listening at the door when the two of you talked yourselves silly – shall-we, shan't-we go to the coppers? Waste of time if you ask me. Much better to seize the bull by the horns.'

'You actually went looking for Hetton?' a disbelieving Lily asked. 'Granddad, you might have got hurt.'

With a disdainful shrug Bert steamed on. 'I may not be as young as I was, Lil, but I'll take my chances with a man like Hetton any day. And it didn't take me long to find out where he was holed up – in a rented room above a bookie's on Canal Road, as it happens.'

'And?' Margie prompted faintly.

'And the horse had already bolted,' came the gruff reply. 'According to his landlord, Hetton had packed his bag and high-tailed it back to Liverpool, to his wife and bairns.'

'And he won't be back?' a relieved Lily asked.

'Not if the coppers have anything to do with it.' The old man paused for effect. 'Don't worry – bringing them into it was nowt to do with me.'

'You didn't go to the police?' Margie checked.

'Not guilty,' Bert growled. 'It turns out Hetton's been a bad lad in more ways than one and they were already after him.'

For a few seconds Margie imagined a long string of victims similar to herself and she felt sick to her stomach. It was left to Lily to ask as calmly as she could, 'Why, what else had he done?'

'The man's a common thief. He stole office supplies from his boss and sold them on the black market – that's why the coppers came knocking. Hetton's landlord gave them a forwarding address. I reckon it won't take them long to collar him.'

'Oh, Granddad, thank you!' Margie's heartfelt cry came out as little more than a whisper.

'Don't thank me, I didn't do owt.'

'You did – you put our minds at rest,' Lily insisted.

'But you still shouldn't have gone there on your own.'

Squaring his stooped shoulders, their grandfather seemed to have sloughed off twenty years. 'I told you – I'd have been a match for him any day of the week.'

'Thank you,' Margie said again.

'Don't mention it,' he said, patting her pale, smooth hand with his gnarled rough one. 'I'd have flattened the bugger as soon as looked at him, don't you worry.'

Lily was still thinking these things through after she'd left Albion Lane and slipped down the alley on to Raglan Road, leaving her grandfather to take Arthur back to Ada Street and Margie to sit with Rhoda until she returned.

Hetton's disappearance meant that Margie was robbed of the chance of going to the local police over it and the man would most likely get off scot-free for that particular crime. That rankled with Lily worse than anything.

'Men!' she said out loud, emerging from the alley into the start of steady snowfall and striding on towards Harry's house. She didn't know where she'd found the courage to do this after a week or more of him ignoring her and acting as if he'd never told her he loved her, but the latest crisis over Billy had made her set aside her doubts. So what if Harry did turn his back on her when she held out the olive branch? She, Lily Briggs, was dealing day in, day out with things far worse than being cold-shouldered by the man she loved. So she knocked on his door and waited for his mother to open it.

'Harry's not in,' Betty Bainbridge said without waiting for Lily to speak but taking in her anxious expression and the sprinkling of snow on her head and shoulders. Harry's mother stood guard – a tall, quiet woman in glasses with her grey hair in a neat bun at the back of her head, dressed in a hand-knitted russet-brown cardigan and a long brown skirt.

'Can you tell me where he is?' Lily asked. Betty's reluctance to look her in the eye made her hold her ground. 'I only want to talk to him. I promise I won't cause trouble.'

'He won't want to speak to you,' Betty insisted un-easily. It sat ill with her to treat Lily like this, but Harry had arrived home early and had gone up to his room insisting that he didn't want to see anyone. Since then, the police had come and gone without a word of explanation from her son.

'But he is here, isn't he?' Lily contradicted gently, looking beyond Betty and up the dark stairway. 'Honestly, Mrs Bainbridge, I only want a quick word.'

'He's not fit to talk to. The police have been. I've no idea what's going on.'

'Is he upstairs?'

Betty nodded and gave way as Lily brushed past and went quickly up then paused on the landing. Would Harry's room be at the back or the front of the house? she wondered.

Harry himself answered the question by opening the door to the back bedroom. 'What do you want?' he demanded, appearing barefoot in shirtsleeves and braces, one end of his collar hanging loose.

In spite of everything, Lily couldn't prevent her heart from skipping a beat at the sight of his handsome face and she realized in a rush how much she'd missed him. 'I only want to know what happened to Billy,' she explained, almost wilting under his angry gaze but somehow finding the strength to go on. 'And to know that you're all right.'

His eyes flickered shut then opened into a defiant stare. 'What does it matter to you whether or not I'm all right?'

'It does matter, Harry. Of course it does.' More than anything, she realized as her heart went out to him, standing pale and angry, his hand grasping the door knob, his shirt open at the throat. 'Let me in, please.'

Swallowing hard and silently working his jaw, Harry finally decided to do as she asked. He stood meekly to one side and allowed her into the room.

Lily felt nevertheless as if she was trespassing. This was a place where she shouldn't be – a foreign country containing Harry's iron bedstead with one of the four brass knobs missing, a mahogany wardrobe with its door hanging open, faded striped wallpaper, a small cast-iron fireplace and shallow, empty grate. Taking a deep breath she turned to face Harry.

'Well?' he wanted to know.

Where to begin? 'Let's start with Billy,' she suggested quietly.

'You know as much as I do,' Harry told her, closing the door. 'More, most likely.'

'Not really. Bob Godwin down at the hospital says it's bad, though.'

'But he hasn't . . . he's still alive?'

'Yes, as far as I know.' She watched his reaction – his eyes flicked shut and he drew a deep breath as he recalled the sight of Billy's bloodstained, con torted body when he'd found him lying unconscious in amongst the Calverts' garden tools. 'I'm sorry, Harry. Billy's your best pal. You must be feeling rotten.'

Harry nodded without opening his eyes. 'I can't help thinking, Why the hell did he have to ride up there after work? Why couldn't he have gone straight home, or to the match? Then none of this would've happened.'

'But even if it's as bad as they say, Billy could still pull through.'

'He could,' Harry agreed through gritted teeth. 'Did you hear that Mr Calvert called me back up to Moor House soon after the ambulance had carted Billy off to hospital and I'd made my way home?'

'Whatever for?' Lily wanted to know.

'Hang on and I'll tell you. I went all the way back up on my push-bike, even though it had started to snow by the time I got there. Anyway, what the boss had to say didn't take five minutes – just enough

352

time for him to come out of the servants' entrance, hand me my cards and tell me not to bother coming back.'

'Oh, Harry!' Lily sighed. She got up and went to stand beside him.

'It's all right, I was expecting it. The coppers had already looked at the damage to the Bentley by the time I got there. Mr Calvert's not the type to look before he leaps – you know what he's like.'

'But he can't blame you, not if you didn't do anything wrong.'

'He can and he did,' Harry argued, staring straight ahead. 'I reckon he or his missis would be the ones who set the coppers on to me in the first place.'

Lily followed his line of vision, out beyond the ash pit and stone outhouses, over the roofs of the houses opposite, into the dark snow-laden sky. 'That's not right,' she said quietly. 'Not without proof.'

'What's proof got to do with anything? A man like Calvert can accuse whoever he likes.'

Closing her eyes to shut out the sight of whirling snowflakes, Lily took courage and slid her hand through the crook of Harry's elbow. She felt him flinch but he let it rest there.

'What are you doing here, Lily?' he asked after a long silence. 'I thought you didn't care anything about me.'

'That's not true.'

'You said you didn't love me.'

'I didn't, Harry. I said I couldn't marry you – that's not the same thing.'

'So you still feel something for me?' He turned to look down at her, his face in shadow. She couldn't make out his mood and had to judge by the softness of his voice.

'Yes,' she whispered.

'You know the coppers will keep on coming after me, don't you?' he murmured.

'No, Harry – don't think like that!'

'They will. They'll say I ran Billy over and hid him in the store room, left him there to die.'

'But you didn't,' she insisted, turning him towards her then resting her hands on his shoulders. 'I know you, Harry. You would never do a thing like that.'

As she spoke, he encircled her wrists with his strong hands then leaned forward to rest his forehead against hers.

'I do love you, and I always will,' she breathed and the relief of her confession brought tears to her eyes.

'Whatever happens?' he murmured, hearing the words and letting them slowly sink in.

'Yes.'

Harry's kiss was slow and gentle, different from the others that they'd exchanged – deeper, sadder, more lingering. It set a seal on how they felt, for better or worse.

*

All Sunday Billy lay unconscious on his hospital bed until, late in the evening, word got out that he'd come round.

'They say he's cracked a few ribs, broken a leg and fractured his skull,' Peggy told Evie and Lily at the door of number 5. She'd struggled through twelve inches of snow and up the deserted street to deliver the news. 'They expect he'll live though.'

'What did I tell you!' Sybil cried when Lily handed on the news to her and Annie during the morning trudge to work next day.

By now the snow had stopped and people had been out with hand-made snow shifters – sheets of plywood nailed to broom handles – clearing the footpaths and banking the heavy snow in rough heaps at the sides of the roads. A freezing wind pinched faces, fingers and toes and most people wore an extra pair of socks and thick mittens, knowing that chilblains and chapped skin would follow if they ignored the icy conditions.

'Yes, it's a big weight off everyone's minds,' Lily admitted – not least because Billy would now be able to give an account of what had happened and Harry would be off the hook. Whether or not Stanley Calvert would give him his job back was another matter.

At twenty-five minutes past seven, the relieved friends parted, each promising to find out as much information as they could about the improvement in Billy's condition. At half past, Lily was at her station and opening her tin of tools, glancing out of the window to see Winifred arriving in a taxi and dodging quickly under the main archway out of sight.

'Not so high and mighty now, is she?' Jennie remarked with evident satisfaction until Miss Valentine caught her eye and made her carry on with a bolt of tweed cloth to Ethel's station on the other side of the room.

Lily thought Winifred had looked upset – pale and drawn – which proved that the events at Moor House had affected everyone involved.

As she settled into work with her burling iron and needle, her thoughts turned to Harry and her heartfelt promise that she would always love him, no matter what.

She was still so absorbed in the memory that she didn't notice the half-past-twelve buzzer sound and it wasn't until the manageress approached her with a brown parcel that she looked up.

'Now then, Lily, it's not like you to be slow off the mark,' Miss Valentine commented. The parcel contained her mother's winter coat which Lily had promised to alter so she placed it under her table and quickly ran along to the canteen, where she joined Sybil and Annie at a table with Jennie and Mary. As expected, the talk was still all about Billy.

'He's come round but he's not saying a lot,' Mary reported. 'I hear they've dosed him up to the eyeballs, that's the reason.'

'He's not out of the woods yet, then,' Jennie opined

above the rattle of cutlery and the hiss of steam from the copper boiler behind the counter. 'And guess what else I heard from one of the Kingsley girls.'

'What?' Annie prompted uneasily.

'They're saying that Billy and Harry got into a fight on Saturday.'

'Before Billy's accident?' Sybil was the first to speak after a general gasp of disbelief.

'So-called "accident",' a sceptical Jennie added *sotto voce*.

Lily, faced with her dinner order of pork pie and peas, froze in alarm. A moment later, she'd recovered enough to leap to Harry's defence. 'Harry never said a word to me about a fight,' she told Annie and Sybil. 'He would have mentioned it, wouldn't he?'

'If it had happened – yes he would,' Annie agreed.

Jennie, though, was in full flow. 'From what I heard, Winifred came out of the house and caught them scrapping on the front lawn. They stopped as soon as they saw her, but that's definitely the way it was.'

'Well, I wouldn't put it past Winifred to make something out of nothing, or anyone else to make it up, come to that,' Annie said before this new rumour got out of hand. 'Let's wait until Billy comes round properly, shall we?'

Her stern remark stemmed the tide of gossip and Lily cast a grateful glance in Annie's direction. Still she felt too queasy to eat her dinner and returned to the mending room with a sense of dread that she couldn't shake off. She worked all afternoon without glancing up once, afraid of risking a told-you-so look from her fellow menders that might eat away at her trust in Harry. At five o'clock she lingered, waiting until the others had gone before picking up the manageress's brown parcel, clocking off and taking her hat and coat from the hook outside Miss Valentine's office.

She was still buttoning up her coat when the click of the phone in its cradle and the turn of the door handle alerted her to the fact that the manageress was emerging into the mending room.

'My dear,' Miss Valentine said in a voice so full of emotion and unlike her own that Lily's fingers stopped on the last-but-one button. 'I'm glad I've caught you before you leave. You'd better come into my office and sit down. I have some bad news.'

It was true – the world slowed almost to a halt just at that moment when it fell apart. Lily heard the tick of the clock in the manageress's office, had time to put down the parcel and rest her gaze on the intricate embossed pattern on Miss Valentine's silver belt buckle. Then she let the question form on her lips: 'Is it about Mother?'

'No, it's not Rhoda,' the manageress said, deliberately sitting Lily in her own chair and waiting until she had her full attention. 'It's Billy.'

'What about him?' Lily stalled. She knew – of course, she knew.

'Mr Calvert was speaking with Mr Wilson on the telephone. There's news from the hospital, which Mr Wilson has just passed on to me. Billy's injuries were worse than we thought. He died two hours ago.'

In a flash Lily recollected Billy's lean, ruddy face the last time she'd seen him, she heard his voice teasing her about being in too much of a hurry, breaking into raucous song about the runaway train.

'He can't have,' she faltered. He was too full of life, too strong and resilient. His young, broken bones would mend and he would soon be back under the lamp post with Harry and Ernie at the top of Albion Lane, kicking a ball around on the Common after the snow had melted, resting his elbows on the bar at the Green Cross on a Friday night, going to watch the match on Saturdays, launching out on to the dance floor with Gladys or Maureen or Sybil.

'I'm afraid it's true,' Iris Valentine insisted gravely. 'It was to do with the injury to his skull. There was bleeding the doctors couldn't see or do anything about and he died without them being able to save him.'

Lily tilted her head back as if somehow this would stop her tears from falling. Poor Billy, with his whole life ahead of him.

'I'm afraid there's worse,' Miss Valentine said as gently as she could. 'I don't go around with my eyes closed, Lily dear – I've noticed along with everyone else here at Calvert's that you've developed a soft spot for Harry Bainbridge.'

359

The clock ticked. Through her tears Lily made out the cream-painted ceiling, the shelves stacked with ledgers, the manageress's glasses glinting on her dainty face, the pattern on her buckle – everything out of focus, every fuzzy detail imprinted on her memory.

'I think you should know that the police have arrested Harry and taken him to Canal Road police station.'

'Whatever for?' Lily cried. She tried to stand up but her legs were too weak so she sat unable to move, wishing for it all to go away like a bad dream.

'They say it was Harry who killed Billy,' came the apologetic reply. 'Unless a miracle happens or some other evidence comes to light, Harry will have to go before the judge charged with murder.'

CHAPTER TWENTY-EIGHT

On Tuesday 14 January 1932, at eleven o'clock on the dot, the order was given to shut down the steam engines that drove the combs and looms in the spinning and weaving sheds at Calvert's Mill. Stokers downed shovels and closed the furnace doors. A thousand bobbins stopped turning; weavers left off winding the warp on to their beams.

Every man, woman, boy and girl put on their coats and walked out under the main archway on to Ghyll Road and stood in silence to watch Billy Robertshaw's funeral procession pass by. The coffin came round the corner from Canal Road inside a glass hearse pulled by two black horses, followed on foot by Billy's solemn-faced mother and sister. Then came Stanley and Winifred Calvert, afforded pride of place after Billy's nearest and dearest – the mill owner dressed in a wide-brimmed black trilby and black overcoat, his daughter in black too, from head to foot – a small hat with a delicate veil covering her eyes, a slim-fitting jacket with a black fur stole and a long, straight skirt. The sombre procession advanced at a slow march with Billy's friends bringing up the rear, everyone walking with hands clasped in front and looking straight ahead towards Calvert's people lining the street.

Hollowed out with grief and with eyes fixed on the flower-strewn coffin, Lily stood at the kerb between Sybil and Annie, all three in tears and only now able to fully comprehend that their old friend was dead and gone.

'Where was Harry?' Vera asked Elsie as they dried their eyes and went back to their stations. 'I didn't see him out there watching the funeral procession, did you?'

'Haven't you heard?' the older woman whispered back, casting a meaningful glance over her shoulder at Lily who followed them up the stairs. 'The coppers didn't waste any time – they came to Harry's house and took him to the station in a van.'

'Never!' Vera gasped.

'Yes, hand on my heart. They moved him sharpish from Canal Road to the remand wing at Armley until the time for the trial comes round.'

'And when will that be?' Vera wondered. Though she and Harry had only walked out to the flicks a couple of times before they'd both decided it was going nowhere, she had fond memories of her short-term beau and struggled with the idea of him being put in prison.

Elsie shrugged. 'Soon, I shouldn't wonder. They say it's an open-and-shut case.'

'Poor Harry,' Vera breathed, casting an anxious look at Lily.

'Poor Billy, more like,' Elsie argued. 'At least Harry's still in the land of the living.'

'Yes, but for how long?' Jennie added her contribution as she laboured past Lily, Vera and Elsie.

'Hush now. We don't even know if Harry's guilty. All we can do is wait and see.'

On the Saturday after Billy's funeral Lily walked up on to Overcliffe Road to visit the cemetery next to Linton Park.

Billy's grave wasn't hard to find – it was freshly dug, under a copper-beech tree at the far side of the graveyard, with only a dry-stone wall separating it from the sweep of moorland beyond.

Lily read the inscription on the plain stone cross. *Billy Robertshaw. 1909–1932. Safe in the arms of our Lord.* There was a rough mound of heavy, black earth with a wreath of white chrysanthemums on top, the flowers already frost-bitten and shrivelled.

Lily stood for a long time looking at Mabel Robertshaw's floral tribute to her son. Sorrow fixed her to the spot as she failed to find words for a prayer that would meet the occasion. Why wouldn't they come? she wondered, looking up and beyond the grave to the dark brown expanse of heather and rock where snow drifts lingered on the tops and in the shaded valleys. Above her head, the bare branches of the old beech tree creaked in the wind and she didn't notice the approach of Annie and Sybil, quietly threading their way between the graves.

'Need some company?' Annie murmured as they came to stand beside her.

Lily nodded.

'We thought you might,' Sybil said. 'Evie told us where to find you.'

'Have you said your goodbyes?' Annie asked after she'd let the wind envelop them for a while and she felt it was time to leave Billy in peace.

Another nod from Lily was their signal to depart: the three women turned from the new grave and made their way out of the cemetery to walk arm in arm back to Albion Lane.

'Tell me to keep my nose out if you like,' Annie said as the wind continued to buffet them and they clutched their hats to their heads, 'but I was wondering if you'd been to see Harry in Armley.'

'I haven't,' Lily confessed, trying to stem the tide of emotion that Harry's name evoked. Harry locked in a cell on a landing patrolled by wardens inside a prison built like a medieval castle, surrounded by a twenty-foot wall topped with barbed wire – it didn't bear thinking about. Neither did the idea that he was charged with actual, cold-blooded murder. No, it just wasn't right.

'Why not?' Annie persisted. 'It's not hard to

364

arrange – you have to get a visiting order, that's all.'

'But you might not fancy doing that,' Sybil real-ized. 'I wouldn't blame you – not if what they say turns out to be true.'

'It isn't.' Lily's denial came from deep within. It broke through the defences she'd erected the moment Miss Valentine had told her the news of Billy's death and Harry's arrest – a double blow to her hopes and dreams. The shock had hit her hard and returned her to that lonely, heart-broken state she'd been in after she'd turned down Harry's proposal. 'Harry told me he didn't do it and I believe him.'

'Anyway, let's not talk any more about it if you don't want to,' Sybil said quickly.

'Yes, let's not,' Annie agreed. 'Shall we think about the sewing jobs we've got lined up instead? The list is as long as my arm.'

'What do you say we make inroads into that for the rest of the afternoon?' Sybil's view coincided with Annie's – that busy hands would help keep Lily's worst fears at bay. 'I have to make a jacket out of that brown velour your Evie picked up for me from the remnant shop. Jean Carson wants it finished by Monday, would you believe, and I haven't even cut out the sleeves and collar for it yet.'

So it was agreed that the three of them should re-turn to Albion Lane and sew, before Annie dashed on from there to Robert's house for tea and Sybil spent a quiet evening at home with her mother.

Inside the house, Evie heard their approach and opened the door for them, taking in their pinched faces and windswept hair. 'I'll put the kettle on,' she offered quickly. 'You all look like you could do with a cup of tea.'

'Make it good and strong, love,' Sybil requested, noticing how sad and worried Evie looked. 'What's up? Where's your little pal today?'

'If you mean Peggy, she's gone away with her mother to her aunty's house in Hadley,' Evie reported briefly.

'Quite right too.' Annie saw the point of Peggy and Betty making themselves scarce until after the dust had settled. 'Well, Evie, if you're at a loose end, why not sew the hem on this dress for Ethel Newby? It's already pinned to the right length. Do you think you can make a neat job of it?'

'I'm sure I can.' Gladly Evie took the almost finished garment, threaded a needle and started work.

'It'll need tacking first,' Sybil reminded her as Lily sat at the machine to sew in the sleeves to Elsie's daughter's blue dress. The smocking had worked a treat and Lily hoped both mother and daughter would be pleased.

'And I'll help you with cutting out the lining for Jean's jacket, since it's a rush job,' Annie told Sybil, and within five minutes all were settled at their tasks. The steady work was only interrupted an hour later by the sounds of movement from upstairs.

'That's Mother,' Evie said with an anxious glance at Lily.

'I'd better go up and see what she wants,' Lily decided.

She found her mother sitting on the side of her bed, arms braced against the mattress to steady herself.

'I thought I might try to get up for a while.' Rhoda sighed and gave Lily a helpless, pathetic look so unlike her old, confident self. 'But I find I don't have the strength.'

Helping her to raise her legs back on to the bed, Lily consoled her as best she could. 'Never mind, Mother, I can bring you up a nice cup of tea if you like.'

'No, no, you sit here with me for a while,' Rhoda decided. 'Who's downstairs with you, pray tell?'

Lily told her about the cottage industry she, Sybil, Annie and Evie had got going in the kitchen. 'We've had ever such a lot of orders recently, Mother. I'd never have believed it.'

'That's grand.' Resting back against her pillow, Rhoda reached for Lily's hand and looked straight at her. 'I see you're wearing Harry's necklace.'

Automatically Lily's free hand flew to the silver locket as if to protect it from spying eyes. 'I never take it off,' she replied.

'Except when you go to bed, I take it?'

'No, Mother, I keep it on at night, too.'

'Is there a picture of him inside?'

Reluctantly Lily undid the tiny fastener to take off the necklace then opened the hinge to reveal the head-and-shoulders photograph of Harry in uniform.

Rhoda took it and studied it carefully. 'He's a handsome lad,' she commented before handing the locket back to Lily. 'Harry never did what they say he did,' she said after what felt like a very long time. 'I don't believe it, do you?'

The question took Lily by surprise and started up anew the whirlwind of panicky emotions that recent events had caused, but she gathered herself and gave a truthful answer. 'No,' she said quietly but firmly.

'Harry's a good boy.'

'He is.'

'He would never run Billy over in cold blood.'

'That's right, he wouldn't.' Listening to Rhoda as she sat with her in the fading light, Lily's trust in Harry gathered strength.

'So you'll tell him that?' Rhoda urged. 'You'll go to see him in prison and say we're behind him every step of the way? He'll want to hear that from you, Lily, and the sooner the better.'

Lily sighed. 'You're right. I know you are.'

'Then what's stopping you?'

'For a start, Harry might not want me to visit him.'

'Don't be daft – of course he will.'

'But, Mother, even thinking about the prison makes me shudder. I don't know if I could do any good and if I broke down in tears in front of Harry, I'd only make things worse for him.'

'You won't, Lily. You're stronger than you think.' Dispelling her daughter's doubts in her no-nonsense way, Rhoda made firm plans for the visit. 'You can catch the bus to Leeds – that's quicker than the train. Take Harry something nice – a block of soap, a couple of new handkerchiefs. Tell him you'll stand by him.'

'I already have,' Lily confessed. 'Before they arrested him – I went round to Raglan Road and promised I'd go on loving him, no matter what.'

'Then say it again.' Rhoda's voice began to fade and she sighed. A while later she asked, 'You can tell me to mind my own business, Lily, but I'd like to know – has Harry asked you to marry him?'

Lily's heart lurched and she avoided looking at Rhoda. 'He has,' she replied, staring down at her hands.

'And what did you say?'

'I said I couldn't, not now.'

Rhoda gave an exasperated shake of her head. 'And that was you, bottling things up and putting others before yourself as usual, was it?'

The sharp question drew Lily's attention back to her mother's face. 'Surely you of all people can see why not.'

'That's you all over, Lily – holding back and not saying what you really feel. And it's true there was a time when I would have said, "That's my girl. I'm proud of you for doing your duty." But not any more, not when all's said and done.'

'Was I wrong to turn him down, then?' The idea, coming from her mother, astonished Lily and she paused to turn things over in her mind. 'What about Arthur? What about Margie? How can they manage without me?'

'They won't be without you,' Rhoda pointed out with another frustrated sigh. 'You can still lend a helping hand, married or not, especially if you and Harry find a house on Albion Lane or Raglan Road and Arthur can come and go as he pleases.'

Rhoda's surprising opinions came like a bolt from the blue and Lily stared at her in disbelief.

'Don't look at me like that,' the dying woman said with her old sharpness. 'I'm only trying to knock some sense into you. And do I need to remind you what I did when I was in your shoes, when Walter went down on one knee at Ada Street and I had my three brothers and your granddad to look after at the time? It didn't stop me from saying yes, did it?'

'No,' Lily said slowly, with ever-increasing wonder.

'I upped and got married, packed my bag and moved out, not without thinking long and hard before I did it, though. I asked myself over and over, was I doing wrong by putting myself first? What would the neighbours say if I left my father and three brothers to cope? But in the end, it was my heart that ruled my head.'

'And you married Father.' The tormented, earth-bound birds in Lily's mind's eye flew up into the sky and soared like skylarks. Tears of gratitude filled her eyes.

'You love Harry, you say?' Rhoda insisted. 'Well, now's the time to show him how much. This is your chance of happiness and I'm saying you should take it, Lily – take it with both hands – never mind what other people say. You're the only ones that matter – you and Harry.'

'Mother, are you sure?' Lily managed to ask in a faltering voice. The birds soared and sang high in a cloudless sky.

'Certain. If Harry's the one for you, don't turn your back on him when he needs you. Give him something to cling on to there in Armley.' Rhoda held Lily's attention with all the passion that remained within her weak frame. 'Do that one thing and let the rest fall into place. And it will – you can rely on that.'

CHAPTER TWENTY-NINE

'Visitor for prisoner number 327!' a clerk called out in the small, airless waiting room at the prison gate. Lily checked her slip of paper with Harry's number printed on, got up and nervously followed a warder down the steps and across a cobbled walkway into the remand wing. Up a narrow stone staircase they went and along an echoing metal landing with cells to either side. Each cell door had a small, barred window with a metal plate that could be drawn across at night from the outside but during the day it was left open, allowing prisoners to press their faces to the bars and call out as visitors passed by. Stiff with fright and refusing to glance to either left or right, Lily ignored the crude catcalls, tightly gripping the bag containing soap, flannel and comb that she'd brought for Harry.

At the end of the landing, the warder led her into a draughty room containing twenty or so remand prisoners and their visitors. He sat her down at a rough deal table by a window covered by an iron grille where she waited with nerves stretched taut for Harry to be fetched. After what felt like an age, he came into the visiting room dressed in grey prison overalls and accompanied by a different uniformed warder who led him to the table where Lily sat.

He sat down opposite her, feeling a mixture of disbelief and relief that she'd finally come to see him after two endless weeks of incarceration. He did his best to assume his old jovial manner. 'What's that you've brought me?' he asked, pointing to the brown paper bag Lily had carried in. 'Is it a cream bun from Sykes' – something I can have for my tea?'

'It's soap,' she replied, studying his face closely, recognizing his attempts to lighten the mood. He looked the same as usual, only paler, she thought, but how he felt inside she couldn't begin to guess.

'What – do I pong that bad?'

'It was Mother's idea. I have to go back home and give her a blow-by-blow account of how you're bearing up.'

'Tell her from me it's cushy in here,' Harry told Lily, still forcing a chipper tone. 'I get all my meals regular as clockwork and a good night's kip. What more can you ask?'

'Harry,' Lily interrupted. She didn't know what she wanted to say, she only knew he didn't have to go on pretending for her sake.

'What?'

Pushing the crumpled bag aside, she leaned

forward and spoke earnestly. 'It's me, Lily, you're talking to.'

Her loving look and soft words broke through the barriers but he didn't trust himself to speak until he'd got control of his emotions. He reached across the table and placed his hands over hers, gazing at her and drinking in every detail of her beautiful, troubled face.

'I can't stop thinking about you, Harry – what you must be thinking locked away in here, if you're eating and sleeping properly, how you manage to pass the time – everything.'

Glancing across the room at the nearest warden as if expecting a reprimand for continuing to clasp Lily's hands between his, Harry at last let his defences come down. 'The powers that be say that they're going to let me work in the library,' he told her softly. 'Sorting out books and putting them back on the shelves, and the like. It'll be better than being locked up in my cell day in, day out.'

'That's something,' she breathed, her heart squeezed by his ongoing attempt at optimism under the shadow of the hangman's noose. 'It's not just Mother who wants to hear how you are – we're all behind you,' she assured him. 'No one thinks for a second that you did it, Harry.'

He nodded and gripped her hands more tightly.

'And I've lain awake at night wondering what I can do to help, but I end up going round and round in circles. I mean to say, why don't the police believe you when you tell them that the accident wasn't anything to do with you?'

Lily's naive belief in him touched Harry deeply but he knew he had to remind her plainly how things stood so that she didn't go away with false hopes. 'The coppers don't think it was an accident. They say Billy was run over deliberately – that's how I ended up here.'

'But you've told them where you were and what you were doing when it happened?'

Harry nodded. 'I was inside the main house, waiting for a list from Mrs Calvert. She'd gone off to ask the cook what they needed from Durant's for their tea and she was going to send me to the shops on my afternoon off as per usual.'

'And the car was in the drive?'

'Yes. I was only inside for five minutes. I even left the engine ticking over.'

'And there was no scuffle between you and Billy?' she checked. 'Because that's what people are saying – that you two had a fight out on the front lawn.'

'That's a load of old codswallop for a start,' he muttered, unnerved by the power of unfounded rumour. 'How could I have a scrap with Billy if I was inside the house, twiddling my thumbs waiting for her ladyship?'

'So that's good.' As Harry explained events, Lily's head began to clear. 'All it needs is for Mrs Calvert to tell the police the facts and you're off the hook. That's right, isn't it?'

'Except that Mrs Calvert left me alone when she went to get the shopping list for me. I could have been up to all sorts while she was gone.'

Lily let out a sigh. Noticing how Harry's hands trembled, she had to overcome a desire to hold him close and tell him that everything would be all right. 'Isn't there anyone else who can vouch for you – Winifred or Mr Calvert, for a start?'

'Winifred did pop her head around the door, but only for a second. Then I heard her go upstairs, but the police are saying she told them she was in her room the whole time. And that's not all. It gets worse.'

'What do you mean?' Lily steeled herself for the next blow, winding her fingers around Harry's and waited for him to go on.

'Right, brace yourself – once the coppers started digging a bit more, they managed to turn up a couple of witnesses who told them other things that can be held against me.'

'What witnesses?'

'Fred Lee for a start. You can bet your life that he wasn't slow to come forward and tell them about our fight in the yard at Calvert's. He said I was a hot-head, known for not being able to keep my temper. Then the coppers got Chalky White to explain how I got my black eye in the Cross during the build-up to Christmas.'

'Oh, Harry.' Knowing that he'd fallen deeper into trouble because of the way he'd stuck up for Evie and Margie hit Lily like a sledgehammer. It took the wind out of her and she fell silent.

'Did you go to the funeral?' he asked after a long time had passed.

She nodded. 'Yes. We were let off work. Don't worry, Billy was given a good send-off.'

'I can't get it out of my mind – the sight of Billy lying bleeding in that garden store,' Harry said in a faltering voice.

'Go ahead, Harry – I'm listening and it'll do you good to get it off your chest.' Lily grasped his hands more tightly.

'I came out of the house with Mrs Calvert's shopping list and saw that the car wasn't where it should have been – someone had moved it. That set alarm bells ringing. Then I spotted it round the side of the house and saw the smashed headlight and all the rest of it. Not that I thought anything was up with Billy, not at first, because up till then I didn't even realize he was there. I just knew something wasn't right.'

Movement at nearby tables – women standing up and embracing their husbands, children clinging to their mothers' skirts and crying – told Lily that visiting time was coming to an end and she felt the familiar panic rise within her. 'Stick to the facts,' she urged. 'Sooner or later they're bound to believe you. And anyway, Harry, I promise we'll keep on digging away to get to the bottom of this.'

'You and whose army?' he said, clearing his throat

and withdrawing his hands from hers as the warden approached.

'Me and the girls – Sybil and Annie. We'll get you out of here.'

Harry allowed himself a small smile. 'I'm glad to have you on my side, Lily Briggs. You're my Boudicca.'

'And what's more I'll marry you,' she announced with defiant suddenness, chin up as he stood and the warder put handcuffs around his wrists, an astonished grin breaking out on Harry's face. 'Are you listening to me, Harry Bainbridge? You'll get out of here and we'll walk down that aisle just as soon as ever you like.'

Back at Albion Lane, Margie sat at her sleeping mother's bedside. She took knitting needles and white wool from her canvas bag and began to knit a baby's matinée jacket, casting on stitches for the back section of the tiny garment and working on with difficulty in the fading light. When it grew too dark to continue, she put the work aside and went to the window to look out at the two lamp lighters coming up the street with ladders and tapers to light the street lamps. Inside her belly she felt an unfamiliar sensation – a twisting or a tumbling that it took her a while to understand. Then, when she placed her hand across her stomach, she knew it must be the baby's first small movements and she felt a surge of joy. 'Mother!' she gasped and turned towards the bed.

Rhoda's eyes were closed, her breathing shallow.

The baby moved again and Margie went and took her mother's hand, stroked her hair back from her cool forehead, leaned in to listen to her shallow intake of breath, ever slower and more uncertain.

Time passed. Perhaps, though her eyes were closed, Rhoda heard the faint click of Margie's knitting needles as she sat back down and resumed her knitting until the bedroom door opened and Lily slipped quietly in.

'How is she?' Lily whispered.

'Peaceful.' Margie laid aside her needles for a second time. 'How was Harry?'

'He's managing all right, considering. I told him we could get married as soon as they let him out.'

Rhoda stirred, and though it might have been Lily's imagination, she fancied their mother had taken in what she'd said.

'Good for you, Lil.' A smile flickered across Margie's face. 'That's the ticket.'

Then the sisters lapsed into a long silence, holding hands and clinging to every laboured breath as their mother's grip on life slackened, while outside in the street the lamp burned steadily.

'Is there anything we should do?' Margie whispered during a great pause between breaths.

'Nothing,' Lily replied. 'All we can do is to be here.'

On and on into the night it went until at last the breathing stopped.

'Mother?' Lily murmured, holding tight to Margie's hand.

Light from the street lamp filled the room. There was no response.

CHAPTER THIRTY

My dearest love,

I write to you with the sad news that Mother
has died. It happened at home on the day of my
prison visit while Margie and I sat with her. The
end was peaceful and we're glad of that. Father
and Arthur have taken it badly, which was to be
expected. Arthur is still with Margie at Granddad's house, where he can be kept separate from
the business of funeral arrangements. The rest of
us – myself, Margie and Evie – are dealing with
the undertakers and the minister at Mother's old
chapel on Ada Street and bear up as best we can.

Harry, love, these are dark days here at
Albion Lane but you mustn't suppose that I have
forgotten you. The fact is, Mother believed in you
as much as I do and it is for both your sakes that
I'll move Heaven and earth to prove that they've
arrested the wrong man for Billy's murder. I love
you, Harry – 'Cross my heart and hope to die',
as we used to say in those carefree days when we

were children playing hide-and-seek together on Overcliffe Common, back when we had no notion of the troubles life heaps on us.

I love you, sweetheart. I say it again, knowing that I'll never give you cause to doubt it and trusting that this letter finds you well in spite of everything.

I'll come to visit you as soon as Mother's funeral is over. Until then, I'll seal this note with loving kisses.

Always true to you, now and forever – your Lily xxxxx

The letter was carefully written, sealed and posted with a heavy heart. Lily pictured it being taken from the red pillar box at the bottom of Albion Lane and sent to the sorting office, arriving at the prison where it would be torn open by the stubby fingers of an unfeeling clerk who would check through it before it was delivered to Harry in his cell. He felt far away from her and unreachable in this the most difficult time of their lives.

On the day of Rhoda's funeral at the end of January, in the deepest, darkest part of a seemingly endless winter, news broke that Harry Bainbridge had been formally charged with the murder of Billy Robertshaw. He would be remanded in custody until he came to trial, making an already sad time unbearably worse for Lily.

The funeral itself was short and simple with three

hymns and a brief sermon about Rhoda's upright character, long service to the women of the neighbourhood and the esteem in which she was held by all who knew her.

From the front pew Lily gazed at the plain coffin. She was dressed in her grey hat and coat, spruced up with a purple silk scarf on loan from Ethel Newby. Margie sat on her left, little Arthur to her right then next to him Evie. At the far end by the window sat her bare-headed grandfather and last of all her father, who hung his head throughout the service with no word of song or prayer escaping his lips. In the pew across the aisle, George and Tommy looked stranded and ill at ease, making it plain that it was duty alone that had brought them here and they couldn't wait to be gone.

Awash with grief, Lily was only dimly aware that Sybil and Annie sat in a pew towards the back of the chapel, along with Iris Valentine and Jennie Shaw from Calvert's and half a dozen other neighbours from Albion Lane and Raglan Road, who sang the hymns heartily in the unadorned, high-roofed chapel. Afterwards everyone filed out on to Ada Street and waited on the cold pavement to express their condolences to the bereaved family.

'To tell the truth, I hardly took it in,' Lily confessed later that evening to her two friends, who had sacrificed an hour or two's pay to be at the funeral and had just now knocked on the door of number 5 to check that she was coping with the aftermath. 'I was so busy worrying about Arthur and Father.'

'Yes, poor little lad,' Annie sympathized, while Sybil glanced around the kitchen in vain for any sign that Walter had returned home with Lily after the service.

'And poor Father,' Lily added, her heart weighed down with sorrow, her eyes heavy with unshed tears. 'What will he do without Mother?'

'He'll carry on as before, I expect,' Sybil commented, making it plain that she hadn't much sympathy to spare for ne'er-do-well Walter Briggs.

Lily didn't have the heart to say it wasn't true, that her father had turned in on himself since Rhoda's death and until now avoided his old haunts. Instead of frequenting the pub, he could be seen wandering the streets in an aimless manner, silent and ashen-faced, oblivious to wind, rain and snow. He'd been up as far as the Common and down along Canal Road past the public baths and on beyond the scrap yard until he'd been spotted spouting nonsense to himself and frogmarched back to Albion Lane by a passing neighbour.

It was Annie who briskly moved the conversation on. 'So now what shall we do for someone who does deserve our help? I mean Harry, of course.'

'I'll pay him another visit the day after tomorrow,' Lily told her, privately doubting her ability to raise his spirits, given her sorrow over the loss of her mother. Still, she would do her best.

'And have we got any more to work on – any fresh

lines of enquiry?' Annie asked, accepting a cup of tea from Lily and the seat closest to the fire.

Lily glanced at Annie sitting in her mother's chair and felt a sharp pang of loss, which she only just managed to overcome. 'Well, Harry is sure that Winifred stuck her head around the door and spotted him waiting for Mrs Calvert's shopping list, but it turns out she gave the police a different story.'

'Hmm, we'll soon see about that,' Annie muttered.

Sybil raised an eyebrow. 'Tomorrow's Friday,' she reminded them. 'What do you say we lie in wait for little Miss Snooty on her way into work?'

Lily's face lit up. 'I must say you're a bright spark, Sybil Dacre.'

'If she's a witness, she has to go to the police station and back up Harry's version of events,' Sybil added, pleased with their new plan. 'We'll collar her tomorrow then Lily, you can visit Harry on Saturday and put him in the picture. That's bound to perk him up.'

'You're right. And I'll ask Harry what happened to the shopping list from Mrs Calvert. If he's still got hold of it, at least it shows the police that part of his story adds up,' Lily agreed. She felt they were definitely on to something and she could hardly wait to set the wheels in motion. The trouble was that when the three women got set to execute their plan, arriving at the mill early next morning and loitering in the main entrance as long as possible on the look-out for the boss's daughter, there was no sign of her or her taxi. Fred Lee soon spotted them, however, and ordered Sybil and Annie to clock on in the nick of time, leaving Lily to climb the stairs to the mending room without catching sight or sound of Winifred Calvert.

'Never mind – we'll nab her at dinner time,' Annie promised as they parted ways.

But again at half past twelve there was no sign of Winifred in the canteen and when Sybil asked Jean Carson why not, she received the surprising reply that Winifred's absence was permanent.

'She won't be back.' Jean's explanation was short and pithy. 'Mrs Calvert never wanted her precious daughter dirtying her hands with dusty files and inky typewriter ribbons in the first place. And we all know who really wears the trousers up at Moor House.'

Lily went to visit Harry in prison next day armed with a motor magazine but with no fresh leads. Her cheerful front became genuine, however, when she learned that one of the first things Harry had done after his arrest was to rescue the crumpled shopping list from his trouser pocket and hand it over to the police. 'That's good, Harry. And you'll never guess what else has happened,' she went on.

'You're right about that – I won't,' he told her with a brief grin.

Lily felt the familiar smile envelop her like a warm glow. 'Miss Valentine told me this morning that she's very satisfied with my work. She's promised to see Mr Wilson on Monday to recommend me for the full mender's wage from now on. That's good news, isn't it?'

Harry's smile broadened. 'Yes and no one deserves it more than you.' Like Lily, he skated cheerfully on thin ice, all too aware of the black waters underneath.

'And Evie's upped her hours at Newby's,' Lily prattled on. 'Dr Moss has given strict instructions for Alice to take things easy and Harold finds Evie a willing worker and quick to learn, which we always knew, didn't we? On top of which, Sybil, Annie and I can afford to pay her a few pennies for hemming work and such like.'

'And how's Margie doing?' Harry wanted to know, storing in his head each little nugget of information that fell from Lily's lips.

Lily paused to think before she answered. 'Margie is growing up fast,' she reported. 'She's knitting a little matinée jacket for the baby and asking Evie to hem winceyette sheets for its cot. She's even promising to drop in on us at a time when Father's likely to be there.'

'To talk him round?' Harry asked.

'That's right. She wants him to know she's looking forward, not back, and hopes she can persuade him to do the same.'

Harry listened and held her hands, nodding and draining her of every scrap of news until she finally ran out. 'You're a sight for sore eyes, you know that?' he told her tenderly. 'The best-looking girl for miles around, so Lord knows what you see in me, especially now.'

'Don't say that,' she protested.

'I mean it. I have a lot of time on my hands in here and I spend most of it worrying how long it'll be before you come to your senses and ditch me good and proper this time, or else there'll soon be somebody coming along and offering you a handy shoulder to cry on.'

'I never ditched you, Harry. Anyway, didn't you hear me last time when I told you I'd marry you as fast as ever I can?'

He longed to believe her, but wouldn't let his doubts be so easily dismissed. 'A girl can change her mind,' he muttered.

Lily leaned across the table and spoke softly. 'Not this one. And if you really want to know what I see in you, Harry Bainbridge, I'll tell you so long as you promise not to let it go to your head.'

'There's not much chance of that. Not here in this place.'

'All right. I see a man who can make me smile even when I'm feeling low and who swept me off my feet the first time he kissed me.'

'Is that right?' he murmured more hopefully.

'It is. And what's more, I tell everyone who asks me that you're someone I can rely on and trust because you'll never let me down.'

'Never in a month of Sundays,' he agreed, slowly letting go of the fears that had built up during the lonely, empty days locked inside his cell.

So they talked on, lightening the mood when Harry told Lily that his mother had visited him during the week and given him the same type of soap that she had brought – Wright's Coal Tar – and had wept buckets when it came time for her to leave.

On her own departure, marked by a soft brushing of lips and reluctant unclasping of hands, Lily had managed to hold back her tears until she was outside the prison gates, where she let them flow freely.

It broke her heart, it really did, to see Harry so cast down, but by the time she sat on the bus home from Leeds she'd dried her tears. I'll keep my promise, she vowed silently, staring out at row upon row of back-to-back houses built into the steep hillsides on the outskirts of the city. I know for a fact that Harry won't ever let me down and now it's up to me to do the same for him – to push on and prove him innocent, whatever it takes.

CHAPTER THIRTY-ONE

January slid into February and winter's back was almost broken as the days grew longer. The snow, when it fell, didn't stick but melted under weak sunlight to allow small green snowdrop shoots to break through the black earth on the edge of the Common. Meanwhile, Lily, Annie and Sybil didn't rest in their attempts to clear Harry's name.

It was the first Saturday in February and Annie had been at Cliff Street market buying reels of cotton when she spotted Winifred Calvert at the next stall, looking at leather gloves.

'I pounced on her and backed her up against the sheepskin mittens,' Annie reported to the others on Monday on their way to work. 'I asked her how was it she refused to give Harry an alibi?'

'And what was her answer?' Lily was eager to know.

'I thought at first she was about to fall into a dead faint from the shock of running into me, but I stuck to my guns and asked, Why not tell the coppers what happened? That she knew perfectly well that Harry had been inside the house when Billy was run over.'

'And did you get her to admit she'd seen him inside the house?' Sybil demanded.

'No, I just got a lot of flannel about going straight upstairs to her room and having nothing to do with what went on,' Annie replied in disgust. 'Then Mrs Calvert came around the corner and saw little miss pressed up against the glove counter and that was the end of that. She whisked her away before you could say Jack Robinson.'

Sybil frowned. 'You know what this means?'

'Yes, we're more and more sure that Winifred is lying.' Lily didn't hesitate to point the finger at the boss's daughter. 'We were right all along – she does have more to do with what happened than she's letting on.'

'You don't say!' Annie and Sybil chorused.

'So there's only one thing to do,' Lily declared. 'We have to track Winifred down and corner her good and proper. And we have to do it sooner rather than later.'

'Yes, because time's ticking on,' Annie agreed as they neared the mill.

'There's no need to remind us,' Sybil said curtly. They all knew but tried not to think about the fact that a date for the trial had been set for the last day of February.

'I'll go up to the Calverts' house tonight after tea,' Lily decided. There was no time to lose.

*

'I'll wait here,' Ernie told Lily as he pulled up outside the open gates to Moor House. He'd requisitioned his father's delivery van in order to give her a lift after work but this was as far as he was willing to go. 'The Calverts are our best customers – they get all their meat from us. If they catch sight of our name on the side of this van and ask what I'm doing here, it could queer our pitch.'

'There's no need to wait,' Lily assured him as she stepped out on to the road. 'I can find my own way back.'

'Yes and you think I'm going to let you walk five miles in the dark along these winding roads?' he argued. 'No. I'll wait.'

She smiled, glad of the back-up. 'Thanks, Ernie. You're a pal.'

Lily trembled as she passed through the gates and set off down the long driveway to where the Calverts' house nestled in a large hollow surrounded by fir trees. The steeply sloping drive was lit by electric lamps and the entrance to the house was illuminated by a brass carriage lamp hanging from a wrought-iron bracket that cast a strong light over the mosaic tiles of the porch and on to the solid oak door.

This must be where Billy was knocked down, Lily thought with a shiver as she took in the scene – clipped evergreen shrubs bordering the drive as it curved around the side of the house, bare flower beds and a glimpse of stone outhouses beyond. Overhead the tall pines were buffeted by the wind and straight ahead at eye level was a lion-head knocker on the door. Her hand shook as she raised it and rapped hard.

Lily waited for what seemed like an age. A downstairs light at the front of the house was flicked on then quickly off. She knocked again. No one came.

But now that she'd plucked up courage, Lily wasn't about to turn away. When her knock wasn't answered, she stepped back on to the drive and followed it into a flagged yard at the side of the house. Once she'd got her bearings, she sidled between two zinc water butts to peer through a ground-floor window into a small ante-room containing rows of wellington boots and stout outdoor shoes. She got the shock of her life when she found a pair of yellow eyes staring back at her, starting backwards at the same time as the Calverts' cat, which jumped from the window sill and vanished through an inner door. Simultaneously another door flew open and, poker in hand, Winifred rushed out into the yard.

'For Heaven's sakes, you frightened the life out of me. I thought you were a burglar!' Winifred exclaimed when she recognized Lily.

Wrong-footed but still able to notice the absurdity of Winifred in a cream lace dress earnestly brandishing a poker, Lily offered a faltering excuse. 'I knocked on the front door. No one answered.'

'We're in the middle of dinner, that's why.' Winifred studied the visitor's pale, determined face. 'You shouldn't have come here,' she said sullenly.

393

'It's about what happened to Billy.'

'Well, what about it?' Winifred snapped.

'I know you saw Harry inside the house so there's no use denying it. And now you have to set the record straight.'

'Not if I don't want to,' Winifred said in the same sullen tone, her face pinched and lips pursed. 'I've said all I have to say to that man – that Sergeant Magson.'

Lily frowned and shook her head. 'Miss Calvert, I know you don't mean Harry any harm but you must realize that things are looking bad for him. If you could just—'

She was cut off mid sentence. 'I've already told you – I can't help you.'

'Can't or won't?' Somehow she held her voice steady and managed to carry on. 'Harry's worked hard for you and never let you down. He needs—'

'For goodness' sake . . .' Winifred's stone-wall defence seemed suddenly to crumble and she left her sentence unfinished, letting the poker clatter to the ground.

'Harry needs our help,' Lily said more softly. 'I know you're not a bad person, Miss Calvert, because you tried to step in and help Evie. Your heart's in the right place and I do believe you can make a difference to Harry's defence.'

Winifred shook her head. 'That's not true – I shouldn't even be talking to you.'

'But you know as well as I do that he didn't do

what they say he's done – running Billy down in cold blood.'

Winifred shuddered. Up shot her defences again, just as noises could be heard in the boot room behind her and Mrs Calvert appeared in the door-way.

Lily saw that Winifred had inherited her mother's looks – they shared the same high carriage of the head and well-defined cheek bones, the same thick, expensively cut hair and clearly the same love of fashion, for Mrs Calvert was dressed for their family dinner in a full-length, low-waisted black dress decorated around the neckline with intricate bead work and in dainty black shoes with high heels.

'Winifred, go back inside this minute,' she com-manded, casting her eyes over Lily. As Winifred obeyed, the mill owner's wife took immediate charge of the situation. 'I heard raised voices,' she told Lily haughtily. 'And now I see we have a trespasser.'

'Mrs Calvert, I only wanted to speak with your daughter about Billy's . . . accident.'

'Winifred has nothing to say on that score. The police sergeant who called here understands that she was upstairs in her room at the time and so she didn't see what happened.'

The fierce formality of Eleanor Calvert's manner was almost too much for Lily but she held her nerve a little while longer. 'You know that's not true, Mrs Calvert. You and Winifred can both vouch for Harry being inside the house when Billy was knocked down.'

The mill owner's wife replied with cold, destructive anger. 'We can do no such thing.'

'But why not?'

'Because, as I told the sergeant, I have no knowledge of what the chauffeur did whilst I was away – whether or not he was in the house as he claims he was, or if, in fact, he slipped outside and entered into an altercation with the gardener, which ended in one man dying and the other being accused of his murder.'

Mrs Calvert's icy reply pushed Lily over the edge. 'But unless you and Winifred speak out, the wrong man will go to the gallows!' she cried, wringing her hands.

'And unless you leave immediately, I will have you forcibly removed,' Eleanor Calvert told her unwelcome visitor, turning on her well-shod heel and closing the door without a backward glance.

'All right – if the Calverts still refuse to help us out of the goodness of their hearts, we have to try a different tack,' the indefatigable Annie decided as she, Sybil and Lily made their daily journey into work next morning. It seemed the more obstacles they met, the greater their determination to overcome them.

Annie's fighting talk buoyed Lily up and she racked her brains to work out what they should do next as they stepped under the arch and went to clock on.

Her first port of call was to return the parcel containing the altered coat to Miss Valentine, who unwrapped the paper to examine the workmanship then promised her more work in future.

'Times must be hard for you,' she commented confidentially, giving Lily the benefit of her penetrating, birdlike stare. 'I'm thinking of poor Rhoda and now this bad business with Harry Bainbridge.'

'We're bearing up quite well, thank you, Miss Valentine.'

'And have the police pinpointed anyone who might have held a grudge against Billy Robertshaw?' the manageress asked, one slim hand on the handle of her office door. Inside the small room, all was orderly as could be – wage packets arranged in neat rows on the desk, Miss Valentine's hat and coat on the stand by the window, a framed copy of the mill's safety rules hanging perfectly level on the wall.

The clear-sighted question took Lily aback. 'I don't know about that, Miss Valentine.' It was something she hadn't considered up till now and she pondered the possible answer for the rest of the morning, sharing her ideas with Vera when the latter caught her lost in thought and demanded to know what was on her mind.

'Miss Valentine has made me wonder – Billy didn't have any enemies, did he?' Lily asked, using the hook of her burling iron to free the end of a broken thread and pull it to the surface of the smooth, dark grey fabric. 'I can't believe that he did.'

'Ah, but everyone has secrets, Billy included,' Vera replied mysteriously, leaning forward to examine a flaw in the cloth she was working on.

'What kind of secrets?' Lily wanted to know. She'd been pals with Billy all her life and he'd never seemed to her anything but cheerful and straight-forward. In fact, the worst thing you could say about him was that he led the girls on a little more than he should – Margie, for instance, and Sybil, who had walked out with him just once or twice until she'd found out he had another sweetheart on the side.

Vera shrugged and pursed her lips, catching Jennie's attention as she carried a ticketed bolt of cloth forward to Ethel's station. 'Lily was wondering if Billy Robertshaw had any enemies,' she whispered.

'It's about time someone got around to asking about that,' Jennie commented.

Lily felt her heart begin to race. 'And did he?'

With one eye on the manageress's office, the older woman paused briefly. 'Ask me again later,' she said with a meaningful wink.

'Wait – don't leave me on tenterhooks!' Lily pleaded.

'And don't you go getting me into trouble with Miss Beady Eyes,' Jennie retorted as she plodded on down the aisle. 'Get hold of me after the buzzer goes and I'll tell you everything you need to know.'

At midday, half an hour before the buzzer was due to signal the end of work for the day, Iris Valentine put down the telephone and came out of her office. She clapped her hands to gain the attention of every worker in the mending department, cleared her throat and made a surprise announcement.

'Mr Wilson says we are to finish work immediately and gather in the canteen for an announcement from Mr Calvert. Please put away your tools and make your way there.'

'What's Calvert up to?' was Jennie's question to no one in particular.

The anxious mill workers found out soon enough once everyone was assembled and Stanley Calvert came into the crowded canteen, flanked by Derek Wilson. Wilson called for quiet but people were bemused by this break in routine and it took a while for the grumbles and mutterings to subside. Across the room, standing next to Fred Lee with other workers from the weaving shed, Sybil and Annie caught Lily's eye.

The mill owner wasn't a tall man so a chair was placed in front of Betty Rowson's serving hatch. Calvert then climbed on to the chair in order to be seen. He was dressed as usual in his good tweed suit, thick gold watch chain looped across his chest, face and hair immaculately barbered, though everyone saw from his expression and from the shadows under his eyes that he was a man under strain.

'Let's have some quiet, please!' Wilson ordered above the muffled exchange of uneasy comments.

At last the room fell silent and the mill owner

spoke, softly at first but then louder and more confidently. 'What I have to say will come as no surprise,' he began, hooking his thumbs into his waistcoat pockets and striking a politician's pose so that he looked confident even if he didn't sound or feel it. 'We're none of us fools – we all know that the country's productivity has been hit hard since the Great War and that no one's buying cloth the way they used to, especially since government orders for army and navy uniforms fell off. That was a bad blow for us here in Yorkshire and it's true to say that there's no prospect of things picking up again, not in the near future.'

'Just you wait – he's going to shut us down!' Jennie muttered, loud enough to be heard by Iris Valentine who shot her a warning glance.

'Orders for high-quality worsted are dropping in favour of cheaper material brought in from abroad,' Calvert continued from his makeshift podium. 'As a result, our order books have hit an all-time low and so far we haven't been able to cut back on our costs as much as we'd like in order to stay afloat.'

'That's it, girls,' a fatalistic Jennie insisted. She was beyond being cowed by the manageress's disapproval. 'We're finished. Come Monday, we'll all be queuing up outside the Unemployment Office!'

Other voices besides Jennie's could now be heard.

'If he's handing us our cards, I wish he'd get on with it.'

'How will Mother and Father manage without my wage coming in?'

'We've done our very best not to go under,' Calvert insisted against a rising swell of unease. A mottled flush had spread from beneath his starched collar, up his neck and across his smooth cheeks. 'My grandfather, Sydney Calvert, started this mill more than fifty years ago and my father built it up to what it is today. For the last twenty years I've worked my fingers to the bone to carry on what they started but there's a tide of cheap imports and mass-produced goods working against me, and that is why it's had to come to this.'

'That's it – we're on the scrap heap,' someone muttered.

'And now we get to the nub – what precisely have we come to?' Calvert unhooked his thumbs and spread the palms of his hands upwards. 'I know you all want an answer.'

'Get on with it,' someone mumbled, followed by a rumbling of 'ayes' from all around the room.

'Rest assured, I'm not shutting down,' Calvert declared. 'I'm not even laying people off, not right away. No, what we have to do to make ends meet is to pull together.'

'How do you reckon we should do that, Mr Calvert?' someone else shouted, throwing caution to the wind.

'Good question.' Calvert turned his hands palms down to quell the rising panic. 'The long and the short of it is . . . we all have to agree to go on to short time, Monday to Friday, nine o'clock until four o'clock with an hour off for dinner. That's a six-hour working day, five days a week, until the beginning of April. According to Mr Wilson's calculations, that should see Calvert's through the present difficulty and out the other side to better times ahead.'

'Says you!' came a cynical cry from the crowd.

'Aye, it's all right for him, but how are the rest of us meant to manage?'

'No, let's count our blessings. At least we still have jobs.'

As Calvert stepped down from his temporary podium and hurried from the canteen, it was Derek Wilson's voice that rose above the hubbub. 'That'll do!' he cried in a tone that no one could argue with. 'Get off home, all of you. And I'll see you back here on Monday, ready and willing to work twice as hard, nine o'clock sharp!'

CHAPTER THIRTY-TWO

'Well, blow me down!' Annie was the first to express her astonishment after Calvert's workers had left the mill and spilled out on to the pavement on Ghyll Road. Everyone else seemed to have been stunned into silence by the sudden change to their hours and wages.

Then Sybil, too, found her voice. 'You can say that again. This cuts our hours by almost a half, down from fifty to thirty. How are people meant to manage?'

'It doesn't look as if I'll get my pay rise after all.' Lily sighed before pulling her shoulders back and addressing Sybil and Annie with renewed determination. 'But you know what, girls – this means we'll have more time to take on extra dressmaking work. You never know, it could be just the thing we need to get us off the ground.'

'If we can find any customers who can still afford to pay,' Sybil pointed out as the crowd began to disperse.

'No, Lily's right,' Annie insisted. 'More spare time is what we need to make a go of this. I think we should pass the word around, stick an advert in Newby's window, maybe even pay to put one in next week's *Gazette*. I could do the wording for that this afternoon if you like.'

Lily and Annie's energy soon brought Sybil into line. 'And I'll knock on doors with price lists written out in my own fair hand,' she suggested. 'We're bound to get some work from doing that.'

On the spur of the moment, the plan was agreed and Lily set off for home to get washed and changed for her visit to Armley. As she drew near, she was startled to see Margie and Arthur approaching the house from the top of Albion Lane.

As soon as Arthur spotted Lily, he broke hands with Margie and sprinted towards her, words tumbling from his mouth. 'Granddad took me to see *Aladdin*!' he proclaimed. 'We went last night. There was the genie of the lamp and puffs of green smoke and everything!'

'You lucky boy!' Lily ruffled his hair, struck by how much he would miss their mother once he grew used to the idea she was never coming back. What did death mean to a boy of his age? she wondered, before giving him an extra big hug and listening as he prattled on. She noticed that Margie quickened her pace to arrive at number 5 at the same time.

'Is Father in?' she asked nervously.

'Would you like him to be?' Lily wondered.

Margie nodded. 'It's high time we kissed and made up.'

'So let's find out, shall we?' Lily and Margie followed Arthur up the steps and into the kitchen.

Sure enough, Walter sat at the table with a cigarette resting on an ashtray and an untouched cup of tea in front of him. Evie was busy peeling vegetables at the sink. 'Margie's here,' Lily announced hurriedly then she took off her coat and sat on the stairs with Arthur while Margie braved the lion's den.

'How are you, Father?' Margie asked, sitting opposite him and getting ready to bolt out of the door if necessary.

It took Walter a long time to focus his distracted gaze on Margie and when he did he knotted his brows into a deep frown. 'Who let you in?' he demanded.

'I let myself in,' she said stoutly, though she quaked in her shoes. 'I came to see how you were getting along.'

'Without your mother, you mean?'

Margie nodded. Walter looked old and grey. She saw too that his chin was unshaven and the rims of his eyes were red, his eyelids swollen. 'I heard you haven't been yourself.'

'Yes, well, give us a chance,' he answered defensively. 'We've only just had the funeral.'

'That's true,' Margie acknowledged, relieved that her father hadn't risen up against her as soon as she set foot in the house. 'It'll take time. Meanwhile,

Arthur's happy with Granddad and me at Ada Street. He's doing well at school – his teacher's pleased with him.'

Out of sight on the bottom step of the stairs, Lily heard this and gave Arthur's hand a proud squeeze.

'Miss Bilton has promised to keep a special eye on him for the next few weeks,' Margie told her father.

'But he'll be coming back home soon, tell him,' Walter said with dogged determination. 'Your mother wouldn't have wanted Arthur to stay up there for weeks on end. Albion Lane is where he belongs.' Raising his cigarette to his lips he took a long drag then exhaled a cloud of blue smoke. 'I don't know about you, though, Margie. Where do you call home these days?'

Taken aback by the open-ended question, Margie leaned away from the table and stole a glance at Evie. Was this a hidden invitation from her father to return to the roost? Or was it a warning to stay away? 'I'm in two minds about that,' she answered cautiously. 'But I reckon I'm settled enough at Ada Street, for the time being at least.'

'I see.' Walter stubbed out his cigarette with an air of finality and stood up to reach for his cap and scarf hanging on the door peg close to where Lily and Arthur sat. 'Why not drop in here every so often to let your sisters check up on you?'

'I will,' she replied, surprised but comforted by his words.

'And we'll see how we go,' he said, making his

way out on to the top step then pausing. 'Find the lad a tanner,' he called out to Lily, then, 'Come on, Arthur, I'll drop you off at Newby's on my way to the Cross.'

'Old habits die hard,' Lily told Harry once they were settled at a table in the same grubby, impersonal prison visitors' room as before. 'Father's always on at me for small change. If it's not for beer money, it's pocket money for Arthur.'

'And you're soft enough to give it, come rain or shine.' Harry hoped that he hadn't revealed the usual struggle to find a cheerful response. He was still determined that Lily shouldn't know what hell he was going through, day in, day out, sharing a cell with two other men who were also due to stand trial for murder – one for killing his wife with a claw hammer after he'd arrived home drunk one night, the other for agreeing to snuff out the life of a rival gang member for the princely sum of five pounds ten shillings. Until now Harry had considered himself streetwise and handy with his fists, but these two cell mates were in an altogether different league, brooding on their bunk beds like ticking bombs waiting to go off.

'I wouldn't mind but every penny counts now that everyone at Calvert's has been put on short time.' The words were out of her mouth before Lily had time to calculate their depressing effect.

'Everyone?' Harry echoed. Even after this short

time in prison, it was hard to take in the idea that life on the outside, with all its ups and downs, went on regardless. He felt stranded and hopelessly out of touch, unable to do much more than simply gaze at Lily and notice every detail about her face, her hair, her clothes and that fresh-soap smell she carried with her.

'Yes but Annie, Sybil and me, we're taking in more dressmaking work to make up for it. They're out scouting for business while I'm here visiting you. Anyway, that's enough about me. We have to talk about you, Harry.'

'What is there to say?' he replied. 'All I've heard is the police found some scraps of metal at the house that don't belong to Billy's bike or the Calverts' car, but that doesn't get us very far. Otherwise, nothing changes in here.' Except that the day for his trial grew closer and the man appointed to represent him had visited Armley to warn him that without firm evidence on which to build his case, the prospects were not good. Harry had decided not to tell Lily this, though.

'But you haven't given up hope?' Lily asked. 'You look so down in the mouth, I'm afraid you have.'

'No,' he lied.

'Is it very bad in here?'

'I've kept better company.'

'But they do let you out of your cell to work in the library like they promised?'

He nodded. 'Yes and I'm reading a book about

Henry Ford and how he built the first mass-production line in America. They say that's the future.'

For a while Lily let the conversation drift – if talking about cars was what Harry wanted, then let him. But time was precious and as usual they were in danger of skirting around some important topics, so with five minutes to go before the end of visiting time, she dragged him back to Billy's death. 'I want to ask you a question,' she began.

'Don't make it too hard,' he warned. 'I didn't pass many exams, remember.'

'Harry, I'm serious. Tell me, what was the reason Billy cycled up to Moor House that day?'

'Search me.' Harry shrugged. 'Why did Billy do anything? It was whatever came into his head, or else he was doing as he was told in order to keep hold of his job.'

'All right, well, here's another question that's been bothering me ever since Vera and Jennie first raised it.'

'What's that?' he asked more sharply.

'I'd have followed it up earlier, only Mr Calvert announced he was cutting our hours and everyone's mind was stuck on that.'

'Come on then, spit it out.'

'It's this: was there any reason why someone should hold a grudge against Billy – something I don't know about?'

'Lily . . .' he protested.

'Think hard,' she insisted. 'Had he done anything wrong? Was he involved in a fight that festered and could have got out of hand – that kind of thing?'

'Lily!' Harry said more strongly. 'We could go on guessing as much as you like but what's the use?'

'We don't have much time and at least this is better than sitting on our hands, Harry. Or would you rather I did that?'

'No,' he muttered, bringing a hand up to cover his face.

'Because I could. I could do nothing and wait for it to happen – you coming up before the judge without anyone standing up for you and letting them say you did it, you killed Billy, and you having to answer for that . . .' The shadow of the noose appeared in her mind's eye and words failed her.

As warders began to clear the room, Harry met Lily's gaze once more and she gathered herself, making ready to leave.

'Thank you for trying your best,' he murmured. 'I don't know what I'd do without you, honest I don't.'

Lily smiled bravely back. She would be strong for his sake, she reminded herself. And so she stood up and embraced him in front of unsmiling men in uniforms, kissing him on the lips to show him she loved him and would never let him down.

Both as good as their word, Sybil and Annie went around the neighbourhood that afternoon and brought in more sewing work so that by the next morning they arrived at Lily's house armed with a request for a baby's christening gown and two orders for girls' dresses to be made up from rosebud-patterned cotton poplin in good time for the Whitsuntide gala on Overcliffe Common.

'We're quite the little hive of industry,' Annie said with satisfaction as they each took up a task.

Patterns were laid out, spools loaded on to the sewing machine, boxes of pins, needles and threads placed at the ready. They were too busy to take much notice of Walter when he came downstairs and went out into the foggy air but glad to stop for five minutes when Evie came back from delivering Sunday papers and offered to put the kettle on for a cup of tea.

'It's about time we had a breather!' Sybil announced, taking care not to set down her tea anywhere near the floral fabric. Her face was flushed from the fire, the sleeves of her dark red blouse rolled up above her elbows.

'And who's this?' Annie wondered when she heard footsteps stop outside the house. She twitched back the net curtain to see the sturdy figure of Jennie Shaw waiting on the doorstep. 'Do you want me to let her in?' she said to Lily.

There was no time for an answer because Jennie gave a sharp knock then entered without waiting to be asked, saying, 'Well I never – cups of tea all round. I couldn't have timed it better if I'd tried.'

'Come in, Jennie, why don't you?' Sybil's exaggerated politeness bounced off the visitor's well-upholstered bosom.

'Yes, come in and sit yourself down.' Lily cleared pieces of paper pattern from the fireside chair. 'Have you come to talk to us about Billy?'

The question changed the mood in the busy kitchen. 'What about Billy?' Annie wanted to know, while Sybil leaned on the mantelpiece and waited with a serious expression to hear what Jennie had to say.

'I was trying to talk to Lily about him before Stanley Calvert dropped his bombshell,' Jennie explained. 'Afterwards I didn't get the chance so when I found I had ten minutes to spare, I thought I'd nip round here and pass on what I meant to tell you yesterday.'

'That's good of you,' Lily told her as calmly as she could.

'But we're still waiting,' Annie pointed out. 'Come on, Jennie, no need to make a meal of it.'

'Right – Billy.' Once she'd eased herself into the chair, rested her hands in her broad lap and accepted a cup of tea from Evie, Jennie was ready to continue. 'You asked me, Lily, if he had any enemies but if I were you I'd be asking myself a different question.'

'Good Lord above, woman!' Annie exclaimed. 'Shall I nip around the block for a breath of fresh air and come back when you're ready to spill the beans?'

'What should we be asking?' Sybil met Jennie's challenge steadily.

'It's this: was Billy walking out with someone in the weeks before he got run over?'

'And was he?' Lily and Annie chorused.

'We know he was,' Sybil reminded them. 'The two of them were seen in town together, remember? That's why I decided to drop him double-quick.'

A knowing look and a nod from Jennie told them that they were in for an especially juicy piece of gossip, still to be delivered in her own good time. 'They probably hoped no one noticed their little, lovey-dovey assignation but you know what it's like round here – word soon got around. And here's something else for you to chew over. What if that someone he was walking out with belonged to a family who thought their daughter could do better for herself? Wouldn't that be the best way for Billy to stir up trouble?'

'This is all very well,' Sybil interrupted crossly, 'but you're not naming names.'

'Yes and if this turns out to be silly tittle-tattle, you'll get the sharp end of my tongue for wasting our time,' Annie added.

But Lily, who was standing by the window, shook her head. 'Jennie doesn't need to name names. We can work it out for ourselves.'

In fact, the answer, when it came to her, was clear as day. Who never came back to work after Billy died? Who walked behind his hearse with a face as white as a sheet behind her lace veil and was later seen weeping at the cemetery gate?

'There, I always knew you were a clever girl,' Jennie said as she saw the truth dawn on Lily.

'Billy was walking out with Winifred Calvert behind her parents' backs,' Lily said with deep certainty. 'She was the reason he nipped up to Moor House on the day he died.'

Suddenly everything made sense. Winifred had been Billy's sweetheart – a romantic pairing that had to be hidden from sight to avoid Mr and Mrs Calvert's wrath.

'Never!' Annie gasped, turning open-mouthed to Sybil then to Jennie for confirmation.

Satisfied that her mission was accomplished, Jennie nodded and handed her empty cup to Evie. 'I'll say cheerio,' were her parting words. 'Now it's up to you girls to make what you can of Winifred's little secret.'

'But did Mr and Mrs Calvert know anything about it?' Annie wondered as soon as their visitor had left. 'Winifred and Billy would do their best to keep it from them, wouldn't they?'

'If they had any sense, they would,' Sybil agreed.

'It's Winifred we need to talk to again,' Lily decided, eager to take the lead in their new mission to wrestle the truth out of the boss's daughter, whether she liked it or not. She quickly began to tidy away her sewing things, thinking all the while how this might be achieved.

'But it's Billy I feel for,' Evie decided. 'He must have loved her more than anything to risk the Calverts finding out. They'd have sacked him on the spot for a start.'

'Yes, it's not easy to work up any sympathy for Winifred,' Sybil agreed as she folded fabric and put the top on her tin of sewing pins. 'There's only you, Lily, who has a soft spot for Miss Snooty.'

'No,' soft-hearted Evie argued. 'There's me too. I feel for them both.' She couldn't help thinking of how badly it had ended and what Winifred Calvert must have suffered since.

'We're all agreed on one thing,' Lily reminded them as they reached for their coats. 'What we have to do now is find Winifred, pin her down and get to the bottom of it. If we hurry, we'll be in time to meet her and Mr and Mrs Calvert coming out of St Luke's.'

It was a quarter to eleven. The Sunday service finished on the hour and it was assumed that the respectable Calverts would be following their routine of attending church like the good Anglicans they were. Now was the time to find out the truth.

Anyone watching from a distance would have seen four determined young women almost running up the steep hill on to Overcliffe Road through a lingering fog that dampened their hair and prevented them from seeing more than twenty yards ahead. Lily led the way, her coat hanging open and with no hat on her head, all thoughts fixed on squeezing the truth out of Winifred Calvert. Had she arranged a tryst with Billy in the garden of Moor House? Had someone found them out and, if so, what exactly had happened next?

They arrived at St Luke's in the nick of time, just as the bells chimed the hour. The verger threw open the big oak doors of the splendid church built with wealthy mill owners' money some fifty years earlier, its fine stonework blackened by soot from factory chimneys and now struggling to attract a congregation large enough to fill its cavernous interior. The first worshippers filtered out into the porch, stopping to shake hands with the vicar and to exchange a few pleasantries with each other. Lily's heart, already racing from running uphill, quickened further as she searched for any sign of the Calverts.

'They're not here after all,' a disappointed Evie said as the church disgorged its worshippers and the vicar stepped inside while the verger prepared to close the doors.

'No – wait!' Sybil saw more figures emerging. As they'd approached the church, she'd made out the mill owner's Bentley parked in the entrance to the cemetery adjacent to the church so was certain they were present. 'Here they come.'

'What do we do now?' Evie wondered. 'There's no point us marching up to them and demanding to know about Billy outright.'

'Leave it to me,' Annie told them, noticing that Stanley and Eleanor Calvert had emerged on to the wide steps before their daughter who had stayed back to talk to the vicar. 'I'll draw them down the steps and out of the way while you lot nip in and nab Winifred.'

'How do you propose to do that?' Sybil demanded.

'I'll let on there's something wrong with their precious car,' Annie decided on the spur of the moment. 'I know – I'll say they've got a flat tyre. That'll put the wind up them.'

No sooner said than she sped up the steps and talked in an animated fashion to the Calverts, pointing towards the place where their car was parked and persuading them to hurry towards it without waiting for their daughter. Immediately, Lily and the others ran to waylay Winifred before she had a chance to follow.

Finding herself surrounded by Evie, Sybil and Lily, Winifred's first reaction was to seek help from the vicar, only to find that he'd already taken off his surplice and was disappearing into the vestry. 'What's the matter now?' she asked, frowning and backing up against the stone wall.

'It's Billy,' Lily answered. Now that the moment of truth had arrived she felt strangely calm so she came straight to the point. 'You two were sweethearts, weren't you?'

'Why won't you leave me alone, Lily Briggs?' Winifred protested weakly. 'I'm sick and tired of being pestered.'

'But you don't deny it.' With fingers crossed, Sybil

went on to take a calculated risk. 'Anyway, you and Billy were seen together. It got my goat because I was walking out with him myself at the time.'

Evie and Lily waited with bated breath as Sybil made the leap of logic. Had it really been Winifred standing with Billy outside the department store?

Winifred shook her head then started to cry, tears rolling down her cheeks. Lily offered her a handkerchief then led her gently inside and sat her down on the nearest pew in order to give her time to pull herself together. 'Wait there a while,' she told the others.

'Be quick then,' Sybil advised as she peered anxiously out of the door. 'We don't have long before Mr and Mrs Calvert come looking for her.'

Lily nodded then sat down next to Winifred. There was a rich scent of pine resin and polish, combined with a musty smell emanating from the worn tapestry kneelers at their feet. 'I know you're upset,' she began. 'But I have to know the truth, for Harry's sake. Did you talk to Billy in the garden just before he died?'

Miserably drying her tears, Winifred shook her head.

'But he had come to see you, hadn't he? That's what you'd arranged. He hoped to slip in without being noticed but the plan went wrong somehow.'

'All right, all right.' Winifred sighed, her resistance crumbling. 'It's true. I loved Billy and he loved me and now my heart is broken. There, is that enough?'

'I'm sorry,' Lily breathed, genuinely moved by Winifred's pain. 'What was the reason you couldn't go out to meet him?'

Winifred wrung the handkerchief between her hands and constantly shook her head as she spoke.

'Mother had found us out on the day before. She came across me writing a billet-doux for Billy, which I meant to give to Harry to deliver. She read the letter out loud from start to finish, mocking me before she tore it into pieces. Then she said I was letting her and Father down and couldn't be trusted to go out of the house without a chaperone from now on – on and on she went.'

Billet-doux? The phrase betrayed a school-girl shallowness in Winifred and Lily felt a flash of anger. 'And Harry was to be your go-between?'

'Yes. Until then I'd made sure Harry knew nothing about me and Billy – we thought nobody did. It was only because Mother had arranged for me to go to tea at Mabel Kingsley's house the next day straight from work and I had to write and tell Billy not to come to the house because I wouldn't be there.'

'But your mother tore up the note so Harry couldn't deliver the message and Billy didn't know about the change of plan. But then you didn't go to tea?'

'No. The next day, I said I wasn't feeling well so I asked Harry to drive me home and he pulled up outside the front door. He went straight into the house but I made sure to take my time getting out of the car.'

'Because you still needed to find Billy and warn him?' Lily asked.

'Exactly. My plan was to sneak round the side of the house, only Mother came out and was angry with me for coming home. She dragged me inside and made me cry until Father came out of his study and then he began to argue with Mother and that almost gave me the chance to give Harry the message for Billy, except that Mother spotted me again and sent me upstairs.'

Lily pictured the scene – a battle royal between the imperious Eleanor and the beleaguered Stanley Calvert, going at it hammer and tongs within the confines of their grand mansion, with Winifred cowering in the background. 'And then what?' she wanted to know, sensing by the continued nervous wringing of Winifred's hands that there was more to come.

'Then I ran to my bedroom window, the one at the side of the house, and looked down on to the yard to see if I could spot Billy. I saw his bike resting against an outhouse door then I saw him with . . . with—'

'He wasn't alone?' Lily interrupted.

'No. He was arguing with two men.'

Lily heard this with clenched jaw and fists. She must stay calm – for Harry's sake she needed to glean every scrap of new information from the distraught Winifred. 'Do you know who they were?'

'I only saw their backs. Billy was facing me but he didn't look up. They seemed to be angry.'

'You're sure you didn't see their faces?' Time was against Lily – the church door had been flung open and she could hear footsteps approaching.

'No, hand on heart,' Winifred sobbed. 'They were wearing caps so their faces were hidden even when they turned around. One was big and strong, a real brute. He threw a punch at Billy and the other one tried to kick him. Billy ducked out of their way and started to run round to the front of the house. That was the last time I saw him.'

'And the men chased him?'

'Yes. And the next thing I knew he'd been knocked over and killed. He's dead and now I shall never see him again!'

CHAPTER THIRTY-THREE

On Albion Lane, in the bedroom she shared with Evie, Lily's mind raced through what she'd learned in St Luke's, trying to come to terms with the one fact that stared her in the face – Billy had got into a fight and been run over all because of Winifred Calvert. She pictured him cheerily cycling up to Moor House, whistling maybe and looking forward to the thrill of a secret tryst with the boss's daughter. Typical, devil-may-care Billy to risk something like that, she thought. Did he really love Winifred, though? Or had he died for the sake of a cheap, celluloid romance, for a girl he would soon have thrown aside like he had so many others?

In any case, the two shadowy figures who had entered the picture were what Lily needed to focus on now, before she, Sybil and Annie were ready to go to the police with as many new pieces of information as they could muster. Who were they and how had they got there? she wondered over and over. Who were these two men wearing caps, one big and strong, the other using his feet to hurt their victim, the rough type who you would commonly see scrapping on street corners or outside the Green Cross? Whoever they were, they held the answers to Billy's death – of that Lily was sure.

She got up next morning before the knocker-up came down Albion Lane, rattling windows with his long pole, and was already dressed and in the kitchen when Evie came down. It was only then that she remembered to delay her departure to fit in with the new clocking-on time of nine o'clock so she kept herself busy with dusting and polishing before leaving the house with fifteen minutes to spare, joining the steady flow of workers down the hill towards the mills on Ghyll Road and beyond. When she arrived at Calvert's, she saw Sybil and Annie waiting under the archway with Fred Lee.

'Fred says we've to go to the office with him,' Annie told Lily with a worried frown. 'He won't say what it's about.'

'Don't worry, you'll soon find out.' Enjoying the three women's unease, the smirking overlooker led the way. 'Some people don't know when they're well off,' he remarked over his shoulder.

'What do you mean by that?' Sybil wanted to know, trying to conceal the nervous knot that was forming in her stomach.

'Having a regular job to come to, for a start. I'd have thought that was well worth toeing the line for.'

'What makes you think we haven't?' Annie asked,

similarly alarmed. Something had put Fred into a good mood this morning, but she couldn't tell what.

'In you go.' He winked, using his foot to hold open Derek Wilson's door for them and all but rubbing his hands with glee.

'That's all, thank you, Fred,' the manager told him. As the overlooker let the door swing to, Wilson gazed without expression at Sybil, Annie and Lily, hands resting on his desk with his fingers interlaced. 'Jean.' He motioned to his secretary, who stood by with three envelopes at the ready.

Hastily Jean Carson came forward and placed the envelopes on the desk.

'That'll be all, thank you, Jean.'

The secretary hurried out with downcast eyes, unable to meet anyone's gaze due to the rising tension in the room.

'I expect you know what these are,' the manager went on drily.

'They're our cards,' Sybil guessed, her heart thudding.

'Correct. I've been instructed to hand them to you as soon as you got here, no ifs or buts.'

At first Lily stood dumbfounded, unable to let the words sink in. This couldn't be happening. How could they be sacked without at least being given a reason?

'But you can't do that,' Annie objected. 'It was only on Saturday that Mr Calvert told us that no one was to be laid off.'

'That was true at the time but now circumstances have changed. Lily, this one is for you.' Wilson pushed the first envelope towards her.

She reached forward and took it from the desk with trembling fingers, staring at the envelope as if it might bite.

'I suppose there's no point asking why?' Sybil muttered.

'None at all. Believe me, I'm simply following orders.' The manager pushed the other two envelopes towards her and Annie.

'But we *know* why,' Annie said, fiercely tearing hers open to check her employment card inside. 'This is us being punished for what happened at the church yesterday – that's what this is.'

Wilson's face remained impassive. 'You are no longer employed at Calvert's Mill. You must collect whatever tools and belongings you have here and be off the premises by half past nine.'

'Don't worry, you won't see us for dust,' Sybil told him with angry determination. 'Come on, Lily. Come on, Annie – we're off!'

'I've never seen Fred look so pleased with himself,' Sybil remarked to Annie and Lily as the three women retreated to Nixon's corner café and commiserated over a cup of tea. 'He was grinning like a Cheshire cat when we went in to collect our aprons and say our goodbyes.'

'Ah, but he won't have the last laugh,' Annie

vowed. 'Wait until he sees our names above the door of that little shop of ours!'

Lily was still reeling from the shock and trying to get to grips with the fact that the one reliable wage in the Briggs household had suddenly vanished. She wondered what her mother would have thought and heard Rhoda's voice saying, 'What are we to do now, pray tell? We can't live on fresh air.'

And it was true – Lily's wage from Calvert's Mill was what had kept the family afloat for six years and the traipse into work each morning, the never-altering view of black walls and grimy windows, the wide arch through which she shuffled had all seeped through her skin and into her bones so that suddenly being cast adrift by the mill owner made her feel very afraid, like a sailor thrown overboard into a vast, empty ocean and flailing his arms to attract rescue.

'How about Miss Valentine?' Sybil drew Lily out of her daze, stirring sugar into her tea and taking note of the steamed-up windows and shabby interior of the once prosperous café. 'How did she take the news?'

'She was knocked for six, just like us,' Lily replied. It was only now as she took her first sip of tea that she was able to stop trembling. 'She shook my hand and wished me well.'

'She knows she's lost one of the best menders she's ever likely to have,' Sybil murmured. 'There's no need to be modest, Lil – we all know it's true.'

There was another pause while they each let the bleak reality of their sacking sink in and the silence was only broken by the hiss of steam from a copper boiler behind the counter and the chink of crockery from a tiny kitchen beyond.

'You know, this latest business could work out well for us in the end, the same as being put on short time. It could be a blessing in disguise.' Overcoming her distress, Lily grew more determined to see a cup half full rather than half empty. 'For a start, losing our jobs sets us free to carry on helping Harry.'

'Without the Calverts breathing down our necks,' Annie agreed. 'Talk about every cloud . . .'

'That's the ticket.' Sybil's voice carried equal conviction. 'Now we have all the time in the world to follow up what Winifred told us. We can be the Dr Watsons to your Sherlock, Lily.'

'That's funny – it's what Harry once called me,' Lily recalled with a faint smile. '"A right little Sherlock Holmes".'

'So we all agree.' Rattling her empty cup down on to the saucer, Annie let it be known she was ready for business. 'The important thing is for us to find out who was laying in wait for Billy in the shrubbery and to heck with the Calverts.'

'That's right, they can't order us around if we're not working for them.' Lily paused, wondering if it had been Eleanor Calvert or her husband who had ordered their dismissal. 'What do you say we move on from here up to number 5. We've plenty of sewing work to get on with while we talk.'

The trio paid for their tea and walked on up Albion Lane, crossing paths with Lily's father, who ducked his head and scuttled sheepishly by.

'No prizes for guessing where he's going,' Annie remarked. 'Look at him – he didn't even stop to ask why we aren't at work.'

'Too busy thinking about his pint, I expect.' Sybil too made it plain that she hadn't shifted in her opinion that Walter Briggs's conduct left a lot to be desired.

As for Lily, the sight of Walter shuffling down the hill well ahead of opening time pulled at her heart strings so she made herself concentrate instead on the task in hand. 'I'll tell you one thing that sticks in my mind,' she admitted as they reached number 5 and stepped inside. 'It's Mrs Calvert learning about Billy's visit ahead of time then arranging for Winifred to be out of the way.'

'That looks dicey,' Sybil agreed. 'Enough to tell me she could be the one behind our two mystery men.'

'Which she'll deny!' Annie reminded them forcefully. 'She'll claim she doesn't know anything about them. And I'd do the same, in her position.'

'The thing is, Winifred is much too frightened of her mother to stand up to her,' Lily pointed out. She found that by methodically setting out her scissors and pins, needles and threads on the kitchen table, she was able to think more logically. 'That means we've got to find out for ourselves who they are.'

'Wait, go back a bit,' said Sybil suddenly. 'Wouldn't the only connection between Eleanor Calvert and the type of roughnecks we're talking about be through the shopkeepers and delivery boys who call at Moor House?'

'Like Ernie,' Lily muttered. 'Durant's deliver meat to the Calverts. He told me so himself.'

'Then let's talk to him,' Sybil proclaimed.

'As soon as he's finished work for the day,' Lily whole-heartedly concurred.

'That's right – we've still got a fight on our hands.' Annie rolled up her sleeves, ready for work. 'We're not ready to give up – you hear?'

'No, we won't ever do that,' Lily agreed, reining back her impatience and inserting neat running stitches into the cream lace material intended for the baby's christening gown.

'We won't let an innocent man go to the gallows.' Snipping and tacking, trimming and gathering the floral fabric for the larger of the two Whitsuntide dresses, Sybil spoke in unusually dramatic terms that made Lily's heart beat so fast it threatened to jump clean out of her chest. 'With or without Mrs Calvert's help, we'll get to the bottom of this.'

'This is where having a telephone would help,' Sybil said when teatime came and they'd got into a fresh huddle outside Newby's. 'We'd be able to ring up Mr Durant and find out where Ernie was.'

429

A quick-thinking Annie nodded then dashed inside the sweet shop, surprising Evie by making a dive across the counter to pick up the receiver and ask the operator for the number of Durant's Butchers. A minute later she'd found out from Ernie's dad that Ernie had indeed finished his deliveries for the day and would no doubt be found propping up the bar at the Green Cross.

'Then that's where we'll head next,' Lily decided once Annie had established the facts.

'Good Lord, the girl's turned into an express train again,' Sybil complained to Annie as Lily sprinted off with them in tow. 'Wait for us, Lily, we can't keep up.'

'She's not listening,' Annie warned.

And it was true – all Lily cared about was tracking down Ernie and firing off the next set of questions about who else went up to Moor House with deliveries. She arrived at the Cross well ahead of Sybil and Annie, swinging open the door and taking in the gas-lit bar with its ornate mirror and rows of spirits. Behind the counter, Chalky White was pulling a pint for Lily's cousin Tommy.

'Now then, what's up?' Tommy called as soon as he spotted her in the doorway. 'Have you come to stand me a pint?'

Lily ignored his well-worn taunt and searched the room for Ernie Durant. There was the usual group of men playing dominoes at a table by the window, two more playing darts and her father and her Uncle

George huddled over their glasses in the darkest corner of the snug, but no sign of their friend.

'Miss Briggs, what can I get you?' Chalky asked as Lily advanced towards the bar.

'Miss Briggs, is it?' Tommy pretended to choke on his light ale. 'Oh yes, I forgot, we have to show respect where it's due now that Lily's a burler and mender!'

'Not any more,' she muttered, realizing that Tommy would find out sooner rather than later. She ignored Frank Summerskill as he emerged from the gents' toilets to join Tommy at the bar. 'I was wondering, Chalky – have you seen Ernie by any chance?'

'Not lately,' the barman answered.

'Ah, she's after the butcher's boy now that Harry Bainbridge has got himself put away for murder,' Tommy mocked, a lock of Brylcreemed hair falling forward on to his forehead. 'You don't hang about, Lily, I must say.'

'Take no notice,' Sybil said, as she and Annie hurried through the door and caught the gist of Tommy's remark. Annie glowered at a sniggering Frank.

'Ernie's not here,' Lily reported, glancing over to her father and seeing how abject he looked. He'd obviously had one over the eight and was oblivious to most of what was going on around him. 'It's no good, I'd better take him home,' she decided reluctantly.

'Yes, tuck him up in bed,' Chalky agreed.

'Rather you than me,' Tommy sneered. 'Uncle Walter's been here that long his backside is glued to the stool he's sitting on.'

Sure enough, it took two of them to get Walter up into a standing position – Lily and Sybil, each supporting one arm and steering the drunken man towards the door which Annie held open.

'If you happen to see Ernie, tell him we want to know who delivers food and coal and such like up to the Calverts at Moor House,' she mentioned to Chalky as she departed.

To her surprise, the remark brought Tommy out of the pub after them. 'Why are you lot poking your noses into what goes on at the Calverts'?' he demanded. 'What's it got to do with you?'

Hearing his raised voice, Lily steadied her father and turned to her cousin. 'And why should you care?'

Thrusting his hands into his pockets, he quickly backed down. 'I don't. Never mind, forget it.'

Walter swayed against Lily, leaning on her with his full weight so that she staggered sideways and had to be helped by both Annie and Sybil.

'Let's get him home,' Sybil insisted.

But Lily was bothered by her cousin's interference. 'What's going on, Tommy? You haven't suddenly got a job as a delivery boy yourself, by any chance?'

The question made him laugh out loud – a sudden, barking sound without any trace of humour. 'Me?' he scoffed. 'No, you won't see me running errands for the Calverts!'

'No – silly me!' Lily was riled by Tommy's smugness. Though her father was swaying and mumbling incoherently, she put off guiding him home. 'I can't see you pedalling a bike along the moor road in this weather. But I can see Frank having to do it if it's his only way to make ends meet.'

'You leave Frank out of it,' Tommy warned.

'Aye, aye – it looks like you hit a nerve there, Lily.' Annie took Walter's weight as he swayed against her. 'Come along, Mr Briggs, stand up nice and straight, there's a good chap.'

'Waste of time talking to the likes of Tommy,' Walter mumbled, slurring his words and ineffectually trying to push Annie away. 'I told him, no . . . scrounging a pint off me . . . no, I said . . . call himself a Rovers supporter . . .'

'Steady now,' Sybil advised, but try as she and Annie might, they couldn't prevent him from letting his knees buckle and his weight was too much for them to keep him on his feet.

Stricken with a sharp sense of shame as her father sank to the ground, Lily hurried to help him back up but was pushed aside by Tommy who roughly took hold of Walter and did the job for her.

'Every week when I was your age . . . at the turnstiles . . . cheering my team on,' Walter rambled, fending off the three women with flailing arms. 'But no, not you, Tommy . . .'

'You shut your trap, old man!' his nephew said, thrusting Walter back against the wall.

'Tommy!' Lily cried, shocked at his rough handling of her father.

'Billy and all,' Walter slurred, eyes unfocused and spit dribbling from his mouth as he slid to the ground once more.

Lily crouched beside him and made him look at her. 'What about Billy?'

Walter returned her earnest gaze with a vacant stare. 'Billy who? What are you on about?'

'Nothing. Don't listen to her.' Tommy moved in again and manhandled him back on his feet then began to march him along Ghyll Road. When Walter stumbled over the kerb, Tommy wrenched his arm so violently that Lily feared he would pull her father's arm out of its socket.

'That'll do, that's enough!' she remonstrated, moving in to rescue him. At last she, Sybil and Annie were able to take charge, leaving Tommy behind as they steered Walter to the bottom of Albion Lane. From there they got him up the hill and into the house where he finally collapsed in the fireside chair.

Warm from the effort of bringing Walter home, Annie, Sybil and Lily took time to catch their breath. Then, while Sybil put the kettle on and Annie hung Walter's scarf and cap on the hook, Lily crouched beside him on the rug to unfasten his collar and straighten him out. 'There, that's better. How are you feeling now, Father?'

'Call themselves Rovers supporters,' he grumbled, on the same incoherent tack as before.

434

'Who?' she asked.

This time he managed a sensible reply. 'You know who. Billy for a start. He'd be alive now if only he'd gone to watch the match.'

'Who else?' she insisted, placing a hand over his and patting it to keep his attention. She sensed that the answer was vitally important.

'Tommy and what's his name – they reckon they go to matches week in, week out, but I know they don't.'

'Tommy and Frank?'

'That's the one.'

Tommy Briggs and Frank Summerskill – two known fist-fighters and fly-by-nights, one lithe and skinny, one tall and with brutish strength. Lily's heart pounded and her eyes widened as she looked up at Sybil and Annie.

'Oh Lord!' Annie breathed as more pieces of the jigsaw slotted into place.

'Jumped-up jackasses, the pair of them,' Walter growled. 'It's only this last week or two that they've had the price of a pint of beer to their name.'

'Mr Briggs!' Sybil said, crouching beside Lily. 'Did Tommy and Frank mention where they'd been the afternoon Billy got hurt?'

'How the hell should I know? I only know they came to the Cross to hand Sam Earby's bike back. They'd taken it for a spin along the canal path, Tommy said.'

'Or up to Moor House,' Annie muttered.

Walter let out a long, loud sigh. 'All I know is, Sam's

face dropped a mile when he went out for his bike. He stormed back in and said it looked like it had been dragged through a hedge backwards – front mudguard missing and spokes all bent to billio.'

'That's it!' Lily threw her arms round a bewildered Walter. 'Thank you, Father. Thank you, thank you!'

'Steady on,' the old man slurred.

Sybil frowned at Annie as they both tried to follow Lily's latest line of thought.

'Don't you see?' she said. 'All the police need to do now is match up the pieces of metal they found at Moor House with Sam's bike. That lands Tommy and Frank in it and lets Harry off the hook once and for all!'

'And it was Father who held the key all along!' Lily told Evie and Margie with a bemused expression that made them smile. 'I'd have been down at the station with Sybil and Annie right this minute, except that Sybil said we should wait until Father has sobered up so that he can back up what we're saying.'

The three sisters sat together in the kitchen after Walter had been put to bed and Annie and Sybil had left in high spirits. Evie was back from a full day's stint behind the counter at Newby's and Margie had dropped by to make the arrangements to bring Arthur home to Albion Lane after school next day.

'Now all I have to do is go to the police station and pass it on to Sergeant Magson first thing tomorrow morning.'

'And you're telling me that this was Mrs Calvert's doing?' Margie fastened on to the aspect that most fascinated her. 'Imagine that – her in her ivory tower looking down on poor Billy and Winifred then paying Tommy and Frank to send him packing.'

'Will she get into trouble when you tell the police?' Evie asked, doing her best to absorb what she'd been told but finding it hard to keep up.

'We'll have to wait and see,' Lily cautioned. 'What she did was definitely against the law even if she didn't expect it to get out of hand the way it did.'

Margie, however, revelled in the prospect of Eleanor Calvert's downfall. 'Women like her think they can dish out orders willy-nilly. Do this, do that, dig my garden, cook my dinner, drive me here and there whenever I like.'

'That's the way of the world.' Lily sighed.

'Not any more, it isn't.' Margie's colour rose as she tore into her subject. 'Times are changing, Evie, you mark my words. These days even the Calverts have to fall into line. There's no use them throwing their weight around – people won't stand for it if they do.'

'Oh yes, and we can walk away and find other jobs at the drop of a hat, can we?' Lily wanted to know. 'Look at what's happened to me, Annie and Sybil. We've no chance of finding mill work now, even if we wanted.'

'Which you don't,' Margie said quickly. 'And that's because you've got something else you can turn your hand to. Calvert and the like don't bargain for that – they're too used to having things all their own way.'

'Since when have you become such a firebrand?' Lily queried.

'Since I had time to think about things,' Margie replied with stout determination. 'And on top of that, I've been racking my brains over what work I can do until the baby comes. Granddad says the tram company is advertising for clerical help while one of their women goes into hospital for an operation. That would suit me, I think.'

'Good for you,' Lily agreed, while Evie crossed her fingers.

'When can I let Peggy know the good news?' Evie asked, bringing the subject back to Mrs Calvert and Tommy.

'After Father and I've been to the police station and they've had time to talk to Sam Earby,' came the advice. 'That should be the proof we need to get Harry out of Armley.'

'How can you be so calm and steady about it?' Margie asked. 'If it was me, I'd be leaping around.'

'Inside I am jumping for joy,' she confessed, her face burning with hidden excitement. 'But I try to think of what Mother would say.'

'What?' Evie wondered, sitting by the fire with her sisters, just as they used to do before the world stood on its head.

Lily issued their mother's warning words exactly as Rhoda would have spoken them. 'She'd have said,

Don't count your chickens before they're hatched.'

It was true that she could already picture Harry's face when the good news broke and almost taste his relief as he walked free, but still she stifled her delight and instead rehearsed word for word what she would tell the police. The time for smiles and kisses was just around the corner, but still out of reach.

CHAPTER THIRTY-FOUR

At ten o'clock that night Margie and Evie left Albion Lane to catch the last tram to Ada Street. Evie was to help Margie pack Arthur's belongings and bring them back home early the next morning so the girls, glad to be the bearers of good news for their little brother, hurried eagerly from the house.

Lily stood on the doorstop to see them off, waiting and waving until they disappeared over the brow of the hill. She was about to step inside and turn the key in the lock for the night when she saw Tommy emerge from the alley and walk purposefully towards her. She stiffened at once to see that the street was otherwise silent and empty.

If she moved inside and locked up, her cousin would come hammering on the door and wake her father. Indecision slowed her reactions, so she was still standing in the open doorway when Tommy broke into a run then leaped up the steps to block her way. Close up, he smelled strongly of beer and tobacco smoke.

'Now then, Lily, I'm glad I caught you before you tucked yourself up in bed,' he began, planting himself between her and the refuge of the warm kitchen.

'Tommy, get out of my way, please.'

'Aren't you happy to see me?' he taunted as he leaned against the door jamb and used one raised leg as a barrier, displaying the swagger of the habitual drinker who has learned how to hold himself without seeming the worse for wear despite his blunted senses.

Lily knew she had to be very careful. 'It's late. I'm tired – I've had a long day.'

'That's what happens when you poke your nose in where it's not wanted,' he sneered. 'It tires you out. I take it you got Uncle Walter back home all right?'

'Tommy, please – it's cold. I want to go inside.'

The more Lily tried to push past him, the more deliberately and forcefully Tommy prevented her. 'Knowing Uncle Walter when he's had too much to drink, his tongue probably ran away with him.'

'Why were you hiding in the alley?' Lily demanded when she found that her efforts to get into the house were useless. Wearing only a blouse and skirt, she stepped down on to the pavement, slippery with black ice, and glanced edgily up and down the street. 'Were you spying on us?'

Tommy held his position on the top step and glared down at her. 'Not that you'd believe a word the old man said,' he went on, taking a packet of cigarettes from his pocket. 'Your head's screwed on too tight for that.'

The throwaway remark somehow made Lily realize the seriousness of her situation. Here she was, alone with Tommy in the dark street, holding information about him that would free Harry and get Tommy and Frank Summerskill put away in prison.

'You realize no one else would believe him either,' Tommy went on as he lit his cigarette. 'It's clear as day that Uncle Walter's not what you'd call reliable.'

As the tip of the cigarette glowed red in the dark, he lowered his head and directed a narrow plume of acrid smoke at her face. Lily's temper suddenly snapped. 'Says you,' she retorted. 'I'd trust Father's word over yours any day of the week, Tommy Briggs, and so will Sergeant Magson!'

Something changed in Tommy's face at her mention of the police. He flicked his cigarette to one side in a flurry of sparks and jumped down on to the pavement, grabbing her arms and dragging her down the hill towards the alley. 'What did the old man say?' he demanded, his breath hot and acrid in her ear, thrusting her out of sight down the dark, foul-smelling tunnel. Tommy jammed his forearm up against her throat, forcing her head back against the cold, greasy wall. 'Tell me, or I'll throttle you, Lily. I swear I will.'

'I know about Sam Earby's bike,' she whispered, her heart racing, her hands around his arm trying to ease the pressure.

Tommy pressed harder. 'Now see what you've done,' he groaned with mock regret. 'You've only gone and forced me to take the wind out of your sails.'

Struggling for breath with his arm still blocking her windpipe, Lily decided that if these moments down the alley were to be her last, she wouldn't give in without a struggle. With a sudden jerk, she turned her head and bit his hand hard.

For a moment he recoiled – long enough for her to shout for help then wriggle out of his grasp and run back on to the street. She slipped on a patch of ice and pitched forward, going down hard. Suddenly he was upon her, one knee in her back, pinning her down. He seemed oblivious to the fact that they were now in full view.

With her head twisted to one side and her cheek pressed against the stone pavement, Lily got a view of cracked slabs and black, shiny cobbles beyond. A light went on in a bedroom across the street.

'It wasn't even me,' Tommy growled. Fuelled by drink and with all judgement long gone, he gave way to a cowardly urge to spout his version of events. 'I was doing the job Mrs Calvert had paid me to do, teaching Billy not to step out of line, and that would have been that.'

'Tommy, you're hurting me!' Lily protested. More lights went on. Somewhere, a door creaked open.

Words poured out of Tommy's mouth. 'But no – Billy wouldn't stay down. He came back at us, kicking and throwing punches, grabbing Sam's bike and flinging it down in Frank's way – red rag to a bull, that was.'

'Tommy!' His knee was crushing her ribs. Once more she struggled for breath.

'After that there was no stopping Frank. He landed a punch that knocked Billy clean out, then he sprinted to the Bentley and jumped in behind the wheel. I was telling him no, Billy was down and out but that didn't stop Frank. He kept on coming. It wasn't me that ran Billy over, it was Frank.'

Lily's head whirled and she was on the point of blacking out when a shadowy figure hove into view.

'You both killed the lad,' Walter hissed as he knocked Tommy sideways with the thick sole of his boot and laid him flat. 'You won't worm your way out of this one, Tommy Briggs. Not after Lily's talked to the coppers and not while there's still breath left in this worn-out body of mine.'

'They'll have to catch me first!' Squirming from under Walter's boot, Tommy sprang to his feet and fled while Lily, weak from lack of air, was only able to prop herself on to her elbows.

'Come on, lass.' Carefully Walter helped her up. 'Do you feel up to coming down the station with me now?'

She nodded then swayed a little.

Her father put his arm around her and supported her as they began to walk. 'Lean on me,' he said. 'That's it – good girl. Just you wait – between us we'll cook Tommy's goose once and for all.'

CHAPTER THIRTY-FIVE

'So it's still a case of wait and see,' Sybil said, ahead of Lily and Annie, as they marched along Canal Road on a clear, frosty morning.

The three women had just emerged from the police station where Sybil and Annie had forcefully backed up what Lily and Walter had reported the night before – that Tommy and Frank were the men who had killed Billy and they should unlock Harry's door and let him walk free.

'Don't worry,' Annie told Lily as she linked arms and they hurried to catch up with Sybil. 'We won't let you out of our sight until the coppers manage to nab the true culprits, which won't be long, not after what we all told the nice sergeant.'

On they went past Calvert's memorial tower, oblivious to faces looking out of the long windows – Jennie and Vera from the calm of the first-floor mending room, Maureen, Florence and Flora from the clattering weaving shed.

'Yoo-hoo, Lily!' Jennie called through an open

window. Then, asking hastily granted permission, she sped down the stairs to accost the passing trio by the main entrance. 'Well?' she asked, all agog.

'We've come from the police station,' Sybil explained. 'Last night Lily and her dad dropped Tommy and Frank right in it and we've been to back them up.'

'It turns out that Mrs Calvert paid them to teach Billy a lesson,' Annie added with beaming satisfaction.

'Blimey!' Jennie gasped, retreating under the arch as quickly as she'd come.

Word spread like wildfire around the mill – Lily's cousin Tommy and his pal, Frank Summerskill, had done the dirty deed under orders from the boss's wife. By dinner time, when the spinners and weavers, warpers and twisters, perchers and packers congregated in the canteen, Jennie and her cronies had all three culprits already strung up for murder.

Out on Ghyll Road, the three women popped into Newby's to reassure Evie that all would be well. 'Even if Tommy and Frank try to scarper, they won't get far,' Lily told her sister. 'Not with every copper in Yorkshire hot on their heels.'

Behind her counter stacked with Turkish delight and mint humbugs, a worried Evie greeted the news with relief. 'What now?' she wanted to know.

'Now Sybil, Annie and I carry on with those orders for dresses and coats while we have the chance,' the ever-practical Lily said with a smile.

446

'And in the meantime we ask about the rent for Henshaw's haberdashers-that-was,' Annie added. 'Come on, slowcoach, we have a pile of orders to be getting on with!' she called over her shoulder, ting-a-linging the shop bell as she retreated through the door.

'About that rent,' Sybil began as they dashed on up Albion Lane, cheeks flushed by the wind, fingers nipped by the frost. 'If the landlord asks for a deposit, it so happens I have a little nest egg saved up.'

'And Robert's sister Ethel has a Singer sewing machine going begging,' Annie reported gaily. 'Before you know it, we'll be set up in our own little shop with so many orders we won't know what to do.'

'What was the nest egg for?' Lily mentioned to Sybil as she unlocked the door to number 5.

'For my bottom drawer, just in case. For silk stockings and satin petticoats and sheets and pillow cases made of Egyptian cotton.' Sybil laughed at herself and winked. 'But now I've decided that marriage isn't for me, I'm free to spend the money on whatever I like.'

Annie and Lily joined in her laughter as they went into the house and found Walter up and dressed, laying a fire then washing his hands at the sink.

'Don't worry, I'll soon be out of your road,' he told them.

'Don't go on our account, Mr Briggs,' Annie told him with new respect.

'No, don't let us turf you out,' Sybil agreed.

Walter put on his cap and buttoned his jacket nevertheless. 'I have to see a man about a dog,' he muttered, eager to escape the women's mysterious snipping and tacking, tucking and gathering. 'I'll be back later this afternoon, in plenty of time for Arthur coming home,' he assured Lily. 'It'll be good to have the littl'un back where he belongs.'

Arthur was home and his bag unpacked when a policeman knocked on the door. 'It's all right, you can relax – we've got 'em!' he announced without preliminaries. 'Frank Summerskill and Tommy Briggs – we cornered 'em in Hadley and brought them straight down to the local nick.'

Lily took in the sight of the officer in his dark uniform with shiny buttons, helmet tucked under his arm. He was fresh faced, with the eager air of a recent recruit. 'That's good to hear,' she said, feeling a wave of unspeakable relief wash over her.

'They were lying low in Frank's brother's house on Westmoreland Street at the back of the Pavilion. We got a tip-off from a neighbour.'

'And have they confessed?' Lily's one lingering worry was that her sneaky cousin and his sidekick would be allowed to weasel their way out, leaving Harry where he was in Armley.

'I can't tell you more than what I've already said,' the young officer replied with almost comical formality that suddenly collapsed when he remembered another piece of vital information. 'Oh, except that Sergeant Magson went up to Moor House to talk to Mrs Calvert but there was no one in.'

'The house was empty?' Lily wanted him to be clear about this.

'Locked up back and front, no sign of life. So the sergeant telephoned the mill and heard there was talk of Mr and Mrs Calvert decamping to Scarborough for a while. The daughter, too.'

'Did they give a reason?'

Replacing his helmet on his head and giving it a firm tap, the policeman indicated that he'd done his duty and was ready to leave. 'Not according to the manager. He said they just upped sticks and left. But, don't worry – it won't stop us from talking to Mrs Calvert about her part in Billy Robertshaw's murder when we do eventually track her down.'

'Thank you,' Lily said in a voice not much above a murmur before closing the door. 'I can't help feeling sorry—' she started to say to her father, seated by the fire, cigarette in hand.

'Don't,' he interrupted.

'Not for Mrs Calvert. For Winifred.'

'Spare me the violins,' Walter warned. 'If you feel sorry for anybody, let it be Billy's mother, his sister and everyone else who's been dragged in.'

'I do, Father,' she agreed, picking up Arthur's aired pyjamas from the fender and handing them to him. 'Believe me, I do.'

*

'Margie's a law unto herself,' Bert Preston complained when, on the longed-for day of Harry's release, he delivered Margie and her suitcase to Albion Lane. 'All of a sudden she's got it into her head that this is her home and she won't stay away a day longer, not for love nor money.'

Walter stood on the top step and glared down at his father-in-law then at Margie. Her chin was up, her brown eyes defiant, daring him to slam the door in her face.

'Well, are you going to let her in or not?' Bert asked, setting the suitcase down.

Lily, who been up long before dawn, waited with Arthur in the kitchen. A glimpse of Margie on the doorstep boldly meeting Walter's hostile gaze made her heart flutter, yet she knew better than to step in. It was up to her father to decide.

Walter had been silent so long Margie was beginning to think that this visit was a waste of time. A lot of things had changed lately, but he hadn't – when it came to forgiveness, it seemed he was still his unfeeling, unbending self. 'Ah well,' she said, ready to turn and flounce away, 'if you're that ashamed of me, I can always carry on living with Granddad like you said.'

'Don't say I didn't warn you,' Bert reminded her as he stooped to pick up the suitcase.

They left and were a few yards up the street, returning the way they'd come when Walter finally spoke. 'That Kenneth Hetton . . .'

Margie's heart was jolted by the abrupt and painful reminder and when she looked over her shoulder, her face was pale under her green velour hat. 'What about him? He's out of the picture now.'

'Where's he buggered off to?'

'To Liverpool, the last I heard.'

Walter frowned. 'That's not the ends of the earth. We can still track him down.'

'He'll be in clink there.' Margie couldn't see where this was leading or why her father should be raking it up now. She and her grandfather retraced their steps to find that Lily had joined Walter on the step.

'In clink for doing what?' he asked. 'Not for what he did to you?'

Margie shook her head. 'No, for thieving from his bosses. Anyway, you tell him, Lily, you know why I've decided to let that lie.'

'She has, Father, and with good reason. I agree with her and Mother – what Margie has to do now is move on from what happened and concentrate on getting ready for the baby.'

Walter thought a while longer. 'And you promise you'll do as you're told from now on?' he asked Margie. 'You won't get up to your old tricks?'

'Such as?' Margie demanded, forgetting for a second that she was in no position to bargain.

'Such as giving me cheek and looking down your nose at me.'

Staring up at him, Margie saw an old man with a wheezy chest, lined face and untidy grey moustache.

Everything about him seemed tired and worn out – his veined hands and blunt nails, the nicotine stains on his fingers, the loose skin of his neck and jutting brows. Her father. 'Cross my heart,' she murmured gently.

'Then come on in out of the cold,' he told her, holding open the door as he stood to one side.

CHAPTER THIRTY-SIX

Harry's footsteps rang out along the metal landing for the last time. He stared straight ahead, following the warder down the steps, out across the perimeter walkway and through the small exit set into the double oak doors.

'Good luck to you, son,' the warder said sincerely as he shook his hand.

Harry turned up his collar and looked for Ernie's van. There it was, parked across the road, with Ernie sitting in it and beside him, in the passenger seat, was Lily.

For a moment she wasn't sure it was Harry. The figure who stepped through the small doorway and shook hands with the uniformed guard seemed too slight, but then as soon as he put up his collar against the wind and turned to look in her direction, she knew him. 'Here he is!' she cried so sharply that she startled Ernie. 'At long last!'

'Watch out for the traffic!' Ernie yelled after her as she jumped down on to the pavement and heedlessly ran across the street between cars and carts, bicycles and big delivery vans.

Lily sped towards Harry, who didn't move from the spot. What he saw was a beautiful woman running towards him, her dark hair flying free. He opened his arms and she flung herself into his embrace.

He closed his arms around her. She laid her head against his shoulder and held him tight.

On Raglan Road, the hastily arranged party for Harry spilled out of Betty Bainbridge's house on to the pavement. While Peggy and Evie carried round trays of sandwiches for the neighbours who had gathered to welcome the freed man home, Harry's mother poured tea.

'It's a pity Jennie and the others couldn't be here,' Sybil commented on the fact that Calvert's looms stopped for no man. 'There's nothing Jennie likes better than a good get-together.'

'I heard that Billy's mother promised to pop in.' Annie looked for Mabel Robertshaw amongst the crowd but didn't see her there. 'From what I hear, she always swore Harry was innocent.'

Sybil nodded. 'Well, it turns out she was right and Lily's proved it, thank goodness. But I'm not surprised the poor thing's stayed away – it'll probably take a bit more time for the dust to settle.'

Annie agreed. 'I wonder how Lily's feeling right this minute,' she went on. 'I'll bet she had to pinch herself when that prison door opened and Harry walked out, large as life.'

'We'll soon find out.' Looking at her watch, Sybil went outside to check for the arrival of Ernie's van. 'What's holding them up?' she wondered.

Craning her neck to get a clear view of the corner on to Ghyll Road, Sybil was the first to spot Durant's van turn on to Raglan Road. 'Here he is!' she cried, amidst a flurry of fresh excitement. The van chugged up the hill and pulled up outside the house.

'Well, I'll be blowed!' Ernie said as he pulled on the handbrake. There'd never been such a crowd in Raglan Road except at coronations and jubilees.

Lily held Harry's hand tight and together they got out of the van, braving the slaps on the back and the cries of 'Welcome home!' as they made their way up the steps into the front room where his mother and Peggy waited.

'Harry's here, Mother,' Peggy whispered to Betty, who seemed to be in a daze.

Harry's mother had heard the news of Frank and Tommy's arrest and her son's release with stunned disbelief. She wouldn't credit it, she said, not until Harry walked through the door and she saw him with her own eyes. And now here he was, thinner and paler, almost a ghost back from the dead.

For a while neither mother nor son spoke a word and everyone who had gathered to welcome Harry fell silent and held their breaths. Lily squeezed

Harry's hand and gave him a nudge of encouragement. He took a reticent step forward, not knowing whether or not he should kiss his mother on the cheek.

Betty saw the baby she'd given birth to who was so like his father, the boy she'd brought up single-handedly. Now he was a handsome, broad-shouldered man uncertain how to act on this, the homecoming to end all homecomings.

Eventually, mastering the rush of tender emotions that threatened to overwhelm her, she was the one to break the silence. 'What are we thinking? Let's give the lad a cup of tea,' she told Peggy as she rushed forward and grasped both of Harry's hands.

'Hello, Mother,' he murmured, leaning in to deliver the kiss he'd hesitated over and finding that her cheek was damp with tears. 'It's good to be back.'

'It's good to have you back, son. Now sit down and tell us all about it, every last little thing.'

CHAPTER THIRTY-SEVEN

'It's all settled. Sybil, Annie and me – we're going to set up shop,' Lily told Harry that evening, as they walked arm in arm along Overcliffe Road.

Ernie had brought in supplies from the Cross and crates of beer had followed tea and sandwiches. By the time their pals working in the mills had clocked off and Evie, Margie and Arthur had joined them after a welcome-home tea for Arthur at number 5, the celebration had got into full swing. It had gone on until well after eight, when eventually well-wishers had started to drift away.

Lily could recall them all now, the jovial voices of friends and family echoing down the street. She smiled at the thought of sensible Margie taking charge back at number 5 – seeing Arthur home to bed and into his pyjamas, straight to sleep without a story. School tomorrow.

'What shop? Where?' Harry wanted to know, as they walked past the Common.

Her face lit up as she described their plans and

how she, Sybil and Annie would achieve them. They ran the risk of it all falling about their ears, she knew – don't think she didn't. 'But we'll give it a go,' she said, striding out under a pitch-black sky.

Like a warrior queen was how Harry thought of her, though she'd never see it herself. A bobbin ligger turned burler and mender, and now a dressmaker with a shop of her own on Chapel Street, marching at the head of an army of brave, free-spirited women into a brighter future.

'Ernie mentioned a job that's going begging at Manby's,' he told her. 'I'm thinking of going after it tomorrow morning.'

'What would it involve?'

'Driving their van, picking up furniture to go to auction, that type of thing. It's not much but what do you think?'

'Get down there first thing,' Lily replied without hesitating. 'Be sure to be at the head of the queue.'

'Look down there,' Harry said after they'd walked a little further, turning to take in their home town in the darkness. He pointed to a thousand glittering lights, to the network of gas-lit streets and the canal winding through. 'What can you hear?'

'Nothing.' Only the wind that drove the clouds through the night sky.

'This is what kept me going,' he confessed. 'The thought of you and me walking up here, free as birds.'

'Together.' Her mind opened to the magical silence

of the moors, to Harry, the man she loved with all her heart.

So they walked on arm in arm, two small figures against the vastness of the night sky.

Acknowledgements

Thanks to Caroline Sheldon, literary agent without compare and, better still, a dear friend. And to Harriet Bourton whose welcome through the doors of Transworld made me feel immediately at home.

If you enjoyed *The Mill Girls of Albion Lane*, look out for the next heartwarming tale from Jenny Holmes

The Shop Girls of Chapel Street

Violet Wheeler is down on her luck. Turfed out of her house after a family tragedy and with no other family to turn to, she has to rely on the goodwill of the local community to help her out.

Working at the Chapel Street drapers, amongst the spools of ribbon, skeins of silk and latest thirties fashions, Violet is given a chance to get back on her feet – and an unexpected chance to find love. It's only when a forgotten piece of jewellery with a mysterious engraving surfaces that Violet starts to wonder if there is more to her family past than she knows, and her future begins to look uncertain . . .

Violet becomes desperate for answers about her family but it could threaten the stable life she's been building.

Can Violet find a happy ending against all odds?

The Shop Girls of Chapel Street
will be available in February 2016